Maiden in Light

A Novel by Kathryn L. Ramage

The Wapshott Press

Maiden in Light

Published by
The Wapshott Press
PO Box 31513
Los Angeles, CA 90031

The Wapshott Press

www.WapshottPress.com

First printing May 2011

ISBN: 978-0-9825813-2-2

06 05 04 034 3 2 1

Wapshott Press logo by Molly Kiely
The Northlands map design by Molly Kiely
Cover design by Michelle Mauk

Also by Kathryn L. Ramage

The Wizard's Son

*Dedicated to Jane Austen
and H.P. Lovecraft,
whose influence may be seen herein*

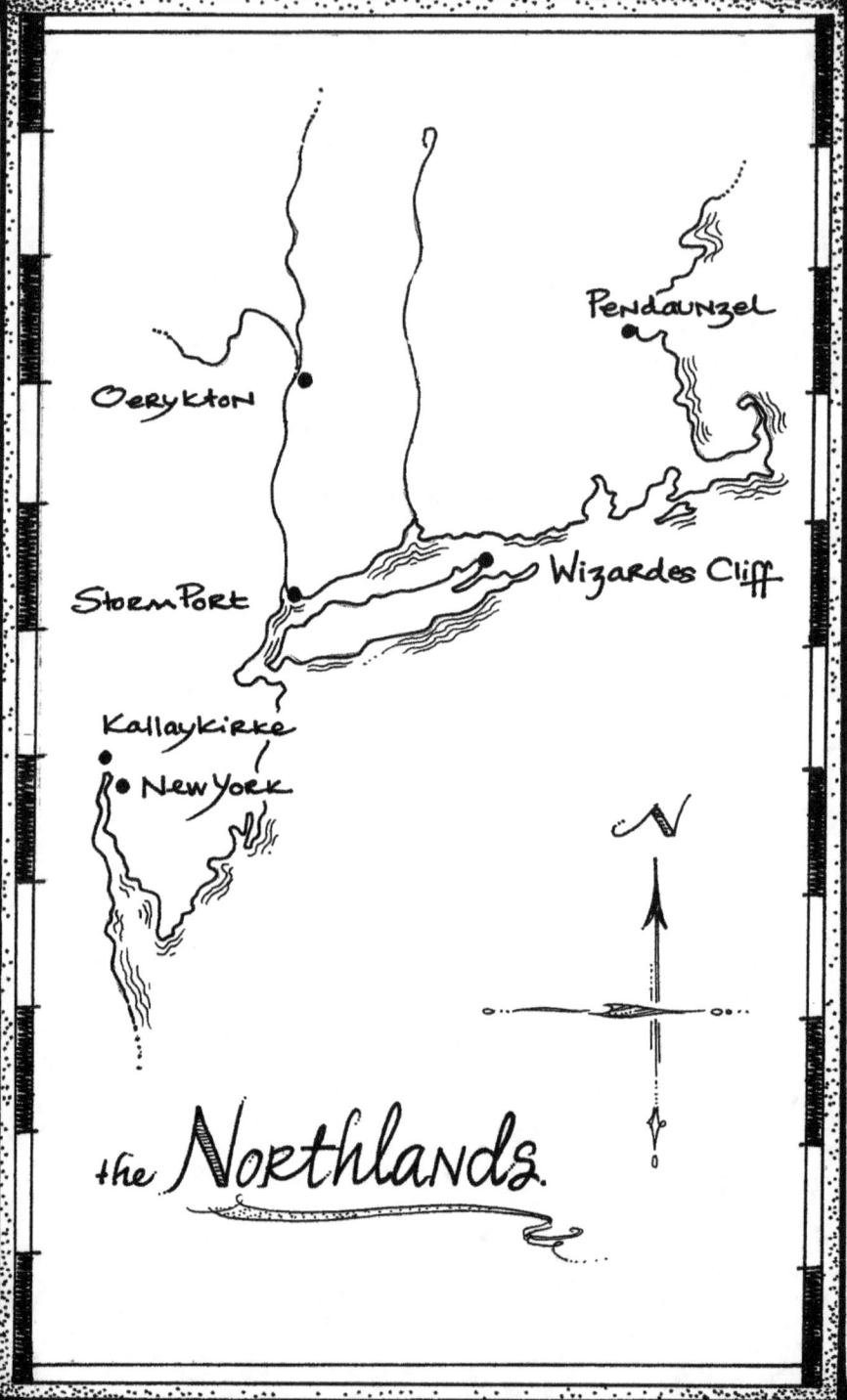

Pendaunzel

Oerykton

Wizardes Cliff

StormPort

Kallaykirke
New York

N

the Northlands.

Maiden in Light

Table of Contents

Ambris
New York
1944

i

Laurel
Wizardes Cliff
1944

Laurel
New York
1949

Igren
Oerykton
1960

281

Ambris

New York

1944

Were there such creatures as the Faerye?

Ambris, called Just, was a gentle soul who would have paused to notice the first spring flowers at the roadside or a glorious sunset or the sparkles of dew on a spider's web—but he did not believe. Occupied by his business in the bustling port of New York, he had no time to dwell upon such fanciful ideas. Yet, this day, he must hesitate and wonder.

A carriage accident draws attention, especially within town walls: the splintering crackle of a broken wheel, the crash, the spew of dust, the horse squeals and human cries. The coach had barely cleared the gates of the Dolphin Inn stable yard, closed from the market square by a tall wooden wall tacked with advertising banners and official proclamations, when one of the forewheels collapsed, its spokes snapped, and one side of the carriage suddenly sagged low. A crowd gathered swiftly about the small disaster, laughing, shouting hearty jests and advice to the coachman in his precarious seat above, offering useless encouragements to the woman shut within. A cheer rose as the axle snapped under the weight of the sagging coach and the entire front end landed with a thud. The woman within howled her outrage. The spectators hooted.

Ambris watched the riotous scene with distaste; it was not his idea of sport. New York was not his home, but he was a nobleman and therefore obliged by long-standing tradition to aid any maid or child or commoner, subject or no, whom he found in distress. Duty compelled him.

He went down from the porch of the Goldbell Inn where he had spent the night, and pressed through the commotion. "Make way!

Make way!" He was a tall and imposing-looking man; even without the blue robes which marked him a Lord of high rank, his was a voice of authority. The crowd gave way.

The woman in the broken coach, a wealthy merchant by her garments, hung out the open window and argued with a youth who sat atop. "Get down from there, brat! You've caused enough trouble!"

"I'm not at fault! Blame the wheelwright for your troubles, not me!"

The youth, in a battered, oversized soldier's cloak, sword agirt, captured his attention. An unusual attendant for a merchant, Ambris thought, a half-grown and boyish bodyguard, then a glimpse of pale chin and brow and silvery hair grown over the collar redoubled his curiosity. Ambris had traveled and seen people dark and fair from all parts of world. What race was this? The look was not entirely unfamiliar; he thought that he'd seen someone like this overfair child before. But when? Where?

He spoke as the youth scrambled over the piles of boxes knotted on the carriage roof. "Lad—" The child laughed and Ambris saw his mistake. Yes, half-grown and boyish, but not a boy. "Your pardon, Maiden. May I offer assistance?"

She dropped easily to stand before him. No maidenly demure here: the gaze which met his was amused and unabashed, the jaw too square and strong for delicate beauty, the tarnished silver brows arch and expressive, and the pale pink mouth not tender. She was out of place, obviously alien to this busy little town and ill-suited for a merchant's service, though Ambris could not say what her proper place might be. What was she? Bold, vigorous, tall, long-limbed, frosty-fair—in commoner's garb of brief brown jerkin and kirtle, she looked like a young swan disguised as a gutter sparrow.

"Gramercies, My Lord. I am unhurt," she answered. "Perhaps you had better speak to Dame Amaris."

The coachman and a porter from the inn were struggling to pry the carriage door from its bent frame and free the furious merchant. A pair of town guards tried to clear the square; the crowd complied by moving back some distance, but remained to watch the show. When the door burst open, another delighted shout went up.

Dame Amaris emerged and paused to assess her injuries and rearrange her rumpled finery before giving orders:

"There are boxes of samples and patterns in the new Orient colors," she announced. "Bring them down, quickly! If there is any damage, I will hold this house responsible! Another coach!

Immediately! I won't stop here another moment!" She turned to the maid. "I knew it was dangerous to receive you!"

"I didn't do anything!" the girl protested.

The dame obviously thought otherwise. "Well, do something now! Make yourself useful." And she swept back into the inn, apologetic porter at her side.

Already, other servants were on the coach like scavengers, climbing to the roof, unknotting ropes, throwing boxes down and bearing them into the yard. The horses were released from the shafts. The maiden watched, but did not offer to help; when the last parcels were down, she stepped to follow the entourage, but the last of the Dolphin's servants frowned menacingly and swung the stable-yard gate shut in her face.

She bit her lip then, finding Ambris watching her in astonishment, flashed a knowing smile. "They won't have me in their yard."

"Surely, they cannot be so cruel to a young maid."

"Can't they?" She twisted to the shut gate. "They say I fright the horses. Dame Amaris blames me for the whole mess, rather than fault her wheelwright." The excitement ended, the crowd began to disperse; some pointed to the girl, made gestures in ancient fashion to ward off evil, crossed themselves.

"She is not your master?"

"No, My Lord, only a traveling companion. I am sent to my uncle at Greenwaters Island, for I have been a cruel, ungrateful girl to my most generous aunt and she bids me go. Dame Amaris returns to Storm Port and agrees to take me so far, if she has not changed her mind."

She spoke as an ordinary maiden might, or with a little more sarcasm, but Ambris was enchanted. Her eyes were stranger than all else; the irises were colorless, like deep, clear, still pools of water, rimmed with bright blue. Gazing, he felt himself drawn into their depths. He might drown at the whim of the nixies hiding beneath that water– Until he blinked and the spell was broken. By all the saints and angels attending, what was this child?

"In truth, I'm glad to leave," said the maid. "If she won't have me, I shall go alone."

"What, will you walk?"

"If I must." She lifted her chin. "I cannot stay here."

"If you like, I may go in and ask after your companion."

"Would you? Oh, but I cannot ask such a boon–"

The gates swung open and a newly equipped coach and four rolled out. The merchant-dame pushed aside the window-curtains and shouted out.

"Laurel!"

"Coming!" the maid shouted in reply. "Fare ye well, My Lord." One foot tucked neatly behind the other, she bobbed in a sort of curtsey, then leapt to the back of the carriage and climbed up to sit behind the coachman. A whip cracked; the horses clattered through the square, driving back pedestrians, and they were gone.

Were there such creatures as the Faerye?

From childhood, Ambris had heard tales of the Fair Folk, of elves and enchanted maidens, of Queen Mab, of Pan, of the banshee and the shape-shifting manitou, but he had never believed their truth. They were only pretty legends, dressed by the fogs of a long-forgotten past and retold for amusement these days. Could such fantastic beings exist in the modern world, in this busy, dirty town in the Duchy of the Northlands, for a rational man such as himself? For one brief, bright, startling moment, he began to think it possible.

Then he descended to the noise and stench and press of bodies on the square with some reluctance. True or no, such moments were meant to be treasured for their brevity as well as beauty, and never extended forever. He had practical matters to attend to and no time to dream after faerye-maids. But he smiled to himself as he walked away.

Ambris's business in New York was a matter of importance to the town's great merchant-houses. Eadeshire, his given land, was an inland county and could claim no seaport for the greater wealth of its people; indeed, the largest town within its borders was the Earl's town of Eadbury, little more than a village gathered about a small castle. But the soil was rich and no one who could work the land was likely to go hungry. They had orchards and vineyards, and therefore ciders and wines which might be used for more than their own refreshment; Ambris had traveled to establish a contract of trade with New York, the nearest port, so that this surplus might be bought and exported. The Mayor Nikholas, himself one of the town's most prominent wine-merchants, saw the advantages of it and was prepared to come to some agreement.

That afternoon, as a scribe diligently made note of the negotiations between the Mayor and visiting nobleman, there was a tentative knock at the door to Nikholas's office.

"Husband?" A woman's voice of rich, warm tones and slight, north-country accents spoke. "Will you come to dinner?"

"Is it so late?" The scribe nodded, but Nikholas turned to the tall mechanical clock atop the bookshelves. "Merciful Mary! Now I think on it, I'm near faint with hunger. We'll finish this on the morrow. You may go," he told the scribe. Then he addressed Ambris: "I had no idea to keep you here all day, My Lord. Will you join our table? I vow that even our meanest fare—which will not be served tonight—is better than the rubbish you'll be given at the inn."

"Mayor, I am grateful to embrace your generosity." The words, perhaps stiff and unnatural, were the height of polite conversation, for Ambris was practiced in all courtly graces. "It isn't inconvenient to come so late and unexpectedly?"

Nikholas laughed. "Oh, you're no surprise to our household. I'll wager My Lady's set a table for a king, no less, in hopes that you'll join us. She's asked after you a dozen times and more since we first had news of your visit. No surprise, I assure you!" He brushed down his merchant-grey tunic before he assumed the bright orange and green mantle of his office, abandoned carelessly on the hearthrug, then took Ambris's arm and escorted him to the private rooms at the back of the Hall.

"Now, My Lord, I will have you meet my good Lady." Nikholas opened the door to the parlor; the sharp whispers beyond ceased abruptly and the woman within dropped into a deep curtsey while the two girls at her side looked alarmed.

Ambris blinked in wonderment, for the enchantment of that morning returned to him now in an unexpected rush. The Lady and her daughters had the look of the Faerye: hair silvery, skin milky fair, eyes colorless. The resemblance between the Lady and the maid he had met that morning was most remarkable; she was tall, indeed, so tall as he and half a head above her husband, and the icy strength of her face showed what that pert young girl might become in thirty year's time, given the exercise of her will and full development of her self-confidence. He recalled, too, that the maiden had mentioned an aunt.

"My Lord," Nikholas performed the introduction. "My wife, the Lady Kaiese. Dearest, I will have you meet Ambris the Just, Earl of Eadeshire."

"My Lady," Ambris bowed gracefully. "A pleasure."

"It is no small honor to welcome such a nobleman to our home," Kaiese replied.

"And our daughters," her husband added. "The elder is Igren, and the little one is Iobethe."

"Girls," Kaiese said through her teeth, so softly that Ambris nearly mistook it for an intake of breath, but the girls responded with swift

Kathryn L. Ramage

curtseys and Ambris bestowed the proper compliments. Igren was a year or two younger than her pert cousin, petite and pink with blushes. Iobethe was perhaps ten and likewise small with a winsome heart-shaped face. Pretty, delicate maids both.

Ambris watched them over dinner. No, he did not believe in faeries. He had not before this day, but he could not account for these unusual women by any more rational means. How could he explain the glamour of them? Surely there was elfish blood in this family, for they were not extraordinary in themselves. Lady Kaiese might look like a marble Juno come to life, but her solicitous hospitality was no different from that which he was accustomed to receive from urban matrons. Iobethe smiled shyly when he met her large, pale blue eyes and replied, giggling, to his questions while her sister, more timid, fixed her attention on her plate; they were not unlike the other little maids of his acquaintance. Had they possessed the dark coloring of ordinary Northlanders instead of complexions of ivory, crystal, and moonlight, they would not have drawn his curiosity. They were not magical—or were they? He recalled where he had seen one of this strange fairness, a lordling pointed out to him at his father's court, a handsome young wizard in the crimson robes worn only by the most powerful of magicians.

"Lady," he said, "I believe am I acquainted with some of your relations. You are aunt to a maiden named Laurel?"

"You know of her?"

"I spoke to her today before the Dolphin."

Kaiese's mouth drew into a thin line. "I apologize, My Lord Ambris, for all she might have said to you."

Ambris was about to protest that he had found Laurel charming, but Kaiese went on:

"That girl can be quite horrid when she chooses, My Lord. She has the worst of her mother—willful, spiteful, wretchedly ungrateful for our generosity. Wickedness itself. 'Tis a disgrace to behave so to one of my own blood, but we were at last called to send her away."

"To her uncle," Nikholas added. "We had rather Lord Redmantyl's tapestries suffer her temper."

Ambris's interest increased, for the young wizard had that title. "Your brother, My Lady?"

"No," she answered bluntly. "He is my cousin to the first degree. I did not like to send her to him, but there was nowhere else she might go and it was impossible to keep her here any longer."

"What has she done?" Ambris asked, but it was immediately

obvious that he had blundered; this was not a question to be asked. "Your pardon, My Lady."

Kaiese's expression lightened. "No, 'tis I who ask your pardon for my indiscretion. I said more than may be said. You must understand that my niece has been a difficulty to us for many years. I should not speak of her. She has gone." She smiled. "Have you been to Pendaunzel recently, My Lord? You must tell us of the doings at court, I pray you. How is My Gracious Lord, your father?"

Laurel was not mentioned again.

Ambris rode home some days later with negotiations between himself and Nikholas settled to advantage of both town and shire. He was pleased that he had arranged this matter so well for all concerned, but honesty forced him to admit that he had only seen that the contract was written in the best legal form, for he had been educated as a lawyer. The idea itself was to his wife's credit.

His marriage to Margaude had been arranged by his father, Dafythe, Duke of the Northlands, and his uncle, Kharles IV, Emperor of the Normans, under rather hasty and embarrassed circumstances. Margaude was the third daughter of the heir to the Kingdom of Bavaria and a distant cousin to the Norman royal family; few nobles—Spaniards included—could not claim some Plantagenet blood. Her first marriage contract had been with the Emperor's son, now Kharles V but then a sullen, self-important boy of seventeen who contested the betrothal violently. He would not marry a maiden five years his senior, plain and retiring, more fond of books than riding to hounds, and once Margaude arrived at the Paris court, he refused her to her face. The princess had been humiliated, her family outraged, and the Norman house disgraced. There was no danger of diplomatic incident: Kharles IV and his brother were men of such power that they could afford to snub a small kingdom in the disjointed remains of the Holy Roman Empire, but they were also men of such honor that they felt the shame of a broken pact. The Prince's behavior embarrassed them as much as if they'd given the insult themselves. As an apology and recompense to the injured bride, they offered a second marriage contract and an alternate bridegroom; Ambris was summoned to Paris and introduced to Margaude as an eligible young man of the Norman house, albeit the wrong side of the blanket.

Of course, the bastard son of the Duke of the Northlands, a young diplomat in the Emperor's service, was not so spectacular a match as the Prince of France and heir to the Norman throne, but the Bavarian princess had accepted him. They wed within the month.

Their marriage had been, on the whole, successful. There was no love between them, but they were of like minds. He left the management of Eadeshire to her while he attended his duties at Pendaunzel and trusted that all would run smoothly in his absence. They were faithful to each other because they had vowed to be so and their children had arrived at regular intervals because children were likely to be born to healthy husbands and wives. On the whole, Ambris did not regret that he had done his duty to his family.

These were warm spring days with little rain; the unpaved roads through the Koefenshire woods and Eadeshire mountains were dry and easily traveled. Ambris gave no thought to greater danger than weather as he rode alone at a leisurely pace. Cutpurses and rogues were commonplace in the cities, but woodland bandits were almost unheard of these days. For five days, he rode untroubled and when, at last, he caught sight of Eadbury cleft between its green hills, his heart rose. A remote place, Eadbury; Ambris welcomed its serenity after the unceasing commotion of New York. The earliest Northlander Christians had found this site as peaceful and secluded, for the castle had once been a monastery, abandoned long ago by the monks and later rebuilt into its new form.

He crossed the shallow river which cut the tiny town in its valley and entered Castle Ellsrood through the park gate. A crucifix of stone-hard wood stood atop the great doors; this was probably not the cross that the castle had been named for in centuries past, but it stood in its place as sign that Eadbury had once been, truly, blessed.

The children playing in the castle courtyard stopped their game and ran up, shouting, as Ambris dismounted. Noble sons, stable-lads, boys of the village—Ambris rumpled hair indiscriminately, teased and answered each according to whom could shout loudest and most distinctly. When free of the clamoring boys, he entered the castle and went up to his private chambers. His wife was there with their youngest and only daughter, Mathilde, wailing at her shoulder.

"Ambris." She kissed his cheek. "Welcome you home."

"Is she ill?"

"The baby? Ah!" Lady Margaude shut her eyes in exaggerated weariness. "'Tis that fool of a nursery-maid. She's given the poor bit her colic again. She knows nothing of children, I tell you, Ambris."

"So you do," he answered, smiling. "At Eadrik's nurse and Eduarde's and at Arthur's and Bertrande's and little Marcius's—"

"Yes, and I shall again at the next babe if we are so fortunate.

How went this business with the York Mayor? Has he agreed to our terms?"

"Let me tell you..." He took the howling infant from her shoulder and soothed it while he explained the details of the contract and listened to his wife lament at the loss of an advantage and praise a clever wording which might bring them some unexpected benefit.

Was he happy with his lot? Surely, he had much to be thankful for. Margaude was a dear friend and a trusted councilor. If there was to be no love in a marriage, then she was all he could desire in a wife. They fared far better than most married couples. The children were healthy; when so many infants died, Ambris knew his good fortune to have fathered six children and not lost one. He had his little shire and his place at the Duke's court; he had earned both. If his career was not so spectacular as that which a legitimate Prince might expect, he had served his emperor and country as a skillful diplomat, loyal councilor and honest magistrate. He was indispensable to his father. What more could a man of reason ask of life? He was content.

But even now his mind turned to more splendid things, to the strange magic which had touched him so briefly in the form of that most remarkable girl. He would not see her like again.

Laurel

Wizardes Cliff
1944

une

At sunset, Amaris Silksmerchant pulled back the window-curtains and called up to the roof: "Girl, come down! The wind grows chill and I will not be blamed if you insist on falling ill in the night air."

The coach was moving slowly on the paved Coast Road; Laurel swung herself down onto the attendants' stand at the rear and stretched to place one booted toe precariously on the step within the carriage door, held obligingly open for her. Once secure, she stretched her other foot to the door, then hand, and hand, and she pulled herself in.

"How far are we from Storm Port?" she asked as she took the seat opposite the fabulous merchant. Amaris's wardrobe was the best advertisement of her trade, for she adorned her impressive figure with yards of summer silks: her misty grey tunic was worked with shining threads of white and robin-egg blue, her spotless wimple covered by a blue lacework veil, her billowing robes gloriously embroidered and lined with soft, watery pink like the clouds at sunrise.

Color signified one's proper place: tradesfolk, farmers, and peasants wore homespun browns and butternut; merchant folk wore light blues and grays; nobles wore darker blue. Government officials wore robes of orange and green, clergy white—the color of purity—and magicians black and red. The correct garb, embellished by guild badges, merchant-family emblems, seals of office, and armorial crests, made it possible to determine the social position of any Norman citizen. Amaris' colors said plainly that she was one of a prominent merchant house and the quality of her garments declared her wealth and personal success. Laurel had been astonished, and a little envious, at her introduction to the Silksmerchant. How marvelous it would be to be such a woman, as near a Lady as a commoner might be, clothed in such wondrous robes!

"We arrive Tuesday afternoon," Amaris answered. "I expect to stop the night at Thornes. Does your uncle know to find you at my house?"

"Yes, Dame. A courier was sent to him."

"You must feel the honor of having relation to a great Lord."

"A great Wizard-Lordling," said Laurel, but her companion did not care to acknowledge the ranks of magic.

"Most folk of common birth do not have so important a connection." Her tone suggested that Laurel did not deserve such importance. For what was Laurel after all? A poor relation, an odd, unmannerly child, a disreputable soldier's daughter, an orphan, a nameless bastard—no one. Amaris was not so impolite to speak her opinion when she had accepted Nikholas' charge, but her meaning was obvious in every implied insult: For the opportunity to establish her own connection with Nikholas, Laurel must be endured; for her own sake, the brat was not worth consideration. Amaris was, in fact, a little frightened. She had been in New York long enough to hear what was said of the Mayor's niece and had expected some catastrophe even before the carriage accident this morning. As they had traveled since without mishap, Amaris had not spoken another harsh word. She hadn't spoken to Laurel at all.

Laurel had felt the sting of such barbs all her life. Did she still resent them? Yes, very much. Did she return the insult? No, she did not.

She shut her eyes as waves of anger coursed through her. In another moment, the curtains or upholstery or the Silksmerchant's cloak would burst into flame. She must control her temper. It was not her nature to submit to any injury. She would love to have her revenge of this insufferable snob, but it was impractical. She must reach Storm Port and the Silksmerchant, for whatever reasons, had agreed to take her. What good would come of Amaris, horrified, throwing her from the carriage onto the night road?

"Who was the nobleman I saw you speaking with at the inn?"

"I don't know his name," answered Laurel. "An Earl, of royal blood. He had golden lions..." She ran a hand diagonally across her chest.

"And he spoke to you. Why?"

"He asked if he might be of service to us after the accident."

"Yes, that's the way of the nobility. They will be kind to even the lowest folk."

"Yes, Dame."

Laurel cared little for people she did not know. This Earl, though he had been pleasant with her, was a stranger and their brief meeting made no great mark on her life. She was far more interested in what would happen once she reached her destination. Though she'd never met Lord Redmantyl, she had heard much of him, so many strange and marvelous tales that she didn't know if she could believe them all.

"Have you met my uncle, Dame Amaris? Is he often at Storm Port?"

"I have not met him," Amaris answered. "He visits the city, but the pursuits of so great a Lordling do not involve my sphere of acquaintance. I have heard that he is a dangerous man to know."

Laurel smiled faintly. Redmantyl was a premiere Wizard-Lordling and possessed of remarkable powers so that all surviving lesser wizards feared him and cursed his name. Tales were told of wizard battles, fierce struggles of mind and magic as fascinating to the folk of the Empire as any clash of sword and shield, for no other battles had been fought on Norman soil in the twentieth century.

The present Redmantyl, so it was said, was once a talented apprentice of the Old Lord and had roused his master's jealousy. Though obliged by time-honored custom to teach the promising youth, the Old Lord conspired to destroy this potential rival before he came into his powers. As journeyman mage, the youth had fled for his life; as full wizard, he was able to defend himself. Alone, he stormed the castle Wizardes Cliff, faced his former master and proved with devastating rage that the Old Lord had a good deal to fear from him after all. Some said that the Old Lord had died in wizard-battle, others that his ancient heart had burst after his fall. Some whispered that the young Lord had murdered him. No one knew; none had seen the final contest. The storm of the young Lord's fury had covered all the sky from Scandinavian Uinlande to Spanish Iardinez, and before the storm cleared astonishing news spread from Wizardes Cliff: an upstart pup, barely more than a boy, had defeated the most powerful of living wizards and claimed the place for himself.

This was challenged, of course. Wizards of power throughout the world traveled to Greenwaters Island to confront the upstart. Alonz of Palefyt, Korbyn the Blind, Dyrkhesse of Anglessey, Inexplicable Kazimir, Skrymos Infidel of Malta—these and a dozen others whom Laurel could not recall fell before the young Redmantyl. Magicians of power were rare at any time, and more rare now. The best of the old days were gone, dead or injured and diminished in their magic, or banished to the borders of madness. Island-seats of wizardry, much coveted for centuries, were empty. Lord Redmantyl had established himself supreme.

In tales of battle he was called Lightmaster, for he brought storms to a clear sky, fires from the heavens, a brightness from his own being that was terrible to see. His fury was as quick as a lightning bolt, and as deadly. So the tales told. None but the fallen wizards had ever seen Redmantyl in a rage; no one had challenged him in the eight years since he had claimed his place and Greenwaters Island was quiet these days. But Laurel wondered at this man who wielded such strange and vast magic.

More and more frequently, she had felt– No, not his influence. His touch upon her mind. She knew that he'd taken an interest in her. He had written to Aunt Kaiese many times since he'd become premier wizard, asking that his niece be allowed to come him. Kaiese had refused him again and again, until now, when she was forced to let Laurel go.

"Merchants do not often have business with wizards," Amaris said. "They are an unsociable lot and do not enjoy the fellowsome pursuits of normal folk." The merchant arranged her robes. "Your uncle is Lord of Greenwaters Island, is he not?"

"Yes, Dame," answered Laurel. "My Lord Dafythe bestowed the fief after the death of the last rightful heir. My uncle is a favorite of the Duke, so 'tis said, when he is at court. But he goes rarely, I would think. Wizards are so reclusive, and Good Heaven only knows what damage *he* may make in the Duke's stable-yard."

Amaris found this last remark pert—"Your tongue, Girl"—and Laurel fell silent.

"If I understand Mayor Nikholas, you shall be one of My Lord Redmantyl's house hereafter?" the Silksmerchant resumed the conversation.

Laurel nodded.

"It is a remote place, I believe. At the far end of the isle." Mild amusement touched her voice. "Perhaps that is best."

Perhaps it was. Laurel was glad to be away from New York. She missed her cousin Igren, for Igren had been her dearest friend. She even missed pettish little Io. A few servants of the Mayor's Hall and a few of the garrison guards had befriended her, but for the rest–!

She'd never been beaten nor mistreated in her aunt's home, only made to feel unwelcome. Uncle Nikholas wasn't unkind, but his household was entirely his wife's business and he would not question

Kaiese on any part of its management. He was never more than indifferent; as she had left, he'd given her a little money for her journey and told her not to be so much trouble to her next home. Laurel would miss him no more than she thought he would miss her.

Aunt Kaiese had received Laurel as an infant at her mother's death, but she called her sister Tomasin an unnatural creature, uncouth to choose a career in soldiery, wicked to bear an illegitimate child; she saw the worst of Tomasin in Laurel and every sign of self-will or temperament was put down as insolence. She gave her niece shelter out of a grudging sense of duty and charity; Laurel might as easily have been a beggar's brat brought in from the streets. And, in her gratitude, Laurel must look after her young cousins and take the punishment if they played some mischief. She ran errands and she received guests to the Hall while the Mayor and his Lady were otherwise occupied. On occasion, she was permitted to join their dinner table.

The town despised her as a witch. Though she had been born in New York, she was always an outsider, shunned and friendless. The merchants, Nikholas's acquaintances, snubbed her and the common folk blessed themselves as she passed. Whatever she might meet in the house of her fearsome wizard-uncle, it could not be worse than that.

Laurel drew her cloak close about herself, tucked up her legs, and reached up to the window-curtain, but the forest had closed in about them and she could see nothing but darkness beyond. "How far is it to Thornes?"

"Not far. Don't fall asleep—I shall want you to carry my baggage in."

"Yes, Dame."

Storm Port was a larger, louder, fiercer city than New York: Amaris drew the curtains shut as they entered through the eastern Lyngate the next afternoon, but Laurel felt the commotion around her as the carriage rolled slowly toward the city's heart. She could hear the babble of a thousand voices and the clatter of hooves and heels, smell the salty sea air and overwhelming perfumes. Curiosity roused, she leaned to the window and peeked out. They were moving past tall buildings, four and five stories high, shops and taverns with painted signs and, as they turned abruptly at one corner, she saw what looked like an enormous marketplace bursting with strange merchants and brightly colored caravans.

"What is that?" she asked, forgetting herself, but Amaris' reply was a swift pulling of the drapery.

The Silksmerchant's house was in a quieter quarter, on a street called the Greenway beneath the west wall lined with trees and small lawns before the private houses. Servants rushed out with vociferous greetings as soon as the coach stopped and swiftly bore away all baggage at the dame's direction. Laurel stood at the carriage block, clutching her bundle of belongings and when the last servant weighted with parcels went into the house, she followed.

Inside, servants pushed past, oblivious; Amaris's husband blinked at her without interest and hurried on, and little yellow balls of fluff trotted underfoot, yipping with excitement. When they discovered Laurel, their yelps grew more fierce and frightened.

Amaris emerged from a room in the hallway above. "What are you doing with my little ones?"

"I wasn't–"

"Here!" the merchant called. Laurel hesitated, thinking that she'd been summoned, but the tiny dogs whimpered and ran up the stairs with their tails tucked beneath them. Amaris shut the door.

The girl retreated to the back hall, out of everyone's way, and pushed open the tall windows to the garden. Overgrown lilacs and bowers of roses lifted themselves against the surrounding walls. Plush beds of pink ladyslippers and bluebells bordered pebbled paths. Laurel wandered awhile and decided that the garden was a pretty place, but confining. Even the most lovely flowers lost their fascination after they had been smelt and fondled twice or thrice. Ought she gather a bouquet? Her hostess would not approve, would in fact be angry that so ill-mannered a maiden had defiled her garden by picking the flowers.

She knelt to gather a handful of the ones she liked best: white aster-like flowers which bloomed beneath the lilac. She didn't know the name of them, but they were like a flower which grew wild in the forests beyond New York along paths where she walked alone. Someone called her name, faintly, but she ignored it. If they would chase her out, then they would have to come and look for her.

She turned her back deliberately and arranged her bouquet with more care than it deserved. Boots crunched on the pebble path behind her.

"Laurel?"

She looked up, "Uncle–?" and stopped suddenly, struck dumb, as she faced the man who had spoken. Lord Redmantyl? Red-mantle indeed! He was robed in scarlet, mantle and riding cloak, and he was tall and fair as she, but his white plaits fell past his shoulders, nearly to his waist, falling freely like a wind-tossed winter rain. Laurel's first impression was that he looked alarmingly like a masculine version of her Aunt Kaiese, for he had the same high brow and same mouth set into firm and uncompromising lines, though his was framed by a close-clipped beard of tarnished silver. They might be sister and brother rather than first cousins. Then she noticed that he was surrounded by a strange and hazy sort of light, as if the very air shimmered in his proximity. Its source seemed to come from within him. He fairly shone with it. Was *this* the magic he was famed for? It must be so.

He *is* a wizard, she thought. A true wizard.

"Uncle Redmantyl?" She would have liked to show herself brave before this powerful being, but her voice betrayed her and faltered. She sounded far more timid than she wished.

The wizard's stern mouth moved into a smile. Unlike Kaiese, he did not despise the sight of her. "You are Laurel, Tomasin's daughter?" But it was obvious that she was, and to Laurel's surprise, he lifted her up in a fierce embrace that seemed to squeeze the breath from her. "Do you know," he said. "I have not seen you since you were four years old." He troubled to recall the circumstances. "At your mother's death, I went to New York to see if there was anything I might do. You were so small then. Do you recall?"

Laurel shook her head.

"I'm sorry not to see you before this. I often wondered. How old are you now?"

"Seventeen, Uncle." She was astonished that his first words should be an apology. Had she truly been afraid of him? Before all heavens, why?

Dogs whimpering at her skirts and servant anxiously at her elbow, Amaris came into the garden. "My Lord— Oh, you've found her. Maiden, where have you been? We've looked all about the house for you."

"I didn't wish to be a hindrance, Dame," Laurel answered. "I took myself to a place where I would cause no trouble."

"You have been no trouble," the merchant insisted. "In truth, she has been a fine companion on this journey, My Lord. The child is a credit to your family in New York."

"I am pleased to hear so," said Redmantyl.

Amaris smiled. "'Tis an honor to offer my service to you, My Lord. I would that I might do more. It is early to dine, but I pray you stay for some refreshment."

"No, gramercies, Goode Amaris. We must go." The wizard bowed briefly. "I am indebted to you for your kindness."

Amaris was taken aback at being addressed as 'Goode,' as if she were a mere shopkeeper, but the wizard had spoken courteously. And he *was,* after all, of the nobility. "I– Gramercies, My Lord."

Redmantyl took Laurel's hand and they left the house of Amaris Silksmerchant.

"She was not so kind to me, Uncle," Laurel told him as they walked down the Greenway.

"Perhaps," he answered. "But we cannot be discourteous to merchant folk." They turned into a narrow sidestreet. The bell towers and golden dome of St. Khrystopher's cathedral loomed directly ahead. A second tantalizing glimpse at the bright colors, the clamor of noise and music, and a hint of exotic perfume from the marketplace renewed Laurel's curiosity.

"What is that?" she asked.

"The bazaar."

"Oh." She looked wistfully to the nearest caravans. "There is a market at New York, but not so large. May we go and look?"

"Not now," said Redmantyl. "You ought not have your baggage about you." They crossed the next street and arrived at the Gray Knightes Inn; the innkeeper escorted them up to their rooms at the back. Laurel left her bundle and traveling cloak, scattered the bouquet on the bed and went out to the bazaar.

The Storm Port bazaar was not so different, after all, from the market of New York; merchants from the city shops and farm folk had come to vend their wares and traveling merchants from near and distant lands—Abyssinia, Napoli, Uinlande, Santiago, Portugal—had set up tents full of exotic and expensive merchandise. The New York market had contained such people, and Laurel had ventured out with Igren to gaze upon such marvels. But this bazaar was so much larger, the wares more marvelous and more expensive, and the clamor more deafening. Merchants shouted for attention and grabbed the sleeves of passersby to draw them in. The natives of the Northlands and its neighbors knew Lord Redmantyl by reputation and avoided him—they would not dare speak to the wizard and risk his wrath—but merchants from faraway lands did not recognize the red robes nor understand their significance; they only thought Redmantyl a great Lord and pestered and cajoled him with the merits of their wares and the good taste a noble patron might show in considering this treasure or that. The wizard, however, was not irritated at their persistence. He bought many gifts, all for Laurel: a tortoise-shell mirror and combs, bittersweet Incan cacao, almonds, the first summer pears, a handful of gaily colored tawdries, a little japanned and gilded box, a bright silk scarf crowded with writhing red and green dragons.

At last, Laurel protested: "Uncle, you mustn't spend so much."

"Nonsense!" Redmantyl replied. "'Tis rare to visit such a place as this, and it ought to be celebrated."

"But the money—"

"Better to spend it than have it gather dust in my purse."

"'Tis so greedy and grasping to choose so many gifts for myself. May I choose for others instead?"

The wizard looked amused. "For whom, Niece?"

"There are people of your household I shall meet soon." They paused at a table laden with bolts of bleached linen and cards of lace from Eirelande. "You have a son? My Aunt Kaiese said so."

"His name is Orlan."

"How old is he?"

"Thirteen."

"Tell me of him? What might he like?" She twisted to look for something appropriate. "Who else is at Wizardes Cliff?"

"Only servants. My chatelaine. The apprentices."

"No one else?"

He shook his head and received a look of sympathy.

"You must be lonesome."

"No, Niece. In truth, there are too many people about the castle for me to find solitude so often as I wish. I must give much time to my craft."

But Laurel believed he was lonely. As a wizard, Redmantyl must needs be set apart from his household, but he could not always like his solitude. He had greeted her so warmly and seemed so pleased to be with her; he made her feel that to be niece and ward to Lord Redmantyl was a far different thing than to be niece and ward to the Uinmerchants of New York.

They made their way across the bazaar, Laurel choosing gifts, until they stood before the great doors of St. Khrystopher's. Minstrels played at the cathedral steps; the maid stopped to toss a penny into the wide-brimmed hat upturned at their feet. She looked up at the towering facade, the arched doorway and the marble angels and saints and snarling gargoyles above, streaked by six centuries of rainwater. "May we go in?"

Redmantyl was not easy with this request, but he consented. Within, he remained oddly cautious while Laurel wandered the nave and transepts. The stained glass windows on the western wall were afire with brilliant color in the late afternoon sun. The memorials and tombstones set into the walls and floor were worn illegible. The bleeding, tortured form on the crucifix over the vestry door was disturbingly lifelike in its agony. Laurel stopped at the votary stands beneath the statue of St. Khrystopher. It was customary for mariners, merchants and wandering Free Folk to light candles and ensure safe journey from Storm Port; she lit one. Evensong chimes began to sing from the towers far overhead.

"Laurel," a voice whispered behind her. "'Tis time we leave."

She turned. "We won't stay for Mass, Uncle?"

"No."

He would not explain and Laurel did not ask. They left the cathedral.

When Lord Redmantyl called for his horses the next morning, the stable-boy brought out two mounts, one a dappled palfrey.

"Uncle, I cannot ride," Laurel protested immediately. "Horses–" she faltered, for it sounded foolish. "Horses fear me. If I draw too near, they cry out and lift their hooves against me."

Her uncle did not seem to think this strange. "These will not." He took her hand and brought it up to stroke the palfrey's nose. Laurel had not touched any animal since her childhood without it shrieking, but the spotted horse lifted its nose into the palm of her hand and snorted complacently. "She is yours, Laurel, for so long as you live at Wizardes Cliff. You'll learn to ride, but for this journey you need only hold fast to the pommel. I'll guide you."

He helped her into the saddle before he swung up onto his own mount; lead rein tied to the palfrey's bridle, he led her down through Storm Port. It was early and the streets were not so crowded as they had been the night before.

"Have animals always feared you, Laurel?" the wizard asked once they had passed through the Dukesgate and were riding through the park to the south of the city.

"No, not when I was small."

Laurel recalled distinctly when it had begun, a month before her eighth birthday. She had always known herself to be different from the other children, but she had not understood how different she was before then. Animals had fled. Her playmates, all save Igren, had taunted her with cruel names—*Imp, Hobgoblin, Witch*—and run away too. Sparks had spit from her fingertips and burst about her when she was twelve, but it was not until after her first menses, last fall, that this fiery magic burst forth uncontrolled. She was quick to anger, and with fury came flame. Aunt Kaiese had been horrified at the scorched tapestries and drapes. The town, which had tolerated her, became more fearful and hostile. They wondered that their chosen Mayor would protect such a creature: those who could write, wrote; those who could not stopped in the street outside the Mayor's Hall and shouted "Put the Witch out!" The common-folk drew their small children away and made wards against evil when they saw her. The town youths threw stones. Laurel had been threatened with eventual banishment for as long as she could remember but this, she knew, was why her aunt had finally agreed to send her away.

"I rather liked animals too. Igren and Iobethe kept a pet cat that slept at the foot of my bed....Do you keep many pets at Wizardes Cliff, Uncle?"

"None at all. Few creatures are so easy to train as horses," Redmantyl explained. "Perhaps dogs and falcons, but I do not hunt. Are you talented in magic, Laurel?"

"Yes, a little."

"Kaiese would not say why she wished you from her house, but I thought that that must be the reason. She wouldn't surrender you to me for any less."

Laurel didn't fully understand this statement, but she replied, "She would have sent me to Tremontegne to be ward to her mother, my gran'ther, but she feared I might be put to harm there."

"Tremontegne is not a place for one such as you, Child," Redmantyl agreed.

She looked up, wondering. Wouldn't Lord Redmantyl have been a child at Tremontegne with Aunt Kaiese and her mother? "You've been there?"

"Not in many years. I left for my apprenticeship to the Old Lord when I was sixteen and I have not returned."

"You were my age," said Laurel. "Did you ride so far alone?"

"Tomasin accompanied me." He turned in the saddle to study her face, as he had several times before. "You are something like her, I fancy."

"Do you think so? Aunt Kaiese says I am like my mother in temper. I am willful, discourteous, impious–"

"Yes, I recall my cousin."

"Tell me of her? What was she like, truly?"

"She was a bold maid," he said after a moment. "Older than I by four years. She was forever scraped and bruised, I recall. She would fight any who challenged her."

"Were you friends?"

"We were oddly matched as playmates," he answered. "But no other children would play with us and we three were left together—Tomasin, Kaiese, and I. Oh, Kaiese preferred her dolls and fineries and I my mother's books, and Tomasin would take up any stick to wield as a sword and chase us about. She struck me horribly once. I still have a scar."

"She meant to be a soldier even then?"

"I was not surprised when she went to the New York garrison, but I think she might've made a fierce, spectacular wizard if she'd possessed the talent. 'Tis in our family, you know. Your grandmother. Your aunt."

Laurel hadn't known this. "Kaiese?"

Redmantyl nodded. "But she fears her abilities and will not use them. In Tremontegne, magic is looked upon as witchery. No wizard is welcome there, and as we are all magical it was wise to either hide the talent or seek a place where magic was more welcome."

"Was my mother talented?"

"No, not so much. She was most envious of my apprenticeship when she accompanied me to Wizardes Cliff. She came particularly from New York for the opportunity of seeing the Old Lord and his castle. I recall when she returned to Tremontegne to escort me. She wore her full gear, that sword of yours. She was but twenty, but I thought her well grown and it was wondrous to travel with her—Along this same road, Laurel! She was proud of me when I came to New York once I was free of my magedom, and she asked after my spell-casting and the strictness of my mage-vows and how I lived in those years, as if she would know all I could tell her of a magician's life. I believe that if she could have been a wizard herself, she would have taken the same course. I did not see her again after that.

"When I heard she was dead, I returned to New York," he went on. "I knew of you, my cousin's child, and I thought I might take you as my ward, but Kaiese wouldn't allow it. It was best." He lifted one hand for silence as Laurel opened her mouth. "I was a young wizard then and not able to take a little child into my protection. I was not fit. You were better left with Kaiese."

"Had I chosen, Uncle, I would've gone with you," said Laurel.

The wizard smiled gently. "There was no choice. I was a wanderer not yet established. Kaiese had a home to keep you and I did not." He urged his horse to a quicker pace; the palfrey followed. "Are you glad to come with me now, Laurel?"

"Oh, yes!" she answered sincerely. "I– I felt you and I wanted so much to be with you. I wondered what you must be like. They tell such tales."

Redmantyl listened with amusement. "What do they say?"

"They speak of your powers," Laurel replied with unabashed enthusiasm. "They say you have marvelous magic as no other wizard before." She hesitated, then boldly ventured: "Will you show me, Uncle?"

"Very well." He lifted one hand and turned his wrist slightly; a small, bright orb of sparkling light appeared upon his fingertips. Then he saw Laurel's crestfallen face. "You are disappointed?"

"Yes," she confessed. "'Tis– Well, I've heard of the great storms at your command and I thought–"

"Laurel, I am a man of quick temper, but I am rarely so angry as that!" Redmantyl answered. "You will not see me in such a rage, I promise you." He pulled his horse to a stop. "But you would have a marvel of magic. What shall I do for you, Niece?"

"You are Lightmaster?"

"I am called so."

"Then I would see something lightsome—bright and wondrous. Please?"

"As you wish." The orb was still balanced upon his fingers; he tossed it into the air, eyes fixed upon it—and it exploded with a *pop*.

Brightness burst about them, forming itself into myriad points of light, fiery reds and oranges, glittering blue and silver, blinding white, like thousands of small suns, from the shadows of the trees to the very clouds, twisting up and up and up into a spire of light.

Laurel's little mare neighed fretfully, but the girl laughed, her senses dazzled. She was breathless, enervated, bathed in glamour. Light burst in her head and through her heart. She was inside it, as if it were hers. Magic ought to be a terrifying and destructive force that thundered and burned and killed; Laurel had not imagined how the same power might be used joyously. She could play with the light, she discovered: the orbs responded to her, shying like living things from her fingertips. She could divert them into frantic, spinning whirls and bounce them against her palms.

The Red-Lord, at the center of the whirling glory, watched her. "Is that satisfactory?"

"'Tis wonderful," she answered. Her hand closed to capture one glittering ball, but the light dissolved through her fingers. "Most

13

wonderful."

Up and up, the spire began to lose its pinnacle. Sparks flew out across the sky and dissolved; orbs struck the trees, the earth, the wizard, herself, and did not emerge. In a minute, all but five were absorbed. This bright quintet, a fairy retinue, remained about Redmantyl.

"What is it like to be a wizard, Uncle?"

"'Tis a profession of marvels," he replied. "But it also has great dangers and heavy burdens. A wizard must live on his guard. Only the most powerful survive. Weakness is death."

Laurel was not discouraged by this warning. "Are you happy in it?"

"Yes," Redmantyl answered. "Shall we go now?"

"Yes, Uncle."

As they rode, Laurel marveled at this strange man. He could create brilliant glories for her amusement and he was so gentle in his manner, yet she knew that he possessed great powers, remarkable and furious. Those tales of storms and fallen wizards were not lies. He had done such things; she knew this as surely as she knew that he'd been calling to her for years, summoning her to Wizardes Cliff.

She did not doubt that life in this wizard's house would be like nothing she knew.

They traveled half the length of Greenwaters Island that first day and journeyed through the next. Foggy twilight lay upon the land when Wizardes Cliff was not ten miles away.

At the barbican, a sleepy-eyed groom took the mounts and Redmantyl took his niece's hand to lead her along an unlit path through dark gardens to an open gate between two squat towers. The castle stood on cliffs before them.

Laurel had never seen a castle before. This one was dreamlike rather than a thing substantial, lower battlements swathed in sea-mist, slender towers bright in the moonlight, pale walls ghostly. From tower tops and windows, dots of fire burned.

"Who would build such a place?" she wondered.

"Haryet Stonecraft," Redmantyl answered. "She was the first Layn Redmantyl to make her home in the Northlands, one hundred and thirty years past. This is her design. Wizards of old lived at Orkeney Castle in Skotslande. 'Tis in ruins these days and not nearly half so large as this."

"How many have lived here?"

"Five, myself included. You shall see how it is to live within the fancy of a great wizard's mind." They stepped forward and Laurel gasped and clutched his arm. She had not realized that the only path from the barbican to the castle was the bridge, a narrow span over a vast chasm. How far was the ground below? Laurel could not see. To look downward into endless darkness was dizzying. Was there ground at all? It seemed to her that she heard waves crashing against distant rocks—but that could be the blood pounding in her ears.

Redmantyl held her against the folds of his cloak. "Don't be afraid."

"There's nothing beneath us!"

"Of course there is." He took her shoulders and turned her gently so that she could see the bridge straight before her. "Look about you, Laurel. Three yards of solid stone to either side! We shan't fall." He brought her forward a single step.

Laurel found it easiest to cross with her eyes fixed upon the tallest tower, directly ahead. If she did not try to look down, she could walk as she might along a woodland path. With each step, they drew nearer the castle.

"'Tis lovely," she whispered, more to herself than to her uncle. "As wondrous as I imagined."

Wizardes Cliff was a magician's hold, given to each Redmantyl in turn. The title and seat were not hereditary, she knew; they were taken by the supreme wizard and held until another more powerful could win them. Laurel was proud that her uncle had claimed the title and defended it against all challengers, for most wizards to attain that level of power were ancient, at least eighty and often near one hundred. The present Redmantyl was forty-seven.

At the end of the bridge, at the tall tower, a portcullis lifted to admit them. They walked down a curving stairway along the inner wall of the tower and into an adjacent hall. A manservant sat in the doorway, half-asleep and wrapped in a cloak.

"Simon!" Redmantyl shoved him into wakefulness. "Have you been here since my departing?"

"No, M'Lord," the young man answered. "I 'eard the trumpeting at the gates an' came right down. Bloody silly 'our t'be coming 'ome if ye'd asked me on it."

"It couldn't be helped, Lad. So much rain today, we had to ride slowly. Are our chambers prepared?"

"Yours're as ready as they were when ye left, M'Lord, and the Lady's are near as right. That is, fit for ye to rest the night if ye don't mind there being no fire, M'Lady." He addressed the maiden politely.

Laurel laughed.

"Of course she must have a fire on a chill and rainy night," Redmantyl said. "Don't wake the gentyl-maid, but see to it yourself."

"Aye, M'Lord." Simon darted down the corridor. The wizard led Laurel along the length of the Hall and into the stairwell at the far end, up three flights, around a corner, and along another corridor. Laurel was quite lost; she only knew that they had passed into a second building, much larger than the first. Redmantyl opened a door.

"These are my chambers. We'll sit here 'til Simon's done."

A low fire glowed in the enormous fireplace and a pot of brown broth bubbled over the coals. Half a loaf of bread and a flask and bowl were left on the nearest table.

"Who was here?" Laurel wondered. "The manservant?"

"Most likely," Redmantyl answered as he swung the iron kettlehook out from the fire and tipped the pot to fill the bowl. "He may have use of this room when I am out. He's slept here as well, I expect." He set the bowl before her. "Are you hungry, Niece?"

She was, and had already broken off a piece of bread. "He speaks so strangely. He is–" Laurel's education was not extensive, but her geography was adequate. The Norman Empire consisted of seven kingdoms: Angelande, Eirelande, Skotslande, Gallys, France, the Northlands and Burgundy. "Is he Irish? English?"

"English, London-born," Redmantyl answered. "I found him on my travels. He had been thrown to the streets by his last master and was in search of a place. He'd never seen a wizard, I believe. Certainly, I was the first likely person the poor beggar had seen that day. He took a liking to me and followed me from the city. I've not been able to lose him since."

He spoke with amusement and affection, which surprised Laurel. So great a Lord would take up a beggar-boy from the streets—and the streets of London, no less!

"Have you traveled much, Uncle?" She lifted her eyes from the empty bowl to look about the room, a traveler's room filled with pagan carvings, enameled boxes of alien design, rich Persian tapestries and Orient silks thrown over chairs and tables.

"Mages and young wizards travel to see the world and learn more of the ways of magic than may be taught by one master," he told her. "A wizard must experience all things."

"You've been all over the world?"

He nodded.

Egypt? Arabia? Spain? Cathay? What manner of people lived there? Could he speak their tongues? Had he seen the Pyramids? Was it true that dragons dwelt in the forests of the Ind? Laurel's questions flew in a furious burst and the wizard tried to answer as many as he could before Simon returned.

"M'Lady," the servant bowed. "Your rooms are ready."

"Gramercy, Simon." Redmantyl rose from his chair. "Laurel, Simon will show you to the chambers chosen for you. If they are not to your liking we shall find you better in the morning. Pleasant night's dreams."

"And you, Uncle." She accompanied Simon out to the corridor. "He's very kind, isn't he?"

"A proper master, 'tis true," Simon agreed. "There's not a one 'ere, maid nor lad, 'oo wouldna say so if ye'd ask." At the end of the corridor, he turned to the stairwell.

"Is it upstairs?"

"Yes, Lady."

"The servants' chambers?"

"Oh, no, M'Lady. Would ye think such a thing in 'Is Lordship's own 'ouse?" They ascended the stairs. "There's no servants in the Magne 'All, save meself, Jem, and yer own gentyl, Dulsye. T'others are in the Turret 'All, below. No, Lady. When there was last little uns in the 'ouse, so 'tis said, they 'ad their rooms above. Yers was a maiden's chambers, the granddaughter to 'Er Laynship Moruen." At the dark corridor at the top of the stairs, Simon took her arm.

"You were not here then."

Simon laughed. "Me? I'm not thirty an' always been with 'Is Lordship. 'Twas the old cook, Edda. She told me of it when we 'ad the 'ouse dusted up for ye, M'Lady, an' she's been 'ere near as long as there's been a castle standing." They passed several doors and he opened one. "'Course, it 'an't been opened since, an' fifty years past."

Candles blazed in the sitting room and a fire burned in the bedchamber beyond. Once Simon had gone, Laurel undressed, throwing cloak, kirtle, shirt, and hose on the squat chest at the foot of the bed. She took her nightshirt from her bundle and pulled it on, then began to explore. It was strange to have such large rooms to herself; her cubby at the Mayor's Hall had only been large enough to keep a narrow bed. This chamber was larger than the room Igren and Iobethe shared.

She examined the riches of her new kingdom, the ivy vines carved on the bedposts and the legs of the tables and chairs, the velvet bed-curtains, the carpets on the polished floors, the tapestries woven with fabulous craftwork. Upon one cloth, centaurs ran past glossy green trees, bows drawn and quivers full; upon another, a fierce, red-eyed knight in gleaming armor stood upon what appeared to be a loose pile of skulls and bones; on a third, an eight-armed woman-creature sat before a burning brazier. Figures from myths and legends Laurel did not know. Her uncle would.

She brought her bundle to the dressing-room to arrange her things, but soon abandoned the effort. A single drawer in the great carven wardrobe contained all her clothes and new treasures. Seated before the vanity table, she combed her hair and pinned up the short silver plaits with her tortoise-shell combs, studying the effect in her new mirror. A large mirror hung on the wall, but the polished metal had grown splotchy with age.

The moon had sunk low in the west and a long shaft of soft light shone in through the dressing-room window and gleamed across the floor. Laurel was not at all sleepy, but she went to bed. Tomorrow, she would see all of Wizardes Cliff, more than darkened passageways and candlelit rooms.

In the night, moonbeams reached into the bedchamber and touched the comforter, then stretched across the bed, but Laurel was asleep.

When she woke, a young boy stood at the chamber doorway, bashful once she blinked at him sleepily. Laurel knew immediately who he must be, for he had the same silver-fairness as Lord Redmantyl and herself. His face was softer than his wizard-father's; the firm, squared jaw was the same, but the lines of his mouth and brow were more rounded, not merely with youth, but with a gentler disposition. His long, silvery hair frothed in wild ringlets, uncombed as boys' would be, and a silver amulet hung on a black ribbon about his throat.

She smiled at him. "Good morrow."

"Father said we mustn't disturb you— I didn't mean to— We only meant to see if you were awake—Olyr, Godefroi, and I," he apologized. "I'm Orlan."

"I guessed." She sat up. "We're cousins. Do you live up here too?"

"No, not me. The 'prentices share rooms up the way and Father said I might come upstairs soon, when Olyr leaves."

"Where are the other boys?"

Orlan glanced back at the doorway. "They didn't dare come in. I would, for we are cousins, as you say, and I thought I might see you.

Godefroi and Olyr wait in the sitting room."

She kicked aside the bedclothes. "Let me alone to dress and I'll be out shortly. Tell them, Cos." She pushed him playfully out the door and shut it.

Her clothes had been left on the chest at the foot of the bed and Laurel dressed quickly, tying gaiters and shirt-laces with swift and nimble fingers. On impulse, she ran to the dressing-room wardrobe and found her box of tawdries. She selected a red ribbon and tied it at her jerkin lacings.

Orlan was in the sitting room with two older boys: One was Laurel's age, a pale, slender boy with dark, curly hair and beautifully large brown eyes; the other was perhaps twenty, a tall, broad-shouldered youth with straight black hair to his shoulders and the piercing eyes and hawkbeak nose particular to the common folk of the Northlands. Both were on their feet as she entered.

"My cousin Laurel," Orlan announced. As he took the tone of a herald, the apprentices were lost to the proper reply.

"An honor, Damosel," the elder spoke.

Laurel smiled; she had been called many names—*Brat* mostly— but never anything so fine as *Damosel* or *Lady*.

"No, you must call me Laurel," she replied. "And you are–?"

"Olyr of Grynstephan," he introduced himself.

"Godefroi Suanesbloode, at your service." The name meant nothing to Laurel, so the younger boy explained: "My mother is Arysbethe Darklingsuan, a wizard, Layn of St. Eduardes Isle."

"My Lord said that we must show you about," said Olyr.

"After breakfast," Orlan tugged at her shirtsleeve. "Come along. I'll show you the way."

"*We'll* show you, Damosel," Olyr corrected.

They went up the corridor in the opposite direction from the way Laurel had come the night before—"That's our room," Godefroi said as they passed one door—then around a corner, along a short passageway at the end of the Magne Hall, and down a stairwell. The boys leapt a step or two ahead, pausing at intervals to be sure that she followed.

After breakfast in the Feast Hall—a great room of long tables and oaken beams strung with scarlet banners and tall windows which looked out over enclosed plazas and the vast ocean beyond the battlements—Laurel saw the castle at a rapid pace, for the boys ran ahead of her, shouting that she must come and see another interesting thing before she had an opportunity to examine the last. They raced up stairways and along mazes of corridors, then out to the brisk, salty air and bright sunlight of the plazas, into the narrow, twisting, steep passageway of a tower, atop the battlements, down into damp catacombs within the cliffs, and up again to stand on the grassy, windswept plateau outside the castle walls.

Laurel's wonder increased. Wizardes Cliff was formidable as a fortress, perched upon high cliffs and bound with stone walls, but it remained unfathomable to her. Certainly a great wizard must keep a house of solitude, but what magical enemy would lay siege as an army might? And why were so many rooms never meant to be occupied? What of the Great Tower, which contained only endless stairways and platforms tangled to form a deliberate maze? Orlan assured her that it was the greatest fun to play in, but he had no more idea of its practical purpose than she did. The Daune Tower, the tallest tower, was another mystery, for it was hollow between the guard's post above the portcullis and its top-most room, where Redmantyl taught his apprentices the arts of magic. A narrow stairway set into the stone wound round and round like a corkscrew and a few platforms and closed rooms interrupted the climb as Laurel and her guides made their dizzying way up, but these were bare of even unused lumber. The tower was silent and the lessons of the apprentices—so the apprentices said—could go on each day without interruption.

While Godefroi and Olyr were at their lessons, Laurel resumed her exploration of Wizardes Cliff. With Orlan, she looked into every room in the Magne Hall. In a hundred chambers and cubbies, they found antique furnishings covered by dusty cloths, rolled-up carpets and tapestries which, once unrolled, revealed patterns colorful and scenes macabre, paintings of red-robed wizards and solemn-faced children and subjects blacked indistinguishably with age, more books filled with minuscule script, rings and amulets engraved with faded spells, jeweled daggers, swords in richly wrought scabbards, sea shells, silver goblets, walking sticks, statuettes of jade and gold and polished wood in shapes human and animal and bizarre—Laurel could not imagine anything on Earth that resembled some of the manikins left on dusty shelves in long-forgotten rooms. Orlan identified some, but not all, for only a wizard would understand such mysteries.

"But I'll learn," he confided. "I'll be a great wizard one day, as Father is."

"You're so sure you'll be magical?"

"I must be," the boy answered simply. "Father says I may 'prentice soon."

"Will you stay here?" Laurel asked. "Or will my uncle send you to another wizard as Godefroi's mother did?"

"Oh, I shall stay with Father," Orlan said. "My Layn Arysbethe has 'prentices and there are no other wizards—none that Father trusts."

Together, they looted chests and wardrobes filled with garments oddly different from the modern fashions: the tunics were cut squarely, the shoes pointy-toed, little gems and pearls worked into fanciful embroidery and ribbons flew everywhere. The stern warrior-Emperor Eduarde Redlyon, who had ruled for most of the nineteenth century, and his ascetic sons, Kharles and Dafythe, had put an end to such frivolous affectations. Laurel had never seen anything to match this ancient finery and she dressed herself, laughing, tripping on the dragging hems of grown folk's robes, running with Orlan from room to room to find more elaborate garb.

"So many people lived here," she observed.

"In Layn Moruen's time," Orlan, lost in blue velvet, replied.

"Simon told me I am given her granddaughter's chambers."

"'Tis true. When she became Redmantyl, she wed a famous courtier of the Duke's court and gathered the talented of her children and grandchildren here—a dozen of them. My Lord Dafythe would come to Greenwaters Island for the hunting and take lodging here in the old days. They had great feasts and even dances on the plazas, so Simon said."

"I didn't know wizards had husbands."

"They don't always," said Orlan. "But it's not forbidden. Wizards may marry if they choose."

"Was your mother Lady of Wizardes Cliff, Cos? I've never heard."

"Mother was no one, not even to Father. He's never married." The words were spoken easily, but the boy was not at ease. "Wizards don't always keep their children. They leave them with kin or at abbeys, or they never know them at all."

"My uncle did not know of you?" Laurel asked, amazed.

"When Mama died, he came to me. He said that he was my father and he brought me here." Orlan struggled to free himself from the velvet robes. "There was no Redmantyl's child in this house before me, not since Layn Moruen's day. No one knew what they must call me or what I ought to wear." He smoothed the scarlet sash across his chest. "I wore Godefroi's gray– Oh, Laurel, the maiden in your room—Moruen's granddaughter—was mother to My Layn Arysbethe, Godefroi's mother, and *she* was a lesser wizard herself, Father says. Blood tells in magic. Father believes so. But there are not many

21

families as ours and Godefroi's. Most of the great wizards of old were unnamed bastards." The boy blushed suddenly. "They couldn't say if their mothers or fathers were magical."

Simon found them amidst this disarray, but he allowed that Laurel might have any antique garb she desired. "'Is Lordship wouldna keep the littlest thing from ye, Dam'sel," he assured her. "'Whate'er she will 'ave.' 'E said as much 'Imself."

Laurel needed no more encouragement and gathered up finery as fit and design caught her fancy: shirts heavy with lace, a long cloak lined with green paisley, a courier's brief, brown jerkin and breeches laced by red ribbons. She found long tunics of dark gray, Orlan's color, with full skirts beneath and she delighted in them until she tried one and found it heavy and cumbersome. The tunics were swiftly put away, but Orlan kept the scarlet sashes, their arabesques of gold thread only a little tarnished.

The Chatelaine Adyna summoned the housemaids to Laurel's chambers and the girl surrendered her treasures to be cleaned and repaired, then continued her games with her cousin. When Olyr returned from the Daune Tower, he stopped at Laurel's doorway to watch the servants at their needlecraft.

"Chyelde Orlan does enjoy digging about the old wardrobes and playing dress-up," he said. "But did you not bring finery of your own to suit, Damosel?"

Laurel scowled. She did not like this apprentice's pert tone, as if he meant every word to insult her. She had endured more than enough insults in New York and she would not here, where everyone had made her so welcome.

"Here, where did you find that?" The youth caught sight of the toy Orlan held, a marionette with a white, painted face and mandarin robes.

"'Tis Laurel's gift to me from Storm Port."

"Let me see." Olyr took it from him and examined it critically. "A pretty toy—the sort to suit you, Chyelde. From Cathay, is it?"

"I bought it of an old Orient man," Laurel answered. "Where is Godefroi?"

"Still at his lessons." He lounged against the mantelpiece, puppet limp across his hand. "I am nearly adept, you know, and I prepare for my mage-vows by testing the strength of my will and learning the spells my master sets for me. Shall I show you, Damosel?"

He let the marionette drop—Orlan gave a cry of dismay—but before the doll body and slender ebony rods clattered on the floor, the apprentice made a gentle motion with his left hand and spoke a string of unfamiliar, liquid syllables. The little figure jerked upright and began to move in a twitching, clumsy dance. Orlan snatched at it; Olyr sent the puppet jumping out of his grasp.

"It's mine, Olyr. Give it to me."

The apprentice laughed. "You could not play with it so even if you knew the spell." Another leap eluded Orlan's grasp. Olyr glanced at Laurel. "Chyelde Orlan will sometimes show a talent for the material medium, but he cannot command it."

The wall behind them gave a great thump, as if struck by an enormous fist. Laurel flinched.

"Orlan." Olyr grinned. "You see his talent for yourself. If it troubles you, Damosel, you must say to him as My Lord does—*Be calm*—and the lad will gain control of himself, if he can."

Orlan's face, usually pale, was pink. The wall thumped again.

"No," Laurel said, rising. "I should not have my cousin distressed at all." A flash of ferocity startled the apprentice; Olyr stepped back and stumbled against the doorframe. Blinking, he retreated.

"Beastly, beastly boy!" she cried after him.

After this, Orlan was always at Laurel's side, taking her for his champion. On Sunday morning, he came to his cousin's room early.

"What shall we do today, Laurel?"

"'Tis a holiday," she reminded him.

"Oh," Orlan answered. "We don't go to Mass."

"Not at all?"

"You may if you wish. Par Raymond, the parish priest at Grynlet, comes to the chapel this afternoon and the servants go to Mass. I would go too 'til my confirmation, then Father said I needn't if I didn't want to. *He* doesn't."

"Where is it?"

"The chapel? At the front halls." He went to her dressing-room window and pointed over the chasm to the barbican on the opposite cliffs. "Do you see that little building in the trees? There. I don't believe Father's ever been in it."

"My uncle is not a Christian?" Laurel thrilled as she recalled how Redmantyl had behaved so oddly in the cathedral at Storm Port. It was said that wizards did not serve any religion. Could this be true?

"I think he is," said Orlan. "He says he believes in God, but he knows other gods too and he will not worship any. Sunday is no different from the other days." The boy jumped down from the broad wainscotting. "We could go riding. Would you like to? I used to ride when Kyarde and Kai were here."

"The Chatelaine's sons?" Laurel had learned that, with her little girl at the castle, the Chatelaine Adyna had two boys, one a novice with the Brothers of St. Yzra in Yrfordeshire and the other squire to the Captain of the Guard at Storm Port.

"They were my friends," Orlan answered. "The apprentices are so much older than I and they never minded me except as Lord Redmantyl's son before Kyarde left, and little more now. Do you ride?"

"Not well," Laurel admitted.

"Nor I," Orlan said, smiling. "But we shan't go far."

Laurel donned her newly repaired cloak and beribboned tunic and breeches while her cousin ran downstairs to change into his riding habit. He returned with the apprentices.

"They want to come along."

"If you will have our company, Laurel," Godefroi said.

"We have nothing else to do," Olyr added.

Laurel could only consent. The stable by the castle gates contained stalls for more than two dozen horses, but only five were kept now: the palfrey, Orlan's shaggy black and white pony, Lord Redmantyl's mount, and two sleek and swift couriers' steeds; a groom saddled all but Redmantyl's horse. Laurel was most concerned with keeping in her saddle when they broke into a trot, but the palfrey was gentle and, with care, she made her way down through the village of Lyges and along the road through the woods beyond. Eventually, the little party stopped at a cove, which the boys announced as Dubbs Beach.

They tied the horses at the edge of the woods. Godefroi pulled off his boots and Orlan threw his riding cloak over a tree branch—then both stopped and looked at her.

"I didn't think–" said Orlan. "I didn't think of you being a girl."

"Oh, there's no fuss to it, Cos," Laurel answered lightly. "You swim here and I'll go down the beach." Before the boys could protest, she disappeared down a footpath at the edge of the wood and did not look back until the forest curved against the sand and the boys were out of sight. There, she undressed and plunged into the water. The cold, salty, cleansing splash embraced her.

Laurel was a strong swimmer and fearless of drowning. Beyond the breakers, she dove, kicking to reach down as far as she could, then burst to the surface, gasping, when she could no longer hold her breath. She laughed for the simple delight of so much cool, open water. She could not feel too guilty about forsaking Mass for this private pleasure; she had done so before.

St. Matthieu's, the favored church of New York, was small in comparison with the cathedral of Kallaykirke across the river; its close nave was cozy enough in winter, but unbearably hot and stuffy on summer days. The merchant folk called it intimate but, of course, the merchants took every opportunity to snub the neighboring French Bishop. Grimacing imps peered down from pillar-perches, windows with small, uncolored diamond-shaped panes let in faint light, and the congregation was especially proud of its one, pale rose window, imported from Rome. The family of Nikholas Uinmerchant had their own pew; Igren was permitted to join her parents in the front once she had been confirmed, but Laurel had always remained with her smaller cousins and the servants at back, in dry and oppressive darkness. She was meant to keep the little maids awake, but often fell asleep herself. The church was an alien place where, try as she might to mimic the faithful, she never truly belonged. The hymns, the ceremonies, the high-toned Latin service were beautiful, but incomprehensible. The images of the martyrs and the tortured form on the crucifix were strange to her. Why would anyone, godling or no, sacrifice themselves for the sake of lesser souls?

Kaiese called her impious for her boredom, but she had not protested too much once Laurel began to leave before Mass on Sunday mornings. Once free, Laurel had gone to her favorite spot along the Froth River, beyond the town. She went alone there too.

The woods had been her element. In the long stretch of wilderness along the river above New York and Kallaykirke, she bathed, ran barefoot in the soft forest carpeting, climbed up into the ancient branches and sat for hours, dreaming that she lived in the treetops and would not so soon, and inevitably, be called back to the town. In the scent of the pines, the brush of meadow grasses against her calves, the cool of green water, the decayed gold of last year's leaves, she touched something crucial. She felt the life around her. In the hushed breeze in the tall birches and pines, she sometimes imagined she heard the last faintly echoed whispers of the roar of the elder gods who had guarded their wild world when it was young—but only a whisper.

Laurel scrambled back to the sand, teeth chattering, and pulled on her shirt, hose and boots. She paced the dry margin of sand, shying stones at the waves or at the gulls to send them screaming into the air, or simply to find out how far she could throw.

A boy shouted from the trees: "Laurel!"

"Here!"

Olyr stepped onto the sand, uncertain and eyes downcast until he saw that she was dressed.

"Where are Godefroi and Orlan?" she asked.

"Orlan's still in the water, but Godefroi and I began to worry. You do not know your way about these woods, Damosel. Godefroi's gone to search–" he pointed northward. "Too timid to look, I'll wager." Olyr laughed. "He's tremendously heart-caught by you. So is Orlan, in a child's way. The little fool, not to see you a maid! But you mustn't think too much on their affection, Damosel. They don't know many girls."

Laurel grinned. "And you, Olyr?"

He shrugged, affecting an indifferent air. "The laundry-lasses and scullions are not beneath my notice. My family are drovers, honest workaday folk." He spoke with pride. "No nobles."

"Olyr, I am no noblewoman."

"You are niece to My Lord Redmantyl–"

"My mother was a swordswoman," Laurel said bluntly. "I have no father. I am a bastard and worse than bastard, for no one may name me."

Olyr was abashed. "I did not know. Your mother. Where is she now?"

"She was sent to the Eduardesmarch." Laurel pronounced this *Eddermark*. "She served in the border guard at Redlyon, and died there. My Aunt Kaiese kept me—but I think I lived there even when my mother was at New York." Olyr stood quietly, listening. "I remember when she came to see me. She had a scar, here." Laurel traced one finger along her forearm, from wrist to elbow. "And she smelled of smoke. She had a pipe! She lit it with little sparks from her fingers. Do you know, Olyr, I wanted to be like her, with bright armor and a sword and a long wooden pipe to make smoke rings. They sent her sword to us and my aunt said I might keep it. I am fairly good with it now."

She took up a white stick of driftwood and swung it to find the balance, then whirled on her toes and drove the point toward Olyr as if she meant to stab him through; Olyr jumped back with a yelp. Laurel leapt again and chased him up the beach, swinging alternately at his head and his legs but taking care not to strike. The apprentice tripped on his own clumsy feet.

Laurel knelt at his side. "Are you hurt?"

"No." Olyr brushed the sand from his breeches, then looked up at her. "You are not at all as I expected," he confessed.

"What did you expect, goode lad?"

Olyr smiled. "My Lord Redmantyl set the house aflutter at your coming. He gave such attention to your rooms, as if you must be particular of your furnishings, and he chose your maid himself. When you first came to the castle, Simon told us that you were a fine Lady. I imagined you must be an over-dainty maiden who would have everyone fuss at her. Everyone's made such a fuss. But you would be a soldier–"

"I think my father might have been a soldier," Laurel told him. "My Aunt Kaiese always looked so angry when I asked."

"You could be, truly, Damosel."

She smiled. "Olyr, you must call me by my right name, if we are friends. Shall we be friends?" She offered a hand: Olyr took it as she helped him regain his feet.

"Of course– ah– Laurel." The boy colored unexpectedly. "If you like." He turned his eyes from hers quickly. "We ought to find Godefroi."

"He can't have gone far. I'll race with you to find him." Laurel scrambled up and ran into the forest, Olyr after her. She flew to keep her lead, determined to show the apprentice that she was no delicate damosel; in New York, there had been no youth she could not outrun nor any she could not defeat in unfair fight. She had defeated Olyr today. She did not fully understand how, but she knew that so long as she stayed ahead of him, her victory was sealed.

By the time she found Godefroi, Olyr was breathless and far behind.

As they rode home, Orlan and Godefroi chattered gaily, competing for her attention, and Olyr was unspeaking but kept his eyes entirely upon her. She had not known boys like this in New York, boys who were not afraid of her and did not hate her. The Sheriff's sons, Peter and Martin, were especially horrid brats who tormented her at every opportunity and she had begun to believe that all boys were just as horrible.

Laurel turned suddenly and Olyr quickly ducked his head and refused to meet her eyes. She had beaten him today. That was pleasant too.

Laurel sat beneath the west window in the Daune Tower. The hexagonal room covered the top floor of the tower and was broken into small compartments by shelves and tables crowded with books and rolls of parchment. A brass-hinged tome lay across her lap—the brown ink was too faint to be read by candlelight—and she did not hear Olyr and Godefroi come up the stairwell.

"My Lord Redmantyl's sent half the household in search of you," the older boy said. "May Eve falls tonight. He must be out of the castle and wants us all at the table before he goes."

"Yes, I'll come," she answered absently. "Olyr, this book says that nothing can be created or destroyed. What does that mean? Everything must die eventually."

"Yes, but it continues in one form or another. Things die, but their bodies remain and return to the earth to feed new life. The elements which make up mortal beings are never lost."

"And magic?"

"Yes, magic too. A spell will hold its essence long after the wizard who cast it has died."

"What happens to the wizard?"

"I don't know what you mean." Olyr glanced at Godefroi, who shook his head.

"Listen to this:

> *The source, therefore, is at the heart. Its beating forces the soul beyond the limits of living flesh, but without the guidance of human will it is no more than the briefest flash: That is, a marvel of God's Work but no art of Humanity. It knows not good nor evil. It is our will as creatures of reason which sets us above the mindless beasts. If the simplest exercises of magic free our souls from*

> *their fleshly houses, then its highest form*
> *shall free us of all physicalities and we*
> *become as angels."*

"Perhaps it means that the soul joins the Angelic Hosts," Olyr suggested.

"Yes, but all souls go to Heaven. Why pick out magicians in particular?" Godefroi asked. "It can't mean that only those with magic are able to free their souls for salvation. We've been called unholy often enough."

"Exactly," Laurel agreed. "It sounds as if the souls of magicians are different from other mortals. A magician may become a pure force of power when he departs his body."

"What book is that?" said Olyr. "It sounds nonsense to me."

"'Tis *The Source of Human Magic* by Uillod of Orkeney."

"You've been reading that? Why?"

"I mean to read every book in this house."

"'Tis a task only the harshest master would set for his 'prentice," Godefroi said, smiling. "My Lord Redmantyl's library is greater than the libraries of Maryesfont and Padua."

"What else have you read?" asked Olyr.

What else? In her quest to know all about magic, she came to the Daune Tower whenever the apprentices were not at their lessons, she took books from her uncle's sitting-room, she explored the vast collections of the Spell Tower. Many of the works were in unfamiliar scripts and languages, but the books she found in the Norman tongue were little more decipherable. She read, though she did not understand: Tests to determine the purity of a unicorn's horn. Reports of the fertility rites of the Druids and the sacrificial rites of the Aztecs. Maps of the human body, noting the influence of planets and signs of the zodiac over each part of the anatomy. Maps of the Earth with layers peeled away like the skins of an onion. A collection of Grail myths gathered by a previous Redmantyl. A debate on the widespread belief that a wizard could transmit magic through the sexual act, with detailed examples to prove and refute which made the maiden blush. Treatises on the true relationship between the written sign and the thing signified. A text of numerics that sounded like impossible conjuring tricks. A book in Arabic prefaced by an enigmatic warning in common Norman—*The Great Lord is not to be Named, for He is Mighty above all Mortals and Lost Immortals and Lord of the Ether between the Worlds. This is his sign*—and the lower half of the page was covered with a black and gold illustration of a huge eye.

"Nothing," she answered. "Nothing that I understand. Magic is so wound up in mystery." Laurel closed the book. "I expect it must be wondrous to be a wizard."

"I cannot tell you truly yet," Olyr replied. "But it must be so."

"What do you study?"

The youth laughed. "Magic, of course."

"No, I mean to ask—What precisely, in the study of magic? I thought you must have magic or not have it and cannot learn it."

"You can't learn it," said Godefroi. "But if you have it, you must learn to command it and so become a true wizard. A 'prentice serves his master in exchange for his education. We gather herbs from the gardens and the woods at My Lord Redmantyl's direction, so we come to know their virtues. We study the stars. We assist in the practice of My Lord's spellcraft and we copy out of the books–" he gestured at the shelves, "to learn the secrets of wizards of old."

"Where does my uncle go tonight?" Laurel asked. "Is it something wizardly?"

"Most wizardly," said Olyr. "May Night is one of the nights of Wizard's Keep."

"What does he do?" But the apprentices could not tell her more.

"Only full wizards have that knowledge," said Godefroi. "I may tell you simply that My Lord Redmantyl leaves the castle on certain nights at dusk and does not return 'til the morrow."

"Only wizards know," Olyr repeated. "We do not yet."

"In truth," the younger apprentice added. "It may be no great matter at all. As you say, magic is full of mysteries. There is so much ceremonial nonsense which we must learn because wizards always have. My Lord Redmantyl answers so many questions by saying 'it is the way,' as if it could never be different."

Olyr grinned. "Hark at his petty heresies! What will you do, Lad—have the world's good order tumble down into chaos?"

"No," Godefroi ducked his head. "But I don't believe things must be as they are now."

"It is the way they are," Olyr answered. "The way they ought to be. If 'twere not, the Good Lord would change it Himself and not leave it to such pups as you. 'Tis pert to ask so many questions which cannot be answered."

Godefroi did not reply. "We ought to go now," he said. "My Lord waits." He turned to the stairs; neither Laurel nor Olyr moved to follow, and he went down without them.

Laurel replaced the book on the shelf. "Olyr, will you show me a spell?"

"You did not like it when I last cast a spell."

"You were cruel to Orlan," she answered.

Olyr could not deny this. "Arts of spellcraft are often past the understanding of magicless minds," he said.

"I am magical!" she insisted. "I will understand. Olyr, I ask for no incantation to call a demon to my service, only a simple trick. Please?" Her eyes were as earnest as a child's but as commanding as a grown wizard's—very like Redmantyl's when he engulfed his apprentice in his greater will.

Olyr surrendered. "Very well." He felt at his pockets for a bit of charcoal, then knelt on the chalk-scarred wooden floor, which was regularly used by the apprentices for such exercises.

Laurel watched as he drew a great circle about himself. "Is that a pentacle or pentagram?" She had discovered both in her readings, but had not yet learned to distinguish between them.

"Pentacle," he answered, proud to display his education. "A pentacle is a star within a circle. A pentagram is a pentagon. Either can be used to fix the elements of a spell. The five-pointed star represents the history of Mankind. God creates the earth." He drew a line down from the top of the circle to the bottom. "We rise from the dust to our mortal state." An upward stroke, to a point midway on the circle's rim. "We live our mortal lives." A third line crossed the circle. "We die and descend to dust." The next line went down. "But we are redeemed and the immortal soul rises again into Heaven." A final stroke joined the starting point at the top.

"I thought that the pentacle was diabolical."

The apprentice laughed. "Laurel, I know no such crafts! My Lord says that necromancy is the corruption of a right magician and 'tis a danger to study such evil. The black arts destroy and pervert. A sorcerer of such arts would draw his star upside-down, pointing hellward. 'Tis all the difference in the world! As we are God's creation, we are protected within this sign. No evil may pass."

He pulled Laurel into the circle with him, wrote about the rim and placed a gyre—"to set motion"—at the top.

The alphabet he used was familiar to Laurel, but the words were strange. "What language is that?"

"Latin."

"Why?"

"That's the way the spell is written. I cannot change it."

"Does it matter? You might write a spell of the same sense in our common Norman or any other language."

Olyr shook his head. "The power begins at the heart," he recited. "It is directed by the mind and it is brought to use by the hand and tongue in spells—That is the litany we apprentices learn upon our first day of lessons. The devices of the spell focus the mind to its purpose and direct our magic. You must perform the words and symbols and rites exactly as they are written. Every mark is very precise—it means something that no other sign can replace. There are subtleties of meaning even in similar words in different languages. The spell would be changed in Norman."

"What if I don't know my Latin?"

"Then it won't work for you. You have to understand the words." He stood beside her, hand at her waist. "But it will for me. Watch." In tones which rang loud in Laurel's ears, he pronounced the words he had written.

For a moment, the air hung heavy about them as the spell began to gel. Something was about to happen—Laurel could feel it—then, as suddenly, the spellcraft shattered, ricocheting from its carefully ordered formation. Sparks flashed before her and she leapt back against Olyr with a cry.

"That isn't what should happen," the boy said in bafflement. "Some erratic catalyst upset the balance—" He looked up. "Laurel, are you hurt?"

"N-no," she answered. With the explosion, she felt something like the tingle that always accompanied a burst of fire, like the electric thrill of enchantment which had engulfed her in the golden spire. And more. A strange, powerful sensation began to spread within her, from her pounding heart to her dizzied head to the burning ends of her fingers, urging her— No, she did not know what she was meant to do, only that she must do it, and soon before she was overtaken.

Olyr blinked at her uncertainly. "Come on, then. We are late."

Laurel rose, legs trembling, and ran after him.

"Olyr, show me more. Show me a spell I might do."

"It didn't work."

"Yes, it did! Only not as you thought it would."

The apprentice frowned thoughtfully as they went down the corkscrew stairway. "Perhaps. It was a spell for the material medium."

"A spell for— What?"

"You see, my magic best commands material," Olyr explained. "That is, I may direct solid objects at my will. Other magicians

33

Kathryn L. Ramage

command other media—water, wind, and light. My Lord Redmantyl is a fabulous wizard of light."

"Lightmaster," said Laurel.

"You may be a magician of light as well. If you are, a spell for the material would react against your nature and go awry."

"How shall I perform a spell of light?"

"I don't know. My Lord Redmantyl only blinks when he wishes to perform some marvel. He has a trick–" He stopped at the door to the Shadu Hall and made the gesture, spreading his fingers and rotating his wrist slightly, but no bright orb appeared.

"I've seen that. 'Tis done so–" She lifted a hand.

"No, left hand, always. My Lord will tell you that spells must be performed with the left hand, nearest the heart." He took her arm, gently, and bent it at the elbow so that her hand stood a few inches from her face. "Now, cup your hand as if you hold a small globe upon the fingertips, and turn your wrist. Focus your attention upon the center and–"

Laurel yelped, for a tiny, bright spot appeared above her palm.

"Don't drop it!"

"I won't. Oh, look!" The spot grew brighter and took on a bluish glitter as it whirled out to meet her fingers. This brightness was part of her, like the involuntary flares, but stronger, deeper, more completely formed. All the blazing energies which had coursed through her had been brought to this one brilliant orb. All her magic was focused there. If she moved her hand, the spell would vanish. Blue darkened to purple and darker, black as a solid ball of onyx. "What do I do with it?"

"Nothing more. 'Tis simply a pretty toy."

"Oh." Laurel tried to repeat her uncle's more spectacular trick and threw the orb into the air, but it dissolved as it left her fingers. "But I can do it."

"Yes," Olyr beamed. "'Tis marvelous." And he kissed her.

Laurel had never kissed a boy before; her stomach gave a strange, funny jump as Olyr pressed his lips to hers. Then he stepped back and looked more surprised than she did.

"Apologies, Laurel," he mumbled, and walked away.

"No, don't be sorry." She ran to catch him. "Have you kissed many girls before?"

"One or two," he answered cautiously. "My Lord does not approve it."

"Why not? What is it to concern him?"

"It interferes with my magic to sport with maids," Olyr said.

34

"Interferes? How?"

"It distracts from the self-command I must achieve to become a proper magician. Love is not a thing 'prentices can enjoy."

"Oh," said Laurel. "Are you truly sorry you kissed me then?"

Olyr's face was dark red. "No, Laurel. But I mustn't."

That night, Laurel turned restlessly in strange dreams. She wandered the evening hour between sunset and night when faint gray light remains to reveal a twilight landscape. Though she could see for miles in the still, clear nightfall, the scene was unfamiliar. She didn't know this place. The sky draped low like a curtain of inky silk and dim glittering stars lay in configurations unlike those she had always known. The earth beneath her feet was cool tar. Shadow-shapes appeared here and there beside her path, obsidian, and trees snatched at her with blackened branches. Hands outstretched, her fingers brushed at shade-cloaked surfaces. A soft glow radiated from the heart of her being—not enough light to give her full sight in the growing darkness, but sufficient to guide her.

With a flurry of movement like a sudden breeze, she was taken up by an invisible throng. Feet stomped and shuffled. Unseen bodies pressed on all sides. Hands plucked her clothing, tugged her, drew her forward. A thousand voices murmured, first so softly that she could hear no more than buzz, then louder and louder until the cry was unmistakable:

"The King! The King! Take her to the King!"

In the way of dreams, she moved slowly, caught in the currents of onflowing motion. Laurel struggled. She pushed at the crowd, but her hands slipped against them; cloth gave way as if no body beneath supported it; shapes melted like mist as she resisted their tug. She stumbled against a black wall, scraped against it, fell. The throng moved on without her.

The stone surface was slick and dark as polished ebony, but she clung to it with the desperation of a shipwreck victim who finds a flotsam spar. She began to climb, pulling and straining upwards. At any moment, she knew, she would slip and fall back to the earth, back into the grip of that unseen crowd. Far beneath her, they chanted.

"The King! The King! The King Comes!"

A hand reached down suddenly; she took it, and was pulled up.

She stood atop a high, broad wall that curved away in the fading light in either direction. Below, the crowd writhed. Sometimes they were human, peasants in ragged garb. Sometimes they were monkeys, howling and leering. Sometimes she thought that they must be sea-things, tentacled, gelatinous. At times, they were a dark, seething mass. They surged toward a great door, miles tall, that loomed against the twilight sky. A man stood at her side. Her uncle? She could see nothing save a tall silhouette, but the large hand still in hers was reassuring.

"There is danger all about you," he said. "But They can't harm you if They don't know you're here."

"They?" she asked. "Who?"

"They are nameless. Call them what you will—it matters not. Their purpose is unchanged."

"The King! The King! The King Comes!"

"They will come, eventually," he told her. "You must protect yourself."

"What must I do?"

"You have the light, Child. It is power enough to defeat Them. Take care how you use it."

"The King! The King! The King Comes!" The chant rose to a howl, fear or delight, as the miserable subjects drove themselves to a frenzy. "The King Comes! The King! The King is Nigh!"

The great door swung open. With a thunderous rumbling, darkness spilled out like inkpots upturned. Laurel felt danger within the blackness, danger like nothing she had ever known. It sought to devour everything. It sought light. It sought life. It sought her.

They can't harm you if They don't know you're here. Laurel crouched against the cold stone, hoping that she might pass unnoticed. Inky tendrils spread like grasping fingers against the sky, blotting out the faint starlight. Below, the crowd ceased its wails and moans as the dark tide swept them into oblivion. It washed through the valley, splashed against the glinting surface of the wall; yet it was alive somehow. There was direction, purpose, in its movements that showed some ghastly, conscious will. Laurel stared at the oncoming horror, frozen with a fascination beyond fear; she had not realized how much light remained in her nightscape before this blacker-than-black descended. In its grasp, there was nothing.

Her magic shone bright about her and made her horribly aware of how conspicuous she was. She would be seen. She would be swallowed with the rest, engulfed, lost—but not without a fight!

Heart blazing, blood pounding in her ears, she waited for the outreaching ribbons of darkness to find her. Danger thrilled through her veins. She felt herself shining like a beacon in the night. The only light in the darkness. Surely, They must see! Endless night stretched over her. The tide rose against the walls below. Darkness filled her vision. They were coming for her.

She burst into a shower of sparks and awoke with the spasms of a violent cough. Her throat rasped and her eyes streamed with tears. This was no dream; the bed was on fire.

Laurel leapt up and shrieked again and again as she slapped frantically at the coverlet. Smoke filled her mouth and nose with every breath; she choked and sobbed as she fought to smother the flames.

Bare feet pattered on her sitting-room floor and hands pounded her door.

"Laurel! Laurel!"

Olyr and Godefroi burst in and joined the battle at her side. Tendrils of flame climbed up the bed-curtains; Olyr pulled them down and beat the smoldering velvet against the floor. Godefroi grabbed the water pitcher from its stand and threw it on the bed. Laurel dragged the sodden mess of charred linen and down off the mattress, and fell to her knees, wretched and dizzy at the sickening, burnt stench.

"Take her out!"

Olyr took her arm and pulled her away.

Godefroi left the smoky bedchamber after them. Tears streaked his cinder-smudged face, but he smiled. "'Tis out now. Are you hurt?"

Laurel, still gasping for clean breath in Olyr's arms, shook her head. She tried to speak, but her voice rasped wordlessly.

"She needs water," said Olyr. "I think the smoke overwhelmed her." His hand was gentle as he pushed her scorched hair from her brow.

They sat on the sitting-room coucherie while Godefroi ran to refill the pitcher. Under the apprentices' worried gaze, Laurel drank a deep draught of the cool water, splashed more on her face and bathed her blistering feet. The boys stayed with her until Lord Redmantyl returned from his Keep in the hour before dawn.

The wizard heard his apprentices' clamorous news, then went into Laurel's bedchamber to examine the scorched curtains and ruined linen. "Niece, you are not injured?"

"No."

"Can you tell me what happened?"

She and Olyr and Godefroi had puzzled over this for hours. "I don't know, Uncle. The candle must have fallen over," she answered. "But I thought I'd put it out!"

"You did," he replied. "And, see, it is still upright." Redmantyl called abruptly to his apprentices. "Olyr, Godefroi, return to your bed. There is no more to be done tonight. The danger is past."

"You know you were the cause yourself," he said once the boys had gone.

True. She *did* know, though she hadn't wanted to confess it, even to herself. Her fire had burst beyond her control, worse than ever before. Her chambers were destroyed. She might have been killed tonight, and might have killed others. Wizardes Cliff might have burned to the ground. This strange power, linked to her unleashed temper, was monstrous. How could she own it? Thought of the damage she could wreak was more than she could bear.

More ashamed than she had been after her outbursts at New York, Laurel covered her eyes. "I'm sorry, Uncle."

But Redmantyl did not seem horrified. Rather, he gazed at her with intense interest as he asked: "Have you caused such fires before?"

"Yes, when I am angry. But I wasn't angry! I was asleep!"

"Did you do anything magical yesterday?"

"Olyr showed me a spell." She lifted her hand, but her uncle quickly captured it and pressed the fingers together.

"No. Not yet, Laurel."

"I can do it."

"You mustn't," he said. "You must learn to command your powers before they may be employed."

Laurel looked up, surprised and hopeful. "Is it true magic?"

"It is a beginning. Come to the `prenticing room after breakfast. We will test then."

"Aunt Kaiese said that I mustn't `prentice."

"She conjured me to this as well, but I did not promise. Will you protest to her if I insist in preventing you from burning my house down?"

Laurel had never willingly obeyed Kaiese before, and this seemed a most unlikely moment to begin. "No, Uncle."

Before the household stirred, Laurel rose and dressed, mindless of her raw throat and scorched feet, and ascended the Daune Tower. When Lord Redmantyl found her amidst his books, studying bright illuminations and diagrams as if she could divine the wizardly writings through them, he smiled.

He began by placing a candle before her. "Laurel, this is a simple test to determine your abilities. Place the thumb and forefinger of your left hand on either side of the wick." He brought her hand up into the proper position. "Create a spark between your fingers and light the candle. Focus. Bring your power to that spot."

Laurel frowned in concentration, then leapt back as the candlewick flamed.

"Very good!" Redmantyl moved the candle to the other side of the table. "Try to light it from where you are, without touching."

This was a little more difficult, but she could do it.

"Can you quell the flame? It is the same spell, reversed. Bring your fingers together as if to pinch the flame between. Think upon the damping and lessening of the fire, not its creation."

Laurel stared at the flame intensely, willing it out; she brought her hand up before her eyes so that the candlewick seemed to be between her fingertips, and she pinched. The flame went out.

"Excellent, Niece! That is no simple trick for a novice." The wizard took up the candle and carried it to another table. "Can you focus from so far away?"

Laurel tried the same trick of sighting the wick between her fingers; she concentrated and pushed, but no flame appeared. Then she saw that scrolls of parchment left on the table beside her were smoldering.

"Oh, Uncle, I'm sorry!" she cried as she leapt up to pat the fire out. Smoke rose from the copybooks on another table. The candle melted into a lump of wax. Laurel turned, helpless at the spreading disaster. Her cloak, thrown over a chair, burst into flame; she yelped as she threw it to the floor and stamped frantically.

"Child, sit down!" Redmantyl commanded. "Be calm."

Laurel sat. "Uncle, I'm so sorry," she said when the last fire was out.

"It is unimportant," he assured her, examining each scroll and sheaf. "Nothing is damaged beyond recovery."

"It's an evil thing!"

The wizard scowled, more angry at these words than the fires. "Certainly not. Laurel, I will tell you once—do not forget. *Magic is no evil. You are not wicked because you bear it.* It is a talent which requires much self-control, else it is dangerous, and it may be put to evil uses, but it is not wrong in itself. All depends upon the magician. You must command it without fear."

He brought down a little wooden box and retrieved a handful of chalky clay balls. "Catch." He tossed one at her. Laurel tried to fix it with her eyes but it came up too swiftly, thudded against her shoulder and fell to her lap. "Try again." A second came at her, struck her chest. "Fix upon it!" Another flew, and another after it.

"I can't!"

"Try!" A ball shot past her ear.

"No! Stop it!" Her temper flared and her power burst with it. The next ball exploded in a cloud of powder. She trembled with the released energies that rushed through her.

"Niece, you have the family temper."

"I didn't mean to–"

"I meant you to. Now I ask you to lose your anger but not your magic. Can you? Breathe deeply. Shut your eyes. Find the power within you."

Laurel shut her eyes. She felt the power about her, within her, a monstrous, enormous, growing force ready to push past her control and burn her body to ashes. It was too strong. A raging demon in her blood. A burst of fire. Evil–

No, magic was not evil. She was not evil. This power was hers and she could command it; the confidence behind Redmantyl's promise gave her the strength to try. He would not expect her to do more than she was capable.

Stubbornly, she wrestled the unrestrained magic to her will. It was only a mindless energy. She understood now. *The power begins at the heart;* she could feel the electric pulses surge there, spread through her veins and nerves from this center. *It is directed by the mind;* as she controlled her rate of breathing, the flex of her limbs, so she could control her heartbeat and through it her magic. The heart could not think. The magic had no will beyond that which she bestowed. Her. Her mind, which thought and felt and knew and contained the things that most made her who she was, possessed this ability. *She* was the conscious force.

Suddenly, her awareness opened *out.* She felt strangely larger, as if the walls and ceiling of the tower-room pressed upon her and the fragments of furniture scraped irritatingly. But her body hadn't changed. Her senses were expanded beyond the limits of physical form. The sky and sea blurred together into a dizzying, all-encompassing blue-green sphere. A hundred voices babbled around her. One blinding being blazed before her, watching her intensely, patiently. *Uncle?* She thought she screamed. This was too much at once. She wasn't ready. She needed time to sort all these new sensations out.

Then, everything fell into place. Her expanded awareness remained, but she could focus upon single elements within it. The rush of impressions ceased to bewilder and overpower her. The demon was caged. She was master of her power. It was no longer an overwhelming thing which would burst out unexpectedly and wreak damage. It was hers to direct. It was a part of her. It was her. She could not be afraid of it.

"Are you in command?"

"Yes, Uncle." She was shaking, damp with sweat, yet her voice was confident.

She opened her eyes. A ball rolled across the floor to rest at her feet. "Can you move that, Laurel?"

Laurel *pushed*, and it rolled away wildly and crashed into the wall.

"Return it to yourself."

The ball rolled back to her.

"Lift it."

She tried, but the ball only twisted on the floor like a living thing. Laurel frowned and pushed harder, and it burst in a spray of chalk dust.

"Enough." Redmantyl knelt beside her. "Laurel, I may tell you that you have no little talent. I would be honored to teach you, if you are willing to 'prentice."

"I might be a wizard one day?"

"You certainly shall be."

"I did not hope—" But she had hoped, from the moment when Kaiese had told her that she would be sent to Wizardes Cliff.

"You have performed splendidly," her uncle told her. "But you have an uneven command of your powers and magic is nothing without self-command. Laurel, listen and remember: the power begins at the heart; it is directed by the mind; and it is brought to use by the hand and tongue in spells. That is our litany."

"Yes, Uncle. Olyr taught me that. And it is through our will as reasoning humans that our magic may free our souls from mortal flesh."

Redmantyl laughed in astonishment. "Did Olyr teach you that as well?"

"I read it."

"Laurel, you are moving too swiftly. Old Uillod! Pan's pipes! Maiden, you cannot leap at the Heavens before you have learned to fly. You will only crash to earth. I shouldn't have left you untended these past weeks. Promise me, no more children's games with Olyr. Magic bears great responsibilities. It is not a thing lightly taken up for amusement's sake. If you will be a wizard, you must give yourself to serious training. We will begin at the beginning..." He brought out a fresh candle and set it before her.

"I can do that."

"Yes, but imperfectly. Keep to this one exercise 'til you can do it without setting the room afire. When you have mastered that, we shall continue."

"But–"

"Laurel, command yourself. Go to."

She spent half the morning lighting and relighting the same candle. Under the wizard's direction, her magic was forced into one narrow channel until it seemed that a thin line of fire grew from her heart to the fingertips of her left hand. Flame. Out. Flame. Out. Again and again, she repeated the exercise. All her attention focused upon that single spark. When Olyr called cheerfully from the top of the stairwell—"He's put you at lessons already?"—she started in surprise. Were the apprentices up so soon?

"We heard you would test," added Godefroi. "I knew you'd be accepted, Laurel, especially after last night. Congratulations!"

As the boys teased that she would able to read all the books she wanted, that her beribboned breeches were not proper 'prentice garb and she'd have to borrow some of their clothes, they also told her of their own work. Laurel realized that they received her as one of their own. They had been her friends before this, but had regarded her as a visitor to the castle, their master's niece, a strange damosel. She remained an outsider and it was assumed that she couldn't understand the nature of their studies; the explanations they gave her questions were always deliberately inexact. Now, she had proved herself a magician, as they were; she was welcome to the secrets of their craft.

Redmantyl called the chattering boys to order and dismissed Laurel for the rest of the day. She leapt down the steps two at a time and ran to find Orlan to tell him her news.

That evening, she set herself to meditate—her uncle had taught her to examine her powers and learn their relationship to her heart and head and the delicate network of nerves and blood vessels that ran through her flesh so that she might achieve mastery—but it was impossible to concentrate. She wasn't the maiden she'd been before her arrival at Wizardes Cliff; indeed, she wasn't the maiden she'd been yesterday. Everything was changed. Her mind was open to every sensation: The walls of her sitting room were cold and hard. The embers in the fireplace glowed and shimmered with intense heat. The fibers of the coucherie cushions and blanket pricked and scratched her bare legs.

Though the bedchamber had been cleaned and aired, a faint, sickly scent of burnt feathers remained to nauseate her. People breathed and moved and murmured. She felt them even when she shut her eyes. They pushed against her, intruding on her peace.

At last, she leapt up, flung cloak about nightshirt, and ran out. She must be free of walls, ceilings, floors; all these hard barriers pressed her, stopped her breath. A confusing jumble of living energies crowded her mind. She could not think.

She flew down the corridor, down the stairs at the back of the Magne Hall, over the castle battlements. She stopped only when she reached the edge of the cliff. Arms wide, fingers extended as if she would grasp every particle in the universe, her newly-born awareness pushed out again. Wizardes Cliff and its distractions rose at her back, but before her was vast sea and sky. Here, the energies were in harmony, soothing. She reached out. She touched the night.

There was so much, so much more than she thought there could be, so much more that remained, enticing, beyond her grasp. Her own light shone about her, a tiny glimmer in the darkness. She could guide herself with it. She was not afraid to seek answers in the enormous and complex mystery around her. She knew herself in this place. She knew what she was at last.

She understood why Lord Redmantyl had taken such an interest in her, why he had called and she had felt his summons. She understood why she had never belonged anywhere but here. She understood her burst of fiery rage—the ordinary manifestations of a young magician's power. She was not weird nor wicked; she saw her promise. She, too, would be a wizard.

tre

Power gave her understanding. As she learned to focus and shield her heightened senses from the onslaught of indiscriminate perception, her world came alive. All the wonders of existence hitherto taken for granted were now small miracles. Colors, music, scents, the most familiar of surroundings, seemed new and enervating. She felt the people around her: the urgent bedlam of worries and erratic rhythms of the castle servants and Lyges peasants as they went through their daily tasks, the peaceful and ordered melodies of Godefroi, the thrilling intensity of Olyr burst in at her in unexpected moments and faded as quickly. These impressions were vague and inconsistent, for her affinity to ordinary folk was negligible and to other magicians only slightly more distinct: the more alien they were to her own nature, the less able she was to feel them. The psychic bond was most strong with blood. She felt Orlan's turmoil as he grew into his first unrestrained powers and the emotions of a boy no longer a child as if she experienced it herself. She felt Lord Redmantyl's unquiet, the tensions he kept carefully under control; he was troubled, but Laurel knew not by what. Though the connection between them was strong, his mind dwelt upon matters past her comprehension—things of darkness and light. Wizardly things. Redmantyl felt her too and understood her thoughts a little better. It embarrassed her that he knew so well how to anticipate her abrupt changes of mood; he knew what would stir her to indignation and what would quiet her.

She saw her own magic, shining like a glimmer of moonlight from the center of her being and radiant on her skin. It was little more than a healthful glow when she was calm, but it blazed with her temper into a bright veneer of flame. The magic itself made her capable of seeing it. She realized that the glamour which cloaked Lord Redmantyl was not visible to all, and that this was how he had seen *her* from the first.

Energies more than human touched her as well. Every living thing held an innate power. Every stone had its subtle energies, every drop of rainwater, every light in the heavens. Laurel had not learned exactly what energy each possessed, but she knew it to be part of the greater flux which ran through all the universe. She felt their influence upon her, and she knew that as she grew into her magic she would be able to influence them.

She understood fire: the air was made of tiny particles, too small to see or feel, but nevertheless there. When she was angry, she touched a few of these minuscules and exploded them—and the air about her would shimmer with points of light. To create flame, she needed more particles, close together about some material that would burn: a candlewick, dry logs upon the hearth, her bedclothes. She had always been able to do this, but now she understood what she did. No second accident occurred; she had that much control.

She understood rain: clouds were made of misted water, like a cold steam. A magician need only choose a fluffy cloud, heavy with moisture, and *squeeze*. Laurel did not yet have power enough for this, but she knew how the trick was done. She sat on the castle battlements for hours, frowning at the sky, but without forming a droplet. Clouds were much easier; they only required moisture. She first cast the spell in her bedchamber with a small dish of water on the floor, and was surprised at how large a cloud so little water made. Fog filled the room within seconds, and her uncle scolded her for attempting this experiment indoors. Thereafter, she made her clouds on the plazas, where the breeze sent them out to sea.

Solid matter was more difficult to command. To levitate objects large or small, one must form an active flux of energy and *push*. More complex tasks were bound by spells, words she must speak, thoughts she must think, to direct the force of her mind. Telekinesis was not innate to her talents—she was unable to lift a thing—but it was Olyr's specialty. He could levitate himself, a difficult trick, and he claimed that he meditated an inch or two above the surface of the floor for maximum comfort and minimal distraction during this intense exercise.

Laurel longed to test the limits of her power, but her uncle always held her back. Driven by impatience and hunger to discover all that a wizard should know, she devoured Redmantyl's collections, beginning with books he had given her, then moving on to whatever she could find in the Norman tongue. Her memory for abstractions good, she absorbed the fundaments of mathematics swiftly. Euclidean geometry was amusing and non-Euclidean more difficult, but satisfying once the equations for conic sections and the circumferences of circles on spheres were conquered. Four-dimensional figures, however, remained baffling: The world only had height and width and breadth; what was the purpose of a shape that extended into the nonexistent? She was often baffled as her education progressed. She read the words, but their sense was not sensible.

Knowledge was rightfully hers, yet tantalizingly beyond her novice grasp. Lord Redmantyl promised that, as a grown wizard, she would be a master of light as he was. She would summon whirling glories at a whim. She would pull lightning from the sky. She would channel her fire into white-hot points and wield it with delicate precision to cauterize infected wounds and cut through wood and stone. All were facets of the same talent. How long must she wait before she came to such powers? Redmantyl's answer was not encouraging: Seven years of apprenticeship. And, after that, five years as a wandering mage and more years as a young wizard. Twenty, thirty years might pass before she achieved full mastery of all her skills and powers. So much time! Laurel could not bear to linger so long; she wanted to know everything now.

As Olyr completed his sixth year of apprenticeship, he retreated to an unoccupied chamber in the Shadu Hall to give himself to undisturbed hours of intense study and meditation. As a mage, he must learn to live and work alone. The room was small and bare, but it had been inhabited not too long ago: ragged copy books crowded the shelves; a great pentacle, a spell of safety, was carved into the floor and small protective wards were cut onto the door and window-latches.

"'Tis a 'prentice's room, so it will suit me perfectly," the youth told his friends. "And look! Best of all—" He opened the small chest at the foot of the bed and brought out a black mantle embellished with red and white. "I found this."

The children gathered to examine it.

"Do you think it is his?" asked Godefroi.

"'Tis too new to belong to an older wizard," Olyr said. "The last Lord Redmantyl left off his black robes fifty years past."

"Father didn't wear the garb of a lesser wizard for very long," Orlan announced with pride. "Twelve years. He told me."

Laurel lifted the heavy folds and spread the cloth over her arms to examine the elaborate embroidery. "Look at the needlecraft."

"Wizards work spells into their robes for protection," Godefroi explained. "A mantle is not effective otherwise."

"Then I must learn to sew," she laughed. Kaiese had made her do needlework, the occupation best fit for well-born maidens, but Laurel was too impatient to sit and push a little silver sliver through cloth. She would work hastily and leave uneven seams and sloppy knots, and most often unfinished pieces. "I could never do such work, and were I a wizard today my protection would be as full of holes as rusty armor."

"Try it on," Olyr suggested.

"Oh, I couldn't." But she did. The mantle was large on her, broad at the shoulders, sleeves over her hands, hem to mid-calf when it should fall at her knees. "How does it look?"

"Wizardly," said Godefroi.

"You look like Father," said Orlan.

No mirrors were in that little room, but Laurel knew from the boys' eyes that this was true. She *felt* like a wizard. The thread-crafted spells about her, faint as they were after so many years, kept some power. If she were a wizard and these her own spells, her magic would join with them; the energy woven into the mantle would be hers. But she was only a novice to the craft. As much as she desired full wizardry, she felt herself too young and unprepared to command such power. Would she ever truly be fit to wear such magical robes?

"Olyr will carry the weight of it better," she said. "He'll be a wizard first of us all." She shed the mantle and offered it to the apprentice.

Olyr looked grand in wizard's robes, manly rather than boyish, fit for the place he would occupy in a few years. Laurel knew that he must feel what she had felt, and was more confident of his suitability to bear the spellcraft.

A blast of horns echoed across the chasm from the front gates. The children forgot the black mantle and ran to the window. The barbican blocked their view of the gardens and stable-yard, but they could hear faint shouts and laughter in the distance.

"What is it?" Laurel wondered. "Have we visitors?"

"Thespers," Orlan answered sullenly.

Laurel stared at her cousin, for a traveling band of actors and musicians was always a delight.

"Come along!" Godefroi tugged her arm. Olyr left the black mantle on the bed and followed the younger apprentice to the stairwell. Laurel and Orlan walked more slowly behind.

"You don't like them, Orlan?" she whispered.

"Not especially," the boy answered. "They are Father's own people, in his patronage. They visit all the time."

As they reached the plaza, the headethesper descended the broad, curving stairway from the Daune-Tower gate. She was a young woman, petite and pretty with a pert, turned-up nose and chestnut hair in long braids. She wore a brief, bright blue tunic, slashed breeches, and broad-brimmed hat with scarlet plumes. A little child with golden curls clung to her hand. Lord Redmantyl waited for them on the cobblestone way below.

"Welcome, Tedora."

They embraced. Orlan, beside Laurel, bit into his lower lip.

"Yryd, you can't know how we've missed you!" the headethesper said with playful affection. "Andemyon's talked of nothing else for months."

But Andemyon, her child, showed no sign of speaking. He had stepped quickly toward Redmantyl with his mother, then paused in shyness and looked up at the wizard with wide, pale blue eyes.

Redmantyl smiled gently. "Come along, Little One. Haven't you a kiss for me too?" Andemyon ran to him and he lifted the little boy to sit in the crook of one arm. Tedora's hand in his, the wizard approached the children gathered at the foot of the Shadu Hall.

"Orlan, my pet!" The thesper embraced the boy, who stiffened against the welcome, and then she regarded the girl. "You are Laurel?"

Laurel was astonished. "You know of me?"

"Yryd has spoken–"

"Tedora, I will have you meet my niece," said Redmantyl. "Laurel, I present you Tedora Headethesper. I am patron of her troupe."

Tedora bowed with sure practice and grace. Laurel did not know the courteous way to speak to a thespian and she repeated Orlan's mumbled "Welcome" in a more clear voice.

Other thespers arrived: Tedora introduced Laurel to a young man named Rymbaughe, another much older named Jareth, and Jareth's daughter Anyse, as they came into the castle with their baggage and packs. Henri, the troupe's fool and jongleur, brought in his clubs and blunted knives. The minstrel Lyse and her son Gilbert carried lute and pipes and tambourine. A plump woman in pink ribbons, Amanda, and half a dozen laughing dancers dragged boxes filled with costumes. The Feast Hall was crowded and noisy that night and the castle was thrown into great commotion as the thespers set their stage on the courtyard beneath the kitchens the next afternoon.

Laurel was fascinated by these strange, boisterous, colorful people. They had a freedom that was wonderful to see, a wild gaiety unknown to workaday folk. They played as easily as children and occupied Wizardes Cliff as if it were their home; they spoke informally to all the household, from the little kitchen-boy to Lord Redmantyl. They drank the wizard's wine and sat at his table and repaid his generosity with pleasant jests and entertainment, careless of responsibility so long as they were in the castle. Their laughter invited any who might be dissatisfied with a dull or commonplace life to come and join the game, but Laurel was not tempted. If she had met such people in New York, she would have gone with them, and swiftly, but she was happy here. Wizardes Cliff was her rightful place.

It did not take Laurel long to discover that Lord Redmantyl was very much in love with Tedora Headethesper, and she with him. They said little not remarkable between performer and patron in company, but she often caught them in unguarded moments which revealed an intimacy passing friendliness or casual flirtation. Their eyes met and they smiled at each other in private jests. When they thought no one was watching, they took hands or exchanged a quick kiss. The thesper's fingers fell gently on the wizard's silvery hair. Laurel felt her uncle relax his vigilant defenses for Tedora; while great wizards were at pains to keep close guard of their secrets and conceal even their right names, she called him Yryd.

And there was Andemyon. The wizard's son? Gossip among the thespers and household had it so, though everyone wondered that Redmantyl did not do the proper thing and make a formal acknowledgment. There was no trace of Redmantyl's silver fairness nor any sign of magic in the pretty child. Yet the wizard's affection for the little boy was undisguised. One tug at the hem of his red robes would summon his attention and he left his work to play a game of catch or listen to whispered confidences. His patience when Andemyon pulled plants from the garden or pens and ink from the tables or books from the shelves was astonishing. Any other child in the house who dared to take such freedoms with Redmantyl's belongings would have had his ears boxed, but Andemyon was the wizard's pet. Andemyon could not be scolded or punished; Redmantyl, for all his intense discipline, faltered at the wounded, abashed look, the trembling lip, the first tears. He could not be harsh. Instead, he received the torn flowers and scrawled and smeared drawings as gifts and explained the illustrations in the books. In the evenings, he cradled the little boy in his arms and read the minuscule letters of manuscripts past a five-year-old's understanding until Andemyon fell asleep, then carried him up to bed. No father was more loving.

As she felt her uncle's love for the thesper and her small son, Laurel loved them as well. She was ready to receive Andemyon as her cousin and Tedora as an aunt. The little boy was shy at first; if Laurel spoke, he fled to his mother. From the safety of Tedora's embrace, he watched the stranger with wide-eyed wonder then, growing bolder, left his mother to follow Laurel at a cautious distance. Before the end of the first week, he would tug at her breech-ribbons and raise his arms in a silent request to be lifted, or climb into her lap if she allowed.

Positive that Redmantyl must marry Tedora soon, Laurel sought the headethesper's friendship, and Tedora seemed as eager to befriend her. Tedora was the first to call her Windswift. Laurel didn't know why at first—the windswift was a little bird that lived in chimneys and darted about the alleys and gardens at dusk—but she soon understood that the name referred to her wind-swift ability with her mother's sword. Her skill became flashy and impressive as she practiced with Rymbaughe, the best swordsmaster of the troupe. Tedora's name was a title of honor, like a battle-name which a knight would take up with pride. Laurel thought it a good name for a wizard.

Orlan, however, was a problem. Though he had been Laurel's constant companion for months, he grew sullen and reclusive after the thespers' arrival. He was more restless and angry than she had ever known him to be, and Orlan was usually turbulent. Unrestrained by wizardly arts of concealment, his emotions were broadcast at an unmistakable intensity: resentment at Tedora's intrusion, outrage at any suggestion that she might become his stepmother, jealousy at Redmantyl's fondness for Andemyon, rejection when Laurel played with the child, and scorn for the little usurper. Oddly, Andemyon worshiped Orlan as any small boy might idolize an older brother and tagged after him, bearing Orlan's insults and slights with determined adoration.

Laurel tried to draw Orlan into games with the young thespers and apprentices, but the boy refused. If she persisted, he withdrew to his room. He would close her out rather than join the others, and Laurel watched his retreat with dismay. She wished she could heal this unexpected breach. Once, she pursued him up.

"Are you angry at me, Cos?"

He was startled at the blunt question, but answered: "No, Laurel."

"Then why won't you come down?"

"You can't miss me," he said. "You have friends enough. *Her.* Her brat."

"But you've been my friend too. Nothing's changed that." She sat at the edge of the bed, where Orlan sprawled with sulky abandon, and patted his arm. "You're being silly. We'd all be just as glad if you behaved yourself better. My uncle would. If you can't like the headethesper and her troupe, at least be courteous. They *are* guests here. And you mustn't be so gruff with Demy. He's only a baby. If he is your brother–"

Orlan whirled and glared—anger stabbed through her—then he put his head down and covered his ears. "Let me be, please!"

Laurel left him.

In torchlight, the thespers performed a play they called *The Women of Paris*. The stage was set in France after the battle of Beauvais in 1331 as the Queen and her ladies awaited their fate. They sat, elegant, in the Lady's chambers and news came to them at dramatic intervals: The battle was lost. The French King was dead. The conqueror, Norman King Eduarde Victor, advanced on the city. The gates of Paris were breached. The invaders committed atrocities in the streets. The palace was besieged. Demands were made. A traitor was discovered and plans to escape cut short. Hope after hope was dashed and despair piled upon disaster, but only one soldier appeared, the Norman guard sent to escort the grieving queen and her daughters to the convent where they would spend the rest of their lives. The Queen plead for the freedom of her children, but the soldier heard her without pity; she must surrender peaceably or be dragged away to prison and never see the little ones again. Weeping, the Lady submitted and was led offstage. The Dauphin Philyppe remained alone. At the end, King Eduarde and his heir Elizabeth arrived triumphant, he in battle-stained armor, she in white princely robes. For love of this firstborn daughter, Eduarde had put aside his infant son and waged war; he promised the little maid she would wed the Dauphin and be named Princess of France to unite the conquered realm to his own lands of Normandy, Aquitaine and Angelande. All kingdoms would be hers. The play concluded with the conqueror almost forcibly bringing the two children together in handfasting.

There were not enough women in the troupe to fill every role. Tedora played the queen, but Jareth was the dowager and both male and female dancers took up the gowns of attendant duchesses and gentyl-maids. Andemyon sat silent on his mother's lap, a little princess. Gilbert was Elizabeth. Anyse played the Dauphin.

"You ought to have put the battle onstage," Laurel told Tedora the next day. "'Twas nothing to the tale but a lot of women sitting and weeping."

"The audience wept too, Swift," the thesper answered, smiling.

"Yes. 'Twas so sad. But I would have liked it better if there'd been a good swordfight. Can you not change it? A headethesper ought to be able to do as she pleases with a play."

"I have. *The Women of Paris* is written exactly as it pleases me."

Laurel was astonished. "You wrote that yourself?"

"Well," Tedora laughed. "Not alone. 'Twas a Greekish play written in ancient times. *Trojan Women.* I changed it so that the battle was in our own history. Years ago, when Jareth was head of the troupe, we performed the tale as originally written and had a magnificent failure. The common folk of the Northlands have never heard of Troy and care less about its ruin. But the story is too good to be lost, so I rewrote it to play upon their patriotism."

Norman citizens delighted in tales of conquest. They would gather again and again to hear ballads sung of legendary battles or tales told of brave knights and shieldmaids. Pageants celebrating the adventures of Eduarde Victor in France or Rikharde Lyonneheart in the Holy Land or the more recent campaigns of Eduarde Redlyon in the Spanish marches were invariably popular. Victorious warfare was the pride of the Empire, even though each kingdom had itself been conquered and assimilated to become part of that great Empire.

"It is the same story. The capture of Paris is the nearest analogy to the fall of Troy—one great nation is overthrown by another and the women and children are left in the hands of Fate. I didn't truly change much, only allowed for the little princesses and the marriage of Philyppe and Elizabeth. There was a prince killed in the original whom I left out, and no one like Helen of Troy in Paris, so *she* must go. Kassandra, the maid raped in the chapel, I brought directly from one tale to other. Were there such poor maids at Paris, as I expect there were, history does not tell us their names.

"Elsewhere, we do put on tales of splendid war with swordplay and blood enough to please a crowd, but Yryd doesn't like them. He says that life is too bloody to watch more of it for diversion's sake."

The girl smiled. "May I ask? I know I have no right reason."

"What is it, Windswift?"

"You love him?"

"Yes," Tedora answered.

"Is that why you are headethesper?"

"No, I was head of the troupe before he was Redmantyl."

"How did you meet him?" Laurel pursued. "Tell? Please?"

"Yryd and I met at Storm Port," the thesper began her tale. "At an inn near the dockyards, which was not *too* expensive and did not protest the lodging of thespers and other odd sorts. We stayed there when I was first in the troupe. We still do a' times in the city.

"When the troupe lodged there that winter, we heard that a wandering wizard lately returned from Europe had also taken rooms, and we were mad with curiosity. A wizard in his prime is a rare sight, you know. But *this* wizard kept to his room, discreet thing, for days. We only saw the little English boy in his service."

"Simon?" cried Laurel. "He has been with my uncle so long?"

"At least so long. For all our pains to see the mysterious wizard, we never caught more than a sight of Simon when he came down for food and drink for his master. Rumor held that the wizard was ill, or that he was shut up for some magician's rite."

Laurel scoffed. "If he was, he wouldn't be in a public inn."

"Not everyone knows that, my pet. We were forced to make our speculations in ignorance of such magical practices. Then, I came to the common room one afternoon and there he sat! He was not Redmantyl then, but a lesser wizard in black. His arm was in bandages and a walking rod lay by the hearth. His white hair—I thought at first he must be an aged man, but when he turned I saw that he was not five and thirty."

"What did you say to him?"

"Nothing. Something stupid. I don't recall. I babble like a simpleton to handsome men. Good Christ knows what Yryd must have thought, but he was all courtesy. He knew that I was one of the troupe and he asked whither we were bound. He asked after our headethesper, Jareth in those days. When we left the inn, he and Simon came with us.

"A magician in our troupe! Imagine, Laurel, our excitement. We women were wild about him and ready to make fools of ourselves—the men would have been in rages of jealousy if Yryd ever played the lover. He simply didn't. Oh, he was friendly, but always a-distant even in our midst. He kept to himself. He played his tricks of light and told tales of his travels for our amusement. If Jareth asked, he'd take part in our performances, but he'd rather not. He was with us, you see, but not one of us. He told us he had come from Malta to Storm Port, but he spoke no more than that. We guessed he had met with some misfortune there. We saw how he had been injured. He was still gaunt and wearied with it. He seemed so very young, yet old in his pain. Helpless. Not at all a fearsome wizard. Dear Simon tended him like a nursery-maid. But we never learned what had happened to him. Yryd and his secrets!

"He traveled with us so far as Maryesfont, and we saw him often in the next years. He knew the inns where we stopped and left messages for us there."

"Did you love him then?"

Tedora laughed. "I loved him the moment I saw him. 'Twas as if I'd fallen into an enchantment and forgot all other men. No other was like him. Magical. Fierce in his pride, yet gentle. So damnably mysterious. When we were apart, I wondered where he was. I worried for him. And when we saw him...I meant to have him, Swift. I will not lie. I thought how it would be to love a wizard."

"You've heard tales of–" asked Laurel. "Of wizards' lovers?"

"Yes, but 'tisn't true, of course. I'm no more magical than I was before we met. I suppose that the myth is made out of the fascination we ordinary folk have for magicians—we hope to receive a little of that magic for ourselves if we are near it."

"What happened? Did you speak to him? Did he–?"

"No, not Yryd. If he thought of me, he would not depart his courtesy to say so. And I was not free.

"Eight years past, the troupe traveled to Greenwaters Island and Yryd went with us. He spoke of visiting the Old Lord—a foolhardy thing in itself and suicide for a young wizard. But Yryd would not listen. Even Simon could not stop him from this madness. He left the caravan at the Redmantyl Road. I did not think I'd see him again.

"When the storms burst from Wizardes Cliff, we imagined the worst had happened and we wept for our friend. Then, a message came from Wizardes Cliff. Lord Redmantyl summoned us."

"You didn't know?"

"We thought it the Old Lord."

"But you went."

"Not all of us. Jareth thought we could not escape the great wizard's wrath. The old Redmantyl would find us if we fled to the ends of the earth. We were terrified, but Jareth and I were Yryd's special friends. We had made him welcome in our troupe and we would not betray him now. I sent the others away to safety and we came to the castle."

"And you found it was my uncle, not the Old Lord?"

"Yes," Tedora laughed. "The young upstart had won. He has been our patron ever since."

"Then he spoke to you?" Laurel persisted.

"No, not 'til some time later. But he *did* speak, Darling. Never fear."

"Will you marry him?"

"I don't know. I would not if he asked today."

Laurel didn't understand. "But why? You love him."

"'Tis not so simple as that," the thesper explained. "When I was a maid at Maryesfont, I was meant to be a scholar and join the Sisters, but I grew weary of forever reading the thoughts of great minds and what lesser minds thought of the great. I do not regret my education, but I could not spend all my life in the libraries of the College of Letters. Did you know that I had been married, Laurel?"

"No. Who to?"

"There was a young thesper. He is not here now—his name was Hybbarde. A charming rogue, but so handsome. Whenever the troupe played at Maryesfont, I came out, at first simply to gaze upon him if I must be honest, but it became more than that. The thespers had a freedom I did not. You've felt that too, from the troupe?"

"They are so at ease with themselves," Laurel answered.

"Exactly. They are people who did not fit the places they were born to, and sought a place where they could be as they wished. I was so unfit myself. If I were meant to be a scholar, I would have welcomed the regularities of a scholar's life and lived content within the cloisters. Instead, I felt bound by them. It didn't seem fair that I must sit still while these Free Folk played and danced and sang the tales I wanted to write. Proper Normans called them immoral and immodest, but the townsfolk came to watch all the same. Some were envious. I wished myself so brave to join them. Hybbarde must have seen this. At least, he noticed how I always attended the plays. And, when the plays were done, he came to me and brought me to the thespians. They weren't wild at all—not so wanton nor decadent as I had expected. They simply live beyond the stifling society we Normans have built for ourselves, where everyone must say the courteous thing and wear the correct colors and always, always, do exactly what everyone else in the same place has done for centuries because that is the way it is properly done. If thespers have rules, they decide them for themselves.

"Hybbarde told me I wasted myself. I was too much a beauty, too spirited to be a Sister. He promised that my place was with the troupe, that they welcomed maids unhappy as I was. He promised excitement I could never know in Maryesfont. Ah, his promises! I've told you once I am a fool for handsome men and I was half in love with him before he ever noticed me. I could not think of staying another day, and Hybbarde smiled and said 'Come along then!' I went with him.

"As it ended, I found my happiness, but not with Hybbarde. Marriage was no freedom. You must remove bits of yourself so that you fit perfectly against the other. For some, I think the price is not too high and they are willing to give over their cares for love. But Hybbarde would have me abandon my imagination and my knowledge—for he had none to match—and I could not surrender so much. I had left Maryesfont to discover them and could not put them away again so soon. As a thesper, I go where I please and reshape my world about me as I see fit and put it on a stage for others to see as well. It is what I am meant to be. I love Yryd more than I ever loved Hybbarde, but I will not leave a place where I belong to try to make myself fit where I do not."

"You won't stay with us."

Tedora took the girl's chin in her hands and smiled gently into her disappointed eyes. "Now what would I do as Lady of Wizardes Cliff, Swift? What do Ladies do? A Lady sits and works her needle while a minstrel strums her favorite ballad. She may ask the chatelaine and steward after her husband's affairs, or the nurse after her children, or the servants after their health, so it seems that she has some concern in the business of the household. Can you see me so? I cannot. It is to Yryd's credit that he understands why I do not wish this. Most men wouldn't."

Laurel had not given much thought to love. She never intended to wed. Who would have her? What man would she have? If she thought of courtship and marriage, she thought of the princesses in countless tales, locked in towers, held prisoner by dragons, entranced under spells, until bold knights won them along with half the kingdom and they lived happy forever after. She thought of brides and grooms in simple white shifts and bare feet kneeling before the altar. She thought of the comedies she had seen where even the most insurmountable difficulties were resolved at the end with a kiss; she thought of the love poems she had sung without knowing what the lyrics truly meant.

She thought that both of Tedora's tales were wonderfully romantic: The scholarly maid who fled with a handsome thesper-lad ought to have an adventurous life. The wizard's beloved ought to be his Lady. If the tales had not been true, they would have ended so. Yet Tedora regretted her marriage and she refused to marry again in spite of her love and Lord Redmantyl's position. Why? Was real-life love so different from the romance?

Some of this must have showed in her face, for Tedora said: "You do not know love on those terms. 'Tis all so pretty, isn't it, like a story with a happy end? Do you have a sweetheart, Laurel?"

Laurel nodded.

"Olyr or Godefroi?"

"Olyr."

"Do you think to wed once you are both wizards?"

They had only kissed once. Laurel blushed. "I don't know. 'Tis so far away. I'm only seventeen."

"Good. You shouldn't think of such things yet. Windswift, you are far too young. I don't mean to frighten you from the delights of love, but know its responsibilities. Marriage bears heavy obligations." She rose. "In truth, I believe Yryd would not have me if I insisted. He must fit to *me* too much to suit himself. A thesper must give up freedom, but a wizard must place magic second to his love, and Yryd tells me that magic must always be first."

The thespers prepared for their second performance on Midsummer Eve and sent the whole castle into commotion as they set their stage, readied their costumes, rehearsed their lines. The play, a comedy, was for the servants and Lyges folk. Lord Redmantyl would not attend, for tonight was a night of Wizard's Keep. While his household bustled about him, he was shut in his rooms throughout the day in meditation and did not emerge even for meals.

There was a lull in late afternoon as the troupe gathered for dinner in the Feast Hall. Weary from running after the thespers and housemaids on countless errands all day, little Andemyon blinked drowsily and nodded over his plate. Tedora had already left the table to oversee some last-minute arrangements, so Laurel took him up to bed.

"Tell me a story," the little boy begged as she tucked him in.

"I know few," she confessed.

"Da has lots," Andemyon answered. "Books and books." He pointed in the direction of the small library adjacent to Redmantyl's sitting room. "Read to me. Please?"

Laurel crossed the passageway and examined the books in the little collection. Most were in languages she could not read; others seemed to be lists and indices. When she found a pamphlet on calfskin, set atop others like it in an unbound pile, which appeared to be a tale in modern Norman, she darted back to Andemyon's room to show him the frontispiece, written with bold, fresh, black ink letters in a large hand.

"What is it?" he asked.

Laurel read aloud: "*Mythos of the Fall. From the Book of Ize. A translation by Yryd Lightmaster, Lord Redmantyl.* Do you see that, Demy? It is his. Has he read this to you?"

Andemyon shook his head. "Uh-uh."

"No? Well then!" The little boy nestled against her arm as she turned to the monkish minuscule within the pamphlet and began: "'In those days, the Most High dwelt in the clouds above the houses of Men and watched their progress from the infancy of the World.'" This sounded a little like passages read from the Bible at Mass, but it was not exactly right. An illustration on the facing page showed the "Most High" watching from the clouds—copied, Laurel imagined, from the original text—a huge Egyptian-styled eye. "'He saw them grow from mute beasts of the wood to beasts of Reason and He saw that the Children of Earth grew well. When Time decreed, He departed from the clouds into the Darkness between the Lights of Heaven. The Children of Earth were not forgotten, but He gave in His Absence the Lesser Gods to care for His Creation and They came to Earth. And these were their names:

"'Luq, the Bringer of Light

"'Asbat, the Crafter of Woods and Tiller of the Fields

"'Gasbat, the Crafter of Words and Song

"'Toloqo, Master of Sleep and Deep Waters

"'Nasthurag, the One who Laughs

"'And Others, lesser angels and minions to the Lords. And They went among the Men and They found the Daughters of Men comely and They took them as wives and so fathered Giants upon the Earth, and Trolls and all manner of Monstrosity.' Andemyon, I oughtn't read this to one so young."

"No, I like it," the child said with sleepy complaisance. "Please?"

Ink-sketched faces bordering the page grinned and leered with inhuman expressions; Laurel tried not to look at them as she found her place and continued. "'They taught their crafts to Men, and the ways of War and Lust and Greed, Drunkenness, Murder and Fire and Worship of Themselves and the False was honored and the Most High Forgotten. The Spawn of the Gods wrought Evil for a thousand years and Blood was upon the Earth. And the Most High returned and saw what had been made of His Children and He called upon the Lesser Ones and said: *You have fallen from My Grace and defiled yourselves with the Mortal beasts, you who have the Power of the Stars and the Secrets of Immortals. You have put your stain upon Man. Accursed you are!*

"'The Lightbringer was cast into eternal Darkness and the Laughter became the Laughter of the Mad. Toloqo sleeps forever beneath his waters and the Crafters make Chaos. Their Legions are vile.

"'And the Most High reached His Hand across the Firmament and

Darkness covered the face of Earth and a wind blasted the Heavens. This was the Wrath of the Most High. The Children of Earth, who knew not, hid in terror but the Lesser Gods and their Spawn were raised in battle and the lightning of their battle split the Darkness asunder and their rage shook the Firmament–'"

"Were they wizards?" Andemyon wondered.

"No, they were gods, and much more powerful. They were immortal—that means that they live forever and never die." She balanced the book on her knees and read on. "'Battle endured for Seven years and the Wretched Offspring of the Fallen Ones were destroyed and their bones scattered as dust and all the defiled cleared from the Earth. The Fallen Gods were cast into the Abyss so that their Evil would not taint the right-made Children of Earth.

"'And the Most High called upon His Children and He lifted one of Man up, the true and most Blessed of Mortal-kind, and taught him Secrets and made him the Voice of all Man, and the Most High spoke unto the Children of Earth through the Chosen One, who was Ize. And the Most High set Guardians, the Wise of Earth and Ize Foremost, to keep the Gates of the Abyss so that the Lost Ones will not return, for Undying They are and They wait from that Time of Old to This. So Saith the Book of Ize of ages past and so say I this day, Yryd Lightmaster, Lord Redmantyl.'"

"What does that mean?" Andemyon asked.

"I don't know. I think it means that the tale was true when it was first written and it was still true when my Uncle Redmantyl translated it."

"But 'tisn't really true?"

"No, of course not. It is only a story from long ago. People were pagan in those days and they made up all sorts of foolishness. This is a pagan tale like the Battle between Good and Evil and the Fall of Lucifer. Do you know that tale from the Bible?"

He nodded. "Mama told me. But–"

"Hush, my pet. No more. You've had your story and must sleep." She kissed his brow and extinguished the candle. "Sleep."

"'Night, Laurel."

Laurel returned to the little library to replace the pamphlet. Then she froze, silent at voices from her uncle's sitting-room. Lord Redmantyl and Tedora spoke together.

"Must you go? It's our last night at the castle."

"I'm sorry that Midsummer falls while you are here, but it can't be helped. This is part of my duties."

"What is it you do at these Keeps, Love? It isn't dangerous, is it?"

"You know I cannot tell you," Redmantyl answered.

"Wizards and their secrets," the thesper said, but affectionately.

"I'll return, and safely, before the household's up tomorrow. I'll be here to bid you farewell."

Tedora laughed softly. "We had a simply marvelous time. I've finally managed to meet your Laurel."

"You like her?"

"She's a wonderful girl. Andemyon adores her. He talks so– He's made her as much a hero as poor little Orlan. Yryd, does she know?"

"No."

"My love, you ought to–"

Laurel tucked the pamphlet into the nearest empty space on the shelves and slipped out. She did not want to eavesdrop on such private matters, especially concerning herself. In another moment, they would be discussing Andemyon. She found Godefroi and Olyr on the stair landing at the end of the corridor, apparently looking for her. "Is the play started?" she asked as she reached them.

"Yes, but it's terribly silly. You haven't missed much." Godefroi shrugged with delicate criticism. "Rymbaughe says it's left from before the days when Tedora was headethesper."

"There's going to be a dance afterwards," added Olyr. "Come down with us!"

"I don't know how to dance," said Laurel.

"Neither do I," Godefroi answered. "But come and watch."

"Please?"

Laurel smiled at the elder apprentice's simple plea. "If you wish." He took her hand and they ran to the plaza. Godefroi smiled after them—abashed, wistful, but incurably hopeful—and followed.

Some minutes later, Lord Redmantyl left his chambers to observe his duties in the night. Tedora went down to join her troupe.

She stood atop an ebony wall that curved away into deepening twilight. Beneath her, a teeming crowd repeated its urgent chant:

"The King! The King! Take her to the King!"

She watched as they surged forward to dash themselves against the great door which loomed against the night sky. A dark, amorphous mass, they blurred and changed: sometimes they were ragged peasants with twisted limbs; sometimes they were howling beasts; sometimes they seemed to be sea-creatures, tentacled and gelatinous. They carried with them a tiny figure, a child lost in garb too large and too long. It struggled and tripped on its oversized cloak and would have fallen, but the crowd swept it up like a bit of flotsam lost in the tide and brought it helplessly on.

"The danger increases, my child," her companion said. "The Forces that work against us have taken another soul into their legion tonight."

"We can't save her?"

"She's already lost."

From far below, the chant rose with frantic urgency: "The King! The King! The King Comes!"

"Their power grows, but so does ours. The time for battle draws near. You must be prepared. You have the light."

"But I don't understand."

"You have the power to deflect Them. You will do what you must to defend yourself."

"The King! The King Comes! The King is Nigh!"

With a blast of clarion trumpet, the door opened. Black spilled out like endless night. Fast-flowing inky tendrils reached out hungrily, seeking light, seeking life, blotting out the stars, engulfing the nightscape, drowning the wailing crowd. A high, thin cry pierced the chaos.

She sank against the dark surface of the wall, knowing They couldn't touch her if They didn't know she was here. But her presence was too conspicuous to escape notice for long; her magic shone like beacon—too bright, too bright. She would be seen.

A shower of sparks burst from her. Fire caught wherever they fell, feeding on the stone, the dead trees, the rags and flesh of the crowd, and grew rapidly, intertwined, rose together in one tower of flame that spurted heavenward. As this raging spire of red-gold surrounded her, the scene melted and changed—no longer a night valley, but the farms and homes of a little village caught afire. She watched, horrified, as thatched roofs went up and walls crashed inward. Chimneys toppled. The tall grass about a well on the common green withered and crumbled to ashes. Yet the screams of the crowd continued unceasing in her ears. And the living darkness spread and spread relentlessly, consuming devastated land and sobbing victims at a touch, smoothing ruin and terror into the peace of oblivion. It would swallow the flame eventually.

Laurel woke. She shrieked and swatted blindly at the bedclothes before she realized that they were not burning. There was no fire.

She felt as she had that other night: Her pulse pounded. Her heart blazed. Her nerves thrilled with released energies and magic glowed bright on her skin. A warning keen of immediate danger rang through her head, yet the night was undisturbed by any menace. No smoke. No sparks. The bed linen was not scorched. There was no fire.

Someone knocked at her door and she leapt up to answer it. Godefroi and Olyr stood in the corridor in their nightshirts, the fear in their eyes only a little relieved at the sight of her unharmed.

"What happened? We heard you cry out."

"Was it another fire?"

"No," she told them. "'Twas only a dream. A bad dream."

"You're not hurt, Laurel?"

"Shall we stay with you?"

"No, I'm fine. I'm sorry I woke you. 'Tis nothing."

Reluctantly, they returned to their beds. Laurel curled on the sitting-room coucherie, too frightened to think of sleep. She wanted to speak to her uncle, to seek the comfort of his presence, but Lord Redmantyl would not return from his Wizard's Keep until dawn. It was still dark, hours before daylight. She must wait.

There *was* a fire. Somewhere. She felt it. She felt the disruption in the flux of energies around her, turbulent as they were after one of her spell-casting lessons. More so. Something had happened. Had she loosed so much unrestrained power to start a fire far away? If so, where? In the castle? In the bed of some poor, sleeping innocent? In a yeoman's barn? In a field or forest? In a village?

The possibilities were too horrible to dwell upon.

These past weeks, she had struggled to keep control of her magic and she believed she had finally mastered it. There had been no smoldering tapestries, no melted candles, no fires save those she deliberately created. She employed all her will and spent long, exhausting hours in rigorous exercises to perfect her skills, but she had been proud at the results. When she commanded her magic, she could claim it as her own and cease to worry at the explosions of her ill-contained temper. She thought she had worked hard enough. But she hadn't, not if this horrible thing could happen, if her powers could burst into a force of great destruction. What if she caused another fire? What if someone had died tonight because of her? Must she always keep guard against it, even in her dreams? What intense levels of discipline must a full wizard attain before she could call her magic safe?

She thought she understood why Lord Redmantyl refused to be distracted from his work even for those he loved best; his powers were like her own and might burst beyond his command as easily if he did not always restrain them. What will he must have! Rather than give his magic to wanton havoc in an unguarded moment, he must put it before everything else—his love for Tedora, his obligations as the Duke's vassal, his responsibilities to his children. She sometimes found him emotionally cool and remote; his thoughts were veiled. Had he set those barriers as a careful, impenetrable line of defense?

Redmantyl knew all there was of young magicians' phenomena. If the worst were true and she had lost control, he could help her regain it. He would understand. He would teach her what to do.

She slept again, and woke well after daybreak when her uncle knocked at her door.

"Laurel, is anything wrong? I thought you were troubled. Godefroi said you had a nightmare."

"No, not a nightmare." She told him as much as she could recall of her dream—the chanting crowd, the wall, the child, the trumpet's blare, the great door and what lay beyond. "'Twas so strange, and I have had it before. What can it mean?"

Redmantyl gave intense attention to her description, but he answered simply: "'Twas only a dream. It may not mean anything."

"Uncle, at the end I saw a fire. There *was* a fire. I felt it."

She expected him to call this a dream as well, but he nodded solemnly. "Yes, I felt it too."

"I– I think I may have caused it."

"No, you didn't. It was very far from here."

"You know what it was?"

"I cannot say."

He would not, thought Laurel. Wizards had their secrets. But this secret was hers too. She felt the fire as an expense of her own magic. She had as much right to know the truth of it as any grown wizard, for she was as much involved. It wasn't fair! Willing or no, she already had a little knowledge, enough to tantalize. Why wouldn't he tell her more?

"Is it part of the Wizard's Keep?"

"I can't explain." Redmantyl patted her rumpled hair. "It was not your doing, Niece. You must trust me and ask no more. You are not distressed?"

"No, Uncle."

"Then bathe and dress and be down at breakfast. Think no more of this."

***

"Olyr, will you marry one day?"

The youth blushed at the question. "My Lord Redmantyl says that wizards shouldn't."

They walked in the gardens before the barbican later that morning. The thespers were preparing to leave; many had already gathered at the stables and Olyr and Laurel could hear their cheerful badinage with the grooms even though they were well out of sight. Andemyon trailed after the pair, pulling up flowers by the roots. He tried to break the stems off shorter, but they only bent and remained unbroken. The dirty ends brushed against his chubby little legs, leaving streaks across his hose and gaiters. Though Andemyon did not follow Laurel as ardently as he tagged after Orlan, Redmantyl encouraged the child, especially when Laurel was with Olyr. The affection between his first apprentice and niece did not escape the wizard's notice. Andemyon was an unobtrusive, but effective, little chaperon.

"But will you?" She was not entirely teasing. "Would you marry me, if I asked?"

"If you asked," he confessed. "I'd not offer for you myself."

"Why not? You do like me?"

Olyr would not meet her eyes. "Yes."

"You said you might marry me if I so wished."

"If you wish. But wizards do not marry well," he explained. "Magic must be most important, or it is nothing."

This answer confirmed her thoughts of the night before. "You speak as my uncle. Tedora told me he believes a wizard must place his work first."

"'Tis true. Magic bears the highest duty. If a wizard weds, he must care for a wife and children too, as any ordinary man. He must put his love of them before his duties as a magician. My Lord will never wed, and he is most powerful of all wizards. My magic is nothing to his and if he fears the threat, then mine must be far more vulnerable."

"What do you think would happen if we did give over magic for love?"

"I don't know. But we must not. Marriage is not for us," the youth finished with less strength than he had begun. "I would like it otherwise, but it can't be. I want to be a great wizard. You are of *his* blood—you would hate to give it up as much as he."

Anyse emerged through the trees. "The troupe's ready to leave. Demy, come along! Your mother's looking for you." Andemyon dropped his ragged bouquet on the grass as she carried him swiftly to the caravan in the stable-yard. Laurel and Olyr followed. Half the household had come to see the troupe's departure; Lord Redmantyl was there, speaking softly with Tedora before she stretched up on tip-toe to kiss him.

"I don't believe I shall marry," Laurel said at last.

cuar

Godefroi raced through the Great Tower, up from the roof of the armory, up to the children on the maze of walkways above, a small ball gripped in his hand. The point of the game was to strike. He threw the ball; Olyr vaulted from the platform where he stood, over the railing to the stairway on the other side to avoid the blow.

"'Tisn't fair!" Orlan shouted. "No jumping!"

Olyr would have ignored this, but Laurel took her cousin's part.

"You have to go back and do it rightly, Olyr."

Olyr returned down the stairway and climbed back onto the platform. "Godefroi, begin again!"

"Wait!" the younger apprentice answered from below. "I cannot find the– Oh, here!" The ball shot up from the dimness unexpectedly, aimed again at Olyr.

The rules of the Hunt were simple: the Hunter pursued the Prey by throwing the ball. If his aim was true, the Prey was captured. If he missed, the game went on. If the intended target caught the ball, the target became Hunter and the Hunter joined the other players as Prey.

The elder apprentice turned quickly and caught the ball. "Hunter!" he shouted. Godefroi disappeared into the shadows and Laurel and Orlan yelped and scrambled to safety.

The Hunt was not a game of magic, for the apprentices' individual powers were ill-matched. Olyr could direct solid objects with great dexterity, but Laurel's and Godefroi's abilities were more erratic and Orlan's growing powers were forceful, but without direction. There were games to exercise each child's particular talent, but none had yet been designed to challenge all at once. Faced with the various amusements of their free hours, Laurel, Olyr and Orlan each favored the games they were best at and could never agree; Godefroi was the only one willing to play at the choice of his friends, knowing he could not win. Arguments were frequent and strident. The Hunt was a compromise. All the children could throw and catch and run and those were the only skills this game required.

Laurel hid behind a length of railing, but Olyr stalked Orlan first.

The boy had run to a slender walkway between two crossing flights of stairs which joined the uppermost tower galley at opposite ends. It was a good strategic position. Laurel had used it herself more than once. Olyr could not strike from either left or right; the stairs blocked long shots from both directions. He could not reach Orlan from below; the walkway was a shield. Nor could he strike from the stairs themselves; Orlan could crouch beneath whichever Olyr chose, or flee to avoid the trap. The only way to rout the prey from this place of safety was to aim from above.

Olyr knew this as well. As Orlan watched, dismayed, the apprentice ran up to the uppermost galley, which curved halfway around the tower beneath rows of arrow-slits. Olyr strode toward the center, pausing now and again to judge the best angle for his shot. Orlan's only defense was to run under the platform before Olyr found his position.

He ran. Olyr leapt to the railing and dropped the ball directly on the boy as he passed beneath. Orlan ducked, but was hit in the small of his back.

"'Tisn't fair!"

"'Tis perfectly fair!" Olyr shouted back, grinning. "I've got you!"

"Laurel?"

"'Tis according to the rules, Cos," she answered.

Orlan kicked the supporting beam and sulkily surrendered.

Olyr waited until the ball had been returned to him before he spun on Laurel. "And now you!" he cried.

The ball flew; she leapt as it rebounded off the wall behind her. Olyr raced down to retrieve it.

"To the top! The top!" Orlan yelped. "Laurel! Run!"

Laurel ran to the nearest steps.

"Look out!"

The ball shot past again, and she sped across the walkway, down, and over the central platform. Godefroi leant unguarded against a railing, shouting with Orlan, more distressed for her safety than his own; the ball struck his shoulder before he saw it coming.

Olyr laughed at his friend's vexation—"Rules of the game, my lad!"—then dashed across the platform after Laurel and up the parallel course to block her escape.

"You won't catch me so easily!" the maiden shouted cheerfully, and turned abruptly back the way she had come, running behind Olyr to the shelter between the two stairways. He continued up, planning to rout her as he had driven out Orlan, but she was under the galley before

Olyr reached his place.

Laurel was good at such games, for she had gained practical experience on the streets of New York. In childhood, she'd learned quickly to dodge her enemies, to run at the first sign of danger, to mislead and lose her pursuers, to hide in the shadows of an alley or doorway, to climb walls and leap from roof to roof, to strike first. They never caught her. Olyr was more easy to elude. As he crossed the galley and came down the other side, she ran down another flight, directly beneath. Orlan and Godefroi cheered, urging her on.

Though she had left New York more than year ago, Laurel had not forgotten. As she ran the tower, she ran those streets. She recalled, too clearly, the jeers of Martin and Peter Sheriffson and the other merchant-children, the sting of humiliation when the shopkeepers' boys flung refuse at her, the mud, the bruises, the furious tears, her aunt's scolding her for misbehavior, as if she were that child again. She *was* that child: Outcast. Stranger. Changeling. Still pursued.

Her laughter stopped.

The ball hit the wall before her. Laurel twisted to fly in the other direction. Olyr caught the ball and flung it again, too hard for playfulness, directly in front of her. It rebounded against the stone with a *twang*.

"Olyr, stop it! It isn't funny!"

"Do you surrender?"

"Never!"

Breathless, she darted down another way. Olyr ran above her; she could hear his feet pound the walkway as he raced to block her path. A stray thought—unexpected, as always—sounded in her head: *I've got her!*

He enjoyed this too much. The younger boys were almost apologetic when they struck against her: little noblemen, they were reluctant to insult a maiden, a kinswoman, a fellow apprentice! Though Laurel, in turn, had no qualms about hunting them down in the course of a game, she gave defeat without humiliation. It was understood that they protected each other when all were pursued. Olyr was different. He stalked Orlan and Godefroi with disturbing glee, taking delight in their capture. He laughed at Laurel's indignation. It stung him a little that she was more successful at games—she knew he suspected that she was a better magician—and he relished her defeat as proof that she could be beaten. For a moment, he had superiority. He was her friend, even her sweetheart, but they were always in competition. How he would triumph at her capture! Laurel hated to lose. She couldn't allow him to win this.

She doubled back abruptly and slipped toward the lowest level, the roof of the armory. The deep shadow there, beneath the central platform, would hide her. If she could reach it before Olyr found her–

"I've got you!"

Olyr was behind her.

Laurel yelped and lifted her hands, but the ball came at her too swiftly. She would be hit.

The tower filled with light. Blinding brilliance shot out around her. Wooden walkways trembled; stone walls shook. Laurel stood perfectly still, frightened at herself. The boys gaped.

"Laurel," said Olyr.

"You can't use magic," Orlan added, voice piping.

"I didn't mean–"

Lord Redmantyl appeared at the highest doorway open to the adjacent Spelle Tower. "Will you tell me what you are doing in here?"

"We were only playing, Father," Orlan, nearest, answered.

"Playing at what—the destruction of the castle?"

"That was my fault, Uncle," Laurel called up meekly. "'Twas an accident."

The wizard was solemn at her words. "What happened, Laurel? Tell me, precisely."

"I don't know."

"She shouted," Olyr offered. "And she exploded into light."

"It was beautiful," said Godefroi.

"My Lord," Olyr spoke again. "What does it mean?"

"It means that Laurel is growing into her magic rapidly, perhaps too rapidly for her self-command. You lads will have to guard yourselves well, for she will have forces to be reckoned against."

Laurel was stunned anew. Since childhood, she had thrilled at tales of wizard-battles and had thrilled more these past months to know that she would be a wizard herself. She looked forward to the time when she would join a foe in combat; it hadn't occurred to her that, when she met in battle, these boys would be her opponents. She and Olyr, Godefroi, Orlan—they were like a pack of tiger cubs, playmates together, but they would grow into deadly enemies. She could kill them.

More than that: They would challenge established wizards to take their rightful places in the ranks of the magical. These wizards were always indistinct in Laurel's imagination, aged, wicked, weak beings in dusty black robes, deserving their downfall. She realized now who they must be. There were so few wizards of power these days. Lord Redmantyl was foremost.

Her uncle had called her very powerful. Powerful enough to be Redmantyl herself?

Did the boys know this? No. They looked at her with awe and new respect—Olyr somewhat envious—but not fearful. Orlan was distinctly proud; he had no thought of future battles. And Lord Redmantyl? Did he know that he nurtured potential assassins in his pupils, his son, herself?

Laurel looked up. The wizard was watching her intently, as if reading her thoughts. She met his eyes. He knew.

The game could not continue thereafter; Redmantyl forbade it. Laurel joined Godefroi and Olyr in the search for the missing ball. When they found it, the rubbery outer surface was charred and peeled away and the whole mass carried a fresh, sickly-sweet burnt smell.

"You needn't have been so distressed, Laurel," Olyr said. "'Twas only a game."

"Laurel, you do not attend to your levitation."

Her copybook, floating a few laconic inches from the surface of the table, fell.

"I thought to separate you and Godefroi so that you both would give full concentration to your lessons."

Since Godefroi had begun his apprenticeship only a few months before her, Lord Redmantyl proposed to teach them together; in spite of the differences in their talents, the first lessons of all apprentices were similar and the wizard might tutor one while leaving the other at a particular exercise. The system was effective when Redmantyl was there to monitor; when he left the two alone, their lessons became chaotic. Godefroi was too easy to tease. In the wizard's absences, Laurel interrupted her friend's studies by scorching the edges of his notebook as he wrote or throwing showers of sparks over him as he sought to achieve his own level of spell-casting intensity. In revenge, he practiced his basic exercises in illusion—the media he mastered—and created chubby imps to distract her or he wrote poems and illustrated the margins of her text to make her laugh when she was meant to concentrate. At levitation, they often sent the objects of their exercise shooting at each other. Yesterday, they had entered a playful battle with chalk balls while Lord Redmantyl was gone to fetch Orlan for his first tests; the wizard had returned to find his Daune Tower room a disaster.

Redmantyl had tested his son and accepted him into apprenticeship, for the boy's powers were increasing rapidly: walls thumped, objects leapt from shelves and tables, and light burst out in bright flashes whenever his emotions were heightened. Godefroi had told her that since Orlan had moved in to share his rooms, their bed linen was often singed and spotted with pinhole burns; Laurel stole to their bedchamber door to watch over the sleeping boys in the night, praying that the bed would not burst into flames. Orlan was fourteen, two or three years younger than the accepted age for a novice, but he had become so disruptive that he had to learn to control himself.

"Your thoughts are elsewhere."

Laurel twisted to face the wizard. "Uncle, how great are my talents?"

"Great indeed," he replied.

"The other day, you said–"

"I spoke truthfully. All the castle felt the force of that burst. I don't doubt it was felt beyond as well. You possess remarkable powers, and that may be a danger to one so young."

"You came into your powers very young."

"Yes," Redmantyl agreed. "And I do not use them so wisely as an older wizard might."

"Have you been in many wizard-battles?" she asked.

"Laurel–"

"Please, tell me. I must hear of it. I shall have such battles one day. Uncle, tell me?"

Redmantyl sighed. "Battle is a fierce thing, Child, for it sets one mind against another as soldiers meet with sword and spear. There are times when your thoughts touch mine—Do you understand that bond, Laurel? You also have this bond with your cousin and perhaps the apprentices, but you haven't yet brought your powers against them. Imagine that you wish to conquer a foe. You have the power to enter that enemy mind forcefully and bend it to your will, if your will is the stronger. In wizard-battle, you test your strength. You use spells to deceive and weaken your foe and brutal force to destroy the power set against you, so that you may prove yourself the better wizard. The battle may last hours, or days, until one wins. Unless your opponent surrenders to your greater power, he will be injured. He may die."

"You have met many in battle?" she asked.

"I have never been defeated."

"Did you enjoy killing?"

Redmantyl was surprised at the question. "Most often, I felt pity for the fallen. I did not kill unless my opponent would fight 'til death and I could end our struggle no better way. 'Tis not a pleasant thing to watch a noble being die at your will, Laurel. I knew some of them well. A few, I confess, I was glad to defeat, for they were my most bloodless foes."

"The Old Lord?"

"Yes, him," the wizard said bitterly. "And others I had once thought friends. Skyrmos of Malta, who welcomed me to his home in order to betray me. 'Tis only due to good fortune that I survived that trap."

"If 'tis so horrid," Laurel wondered, "why must you battle at all?"

"We test each other to banish the weak and unguarded. 'Tis harsh, yes, but it is the way of things."

"Would you have joined in battle against one who 'prenticed with you?"

"I did. Arysbethe Darklingsuan."

"Godefroi's mother? When? I haven't heard the tale."

"Arysbethe was not known in those days," he said. "I fought many of greater reputation at the same time, but she was one who stood well in the challenge and departed uninjured."

"Were you friends before?"

"Arysbethe was in the year before her mage-vows when I began here. We were not dear companions."

"Olyr and Godefroi are my friends," said Laurel. "Orlan is a brother to me. I would die rather than hurt them. Must we fight when we are grown?"

"If they challenge you," the wizard answered solemnly. "But I do not believe any one of them would. Even if they were not so much your admirers, Maiden, they are not your equals. You will have to fight other wizards one day—if not your playmates, then others. Death is part of the profession and you must face that. You are more than a match for most."

"How might I match against you, Uncle?"

Knowledge touched his depthless eyes again and confirmed her worst fears, but his words were untroubled: "You are the best of my pupils and unless another wizard nurses a greater power unknown to me, you will be my successor."

"You are pleased at this?"

"I accept it as a possibility preferable to all others. I must fall eventually."

"Uncle—"

"Do not fret for that now, Laurel. You aren't so strong yet, and you will not be for many years." He took up the book upon the table and opened it to a page near the middle. "To your Latin."

As she translated *The Colloquy on the Occupations*, Laurel allowed her mind to discreetly seek Redmantyl's. She knew he must be aware of her questioning touch and would only allow her to seek so far. Yet she sensed enough: He had not lied; there was little sorrow, fear, or jealousy in him at the possibility of her powers growing greater than his. She felt mostly his resignation to Fate, colored by hints of a less expected emotion. Pride? Yes, he was proud that when he must inevitably fall, she would succeed. Certainly, that was preferable to defeat by an enemy's hobgoblin apprentice. He believed, as she did, that she might challenge him without meaning his death.

Laurel hoped that, if she must meet Godefroi or Olyr in battle one day, she could likewise defeat them without causing their destruction. She had to consider the possibility. At this moment, it seemed unlikely that either boy would set himself against her, but they were only children; what sort of men might they be when they were grown? Could they forget that they'd been apprentices together, that they'd once been friends?

"Uncle, this word in the conversation with the falconer—*trade*," she asked. "Is that meant to be *give* it to me, or *sell* it?"

"Give," he answered without turning to her.

"Give as in trade?"

"No, simply give over."

She laughed. "'Tis greedy then! He has no right to take the falcon from its master."

Redmantyl smiled. "You aren't meant to think upon the colloquy, Maid. It is an exercise in grammar, not a grand tale."

"I don't see why I must translate such beastly, boring rubbish in the first place. What has this conversation with fishers and ironsmiths to do with magic?"

"It contains the rudiments of Latin grammar, Laurel. Many of the important texts of wizardry are written in that tongue."

"Then why can't I study from them?"

"You haven't the skill," the wizard's voice was solemn but his eyes twinkled in amusement. "My impatient maid. In a year or so, when you have more mastery, I will give them to you. Until that time—" he stopped suddenly. "Enough. Leave that, Laurel. We must go down."

"What is it?"

"Tedora is here."

Lessons were abandoned for that day. As the thespers came into Wizardes Cliff, servants, apprentices, even Orlan, were sent to assist them. Baggage must be brought in from the stable-yard. A suitable spot for the performance must be found: it was a rainy late May and too chill to set the stage out-of-doors.

Laurel was given charge of Andemyon, for she had become his special guardian at the castle. The little boy did not cease his worship of Orlan, but he'd endured too many rebuffs to do more than shyly follow his sullen idol. Laurel, on the other hand, would play with him, read to him, attend to him while Tedora and Lord Redmantyl were elsewhere. She could draw him away from Orlan, for which her cousin was grateful.

The child was in danger of being lost underfoot in the rush on the castle yard or struck unwary by a heavy trunk or parcel. Laurel could not both help the thespers and watch over him; she took him up to Redmantyl's chambers, safely out of the way, and retrieved a book from the wizard's library.

The pamphlets Redmantyl had been collecting the previous summer were now bound into a complete volume of odd myths from a dozen ancient and lost civilizations, telling of the beginnings of the gods, the creation of the Earth and of humanity, the origins of evil. Laurel was not certain that they were appropriate for a child of six— some contained strange and beautiful images, but others were disturbing even to her—but there were few other tales in the Norman tongue and Andemyon seemed to enjoy these. They read one or two at each visit.

Seated by the hearth in Redmantyl's sitting-room, she read of Prometheus' theft of the sacred fires from Olympus to bring light to the mortals and of Pandora's box filled with tiny horrors. Andemyon curled half in her lap, eyes shut, but listening intensely. Whenever Laurel paused, he plead for her to go on.

Laurel hadn't been reading long before a young man with short, reddish hair wandered past the open door, then he stopped and stepped back and smiled at her. "Your pardon, Maiden," he said. "I find myself lost. Can you show me to the Bottom Hall?"

"You are truly lost, Thesper. Go down," she pointed to the end of the corridor. "And down the stairs to the lowest floor. The Hall is just there."

"Gramercies." And he was gone again.

"Demy, who was that?" she asked. But the little boy was sleeping.

A little later, Olyr came to the doorway. "Is this where you'd gone, Laurel? We were beginning to wonder."

"Yes, and hush." She extracted herself from beneath the little arm thrown across her lap, and went out, carefully closing the door. "Andemyon's asleep. Are you finished with the thespers?" she whispered.

Olyr nodded. "You were fortunate to miss out on that," he said. "Everyone's gone to the Bottom Hall. They'll be performing the tale of Parsyfal and the Sangrael tonight. Rymbaughe said we might help the troupe set stage. Godefroi's already gone. My Lord left Orlan to direct the thespers, but *he* disappeared even before we brought the first cart over."

"Gone to practice his magic," said Laurel. "He's been working so hard these past weeks to show my uncle he's fit for 'prenticing."

"Well, he's in now. There's no need to shut himself away all day."

They went to the top of the stairwell at the north end of the Magne Hall; three flights below, the troupe laughed and shouted as they dragged their boxes and baggage down the corridor. "They've been short-handed this last circuit," said Olyr. "There's a new thesper or two, but others have gone—Lyse, Gilbert, Amanda, half the dancers."

"I met one of them."

"Who?"

"The new thespers. Did you not see him? A handsome youth, red-headed."

Olyr scowled. "Yes, that one. I don't know his name. You think him handsome?"

Laurel laughed.

"I thought him a pert beggar." He wound her silvery hair around his fingers. "He asked so many questions of My Lord Redmantyl of us all, 'til Rymbaughe bid him shut up his gabble."

From below, Rymbaughe's voice rose in an urgent command and Henri, the jongleur, replied with some indistinguishable jest. Wood scraped against the stone floor.

"We ought to go down," said Laurel.

"Wait." Olyr slipped an arm about her waist. "Let's not, yet." He tried to draw her close for a kiss, but Laurel put her hand on his chest and held him away.

"Olyr, no."

The youth frowned in confusion. "What's wrong? You've been so cool. Have I made you angry, Laurel? That day– When we played at Hunt and you blasted the Great Tower? I didn't mean to strike you hard. 'Twas only in play."

"No, Olyr, I'm not angry at that. 'Tis simply..."

Could she explain? Of all the thoughts which had troubled her the past few days, this was the most disturbing. She didn't fear so much for her uncle; if she challenged him one day, that time and place would be of her own choosing and she was assured that they could meet without meaning death to each other. She didn't fear for Orlan or Godefroi; they could never hurt her and she wouldn't harm them. But what of Olyr?

Though she wanted to trust this boy wholeheartedly, she could not. His mind was veiled from hers, and the unpredicted, lucid glimpses revealed thoughts which did not quiet her unease. When she was near Olyr after that last game in the Great Tower, Laurel recalled too well what she'd seen in him: his jealousy at her powers, his ferocity in competition, his glee as he sought to capture her. It was only in play, but if he felt so now, even for a moment, such feelings might declare themselves more strongly when they met as grown wizards. The stakes then would be higher. He must win. So must she. In battle, as in these children's games, they might forget what they were to each other.

And what were they? In truth, there was only the lightest of bonds between them, a pretty game between boy and girl. For all their claims of "liking" and "having preference," they did not speak of love. They exchanged stolen kisses, but were always restrained from more. They were not lovers, not a young woman and man who would handfast to pledge the rest of their lives; such relationships were unwise for magicians. Their training discouraged intimacies both physical and emotional. Lord Redmantyl discouraged this infatuation—perhaps, Laurel realized, to save them from the doubt and sorrow she felt as much as to reinforce their dedication to the magicians' undistracted state. They were apprentices together, playmates, sweethearts. Nothing bound them to each other except what they felt right now, and the time for this innocent pleasure was already slipping away.

"I've been thinking," she confessed. "My uncle and I spoke of wizard-battle this morning."

Olyr laughed. "And you're afraid of it? You? I'll wager you'll thrash any who challenge you!"

She shook her head. "Olyr, has it not occurred to you who I will battle? It will be you."

Olyr hadn't thought of this, and he was shocked at her suggestion.

"No, never!"

"Who then? Wizards must challenge each other to test their powers and expel the weak from their ranks. You know this as well as I. Magicians battle other magicians, and there are no other magicians—only my uncle and Godefroi's mother, and Godefroi and Orlan. Do you think them more likely?"

"But I am no more your foe than any of them. Do you believe I could hurt you?" He paused. "Could you hurt me?"

"I could not now, but we may feel differently when we are older."

"No." Olyr refused to believe this. "I shan't. It will never happen. Laurel, I promise you."

There was so little time. Olyr would take his mage-vows soon and leave Wizardes Cliff. She kissed him. "I pray you will remember that."

"Laurel!" Orlan called out nearby.

She left her sweetheart's arms and rushed to the corridor, brushing her hair from her face. Her cousin stood outside Lord Redmantyl's chambers. Andemyon was awake, clinging to the doorjamb, staring up at the older boy with wide eyes. "What is it?"

"What did you do?" Olyr demanded.

"Nothing! The imp was here, waiting for me." Orlan frowned fiercely, and Andemyon ran to hide at Laurel's legs. "Where's Father? He promised we'd begin my lessons this afternoon."

"Didn't you hear, Orlan?" said Laurel. "There'll be no lessons this sennight, at least so long as the thespers are here."

"But I–"

"You must know that My Lord wishes to spend his days with the headethesper while he can, rather than stay in that dusty room," Olyr added.

"But Father said we would begin today," the boy protested. "Why does she have to come, and he always abandons everything for her? 'Tisn't fair!"

And why, Laurel wondered, did her cousin always have to be so troublesome when the thespers visited? He couldn't bear Tedora, even for her briefest visits. "He loves her, Orlan. Aren't you grown enough to understand that?"

"Soon enough, Laurel," Olyr said.

Laurel felt her cousin's disappointment and anger as if they were her own, but there was no help for it. "Orlan, it's no great matter," she said easily. "There's little any of us will miss in a sennight, and you least of all." The boy was more sullen at her words, so she added quickly: "Uncle Redmantyl would only have taught you exercises to focus and direct your power. Olyr can show you the same if you must know them immediately."

"If you like," Olyr offered. This was obviously more for Laurel's sake than Orlan's, and she smiled at him.

"There you are, Cos. Nothing's lost."

Orlan did not look any happier.

"The troupe will play the tale of St. Parsyfal in the Bottom Hall tonight and Rymbaughe said we might help set the stage," she announced, then turned, teasing, to Olyr. "I imagine that new young thespian, the handsome one, will play Parsyfal. Coming, Lads?" And she ran, hoping they would follow.

On the stairwell, she heard the walls thumping above her with Orlan's uncontrolled rage.

Rymbaughe had sent the thespers through the Magne Hall to the carpenter's shop and lower rooms in search of unused furniture to supplement the troupe's props. Trunks and boxes, chairs and benches crowded the end of the lowest corridor before the Bottom Hall. A large table with a splintered and repaired leg was jammed firmly in the doorway; Henri and a tall, tawny woman, one of the new thespers, struggled and shoved without success.

Rymbaughe was in despair: "Henri, curse you!"

"It looked like the perfect thing!" cried the jongleur in his defense. "We'd never fit such a one on our carts."

"We can't fit this one into the bloody Hall!"

"Can't we turn it on its side?" the new thesper offered.

"We might've," Henri agreed, "but not now. It's proper stuck!"

"Well, push! We can't leave it here. Push!" At the sound of Laurel's footsteps on the stairs, Rymbaughe looked up. "Ah, good! You will give your hands– You two?" For Olyr had arrived after her.

"Yes, of course."

Laurel leapt onto the table and scrambled on hands and knees across and into the Hall. Within, Anyse and the remaining dancers scattered the contents of their parcels to find the costumes for the production. Jareth gathered a bundle of robes and gowns to be sent to the laundry to be brushed and pressed. Godefroi knelt amid paint pots, brushing green and brown patches on an enormous expanse of canvas spread on the floor. The headethesper was not there.

"Where's Tedora?" she asked.

"With My Lord Redmantyl," Rymbaughe answered. "My Lord

said we might set stage here, then they went on their way. 'Twould be impudent to ask to where. I've been left as headethesper in her absence. Take hold of the legs, if you please, Damosel, and pull with all your might. Robby! Anyse! Tally! Give a hand! Klyff!" This was directed at the red-headed thesper, loitering in the stairwell beyond. "In here, you lout. Where have you been?"

"I was lost," the youth answered simply, and smiled when he saw Laurel. He climbed over the table to help pull, but seemed to give little effort, for the others pushed and yanked and puffed far more to squeeze the table through. Once it shot free, Rymbaughe examined the scraped sides ruefully.

"All the varnish is off. We'll have to– Where's the white baize?" He sent the dancers on a frantic search. The red-headed boy remained near Laurel, enjoying the commotion. She looked up once, and met his eyes.

"Why did it take you so long to find the Hall, Thesper? I gave you very good directions above an hour ago."

"Yes, but I didn't take them," he answered with a grin. "There was too much to see on my way along. May I ask your name, Maiden? We haven't been properly introduced, but I perceive that you must be a lady of the household."

Anyse made the introduction: "Laurel, this is Klyffaude, who joined us when we were at Maryesfont last. Klyffaude," The youth bowed. "I have the honor to present you to My Lord Redmantyl's niece, Laurel Windswift."

"Your servant, Damosel." He took her hand, but instead of pressing his forehead to her fingers, brushed his lips against the palm. Laurel snatched her hand away. The white baize was found, and Rymbaughe determined that they needed more chairs and departed to search for some. Orlan came in and sat at the window in the back corner, Andemyon at his feet, and watched the proceedings sullenly.

"How long will you stay?" Laurel asked as she helped to tack the baize around the table to conceal the scratches and broken leg.

"So long as Tedora wishes and My Lord allows," Jareth answered.

"Wizardes Cliff has become a home to us all," his daughter added. "So near as we have one. If our headethesper thinks to have us stop here a sennight or more, we are glad to."

Orlan, at his window, scowled.

Godefroi had finished his canvases: one was painted to represent a greenwood; one featured a crenellated wall and pennant-capped towers; the third was a field of bleak gray cut by jagged black lines like dead branches.

"Yes, that's good," Rymbaughe approved when he returned. "What is that last one meant to be?"

"The Wasteland."

The thesper shuddered. "It *feels* like it. You know, you might join us, Lad, with a talent like that. We've need of a good limner now that Lyse is gone." The apprentice seemed pleased, but not ready to accept this invitation. "When the paint's dry, we'll have those hung here–" Rymbaughe gestured broadly across the western wall of the room. "In proper order."

Laurel climbed onto the table, pulling a corner of the gray canvas with her; Tallyra, standing on a bench at the opposite corner, did the same. They stopped in the middle of their effort as some of the others returned with chairs, then pulled again. Laurel reached to fasten the tapestry loop, and Klyffaude leapt up to help her. She was tall, but he taller still and easily able to slip the loop over the little iron hook that had been pounded into the wall a foot or so from the corner—the canvases would not block the door and the thespers could make their exits and entrances in this narrow gap. "Gramercies, Thesper."

The boy continued to look upwards. "In truth, I doubted I could stretch up any better than you, but 'twould be discourteous not to offer assistance to a fair damosel. How high a ceiling is this, would you say?"

She looked up. "Three yards, or a foot more. 'Tis not so high as the ceilings of the Great Hall and Feast Hall, directly above. There, the beams cross twenty feet above the floor."

"Are there many rooms so large here?"

"A few others."

Klyffaude jumped down. "The size of this place!" he said in genuine amazement. "I could not believe my own sight as I crossed the great bridge and saw the castle before me. You mustn't wonder that I could be lost so long, Damosel. I fear I should be again if I were sent alone from this hall." He sat on the table. "Rymbaughe tells me that we perform for My Lord's household tonight, but that may be hundreds of people!" He took a playful tone of alarm.

"Not so many," Laurel answered. Tallyra was waiting for her to take up the castle canvas. "We haven't more than fifty servants together, and ourselves—the 'prentices, myself, my cousin Orlan." She jerked her chin toward the sullen boy in the corner. "He is Lord Redmantyl's son. Oh, and my uncle will attend, certainly." She took up the tapestry, but Klyffaude took it from her and climbed up again.

"I've heard much of your uncle, Damosel," he said. "They say My Lord Redmantyl is a fearsome wizard. All through this winter, I listened to the thespers' tale and I imagined how it would be at Wizardes Cliff and to meet a great Lord. Now I am here and I am not yet properly presented." He glanced about; everyone was occupied with their own tasks. "I'd heard much of My Lord long before, from Tedora. She is my cousin, did you know?"

"No. She's never spoken of her family." But Laurel could see a certain resemblance; both had a playful charm, snub, upturned noses, and an elfish wildness in their manner that suggested they could only be Free Folk. "You are near kin?"

"Her father and my mother are brother and sister." His grin flashed again. "We may be kin ourselves, Damosel, if I understand things rightly."

"How so?"

"There are rumors among the troupe," his voice dropped lower. "Of the love of Tedora Headethesper and a great wizard, her patron."

Laurel nodded.

"'Tis true then?" He grinned. "My cos may become Lady of Wizardes Cliff. Now, I am her cousin to the first degree, and you are My Lord's– ah– sister's child?"

"My mother was his cousin, to the first degree."

"Then you are also his first cousin, but to the second order of blood. Therefore, should My Lord and Teddy wed, you and I shall be second cousins, in the second order."

"That's not how 'tis worked." But she saw that he plainly spoke nonsense and she would have no more such silly conversation. Rymbaughe and Olyr returned, dragging a long bench between them.

"Klyff, go about your business!" the acting headethesper ordered, and Klyffaude departed with one last grin.

Laurel picked up the corner of the forest canvas.

"You mustn't mind him," Rymbaughe said, as an apology. "He's a nuisance, I know, but he's harmless if you push him down now and again and make him behave himself."

"I don't mind at all," she answered. "But he's pert enough for a dozen lads! I've never met such a one before."

Rymbaughe laughed.

Lord Redmantyl and Tedora returned at sunset and the thespers gathered in the Feast Hall. After the last platter had been cleared and the last kettle scrubbed in the scullery, the household went down to watch the troupe's version of the tale of St. Parsyfal.

The play began with two people alone in a forest: Tedora, dressed as an old woodswoman in a snowy-white wig and a long, green shawl, and Klyffaude, a young forester in tall boots and a short tunic of green.

The old woman spoke: "Now that you have come of age, my dearest child, 'tis time for you to learn the truth. Your father was a knight, brave and true, the finest champion of King Arthur's court. I loved him dearly. When he died, I abandoned all worldly goods and you were born to me alone."

The boy asked many questions, for he was oddly ignorant of even the most simple matters: What were knights? Who was King Arthur? His mother's answers only intrigued him to learn more and go and see the world. He insisted that he must go until, at last, she bid him farewell and sent him out in his father's rusted armor.

He arrived at the court of Camelot, where his social errors there made the audience scream with laughter. He rode his nag into the palace courtyard and demanded that Arthur make him a true knight, then introduced himself by the name of "Dearest Child," for that was what his mother had always called him. He robbed a damosel of a ring and a kiss, for he'd been told that knights may have such tokens of love. At the King's banquet, he spit on the table, picked his teeth with a knife, and spilled wine all over Queen Guenivere when he rose to toast the Lady. A riotous scene followed when Sir Gauiane, the courteous knight, and Sir Launfal, Guenivere's champion, tried to teach this rustic newcomer the arts of love and courtly behavior. They showed him how to dance, how to speak respectfully, yet prettily, to a maiden—Rymbaughe, as the bearded Gauiane, simpered as the rough youth paid him court—and how to show gracious table manners and not grab and gulp like a hungry wolf. Then, Gauiane, Sir Bors and Sir Yfein taught the boy how to fight; a daring play-battle followed, with the knights chasing their yelping student up and down the stage and around the audience. Then there was a solemn moment as the Mother Abbess taught the boy of Christ and he took the name of Parsyfal at his confirmation.

As Arthur's knight, Parsyfal rode out in search of adventure. He met a fisher, an ancient man in white, who was King Pellas of the Wasteland. Pellas invited Parsyfal to take lodging at his castle; the castle was in ruins, dusty and unoccupied except for the crippled king. As they shared a silent dinner, three glowing maidens in white walked past, one bearing a spear, the next a silver bowl, and the last a covered chalice bright from within. Parsyfal gaped at them as they passed, but didn't ask his host who they were.

After the last maid had gone, Pellas said to him: "Why did you not speak?" But Parsyfal could not answer. The King then explained that the third maid had carried the Holy Grail, the chalice used by Christ at the Last Supper, brought to Britain by Joseph of Arimanthea, and afterwards lost to the world through wickedness. Only the most pure and holy of knights could recover it. If Parsyfal had spoken, the maids would have stopped.

"Am I not worthy?" the young knight asked.

"'Twas error that stopped your tongue, Child. But all is not lost. You may redeem yourself. The way is not easy. Have a care."

Parsyfal ran after the maids, and so began his quest to recover the Grail. He followed them from castle to castle, repelling temptation, battling evil, and speaking with Holy Folk. He joined the battle at Castle Grimolin and freed the imprisoned maid Blanchefleure; they spoke together in pretty love-talk, as Gauiane and Launfal had taught him. But when he left Grimolin to resume his quest, he lost his way. Memories of Blanchefleure always distracted him. In one particularly heart-touching scene, after battle with an evil knight, the blood on fresh snow and the early daffodils peeking through reminded him of the golden hair, crimson lips, and fair complexion of his beloved. While he stood lost in this idle imagining, the three Grail Maidens stepped quietly behind him, but Parsyfal did not see. At last, they walked away.

At the end, Parsyfal returned to Blanchefleure, disappointed in his quest, but he told his love that she was worth the loss. They promised to marry, but the Lady died and the young knight went to a monastery to repent his fall. He said that he had sought worldly pleasures above the holy, and lost both. This was a surprise, for it wasn't one of the traditional conclusions of St. Parsyfal's tale. Usually, Parsyfal succeeded in his quest and ascended to Heaven, or he wed Blanchefleure, so that the story ended happily.

Backstage, in the stairwell and broad corridor below the Magne Hall, the thespers removed their costumes. Tedora rested in loose shirt and ungaitered hose. Marsyegaulte, Tallyra, and Anyse washed the glowing phosphor from their arms and faces. The long, blonde tresses of a wig thrown on the stairway spilled down like a waterfall of liquid gold. Jareth stripped away the white beard of King Pellas and Klyffaude stripped away his monk's robe as casually, leaving himself in nothing more than brown hose. He was the first to drop to one knee as Lord Redmantyl, Laurel, Godefroi, and Olyr entered. Orlan had not wished to accompany them.

The wizard went among the thespers, paying his compliments, and the apprentices followed, muttering less eloquent praise.

"It was wonderful," Laurel said to Tedora, then turned, teasing, to Klyffaude. "'Tis a surprise that you act so well, Thesper. But you do."

"You think so?"

"In truth. When you went to the Brothers and prayed for forgiveness, you wept—you truly wept."

He smiled that she should notice. "Gramercies, Damosel."

"'Twas a strange ending, I think."

"'Tis Teddy's own work. She always had a liking for Greekish tragedies—Oedipus and such-like." He grinned at his cousin. "The speeches I must learn!"

"When he troubles to learn them," Tedora answered.

"Well, they are so deep in misery that I must weep to read them, and my tears will run the ink. You have seen such plays, have you not, Damosel Laurel? Do you weep at them as much as I?"

Laurel laughed at his absurdity, then she saw that Olyr was nearby, and his eyes were dark and stormy.

"Olyr, you mustn't fuss so," she said as they went upstairs. "You know how thespers say such nonsense in play. It didn't meant a thing. He was marvelous as Parsyfal, didn't you think?"

Olyr didn't think so.

"Yes, he was. But he is nothing to me." She kissed him quickly. "Are you angry?"

He shook his head, then thought, then shook again. "He does like you, though. But he can't be spited for that."

"He's only a pretty thesper."

"Yes, but he'll come here again and again. Laurel?" There was an anxious note in his voice that made her pause. "What will happen when I am gone?"

The next night was as cold and rainy, and the children and thespers met after dinner about the fire in the Great Hall. Serving maids brought in pinked wine and steamy mint tea and platters full of little cakes warm from the kitchen, and loitered until Adyna sent them away. For Tedora told stories; she was as gifted a bard as a thesper and even tales they had all heard countless times seemed wrought anew by her lips. She was at home center stage, weaving wordcraft, and she held the room enthralled until she was done. Then, growing hoarse, she took a deep drink of wine and asked if the company would like to see a feat of *prestidigitation.* No one had any idea what that could mean, but they clamored for it.

Tedora produced a two-penny piece with a flick of her hand, balanced it between her knuckles and, with intense concentration, juggled it across the back of her hand, from knuckle to knuckle, and back again. Then she tossed it up, flipped her hand palm up, and swatted the coin high into the air; it glittered in the firelight as it spun up toward the rafters and down again. She caught it between her hands. But when she unfolded her clasp, the tuppence was not there.

"You must have dropped it," Olyr said.

Tedora grinned. "And perhaps, my lad, you've caught it." She gripped his nose between her fingers, pulled gently, and two penny-pieces fell to the floor at his feet. There was a uproar of astonishment.

"'Tis magic!" Laurel cried.

The headethesper was much amused by this.

Lord Redmantyl had been watching from the dark end of the room. "I had no idea you had such a talent, Teddy."

"Hybbarde taught me," she answered. "He was 'specially good at such tricks—the disappearance of money."

The entertainment ended, Godefroi and Orlan began a game of Naughts and Crosses on the hearthstones, Anyse teased the dancer Robert, and Tedora joined Redmantyl in the corner. Laurel went out to the stairwell for a fresh breath, and Klyffaude followed her.

"Do I disturb you, Damosel?"

"You vex," she answered. "Leave me, I pray."

Klyffaude did not leave. "That boy, the 'prentice who makes such moon-eyes at you, is your sweetheart?"

"Perhaps."

"'Tis said that he goes on his mage-travels soon."

"He will take his vows this summer," Laurel acknowledged.

"Poor thing," Klyffaude said. "It must be a sore stretch to live starving and chaste for five full years!"

"But once it is done, you are a wizard."

"Will you take these vows yourself, Laurel?"

"Of course, and live in them easily."

"I could not."

"You wouldn't be able to," she answered swiftly. "Thespers have no more self-command than squirrels."

"You think so, do you? You think there is no effort to memorize lines and lines of speech and then speak them before a crowd as easily as if they had come to your mind that very moment?"

"No," Laurel admitted. "But I am no actor."

He smiled. "I might teach you."

She couldn't help smiling in return. "You may try." She sat on the steps and folded her hands. "Where shall we begin?"

"My best speech is Parsyfal's when he thinks of Blanchefleure."

"The poem near the end, of snow and daffodils?"

"'Tis my favorite." Klyffaude knelt before her, took her hands, and looked into her eyes. His sparkled merrily in the dim candlelight, and they were so blue. So blue, she thought, as Andemyon's. "Listen, Damosel:

I have seen these before, the colors of my love.

The blooms are brighter than all golden things
Save the glory of her hair.
Oh, if she were here that I might comb that brightness!

The snow is whiter than all pure things
Save her fairest skin.
Oh, if she were here that I might embrace that purity!

The blood, cut fresh from my own heart,
Is ruby-red as her fair mouth.
Oh, if she were here that I might kiss that redness!

If the Earth were dark and the Heavens full
And I left behind, a soul forgot and unsaved,
I would find my comfort here.

My love would keep this place with me,
As the blood on the snow and the daffodils in new bloom.
Nothing in Heaven or Earth could be more rare.

Tedora wrote that. To learn the words, you must repeat them. Can you?"

This was no more difficult, and more easily understood, than the exercises Redmantyl had her recite. She began quickly—"I have seen these before, the colors of my love"—and continued without pause to the end.

"Well done!" Klyffaude sat back on his heels. "But you speak the words as if they mean nothing to you. Know you no poetry?"

"I know many poems, but I do not recite with a bard's feeling."

"To be a thesper, you must speak the words as if your heart were rent at the memory of your true love. You clutch your chest with the pain." He demonstrated. "When you speak of the kiss, it must be as if you desire it more than anything. Parsyfal has abandoned his quest in the dream of it. Can you imagine yourself a young man so much in love?"

"Young man?" Laurel smiled. "No."

"Thespers often do so, when one more suited for the role cannot be found. A pretty youth may take the maid's part, or a woman may fix a beard to her chin to play a man."

"I've seen them do it."

"True enough. Anyse would play the young lads before I came to the troupe. Could you not be Parsyfal?"

"Never!"

"Then, if you'll not be a lovesome youth, you must imagine yourself longing for one. Say the words and think of your true love." He grinned. "Think of Olyr, who will be gone from you."

Laurel laughed. "Olyr? With golden hair and ruby lips?" The image was so strange that she could not stop her laughter and Klyffaude began to laugh too, until tears flowed down his face.

"Who would you imagine then?" he asked, blotting his eyes with his sleeve.

"Who indeed! Are there youths so fair as a maid?"

"Not many," he agreed. "Little Andemyon, if he does not change."

"If Andemyon, then yourself as easily," she answered pertly.

The youth blushed. "Me?"

"You are like Andemyon may grow to be one day—a pretty lad, rosy and fair." She rumpled his hair. "'Oh, that I might comb that brightness.' Shall I say the words to you, Klyffaude?"

"If you mean them, My Lady." The earnest look in his eyes disturbed her; it was time to end this game.

Laughing, she slipped past him with a little dance, and bumped into Simon. The young thesper's complexion darkened and he excused himself. Simon remained, blinking at her, rather surprised, in the dim light.

"What is it?" Laurel demanded.

"Ye look much like 'Is Lordship," the manservant replied. "Taking to be'ave too much like 'im too."

"I wasn't doing anything wrong."

"Then ye've nought to fret for," Simon told her. "But I bid ye back to the `All, Dam'sel, before `Is Lordship misses ye."

He'd never spoken so to her before, but Laurel often heard him use this tone to his master when he was dissatisfied with the wizard's conduct. At first, she'd been surprised by the familiarity with which the servant dared address his master, and more surprised that Redmantyl received these scoldings humbly and followed Simon's advice. She had since learned that the young Englishman was her uncle's closest friend; he'd been with Lord Redmantyl longer than anyone else, had witnessed all the adventures the wizard would not speak of, and was trusted at least as much as Tedora. If anyone might safely criticize Lord Redmantyl, it was he. And, if Redmantyl listened, so ought she.

She returned to the Hall.

Laurel and Olyr watched the thespers' departure from the top of the Shadu Hall days later. "I know now how Orlan must feel to see them go," Olyr said. "Thespers are only trouble."

"`Tis not their doing, Olyr. They only mean to be jolly."

"Perhaps." The apprentice leaned upon the parapet, his back to her. "Laurel, I shall go from Wizardes Cliff soon."

"Yes, I know."

"We won't see each other for five years, `til I confirm myself a full wizard. My Lord Redmantyl thinks that best."

"It may be," Laurel answered with coolness she didn't feel. "Five years from now, I shall complete my apprenticeship and take mage-vows myself. We will not be together for many years."

Olyr nodded. Laurel waited for him to speak. She'd observed his unrest this week. He, too, was troubled by the thoughts which had troubled her; she'd made him think: They would be parted for ten years. When they were grown wizards, they wouldn't be the same. They wouldn't feel the same about each other. They might forget.

"Olyr–"

As he turned, it was as if the barriers between them fell and she saw more deeply into him than she ever had before. Sorrow lay upon him like a shadow of darkest night; he knew that they might one day be rivals, and it frightened him more that it had her. *She has such powers,* he thought. *She might challenge the Red-Lord himself when she comes to her own. Can I survive? Can I win against her?* He hated himself for the thought. *Yet, she is so beautiful. Glamour so bright. What moth would not be glad to perish in that flame?*

"I will remember you, Laurel."

"And I you," she said softly, for she didn't know if they told the truth.

cinq

In the summer of 1946, Igren and Iobethe were sent to Wizardes Cliff. Plague had come to New York. Though New York's plagues weren't so frequent nor so fierce as those in Storm Port, when the warm weather, open sewers and increasing number of fleas brought disease to the little town, wealthy merchants sent their families to places of safety. Normally, Kaiese's daughters went to the Abbey of St. Samandra in times of danger, but this year plague had entered the nearby haven and children there died as quickly as children in New York. The Mayor's coach brought the girls to Storm Port and Redmantyl's steward rode with Laurel's palfrey and Orlan's pony to escort his nieces to his home.

Igren had left her childhood during Laurel's years away; now seventeen, with a petite young woman's figure, demure manner, and hair grown long to cover her like an enchantress's cloak, she was at the point of bursting into remarkable and exotic beauty. Iobethe, twelve, was the same frail creature with little chin, large pale blue eyes and ribbon-bound ringlets she'd been at ten. Both maidens inched near each other as Steward Alfryda brought them to the Great Hall where Lord Redmantyl waited to greet them. They were obviously weary from their long journey and unsettled by crossing the bridge, but more frightened at this introduction. Igren, indeed, looked pale and ill until she found Laurel at the wizard's side, and smiled slightly.

After the ceremonies of formal welcome, Laurel took the visitors up to their room across the hall from her own. Iobethe immediately began to change from her riding breeches and traveling cloak, but Igren followed her cousin out.

"Do you like it here, Laurel?" she asked once they were alone. "You are so– You are changed. Not so angry as you once were."

"I'm not angry," Laurel agreed. "I am among friends. My Uncle Redmantyl has made this my home as much as his."

"He isn't at all as Mama said," Igren confessed, shamed at her foolishness. "I thought he must be like a demon with fire shooting from his eyes. But he is– He is like us. Io and I may go home in

October, if the plague has passed, but Mama made us vow we would be no more than courteous here. I was not to tell–" The maiden blushed.

"Tell what?" But Laurel had guessed already. Her eyes, searching, expectant, ran over her cousin's frame. Did she detect a faint glimmer?

Igren ducked her head. "You mustn't tell anyone."

"Cos, it is nothing for shame!" She embraced the girl with swift affection. "This is a house for magic." The word hadn't been spoken until then; Igren shied, but Laurel's confidence emboldened her.

"'Tis not so much. 'Tis nothing. I am not even so magical as you were before you were sent away. You are my uncle's 'prentice, aren't you? Mama thought you might be. She said you mustn't– But she knew you would for you did not obey her even at home. I am to tell her if I see that you practice magic. But, Laurel, I shan't."

"It wouldn't signify if you did. I am my uncle's ward, and not hers."

Admiration touched Igren's eyes. "You won't ever come back, Laurel?"

"Not ever."

"I've missed you." Memories of friendship rekindled, she spoke rapidly, spilling months of secrets at once: "'Tis so dull at home. I never go out as we used to. Remember the marketplace? I don't go– It isn't so much fun without you. Mama has me to sit with her when she receives her guests, as she says I am out of the nursery now, but I daren't speak unless they speak to me. Do you know there is a nobleman who always asks after you when he visits? I never know what to say–"

"Laurel!" The boys stopped at the sitting-room door, suddenly abashed, for Igren looked alarmed at the interruption. They had come up wishing to see more of this strange, silent maid, so like yet unlike the girl they knew.

Godefroi spoke: "Laurel, ah– Damosel Igren, pardon. We thought we might show you about the castle, if you will, if you are not weary?"

"We rode so long," Igren said helplessly, turning to Laurel.

"Not today," the elder girl answered. "Igren and Io are unused to such travels and, you see, my cousin is still in her riding garb."

"Perhaps in the morning?" Orlan suggested.

"Perhaps." Laurel shooed the pair away, and Igren looked plainly relieved.

"Those boys." She kept her eyes upon the door, as if these unfamiliar, dangerous creatures might burst in again. "I saw them with my uncle, when we were brought to him."

"They've been impatient to see you since we heard that you would come," Laurel answered. "I told them everything about you."

Igren covered her mouth with both hands. "Oh. What did you say?"

"I said that you were my only friend in New York, and as dear and dovesome a maid as could be," Laurel laughed. "My uncle said there could not be such a creature in our family. Orlan, the fair one, is your cousin as much as I am, and Godefroi is nearly a kinsman too. You'll like them if you will not be so timid. They didn't mean to frighten you."

"I don't know many boys," Igren said softly. But Laurel thought that this would change, and soon.

At dinner that evening, Iobethe talked spiritedly with the boys and laughed as Godefroi and Orlan made jests. Laurel, seated beside her uncle, discussed Adyna's departure to Storm Port and Simon's promotion to Chatelaine. Igren turned her eyes from one conversation to the other, then to her plate, discomfited by this playful familiarity. Laurel pitied her cousin. When Lord Redmantyl tried to engage her in conversation, asking after his cousin Kaiese and whatever news she might have from New York and Storm Port, Igren only responded with wide-eyed, taciturn replies. Likewise, when Godefroi and Orlan and her sister invited her to join them, she refused. It was painful to see her so afraid; Igren dreaded that she might be asked to speak and not know what to say. The gentle maid found it too difficult to make light-hearted jests with boys. She was shocked to see Laurel speak so freely with their fearsome wizard-uncle, even tease him with the suggestion that if he wouldn't have Orlan's servant Jem receive Simon's duties, perhaps he would prefer to share her own Dulsye. Yet, even in this diffidence, Laurel sensed a wistful envy: Igren would like to be so brave, but she could not. She didn't possess the self-assurance. Her silence was more safe.

Laurel determined to help. There must be a way to put Igren at ease.

"Uncle, I have a request. Will you test Igren?"

"I cannot have her 'prentice without her mother's consent," the wizard answered.

"I do not ask that. Only see her."

"You think she possesses some magical ability?"

Laurel nodded.

Kathryn L. Ramage

"What have you seen?"

"Nothing," she confessed. "But Igren says so and she wouldn't lie. And my Aunt Kaiese had her promise not to speak of it while she stayed here, so *she* must fear you'd learn of my cousin's talent. Also, you were called not to teach me of magic when I came here, yet you have."

"The circumstance is different. You are not Kaiese's to command when you are in my house and your powers are too valuable to keep idle. If Igren had any such ability, I would see it."

"You haven't seen any magic in her? Not the least bit?"

Redmantyl laughed at her persistence. "Oh, very well. It will do no harm if I speak to Igren. If only she would not look so frightened of me."

Days passed before Laurel found her opportunity. When she wasn't at her lessons, Orlan took the time to show his cousins about the castle at a leisurely pace; they visited the Great Tower one day, the battlements and cliffs' edge another, the gardens the next. When Igren was at liberty, Lord Redmantyl had more important business to consider.

In the meantime, Laurel brought her cousin to the libraries. They explored the cochlear compartments of the Spelle Tower together, Laurel taking fanciful, illustrated tomes from the shelves in hopes of igniting her cousin's curiosity; she chose the books which had attracted her most in her own early days at the castle and those which would be least likely to cause alarm: myths and legends of classical, Christian, Arabian and Oriental origins, botanies, bestiaries, poetry, thaumaturgical treatises of the most harmless and abstract topics—in short, nothing that might be taken as wicked by a girl who'd been brought up to fear and despise magic. In the Daune Tower, they turned through apprentices' lesson-books and Laurel explained the nature of her exercises. Igren expressed a little interest in the collection, and was even induced to carry a book or two to her chambers for further study, but she had none of Laurel's voracious appetite. The maid modestly assumed that wizardly knowledge which was not actually diabolical and therefore forbidden was still beyond her understanding. She insisted she could never learn Greek or algebra and she was astonished as Laurel displayed her own education; at her cousin's enthusiastic explanations, she nodded with incomprehension. She admired the small feats of magic Laurel and Godefroi and Orlan performed for her and even wished she might cast such spells herself, but she knew she wasn't able. Igren was a spectator to magic, vaguely interested in its workings, but not ready to belong to it.

At last, as they came to the small library in the wizard's chambers, they found Lord Redmantyl in his sitting-room. The wizard was occupied by his own reading, but he set this work aside when Laurel led her cousin in.

"I have been waiting for you."

"Mama said I mustn't–" Igren began reluctantly, seeing their purpose.

"You will not be made to do anything you do not wish." The wizard offered a hand. "I only require that you speak. Will you, Niece?"

Igren was unable to refuse and she let herself be escorted to a seat.

"Laurel tells me that you have some ability in magic. Is it so?"

The girl fluttered and twisted to look up at Laurel.

"Igren, tell him. Honestly. You mustn't be ashamed!" Laurel insisted.

"Laurel," Redmantyl glanced at her with a warning.

"I'm not," Igren said softly.

"If you wish to leave, Maiden, you may," he told her. "Nothing more will be said."

"No." She turned again to Laurel. "I don't know if I– I have– I feel– A little. Not so much."

"Have you ever created sparks or bright lights when you are angry?"

"No, Uncle."

"Do the walls thump about you? Have you head-pains? Nosebleeds?"

"A pain, here." She touched her temple. "When I am fretted."

"That is not necessarily magical," said Redmantyl. "Why do you believe you have the talent, Niece?"

"I *feel* it," she whispered.

"May we test?"

Laurel watched what followed with disappointment: Igren could not light the candle set on the table before her, nor could she roll a ball on the same surface. Even when she concentrated as best she could, her heart shone with no more than the faintest glamour. It was as if Igren had no energy, no will to bring her little power to light; magically perceived, she was barely there. Each failure brought tears and, at the end, Laurel nearly wept too.

Redmantyl looked at both girls, and sighed. "Igren, one last test. This will not be so difficult." He turned his hand slowly and a glittering orb of bright blue appeared upon his fingertips. "I know you are not capable of performing this trick."

"Laurel can do it."

"Yes, but you are not Laurel. She is a most remarkable young magician and I do not ask you to match her. I shall maintain the shape of the sphere. Take it into your own hands, Niece. Carefully."

Igren, wide-eyed, took the orb, cupping it as delicately as a bright and precious gem.

"Do you have it?"

"Yes." Her lips moved with barely a sound.

"Bring all of your attention to that spot, Igren. Don't fret yourself. You must relax." He waited until her quickened breath became more slow, her intense, colorless eyes blinked once, and a little color returned to her ivory cheeks. "What color is the sphere?"

"Blue."

"Say it is another color. Yellow. Wish it to be yellow. Make it so."

"H-how?"

"Will it. You've brought your concentration to it—Have it be yellow."

The color drained from the orb abruptly; it became a misty thing, barely visible to Laurel in her seat by the hearth. Then it began to glow with palest gold. Igren laughed, embarrassed, and the fragile spell collapsed.

"Uncle, I didn't mean–"

"You did as I asked. I do not expect the self-command of a grown wizard from a young maid, even Laurel."

The girl glanced at her cousin. "I'm not so strong as Laurel."

"Nor is Godefroi, but he is my apprentice."

"I could not 'prentice," Igren protested. "I'm not clever. All those lessons. My mother–"

"I cannot teach you," Lord Redmantyl agreed. "Kaiese wouldn't approve such a thing. Even so, Niece, you do not yet require apprenticeship. You possess a most delicate ability. It may prove more promising as you mature and come into your full powers, but you will not grow so much in your months here."

Igren was a little sad at this judgment, but relieved that she wouldn't be forced between loyalty to her mother and to Laurel. She thanked her uncle quietly before he sent them both away.

As they returned to their rooms, she said, "You shouldn't have done this, Laurel. I was not to speak to my uncle of magic."

"You didn't have to test if you were afraid to."

"You made me–" She stopped, for Iobethe waited on the landing above, eyes bright upon them.

"What did you do?" she whispered, hissing, as they came up.

"You've been listening!" Laurel accused.

"No one said I mustn't," the child answered pertly. "Igren, you spoke with my uncle? What did he want?"

"He is kind. I am not so afraid of him," Igren answered cautiously. "We talked of magic–"

"Did you?" Iobethe asked. "Did you do magic?"

"I did. Io, I could!"

"Oh!" her small sister gasped. "Mama wouldn't like that."

"You mustn't tell," Igren insisted, a little frightened. Laurel's frown reinforced this plea.

"If you do, Imp," Laurel warned her.

"You can't hurt me," the little girl protested, but her voice squeaked. "I'll tell Mama if you do! I'll tell my uncle!"

They were in the corridor now and Orlan, slouched against Laurel's chamber door, looked up hopefully at their voices. Laurel pinched the girl to be silent.

"I was looking for you." He addressed all three, but his eyes remained tentatively on Igren. "There is a little time before my lessons and I would ask you to come along for a walk in the wood. 'Tis beyond the village," he explained. "Remember, as you came to the castle?"

"Like the woods about New York," Iobethe said. "We are not permitted there. Laurel, can't we go?"

"You may," Laurel answered. "Igren and I have other business."

"Business?" Orlan wondered. "At what?"

"'Tis a secret." She pushed past the boy to reach her door. "Only maids may know."

Orlan turned, baffled, to Igren; she shook her head and retreated after Laurel. "Girls," he said in disgust and went to find Godefroi. Iobethe tagged after him.

Laurel shut the sitting-room door. "You were willing to test, Igren," she resumed their interrupted exchange. I may have brought you to meet my uncle, but I didn't force you to stay and you cannot pretend otherwise."

"You meant for me to test all along," Igren answered. "Those books."

"You read them."

"I wanted to know. Magic seems so wonderful." Igren bowed her head. "I wondered," she confessed.

"And you have an answer. 'Tis better than never knowing certainly. You may not be afraid of what you are, once you truly know. You are magical."

"Not so magical."

"You'll grow stronger, Cos. I know you shall," Laurel promised. "But the talent must be developed. I wasn't half so powerful a magician before I began my 'prenticing, and you must practice too. Shall I show you?"

"You know I mustn't–"

"My Uncle Redmantyl mustn't teach you, and he shan't. I shall." She pulled Igren to sit beside her. "We'll begin where my uncle left off." She produced an orb of iridescent blue as quickly as Redmantyl had, then let it roll from her fingertips to the palm of her hand. There was no sense of surface nor of weight as she lifted it to Igren's cupped hands. The spell held and the orb did not burst. "Now, the sphere is blue, Igren..."

Lord Redmantyl might be satisfied with his judgment of Igren's abilities, but Laurel was not. She couldn't be, especially as she observed her cousin in the weeks that followed. It wasn't so strange that Igren didn't glow with the force of her powers like other magicians; her talents were peculiar, even among the magical. Animals feared magic. In the village, geese and chickens would squawk and dogs would howl at the wizard's apprentices; the castle horses were always skittish with their magical riders; in the woods, wild things fled. But Igren seemed to quiet the beasts. The Lyges dogs would come to her, tails wagging, and Laurel's palfrey preferred to bear the more gentle girl, leaving Laurel to take Redmantyl's mount when they rode. Although Igren couldn't tame the woodland creatures, she left them unafraid. When she ventured into the Greenwaters Island forest, apart from her companions, the birds continued their songs in the nearest trees and the deer kept their grazing at the side of the path as she passed, while another human intruder would make them scatter. If this was magic, it was not like any other talent Laurel had ever encountered.

Laurel wasn't the only one to notice. Godefroi, watching Igren one afternoon, confided, "She could catch a unicorn if there were one about. But she'd free it as quickly."

Igren sat on the sunlit Seayrifte Plaza below the windows of the Great Hall; a little speckled sparrow fluttered down to perch upon her hand. She smiled and spoke sweetly to it, but the apprentices were too far away to hear her words.

"Is it magic?" Laurel wondered, not for the first time.

"Of a sort, perhaps," Godefroi thought. "But not as you and I possess. She casts no spell to make the creatures love her. They simply know that she will do no harm." Iobethe ran out to her sister, and the sparrow flew away. "I think of her like the figure of a maid in a unicorn tapestry. Or–" He blushed that he should have such ideas but, emboldened, spoke: "Like a Lady in the tales of Old Days. We hear of the fabulous fairness of Guenivere and Isolde and Oluen and we believe that such beauty is no longer found upon this world. But I think that if any such women ever truly walked, then they were as Igren—passing fair and always so gentle that their grace must have magic in it. They did not *do* things, but were simply lovely beyond compare. Igren will be greatly admired."

"She is already," Laurel laughed. "What words from you, Godefroi! If bards will sing my pretty cos's praise, you shall be first among them. You might make a song of this. You could, if you choose."

"I have thought of it," the boy confessed. "But I don't have the words—they sound so silly spoken. 'Tis only the image of beauty."

Laurel understood: Godefroi saw beauty. He was forever looking at the shadows on the Summer Plaza and the patches of green and brown that made up Greenwaters Island; he studied the stars, the frost upon the windowpanes, the bare branches of winter trees as if they hid some pattern and he tried to copy them, first with sketches, then with carefully crafted illusionary spells of his own design. Now, Igren was the beauty to gaze upon and think of.

Laurel wondered if Igren charmed males as easily as mute beasts, or if Godefroi and Orlan too were simply fascinated by an extremely pretty girl. Igren didn't encourage Godefroi's poetry nor her cousin's boyish admiration—she was startled when they spoke to her—but both had stared and smiled and offered bashful invitations for Igren's company since her first day at Wizardes Cliff.

If there was magic in this, Laurel was determined to discover it.

"Igren, will you have another lesson?"

"If you wish." The girl rose from the coucherie by her dressing-room windows, where she'd been watching the rain, and came to Laurel. "What shall we do?"

"We must test the nature of your ability. You may command best within the mental medium."

"The– What–?"

"Some magic has no influence in the material world," Laurel explained, simplifying the lengthy and tortuous passages she'd gathered from a dozen sources on the subject in her quest to discover an answer for Igren's talents. "A mental magician exerts her will only in the mental energies of other people and living creatures. She senses them—she reads the thoughts which pass through another mind and she can disrupt them and command their actions."

"Another of your books," said Igren, with a smile. "What does it mean?"

"Such magicians cannot cast spells and so are not counted as true wizards, but they are no less magical."

"You believe I may be such a creature?"

"You certainly have something of the ability. I've seen it. But we must test to see how powerful it is."

"What must I do?" Igren asked, simply willing to do what her cousin required. She would never ask Laurel to create such an exercise for her, but she wouldn't resist if one were given her.

"You must try to pass your thoughts to me. Think of something, but you mustn't say what it is. *Think* at me."

"But, Laurel, how shall we know that it is my power, and not yours?"

"Yes," Laurel agreed. How would they be able to determine if Igren had sent a thought to her, or if she had plucked it from her cousin's passive mind? She was often able to sense the thoughts of her kin and Igren was closer to her than either Orlan or Lord Redmantyl. "There must be another– Oh, I know! You must have me do something. Don't tell me. Think it. Will it me."

"Is that different?" the girl asked. "You will know what I think."

Laurel shook her head. "No, you must command me. You may not know it from my own will, but I shall. You must trust me for that. I shan't put myself up against you, Cos." She sat down on the steps of the platform beneath the bed Igren and Iobethe shared and waited, but Igren hesitated; the gentle maid had never ordered anyone about and to command Laurel was nearly unthinkable. "Igren, do it."

Reluctantly, she obeyed. Her fingers brushed Laurel's temples. Her eyes shone solemnly into her cousin's. The fair brow creased with some effort. Laurel waited, wondering what the unspoken command might be, and then she felt it: she was suddenly dizzy, weary, heavy-limbed, as if she had kept herself awake for many long hours and could refuse sleep no longer. A dark, sparkling whirled up into her head and overtook her. Her eyes blinked once, again, then shut. She slumped against the bedpost.

"You aren't playing to tease me, Laurel?" her cousin's voice awoke her.

"Honestly, I'm not." Laurel brushed her hair from her eyes as the mists dissipated. "You bid me sleep and I vow I did! I would've slept if you'd not left off." She yawned and Igren smiled, timorous but pleased. "Now try again, and I shall resist. We'll see how strong your powers are."

Again, she felt the tentative touch of Igren's thoughts within her own, the whispered urge of *sleep, sleep.* At the first tingling, drowsy sensation, she rebelled. Igren jumped back, startled.

"You push so fiercely."

"Most folk will if you use such influence upon them," Laurel answered. "You cannot always find them willing, or catch them unawares."

"Then it is a useless talent," said Igren.

"No. 'Tis simply feeble and so must be strengthened to have its full effect. You must push back against me. Try again and if I resist you, you must push harder, as much as you can. You shan't hurt me."

Igren stood silently before Laurel, preparing herself for this battle of will against will, then began to assert her subtle influence. At the first timid urgings, Laurel rebelled; the young maid retreated immediately.

"Igren," she spoke impatiently and pushed out to provoke her cousin to use the powers that must be there. But Igren didn't resist and suddenly Laurel was no longer defending her own will, but engulfing Igren's. She saw into that quiet mind, so different from hers, so different from any other she'd glimpsed. She could barely understand what she felt—No single thought was clear. Instead, there was a strange, thrilled fear as that lesser will fell beneath her crushing strength, the sensation of a single spark dimmed, the image of a fluttering bird in her grasp. She could feel the race of Igren's heart.

Igren shrieked. "No!"

Laurel leapt up. "Igren, I didn't mean–" As she reached out, her cousin eluded her hands and fled to the dressing-room. Laurel caught her there.

"I could feel you! You–" Sobbing, Igren covered her face and fell to the windows. "Why do you press me so?"

"To make you magical," Laurel answered, ashamed of herself. She hadn't meant to be brutal; she'd never imagined that Igren was so fragile. Their struggle had been no different from those Laurel engaged in with Lord Redmantyl during her lessons, but where she repulsed all attempts to subdue her will and grew stronger for the exercise, Igren grew more faint. It wasn't Laurel's nature to submit, even when threatened by forces greater than her own. But Igren-

"I am not like you. Sweet Marye, I could never be! I–" The girl twisted to press her face to the coucherie cushions. "I didn't know what your magic was– I must disappoint you, Laurel. I cannot be more than I am."

Laurel felt the misery behind these words stab through her. Igren had never been enthusiastic at these informal lessons and she hadn't realized until now how much it meant to her cousin to be magical, at least a little. She sat down beside Igren and tenderly lifted her. "It's not for me to be disappointed, Pet. I only wish you to be what you may be."

"Beside you, I am nothing at all."

"That isn't so," Laurel insisted, but Igren continued to sob in her arms. The windows beaded with raindrops like tears.

On the holy day of Assumption, also called Maryemas, Laurel accompanied her cousins to Mass. Though she heard Iobethe tell her rosary beads each night and watched both girls cross to the chapel every Sunday, she hadn't thought to join them until Igren invited her this morning.

Laurel had never entered the chapel before, had never been nearer than the gardens about it. Once she'd come to Wizardes Cliff and the pressure to attend Mass was relaxed, her tenuous belief lapsed completely. The loss wasn't felt. The tenets of the Christianity which had constrained her in her ignorance were loosened as she learned more of them. In their studies, she and Godefroi often analyzed the quaint rituals practiced by Norman common folk and wondered why, if the Church was universal, the French enacted one ceremony to celebrate a certain holy day, the Irish another, the Northlanders a third, and the Prelate in Rome proscribed something which didn't resemble any of these? Godefroi said that each had combined the pagan rites of their ancestors with the teachings of the Church at the time of conversion and carried the amalgamation on through the centuries without understanding; he called them meaningless, but then, Godefroi called all rites meaningless. Laurel began to think that this was true. She compared the hagiographies to older mythologies. St. Anne's virtues were very much like those of Vesta. St. Khrystopher, the patron of travelers, echoed Hermes or Mercury. Even the attributes which named the Blessed Virgin Mother, Seat of Wisdom, Queen of Heaven, had once named forgotten and fallen goddesses, Demeter, Isis, Athene, Juno, Ystre. As she learned Latin and Greek and Hebrew and read the scriptures for herself, Laurel's questions multiplied but no satisfying answers followed. The Church demanded blind obedience but she could not, had never been able to, submit without question. She doubted, then scorned. If there was no truth in the ceremonies, why should she attend? Her uncle didn't discourage this skepticism; contrary in fact, he said that wizards ought not offer service to any higher power and it was just as well if she abandoned all religion now rather than wrestle with such spiritual conflicts later in her career. Laurel needed to hear no more. Faith receded.

Par Raymonde, the parish priest, was pleased to see her and attributed her recovery to the piety of her well-behaved cousins. Laurel went through the motions of Mass as smoothly as she always had in New York. Afterwards, as the servants returned to the castle and the priest returned to the little rectory in Lyges, the girls played in the garden. This bright and fragrant patch, hidden from the chapel on one side and the stableyard on the other by its sheltering rows of trees, was the one place in all of Wizardes Cliff that reminded Igren and Iobethe most of home, for there was a small garden behind the Mayor's Hall. Here, the paths were soft beneath their feet and the sunlight through the trees was more warm than when it gleamed on the pale stone of the castle. They gathered armloads of flowers and laughed more freely than they would in the wizard's house.

Laurel remained with them, although she'd left behind such girlish games years ago. She didn't think of the garden as pretty flora. As part of her education, she learned the virtue of every plant here as well as the uses of many plants that grew wild on Greenwaters Island; she went out frequently to pluck petals, dig up roots, gather herbs and leaves and seeds. The root of that broad-leafed plant beneath the yew trees was chewed to comfort a toothache. Tansy leaves were brewed into an ointment for spider bites and rashes; the yellow flowers made a potion to relieve stomachache. The little blue flowers Io gathered eased a fever. The juice from the stalks of touch-me-nots made a soothing balm. Poppy seeds, ground into powder or boiled into black paste, were used to dull pain; a small amount relieved a headache, a larger amount eased severe injury, and larger still created fantastic visions. Her uncle had cautioned her against taking up this last practice, for it was more destructive to self-command and the senses than even wine. A massive dose could cause death. Others here—foxglove, nightshade, rhododendron, and those large, white horrid-smelling flowers—could also kill. Igren and Io played among them, but Laurel knew what they were.

Then she heard the familiar voice of Tedora Headethesper call up to the guards on the wall, and the laughter and jangling music of the troupe as they drove up through Lyges, and she ran to meet them at the gate.

The next evening, Laurel pulled on an antique costume worn by the granddaughter of Layn Moruen. The velvet gown was ashen gray, but she didn't think her uncle would object to her use of Orlan's color; nothing so fine was ever made in brown. Scarlet and gold needlework covered the bodice with an elaborate arabesque of leaves and flowers and golden ribbons laced the front and tied the sleeves, which were tight from wrist to elbow, then slashed open to the shoulder. There was also a veil to pin over her hair, but the lace had not worn so well. She was unaccustomed to such garments, for she held such decorative, maidenly things in contempt and despised dainty slippers and hair ribbons and frilly petticoats. But tonight, she would wear this. She wanted to be pretty, if simply to find out that she could be.

It had begun when she met the troupe at the gates.

"Swift!" Tedora had cried as she reached up to embrace her. "Why, you've grown half a span since this spring! How are you, my darling? Do you think this lovely weather will hold so we can put on a performance tonight?"

"I hope not," Laurel had replied. "My uncle will be out of the castle. 'Tis Maryemas."

"Blasted Wizard's Keep."

Igren and Iobethe had followed her from the garden; Laurel urged them forward and introduced them to the headethesper and the others as the caravan rolled into the yard. Igren, shy at so many strangers, unsure what courtesy called for in the greeting of thespers, met each with a few words and offered her flowers.

Klyffaude leapt out of the last wagon as it passed. "Laurel!" He grinned at her. "I thought 'twas your voice, but now I see I am mistaken and truly hear your sister."

"No," Laurel answered. "My cousin. Igren Uindaughter of New York."

"Near enough. More of your wondrous family." He gave Igren his best smile, and Laurel did not think the young thesper so charming as usual. But Igren pinked prettily.

Other compliments followed: how lovely her cousins were, how fair, how sweet, how well-bred. Igren and Iobethe had attended Mass in their best clothes, while hers were as shabby as a strolling minstrel's. When her antique courier's garb had grown ragged, the castle tailor had cut others in similar fashion: short tunics like the brief brown jerkin of an apprentice, with a scrolling red *R* sewn on the left breast, breeches with red-ribbon laces up the thigh, linen shirts featuring little edges of lace which appealed to her thesperish fancy but were in no danger of dipping accidentally into an inkwell or sweeping the chalk lines of a spell from the floor or catching fire over a candle in the exercise of her magic. Comfortable and practical, she wore them daily and gave no thought to her appearance.

For the first time, Laurel was struck by an unpleasant self-awareness. She knew she was not like her dainty cousins; throughout their visit and even on that day of Maryemas, she observed how her magic, her education, her strength and athletic vigor, her lack of religious faith made her different from them. The knowledge had never disturbed her before. She didn't want to be demure and well-mannered. She'd always pitied the little maids who were taught needlecrafts instead of reading and writing and were praised more for their beauty than their intelligence. She laughed at the young women who did nothing but chatter about the men they would wed and thought them foolish, useless creatures. But now she felt as if *they* were what maidens ought to be and *she* was in error. Women were generally, by nature, small and soft in physical form and tender in heart. Examples were obvious and plentiful. One didn't have to be so beautiful, delicate and gentle as Igren: the servant-maids of the castle were meek and modest; Marsyegaulte was graceful in her yellow wisps of dancer's gown; Anyse was lively but as pleasant and comely as any girl of the village; even her much admired Tedora was a pretty little woman. They shared the common traits of a femininity she didn't possess. Even clever or strong, they couldn't be mistaken for anything but women. No one would call them "Lad." Beside them, she felt ungainly and somehow wrong. She was too tall, too quick, too boyish, too rough. She was not a proper maiden.

As she escorted the troupe into the castle, she noticed with increased embarrassment that Tedora was correct; she was now taller than Klyffaude.

And that had brought her to this. The skirt of the damosel's dress was too short—above her ankles when she'd first tried it on two years past and only a few inches below her knees now—the bodice was tight across her breasts and tight about her waist, and the sleeves didn't stretch all the way from her wrists to her shoulders, but loose lacing gave her room to breathe. Before her mirror, hair combed and braided, she could almost imagine herself a proper young noblewoman, the niece of a lordling and not a vagabond and untamed child. But her own reflected, self-conscious smile was mocking: *Silly girl*, it chided, *do you think you can pose as an ordinary maiden? No fine gown will make you a beauty. One word from this mouth will betray your true nature.*

She went down to the dining hall; the layers of lacy petticoats beneath the skirt were heavy and hindered her usual quick steps. Laurel no longer wondered why merchant-dames moved so slowly and stately: they could walk no other way.

In her seat at her uncle's left, she remained more stiff and silent than necessary, half-hoping that no one would notice her, half-afraid that no one would. The thespers caused enough commotion about the crowded table as they laughed and called for platters and pitchers and exchanged friendly insults. Orlan sulkily played with his food. Iobethe was in helpless giggles. Lord Redmantyl's attention was occupied by Tedora as he adroitly fended off her teasing questions on his absence the night before.

At last, Godefroi spoke—no great intrusion upon the uproar, but it seemed to her that he shouted: "Laurel, why the fancy dress?"

"'Tis magnificent," added Tedora, distracted from her ineffective siege upon the wizard. "I thought so when you came in, how different you seemed. Gray ought to be your color, Swift, not brown." At Redmantyl's frown, the headethesper laughed. "Where did you find it?"

"In an old wardrobe somewhere. Simon once told me it belonged to the maid who lived in my chambers long ago."

"My grandmother," said Godefroi. "Maidens wore those fanciful gowns in the olden days. 'Tis pretty enough, but I wonder that anyone would have it in modern times. Is there a reason, Laurel? I didn't think you cared for such fripperies."

"Perhaps you think to join our performance tonight," Jareth said in jest. "'Tis a Romance of the Eduardian days."

Rymbaughe agreed: "Diana Hartsrider tearing about on her steed, leading her Northlander troops to drive the Spaniards from the marches. Tedora's meant to take the role, but you're far more credible as a warrior-maid, Damosel. You'd tear the make-believe to pieces."

"Well, she can't tonight. Diana is already wed to Eduarde Redlyon in our tale. She took to no battles after he captured her."

Laurel smiled uncertainly, suspecting that they drew her into an elaborate prank. "I'd never be able to at any rate," she retorted. "Klyffaude says I recite like Judy-on-a-stick."

Klyffaude did not deny nor cheerfully agree to this; he was engaged in soft conversation with Igren at the far end of the table and had heard no word.

"'Tis pity now I think on that," said Tedora. "Poor Diana."

"She birthed the last Emperor and My Liege Dafythe, fine men and good sovereigns both," Lord Redmantyl answered. "You can't call that a tragedy."

"Nonetheless, I'm grateful women aren't called to give over everything upon marriage these days. Was I willing to surrender for Hybbarde's sake? Will our Laurel leave her wizardry for love of a lesser magician? Do you think Prince Margueryt will be content put up her sword upon marriage? They say Dafythe's daughter bears the fire of the Redlyon's spirit. A maiden of just four and twenty, yet she's ready to carry on the old feuds with Spain. If she's half so bold as her gran'thers, there's no man in a Christian kingdom today to match her. No man of reason would think to ask for such sacrifice. 'Tis a woman's worst sorrow to marry beneath her. Her husband's jealousy keeps her from what she ought to be, if that is more than he is. We are fortunate to escape that peril."

"All marriages are not so bad as yours was, Tedora," Jareth said gently. "My Rose and I were happy enough."

"Would you have let her go to war?"

"She wasn't that sort. And if she were fit for it and would go, I'd have no way to hold her. You know the old saying—*A disappointed woman is more dangerous than a wounded lion.* I wouldn't be fool enough to test its truth, especially if I were wed to a swordswoman."

"Do you think Margueryt will bring us to war once My Lord Dafythe has gone?" wondered Rymbaughe.

"I pray not," Godefroi replied with one of his little heresies. "Why does anyone, female or male, want a war? 'Tis bloody misery and pain over the most feeble of reasons from all I've read."

The company was surprised, amused. After all, the Norman Empire was built upon its history of conquest and legends of courageous warriors. But Lord Redmantyl took his apprentice's part: "I shall give my service to the Prince when she is my liege if she requires it, but I too hope it will not come to that. I have fought and do not wish for another battle. It is no game. We've had peace for fifty years and ought to be glad of that."

The memory of Eduarde Redlyon, the fierce, spectacular warrior-king of the century past, fell like a shadow across the Empire and cast the administration of his sons Kharles and Dafythe into fainter light. If modern Normans spoke with pride of their warfare, it was in remembrance of the Redlyon's campaigns. If they thought of the Spanish with contempt, it was also because they hadn't forgotten their hatred of this former foe. Every good Norman could recite how the young Eduarde, outraged by the tragic death of his elder brother Denys in battle against the Spanish at Princemarch, sought a vengeance that carried over the next seventy years at the Northlands' marches, at Madehef in North Africa, and in the Pyrennes mountains until at last, past ninety, he proposed a treaty of peace at the request of his sons and wed the Infanta Marianne of Navarre to seal his pact. Every good Norman heard tales of clashing swords and brave warriors marching in their Lord's name and the spilt blood of defeated enemies, and they imagined what it was like to live in such wonderful days. Ancient knights and soldiers who'd fought with the Redlyon were revered and envied. The *pax normania* established by the late Emperor Kharles and Duke Dafythe, with its unmolested trade routes, lighter taxes, and relaxed policies was scorned as dull and the men who'd kept the seven kingdoms secure for half a century were called pale echoes of their forceful father. The Normans looked hopefully to the next generation—the young Emperor, Dafythe's daughter Margueryt, and the Irish Prince Kat—for a return to the glory days now lost.

The thespers made their living upon this hope, for *The History of the Redlyon* was their most popular play outside of Wizardes Cliff. And, while Lord Redmantyl didn't care for such tales, many of his household did. In the light of torches on the plaza, they relived the times of old and recreated Eduarde's battles and court intrigues and, finally, presented a royal pageant: rows of guards in tin armor and jangling swords, blue-robed courtiers, the black-bearded, scowling Spanish ambassador, the cheering crowd supplemented by the audience. Laurel watched with aching heart and shining eyes.

Andemyon was to have a speaking role in the performance that night. Though he'd been on stage often while an infant in roles such as the baby Jesus, infant Arthur, and various little princes, he grew too frightened to appear once he was old enough to be aware of the dozens of eyes upon him. The troupe's latest attempts to bring him out were disastrous, but he was seven now and Tedora had rehearsed him all afternoon in hopes that he would prove himself a thesper after all.

The little boy made his entrance in the gold and purple tabard of a royal herald. His announcement, "Eduarde, Emperor of the Normans," would bring Rymbaughe out as the fabulous king. But when the moment to deliver this speech arrived, Andemyon didn't speak. Wide and blinking blue eyes fixed on the faces of Redmantyl's household and the guests from Lyges, lips moving soundlessly, he stood petrified.

"Andemyon," his mother urged from the unlit edge of the stage, but the child remained silent. Tears spilled onto his painted cheeks and the rosy dust smeared and spattered on his costume. Rymbaughe, waiting for a cue that would never come, stepped up behind him.

"You mustn't weep, Little One," he whispered. "'Tis nothing to fear." He looked up at Redmantyl. "Apologies, My Lord."

The wizard only held out his hand. "Andemyon, come here." The little boy ran to him. The play continued, the thespers skillfully covering the absence of one minor player.

Afterwards, as the audience dispersed, Tedora came down. Andemyon, still in the wizard's lap, looked up mournfully.

"Mama–" He reached for her.

Tedora took him up. "Hush, my pixie. You won't have to go up again."

"The people–"

"Yes, I know." Together, wizard and thesper brought the child into the Bottom Hall. The summer evening had grown chill and the winds from the sea swept in over the battlements to rumple the people left on the stage and plaza. Klyffaude offered his cloak to Igren as they went in.

"My poor little cos," he said. "I don't imagine he'll ever be a great thesper, or any sort of thesper. He's far too timid and he'll never stand before an audience. A pity too—he'll be a handsome lad and the maids love a handsome lad. Don't you think?"

Igren smiled shyly. "I think he has a lovely name," she said. "'Tis from one of my favorite tales."

"What tale?"

"Of Artemis and her sleeping love." Her sparkling laugh rose through the Hall, then she stopped, ashamed at her forwardness. "Do you not know the old Greek myths? I had heard you were at Maryesfont."

"No," Klyffaude grinned. "My home is Maryesfont, but I am no scholar."

Tedora gave orders to her troupe to bring their props in from the courtyard, and quickly. She kissed Lord Redmantyl and prepared to take Andemyon up to bed, but the child was heavy for her. Laurel offered to help.

"My pert cos is right, of course," Tedora confided as they ascended to the boy's bedchamber. "Andemyon is no thesper."

"What will become of him?"

"What can be done with one who is out of place among the Free Folk?" She kissed his curls. "He wants another way and must find it for himself when he is of an age to decide. I would keep him here, but I couldn't bear to leave him. 'Tis best to have your children near, especially when they are small. I wouldn't like to meet my own little one only after he had half grown." She patted Laurel's cheek. "I think that unnatural and hurtful."

Andemyon was put to bed and Tedora stayed with him until he fell asleep. Laurel returned to the Bottom Hall. Rain battered the castle; the thespers had taken down the stage and were packing their costumes and tapestries. Orlan sat sullenly at the window with Rymbaughe, the only thesper he seemed to find tolerable. Redmantyl was at the fireside, gazing into the flames as if he could divine some truth in their flicker, and Iobethe embroidered near the light. Igren and Klyffaude were in the same conversation.

"It is not your true name?"

"No, Damosel," the youth answered. "But you may wager half the Free Folk, and more, call themselves by names far different from those they received at christening. You'll find a good many Maryes, Toms, and Jacks about."

"Which are you?" asked Igren. "Tom or Jack?"

"Neither. At home, I am called Leod."

"'Tis not so common."

"Perhaps not, but I grew weary of it all the same and thought to find another to befit my new-found trade. A thesper's name ought to be suited to his place, dear maid, as an alekeeper's is to his."

"Alekeeper?"

"My mother and father keep a tavern at Maryesfont, in the town, and I would have kept it after them if I had not left with my cos." He chuckled. "Goode Keeper Leod, beer-paunched and red-nosed and ever-so jolly with his customers. Can you see me so, Damosel Igren?"

Igren smiled. "No, indeed."

"Nor can I. And could never. My mother would welcome Teddy's troupe at our inn, though she knew my cos would win away one or two of us. `Tis only myself so far."

"Is it a large family?"

"Three brothers and two sisters. I am eldest, and one of my sisters is meant for the Abbey, but there will always be at least one left to take up the trade."

As Laurel watched the two, she thought that Klyffaude had told Igren more in one playful conversation than he'd told her in his three previous visits to Wizardes Cliff, and that she had never seen Igren so merry.

"I haven't been so far south as New York, Damosel," the thesper said. "Before I joined the troupe, they would travel down to Lyngreen but of course we cannot visit it any longer."

"I recall," the maid answered. "We passed it on our way to Storm Port, my sister and I. `Tis burned to the ground."

"Not a house left standing," Klyffaude agreed. "They say a child caused it. I heard it was a pleasant town, upon the river, and the people were generous to weary wanderers. Is it so in the southlands? If our little troupe made its way to New York in better times, would you welcome us?"

"My father is not patron to thespers as my uncle is, but he invites a performance sometimes."

"And would you come to see us play, Damosel?"

Igren blushed and ducked her head, then glanced up to find Klyffaude gazing at her, hopefully, earnestly. She smiled.

Laurel flew back upstairs, up to her chambers, and pulled furiously at the ribbons and lacings which bound her, mindless of the seams, until she tore herself free and flung the velvet gown aside. She felt more awkward than before, ridiculous for trying to be a woman she was not, humiliated that she'd made such a fool of herself before so many people. She would never wear such beastly garb again.

"Laurel, you are changed."

"Am I?" Klyffaude had barely spoken to her all week, and these were his words?

She slashed at the branches of the garden birches and shrubs with her sword, heedless of the berries and leaves that showered down about her. Her fencing was practiced infrequently when the troupe was away, for there were few potential partners at hand. The gate guards, sons and daughters of the neighboring farmers, were barely trained. Orlan was willing, but as a pupil, and Lord Redmantyl would spar with her on rare occasions; the wizard was not remarkably skilled himself and not inclined to give his discipline to physical battle, but he understood that Laurel was a fighter—"like your mother"—and he encouraged the instinct for its own sake. When the troupe visited, Laurel sparred with Rymbaughe, the best swordsmaster among them, whenever he had the time to indulge her. She'd worked with the young man daily this sennight past; indeed, he had left her minutes before Klyffaude's approach.

"You were more gracious when we were here last. I imagined we parted as friends. Is it that you pine for your Olyr?" But Laurel did not find this amusing and Klyffaude quickly lost his grin. "I beg your pardon if I imagine wrongly."

Blade slicing the air with a satisfying whistle, she answered: "You are not entirely wrong, Klyffaude. I have new duties and little time for games. If you like, join me now." The sword Rymbaughe had left was a stage prop of tin which would bend at one good stroke of steel, but the boy took it up.

"What duties do you have?" he asked after the first tentative feints.

"I am no longer a novice." She returned these effortless strikes and, with more aggressive clips, guided him out of the sheltering trees to the narrow greensward before the barbican. "The lessons of a third-year proficient are more intense. I am given to my studies even when my uncle has called a holiday. And I must provide chaperonage for my cousin Igren." Her voice was not so smooth as she might have wished. "She much needs me."

"I do not doubt it." His smile returned. "Are your cousins here long?"

"'Til October. They'll be gone before you visit again."

"A pity."

"You'll miss Igren?"

He shrugged. "She's a pretty maid and sweet to speak to."

Laurel wanted to be angry, but it was useless. Neither she nor Igren meant a thing to this boy. He must flirt with every maiden he met on his travels. His lovesome talk was only pleasant sport.

Up to this point, they played a half-hearted game. Though Klyffaude enacted swordplay for his living, he rarely took up a sword offstage and never with serious intent. He knew how to make polished metal flash thrillingly in torchlight, but not how strike against an ardent opponent. Preferring the role of courtier to that of knight, he enjoyed contests of words more than weaponry and so took more interest in the conversation than the sport. His casual attitude was exasperating and

Laurel soon outreached herself in trying to knock him from this lazy, complacent stance. By accident—her error, not his dexterity—he stung her wrist and the hilt slipped from her hand.

"First touch!" he laughed. "Do I win?"

"No, not yet." Laurel picked up her sword and began again.

"I am surprised, Klyffaude," she said. "I did not think a lad so lively as yourself would find a preference above all others for a gentle girl such as Igren."

Turning swiftly, she swung. Klyffaude's tin blade shot up to deflect the blow.

"Heavens above!" the youth cried. "Laurel, trouble not over Igren. Oh, she's a beauteous little maiden—you cannot deny it." He parried again and again, springing to elude Laurel's unrelenting attack. "In truth, I would say that you and she are very like in physical feature, but she lacks your spirit. Do I prefer her to all others? No."

Laurel slapped his unprotected flank with the flat edge. "Yet you'll tease her heart."

"A pretty maid's heart is meant to be teased." He leapt back. "No harm to that. 'Tis a pleasure to hear 'em laugh. I do not give my heart so quickly as my words."

"Words must not be spoken lightly," Laurel replied solemnly. "The heart should be with them."

Wrist rotating rapidly to and fro, she brought her blade up and down and up again in wide, fast arcs, leaving Klyffaude to duck and jump as his own blade rebounded in frantic defense. One blow aimed for his head; the next, his knees. Clash and clatter rang in their ears, yet in a vivacious rhythm. Laurel did not strike to harm him, but to tease. She played in the manner of a thespers' mock battle, flailing to look dangerous without a single threatening touch. This was the sort of swordplay Klyffaude was familiar with and, ever aware of the steel edge, he dodged and parried, laughing with her.

"How shall I make my living then? A thesper speaks a thousand words he doesn't mean by his soul's own each night."

"That is not what I meant," she said. "I do not fault you–"

Breathless, tin point forward in a wary attempt to keep her at bay, he grinned. "You do not?"

Laurel lowered her sword. "Not for your craft. When you play at being someone else, you cannot speak as yourself. When you speak as yourself and still play, you are false."

"I? False?"

"You deceive maidens as an amusement." The blade swung up

abruptly, knocking Klyffaude's relaxed foil aside. "You confess so much freely. My poor, innocent Igren!" She lunged at his unguarded chest. "How can I know if you've ever spoken once in truth?"

"I vow to you–" He leapt clear of the oncoming blade.

"If you have lied throughout," Laurel pursued mercilessly, "how shall I trust this vow?" Short, swift jabs cut his defenses, yet never grazed him. Klyffaude jumped back, and back again. They spun in a macabre dance, a swords-length apart, turning about each other in dizzying orbits. Klyffaude put on a valiant show, but Laurel moved too swiftly, breaking through his guard more than once and pulling back before she made the lightest touch. Defeat was imminent, but he would not yield. Eyes on the flashing steel, watching for her next strike, panting, dodging, he never lost his baffled smile as Laurel drove him across the lawn.

Then he laughed. "Damosel, you sport most cruelly!"

"And you have not, my pretty lad? Only think, Klyffaude, how I do your heart good to toy with it." With a sudden lunge, she pricked his tunic front. Klyffaude leapt, off balance. Laurel grabbed his free arm and, briefly, caught him to her before he stumbled against the trunk of a willow tree. Blade a bar across his chest, she pinned him. "'Tis pleasure to hear you laugh."

"Wizardling!"

"I do not deny it."

Klyffaude dropped his sword to the grass. "How shall I have you believe me?" he asked.

"You cannot, false creature, and there's an end to it."

"You will not think I speak in truth if I say I prefer you to all others?"

She slapped his cheek lightly. "A raise-hell such as you would say these words to every girl. When you speak to Igren, to Marsyegaulte, to the poor maidens of Storm Port and Maryesfont and the villages between, you promise each in turn that she is all, but when she is not with you–" She made as if to brush dust from his shoulder. "Were I to speak of love, I would be most sincere."

"As I am, Laurel," Klyffaude promised with bright earnestness. "I do not promise wildly, unless I must do so in performance."

Laurel bit her lip to keep from laughing. "Silly, wicked boy."

"No, My Lady, I am true. I vow that I do love you best, 'pon my most sacred honor. Do you believe me?"

She took his chin and lifted his face as if to kiss him, but only brushed her mouth near and whispered, "No."

114

"Laurel–!"

The young woman walked away.

Olyr had been gone a year. He'd taken his mage-vows on Midsummer day and gone on whatever adventures his own interests and fate determined: to Cairo to dig among the hieroglyph-carved obelisks and pharaohs gone to dust, to the forests of Breton and the plains of Wessex to map the prehistoric standing stones, to the Mountains of the Moon in quest of the unicorn, to Malta and Lindisfarne and Isla Terrefina to examine the treasures once kept by Redmantyl's defeated foes, all in search of the arcane lore which made up a wizard's education. Olyr had read of such things for seven years; now he would travel to see them for himself. As Lord Redmantyl explained, magedom provided a young magician with an opportunity learn more than one master could teach. It was also a time for the young magician to remove himself from his master and fellow apprentices and to test his self-command against the temptations of the harsh world. As a wizard, he must learn to live alone.

In the final months of his apprenticeship, his intimacy with Laurel was badly shaken. There were no more sweethearts' private conversations nor surreptitious embraces. No more stray thoughts burst into her head. They avoided each other. Even before Olyr had gone, their little romance was at an end. Yet, from time to time, an unexpected confidence revealed that this coolness was not entirely what Olyr wanted; he simply had no other choice if he wanted to be a wizard.

"My Lord Redmantyl will have me keep vigil at Midsummer," he told her one day in June immediately before his departure.

"You're going with him?" Laurel had asked, a little envious.

"No," Olyr answered reluctantly. "I am to meditate in my chambers. When I am confirmed a wizard I shall receive all the secrets of Wizard's Keep. Not before. My Lord says I must learn vigilance during my mage-years. This is my final test before I take my vows."

"'Tis strange. A Keep, yet not a Keep," she said. "But the vows are strange as well. Do you understand them? We vow to refuse wine—*That*, I see the sense of, for a drunken wizard is a dangerous fool. But sugar? Roast beef? Salt? Why foreswear these things? There's no reason I can discover."

"Yet I will take them. So will you," answered Olyr. "What matter what we swear to if it is the way to wizardry? Do you know, Laurel, I was afraid of this vow-taking. Leaving. Thinking of everything I must lose in my magedom. But as we are nearly upon the day, I begin to believe I *shall* succeed. If I can do this, I can be so firm of will for all my life afterwards. I shall prove myself a true wizard." He gave her a tremulous smile. "That is all I want to be. I will give over all else for it. I am willing to endure the test."

"As am I," Laurel replied in honesty. "But I can't help if I think the rite itself is nonsense. I would take my vows in good purpose so that I may keep to them and know *why*. This– `Tis one of Godefroi's pointless ceremonies."

"Sometimes you are as bad as Godefroi," he laughed. "Questions! Questions! Why? I don't know, and don't care to know. Things are as they are. No more questions, Laurel, I pray!" His arm about her shoulders, they went in to dinner.

"Simon's promised me everything I will not taste again," said Olyr. "My last wine. My last joint of venison. My last honey-cakes." He kissed her. "When I am free, it will not be the same."

"No," Laurel agreed. "It won't."

Olyr shut himself in his room for three days and two nights, fasting, sleepless, in deep meditation. Laurel, Godefroi, and Orlan paused at his locked door and listened to the whispered chants within, the furniture scraping and bumping on the floor, the books flung against the walls. The atmosphere was thick with spellcraft; by dusk of Midsummer Eve, the wards Olyr had wound for himself were so dense that the apprentices could not venture into the Shadu Hall, though their speculations grew more elaborate through that night.

On Midsummer morning, the adept rose from his rigorous exercise pale and gaunt, as grim as Lord Redmantyl always was after the performance of this strange duty. He didn't answer their questions. He ignored them as he went to the Great Hall. The psychic barriers of a well-guarded grown wizard were firmly fixed and no invading mind could penetrate his thoughts without his consent unless they met for wizard-battle and he was overpowered. He was no longer one of them. He was no longer hers. Friend, companion, playmate, sweetheart—All had gone in those days of vigil. Only the mage emerged.

Before the wizard, Olyr took his vows. He knelt at the point of a triangle. Lord Redmantyl stood at the base, arms extended over his apprentice, as he chanted the lines of the ritual.

"As child becomes adult, fledgling hawk, cub lion, sapling oak, so pupil becomes master. One departs instruction at a master's hand and enters the ranks of the magical as a wanderer. It is a time of great observance. All witness that a young magician joins the battle. As it has been from the time of Kornelys Magnus, he who was first Redmantyl, we make solemn vows upon this event, and we suffer penalties most terrible for their lapse. I charge you, Olyr, first of my apprentices. Will you speak?"

"I shall, My Lord."

"Do you eschew the taste of blooded meats and such spices which unbalance the humors of the body and so disturb the balance of the mind?"

"I vow," Olyr responded. "No blood, no salt, no sweet, no spice shall pass my tongue to the corruption of my will for the span of my years as a mage 'til I am confirmed a true wizard."

"Do you eschew the liquors of fermented grains and fruits and such physics which confound the senses?"

"I vow. No ale, no wine, no poppy, no coca shall pass my tongue to the corruption of my will for the span of my years as a mage 'til I am confirmed a true wizard."

"Do you hold yourself in chastity and spurn the distractions of fleshly pleasure?"

"I vow. No temptations of the flesh shall draw me to the corruption of my will for the span of my years as a mage 'til I am confirmed a true wizard."

"Will you attend the nights of Wizard's Keep—*id est*, Midsummer, Maryemas, Matthieu's Eve, All Hallows, Midwinter, Candlemas, Benedict's Eve, and May Eve—in sleepless vigil and fast?"

"I will, for all my life hereafter." Olyr's voice shook a little at this last vow, but he continued, faultless, through the litany which followed.

"Speak the pact, Olyr, and seal it."

"In my right name, Olyr Droverson of Grynstephan, I speak these vows upon the completion of my seventh year of apprenticeship, having proved my worthiness to the satisfaction of my master Yryd Lightmaster, Lord Redmantyl. So am I bound 'til I am called a wizard of true name and power. So am I doomed to call myself no wizard if I prove false."

This was a spell as much as a promise; its breach would be disastrous. For the single infringement of one vow, a mage was expelled and cast from the ranks of wizardry forever.

"It is done," Lord Redmantyl proclaimed. "Olyr, I call you mage."

Exhausted, Olyr received the herbal tea and unsalted bread offered by the wizard. He must have been ravenous after three days of fast, but as a magician in control of himself, he sipped and tore off small bits one at a time as if this meal were no different from his last feast. He

117

rested that night and departed in the morning with few words of farewell to his friends. Wizardes Cliff had not seen him since.

At times, Laurel studied maps or read of faraway mysteries and she wondered where he was. She worried for him. She missed him. What sort of man would his adventures make him? What would be when they met again?

Since Olyr had gone, she played with Klyffaude, though guilt had always colored their friendship; she saw Simon's disapproving looks and her uncle's cool observation and she thought of Olyr's stormy, hurt eyes and she felt that her conduct might be immodest and unmaidenly. Perhaps it was. But she'd learned this summer she was nothing like ordinary maids, could never be. She would not waste her time to try.

Why should she feel guilty? She didn't betray Igren, for her cousin was not in love. Igren was encouraged by the attentions of so handsome and vivacious a boy, but bedchamber confidences, punctuated by some blushes and much giggling, assured Laurel that the maid didn't trust the young thesper's honesty any more than she did. Igren was too prudent to give her heart to a wandering thesper; she wouldn't think of Klyffaude once he had gone.

She didn't betray Olyr. They'd made no promises to be true to each other in their years apart, for such lovers' vows were meaningless to those who desired wizardry above all else. Olyr was a mage. He must be nothing to her. Whatever they'd shared as innocent boy and girl was lost forever.

She didn't deceive Klyffaude. He was an engaging youth, no more; he could not be sincere and he gave her no reason to treat him seriously. She didn't risk her dedication to her magic with him.

There was some attraction, true. He was handsome—*that* could not be denied: his lightborn wit and indefatigable charm, his irrepressible grin, his tangle of russet hair, his long legs displayed by short thesper's tunics, his bony, adolescent, too-large hands, his tip-tilted nose, his nonsense, his cheerful, lazy energy, his audacity which she was provoked to conquer. She enjoyed the bafflement in his blue eyes when she parried his jesting words as easily as she wielded her sword: to thrust and block, to cut in delicate strokes, to trap and defeat even if she could not completely, permanently quell his impudence. The fact that he sought her out to play these games when there were so many pretty, dainty maidens who succumbed to his banter flattered her in a way she didn't know she could be flattered. Yet her unformed yearnings for Olyr had been more disconcerting than anything she felt for this pretty thesper. This was no courtship, no dalliance. She wasn't distracted by Klyffaude, only amused.

As the troupe prepared to depart, Laurel watched Klyffaude make his farewells with Igren. "It has been an honor to be welcome in your presence, my lovely damosel. I hope we may meet again." He ducked his head and bestowed a quick kiss, which took Igren completely by surprise.

Then he turned to Laurel, but did not offer to kiss her. "And you, My Lady! I look forward to our next match!"

"As do I, Klyffaude," she answered. "I shall not be so gentle then."

Igren and Iobethe left in October. Redmantyl and Laurel rode with them to the harbor at Keyfinsands, avoiding Storm Port where the plague had struck in full force. The girls were homesick and ready to return to New York. Though they enjoyed the magic and strange people at Wizardes Cliff and were a little sad to leave their cousin and new friends, Igren and Iobethe had only been visitors to the castle. Wizard's ways were forever strange to them. They didn't belong here, as Laurel was always alien to New York.

On the journey home, her uncle said, "I compliment you on Igren. I was in error of her potential. She did develop with your assistance."

"You knew?"

"I knew that you would judge her talents for yourself and not regard my opinion."

Laurel sighed. "Our lessons weren't so successful as I would wish. She might've been a mental magician, but she was afraid. I hurt her. I didn't mean to. Uncle, tell me in truth—Am I too terribly rough? I think I must be improper as a woman."

"That depends upon what a woman is in her proper place," Lord Redmantyl answered after some thought. "It would be different if your future was that of a merchant-dame or Lady. I would say then that you are willful and insolent and much in need of courtesy. But a great wizard must needs be strong. There is no place for the infirm of will in our profession. Your Igren is a sweet and tender maid and I do not doubt she will be a most loving wife and mother when she is of an age to wed, but she could not survive where you must."

"You don't think Igren will ever return?"

"No. Even once she is able to choose for herself, Kaiese will keep her from it. Whatever she might have otherwise been is lost. A pity. The child desires her magic, but she fears it more."

syx

The troupe returned in June, full of laughter and games. Thespers wandered the castle morning and night, creating spectacular pageants on the courtyard above the Seayrifte Plaza and attending banquets in the Feast Hall. Lord Redmantyl and Tedora spent their time together. Orlan sulked. Godefroi painted new canvases at Rymbaughe's direction. Laurel found books for Andemyon—the little boy could read quite well now—and she teased Klyffaude unmercifully.

The thespers chose to unveil a new play, *The Chevrefoil*, at their patron's home. Tedora had found this pretty lai, part of the lengthy, tragic tale of Tristan and Isolde, in the libraries at Maryesfont and made it into a romance of costume and courtly pageantry. The performance ended before sunset and the new minstrels struck up a sad song to accompany the lost lovers' dance; all the troupe came out to join them and the circle was soon enlarged by castle folk and Lyges guests. Great spinning figures formed on the plaza and the music grew loud and merry.

"They always have tales of love," Orlan complained. "No more dragons or knights—'Tis a bore."

"I prefer the lovesome tales," said Godefroi.

"You?" Laurel smiled. "You scorn everything that's done again and again."

"Only if 'tis made meaningless by the repetition," the youth replied. "Love tales are true."

"How would you know?" Orlan said.

"As well as you do, Lad. If you seek to learn of love, you may see it all about tonight." He waved to the whirling figures. "'Tis always the same, because it is always right."

"Do you think you'll ever marry, Godefroi?"

"I think not. There's no one–" He glanced at Laurel, but she was watching the dancers with similar hopefulness. "Wizards are not meant to wed. My mother was forced to expel my father from her house to save her magic. She sent me away. I took too much time from her work once I grew to my own powers."

"It seems so odd that I'm near one and twenty. Many girls my age are already wed and caring for a house and children," Laurel said. "Tell me, do you ever think that once we finish our 'prenticing we must spend five years in celibacy?"

Godefroi laughed. "I would give it a good deal more thought if I'd ever been in another state. Have you–?"

"No," she answered.

"My Lord Redmantyl says it is easier to not know of love than to abandon it. But I *think*–"

Klyffaude had shed the trappings of his costume and crossed the plaza, dodging dancers, to reach them. "Will you dance, Damosel?" he offered with a little bow.

"I cannot," said Laurel.

"You mean you will not?"

"No, I mean that I do not know how."

The thesper looked surprised. "Not a step? Have you never joined a festival circle?"

"At my aunt's house, I was called unfit for society and kept from the dances and festivals."

"'Tis pity for a maid to never know a dance."

"My cousin Igren dances beautifully."

Klyffaude grinned. "Igren isn't here, and I cannot bear to hear the music and stand still. You must join me." He held out a hand. "Will you, Laurel?"

Godefroi and Orlan expected her to cut this impertinent boy to the quick; they were astonished when Laurel accepted. Klyffaude led her to the nearest circle, gripped both her hands and pulled her in. Laurel followed the youth's quick steps, but her feet were not as nimble.

"Don't fret so," he whispered. "Watch me and listen to the music."

"You make it look so simple."

"It is. It will be, if you relax."

The music was bright and fast and Klyffaude moved easily with it, as if he felt the music through his limbs and did not need to think. Step, step, kick, step. The dancers around her—thespers, cowherds, laundry-maids—were so graceful. Laurel tried to mimic their movements. She pointed her toes and leapt after the others, always a little behind the beat. Side-step, then back again, and round and round until she was dizzy. Laughing blue eyes shone into hers; she stumbled. Klyffaude caught her by the waist, and she pushed herself away.

"No more. I can't–" Another whirling dancer struck her, and she fled the circle, losing Klyffaude in the confusion. At the open door to the Bottom Hall, she stopped. There were voices within; Tedora and Redmantyl had also left the figure.

"—once more!" the headethesper cried. "Why must you always be out when I am here?"

"It can't be helped," the wizard answered more quietly.

"We have so little time. You can't forget your duty for one night?"

"The Keep is a wizard's most solemn duty."

"So you tell me."

"I can tell you no more. Tedora, I regret that Midsummer eve falls tomorrow, but I cannot alter the course of time, even for you. I shall return before midday, I promise."

Laurel tried to slip away, but her uncle glanced up suddenly, aware that someone was nearby. Trapped, she emboldened herself to ask, "What *do* you do at Wizard's Keep, Uncle?"

"The Keep is a wizard's business," Redmantyl told her simply, firmly. "Vex me no longer with unanswerable questions, both of you."

"Bloody Keeps," Tedora said as he left them. "What do you imagine he does all night at his secret rites?"

Laurel shook her head. "'Prentices aren't meant to know."

"I'd die to find out for myself. I expect you'll learn soon enough, and never tell me either." She laughed. "You're so much like that blasted secretive wizard sometimes 'tis frightful."

Klyffaude was at the doorway. "There you are! Laurel, why did you fly? Your dancing wasn't *so* horrible!" He flashed a smile at his cousin. "In truth, I believe she's angry that she can't best me at everything."

"Angry?" answered Laurel. "Why should I care for such a foolish waste of time? It's not fitting for magicians to make merry at a dance."

"Your uncle dances."

"Quite elegantly," Tedora added, smiling.

"My uncle does many things I do not."

"I imagine he does." The youth grinned. "Tell me, Laurel, if you are admitted to such wizardly mysteries, is it true what they say of the kiss of a magician?" He drew near as if he meant to experiment.

This was the tone of their usual banter but, after the damnable dancing, Laurel was in no mood to play. Blushing, she pushed him back. "Hush your prattle, stupid boy!"

After sunset on Midsummer eve, as twilight deepened, Laurel hid and waited impatiently in the shadowed thickets of the chapel garden. Was it yet time?

She meant to solve the secret of Wizard's Keep. From her first days at the castle, she'd watched Lord Redmantyl go out on the nights of Equinox and Solstice, on May Night, Maryemas, Candlemas, and All Hallows, and she wondered each time where he went. The wizard would never tell. If she looked out of her dressing-room window in the late hours, she sometimes saw strange, glowing lights out on Greenwaters Island—the unnatural color of wizard-fire. Something spectacular was happening and she was eager to discover what it was.

Her uncle's promises that she would understand when she was a wizard herself did not satisfy. She sensed a tantalizing, ominous truth behind this mystery. Her training told her that she was being prepared for great vigilance. She hardened her will against all weakness. She guarded her power's source, for magic was drawn from the heart and directed by the mind and these must not be damaged by the smallest disturbance. She cast spells of protection, wards as impervious as iron. Again and again, she heard that a wizard must be set apart from other mortals and never give herself in complete trust to any lover, friend, or child. She was encouraged to be stern and unfeeling, to fight her fellow apprentices and even Lord Redmantyl unflinchingly if challenge demanded it, to abandon all bonds of affection if they became too dear, too dangerous. Each exercise, each warning, indicated a magical purpose which required enormous power uncontaminated by external influences. She was armed as a knight errant for battle, but against whom? Redmantyl spoke of rivals, but there were no rival wizards these days. What foe did she defend herself against? Wizard's Keep was the key.

She couldn't wait until she became a wizard; she must know now. She hadn't told Tedora, but twice before she had tried to follow Redmantyl to his private ceremony and, both times, lost him in the forest.

Lord Redmantyl passed her. Laurel crept through the gardens to the stairs behind the stable. As the gates opened and he went out, the guards were turned away; she scrambled to the walkway atop the wall and lowered herself over the other side to the roof of a cottage below. The eaves were low at the back and she jumped again. She had practiced this part of her quest before. It wasn't difficult to slip out of the castle unseen. Redmantyl walked down the central street of Lyges and she followed, slipping through narrow, parallel alleys until she reached the lowest terrace. But where was the wizard? Had she lost him already?

She hadn't. She had run ahead of him. Quickly, she crouched to hide behind a cowshed as he crossed the village green.

Lord Redmantyl disappeared down the dark road out of Lyges. Laurel climbed over the low wall at the edge of the green and crept through the forest, keeping a safe distance behind. If she was discovered, she knew, he would send her back and be more cautious if she attempted this trick again. She would never have another opportunity such as this. She dove into the bushes as he turned– No, not to find her, but to look up at the sky. A full moon was rising.

Two, three, five miles, they walked past the neighboring farms, past the lane to Dubbin-on-Pont, until she no longer knew how far they traveled. Lord Redmantyl left the road to cross a meadow; Laurel crept behind, keeping low in the tall grass. They passed through woods so thick with bushes and brambles that Laurel soon lost her way in the tangle. The trees closed in, leaving her without a hint of light. Her breeches were torn and her bare arms and face scratched. Her heart beat loudly with fear and frustration and her magic shone on her skin so that she was certain he must see her if he were anywhere nearby. She was about to turn back through the hindering darkness when a silvery gleam flashed before her. She found him.

The wizard had entered a broad clearing without a blade of grass nor pebble, ringed by a circle of small standing stones. Here, the light was bright. Laurel watched as Redmantyl cut a circle in the dirt, a pentacle so large that it filled the clearing, and in the pentagon at the center of the huge five-point star, a smaller star, a pentagram. Now and again, he paused in his work to check the position of the moon. Laurel, concealed in the underbrush, glanced up also. It had risen during their walk, and she knew from her astronomy that it would soon reach its zenith in the dark sky.

The weaving of his spells completed, Redmantyl seated himself in the inner pentagram like a tailor, legs folded beneath him. He brought twists of white linen, a small silver chalice, and a knife—she saw the glint of the blade as he set it before him—from the pockets of his mantle. The contents of the linen packets were poured into the chalice and, knife at his left wrist, eyes up to the rising moon, he waited. Silent minutes passed. Even the crickets were quiet. Laurel watched through the trees. She didn't see a change in the sky, but she knew that the wizard must be aware of the precise time. The moon crept slowly up toward the appropriate point overhead.

The moment arrived. He cut the side of his wrist; blood spilled into the chalice, onto the dirt about it. A sudden flare shot upwards, a tall spire of flame, then died down and left only its heat. Radiance shone through the silver cup, pulsating with furious energy. Laurel felt its intensity from yards away.

The wizard bandaged his wrist with one of the linen scraps and rested his loosely clenched hands on his knees. Bathed in his own glamour, a softer glow than moonlight or fire, he intoned a chant, words spoken so softly that Laurel could not hear them. Long minutes passed. Redmantyl remained unmoving, his whispered song unceasing. Laurel waited, wondering if there was no more to the ceremony than this. It had been a fascinating thing to see, but surely her uncle didn't need to be so secretive. Where was the terrible battle she had sought? Where was the foe?

A horrible thought occurred to her: Were all the rites of wizardry a game that magicians played to justify their own power? Was her apprenticeship without meaning? Her magic a sport? Could it truly be as Godefroi claimed of so many ancient and honored traditions—that spellcraft was no more than a collection of rituals enacted through long centuries by fools who didn't know their original purpose? Was this all there was?

Laurel refused to believe it. There *must* be meaning. She was here, and she would stay until the vigil was finished. Shifting ever-so slightly, to avoid disturbing the entranced wizard, she tried to make herself comfortable amid the damp dead leaves and twigs of her covert. She'd come to satisfy her curiosity and must see this adventure, disappointing as it was, through.

The night went on, warm and windless, in unnatural silence. Lord Redmantyl's breath fell rapidly and his fists clenched, but Laurel didn't see. She was near sleep, when she was suddenly aware of a shadow cast over her.

She started up. No one was there. She looked to the pentacle; Redmantyl had gone. Yet he *was* here; she could sense his presence nearby. She felt another presence too, strong, about her. The sensation overwhelmed her. It was–

It touched her—a thing alive somehow, yet not human, nor beast nor plant. It was nothing she could understand, only hunger and a sort of glee as it pressed in to quiet her beating heart and numb the edges of her mind with icy cold and the black of endless night. Still, there was no one.

She screamed.

Lord Redmantyl was within his pentacle as if had never left it.

"Laurel!" He rose, but did not cross the protective wards. "Laurel, come to me, quickly! Into the circle! You will be safe!"

She wanted to fly but the unseen thing held her, frozen, too frightened to move. A roaring wind burst through the trees, up from nowhere. The forest was ablaze, the sky bright with furious light. Myriad dots swarmed and buzzed like a million golden bees. Redmantyl was afire as well: eyes as bright as the moon, being bright with unleashed energies. He stood huge and horrible, a beacon of power. There was a sudden shock of fury not directed at her; a rough blow struck, knocking her aside. She was free.

"Laurel, here!" he shouted, and she ran through the underbrush, falling over grasping brambles and tree roots. The pentacle traced in the dirt gleamed as if it were molten metal. Low fires rose from the rim. The wind howled like a living thing outraged. The wizard reached out and she crawled to the clearing, to the circle, to him. Thunder roared, and as he took her up, into safety, she fell into nothingness.

"The King! The King! The King is Nigh!"

She stood atop the wall. The great door, miles high, had opened and darkness spilled out, swallowing light and life. She crouched down against the ebon stone to hide herself from that engulfing force, but her magic shone like a beacon. Ribbons of ink, like tentacles, drew toward her.

She fought with the fury of a being struggling for its life. She surprised herself, for she called to powers she hadn't known she possessed. The wall beneath her feet trembled—with her own power, not theirs. Darkness pressed on all sides, but a blast of silvery fire stood around her to burn away the night. She cut the outreaching tendrils and held that engulfing force at bay. They couldn't take her; the bright fortress held.

When she woke, the moon hung low and the eastern sky was gray with dawn. She lay on a red cloak spread on the clipped grass of a meadow near the road. Lord Redmantyl sat by her feet.

"The danger is past," he said. "How do you feel?"

Her head ached and her hands and knees were raw and torn, but she knew that was not his concern. "I am well."

The wizard looked into her eyes; she felt an odd pressure within her skull as he searched and determined that she told the truth. He traced a device on her brow with the smallest finger of his left hand, then went to a stream that flowed through a nearby copse and brought her a drink of water.

"I should be furious with you, Laurel. You deserve to have your ears boxed for meddling in wizard's affairs, but I am more glad to find you unharmed."

"Yes, Uncle," she answered meekly.

"You've endangered your life—and mine!—our souls, our sanity, the safety of this little world, and for your damned desire to seek knowledge not rightfully yours!"

"I didn't know!"

"You shouldn't, not yet." He took her into his arms. "You've seen more than any not a full wizard should. And, by the right gods, They touched you!"

"W-what–?"

"You shouldn't know. It is too soon. I may say that there is power in this universe, great evil beyond mortal understanding."

"They are demons?"

"They've been called so before. They are creatures of the Ether and cannot take material form. They are trapped Outside and have no true power in this realm, but their influence may be felt."

Laurel shuddered.

Redmantyl observed her, pained with turbulent thoughts; Laurel, too ashamed to meet his gaze, felt his bewilderment in the face of a dilemma where neither choice was right. It was her fault, she knew. She'd broken the secrecy of the Keep. She'd uncovered those rites which magicians held forbidden to all but their strongest ranks. She had placed so much in incalculable jeopardy for her curiosity. Her crimes against wizardry were enormous and Lord Redmantyl, the greatest of all living wizards, magistrate of magical lore, supreme upholder of their laws, her uncle, must decide what to do. What punishment could there be for such transgression?

He rose suddenly, resolved in his course, and began to speak. He gave her the secrets she sought: "You perceive now the purpose of Wizard's Keep. We who possess magic are guardians. We protect, for we know the danger and would not see our world despoiled by such evil. We stand watch to keep intruders from stealing in. There are gateways to the Outside of which lesser mortals are unaware. 'Tis fortunate it is so. We must see that it continues in this way. *It is important—We do not go beyond the door.* It is madness to look over the threshold. Those who do are lost.

"On certain nights, the alignment of the heavens provides these outcast beings with means to enter our sphere. Our earthly magic attracts Them and keeps Them– ah– occupied `til the door is shut and the opportunity lost. They do not always take the opportunity. One may sit in vigilance through Wizard's Keep without incident year after year. But on other nights..."

"As tonight?"

He nodded. "They were drawn to me, but I was warded. A circle is not easily broken. We learn what is required to defend ourselves. More than that is necromancy—the dark arts which no right wizard will entertain. They are a temptation to more power than a human can safely command and a corruption to the soul. A magician can have no dealings with the Outsiders, for they are masters of deceit and malign arts, nor receive their favors. We can't control Them. If you are so foolish, They will control you and bring you to evil regardless of your first intentions. That is their nature. They may take a soul for their purposes if the mortal is so weak, or willing to be taken. A wizard who falls to Them is a dangerous thing. We cannot be weak! Our power bears responsibility, Laurel. I pay this price for my place—I am sworn to forever keep my guard."

"Uncle," she asked. "Where did you go when you left the clearing? Not Outside?"

"No, not Outside. There is a space between, where the two spheres intersect. I– You cannot yet understand. It is something you will learn when you keep guard also."

"When I am confirmed a true wizard."

"There is no time for a proper initiation," Redmantyl answered. "You must begin immediately. At the next Keep."

Laurel had not expected this. "But I can't!" she protested. "I'm not ready."

"Nonetheless, after this night you must take your place. You are too vulnerable as you are. You know more than you ought. A mistake will be most perilous for a child such as you. There is no other way. Before the ranks of wizardry, you must be counted a true magician. You are privileged to the secrets of our craft and sworn to the duties we bear. Laurel, you mustn't speak of this to anyone!"

There, on the meadow, he performed impromptu rites of confirmation and Laurel took a most solemn vow. She was bound as he was.

"What is done cannot be undone. So it is." He helped her to her feet. "I would not have you endangered for anything, my child. You are so young, yet I cannot leave you ignorant and unprotected. You will need great vigilance and enormous self-command. They know of you now, that you are a great power unready."

He threw his cloak about her shoulders and they walked home in the summer dawn. Dew sparkled on the grass. Cool breezes brushed their faces and a fresh, rainy scent clung to the air. Birds sang in the trees and farm-folk shouted as they drove their cows and sheep to pasture. Wispy pink clouds glowed behind Wizardes Cliff's pale towers. A morning like any other morning. Laurel thought how beautiful it was.

She returned to the castle, but her life was not as it had been. She was changed; knowledge of what the world truly was stayed upon her like the dark shadow of a cloud blotting the sunlight. She was no longer innocent. She couldn't feel safe. Nothing was safe. How could she think to be merry when she knew how close they all were to infinite peril?

They had touched her. She could only forget the chill that had coursed through her soul by an intense act of will. Her thoughts were forced into other, more comforting, directions—she didn't dare remember—but her will was not always so firm. The memory crept back upon her whenever she left herself unguarded. They slipped into her dreams.

There was no comfort to ease her fear. She would face this same crisis eight times each year for the rest of her life. She must learn to live with it. It wasn't in Laurel's nature to endure patiently; she wanted to stand against the danger, shout, and strike until she had defeated her foe, but this was no battle quickly won. She might as well fling herself at the evening fog as struggle with the unseen forces that haunted her mind. She would have liked to seek her uncle's counsel but, save for his discreet references to *Others*, he didn't acknowledge their existence and he didn't encourage her to speak. Her fears could not be confided elsewhere; her vow, given with dreadful purpose, could not be broken.

She prepared for Maryemas in August: Redmantyl impressed her daily with the importance of self-command. He taught her to maintain her intense vigilance and crammed her brain with every defense she was capable of exercising. She read warding spells from texts that had been hitherto forbidden her, but only carefully selected pages. Lord Redmantyl wouldn't allow her to examine them completely; he didn't dare look upon certain chapters himself lest he be tempted by the forbidden knowledge written there.

Though she was technically still an apprentice and must endure the years of magedom before she was fully acknowledged, her duties became those of a wizard; she assumed the protection of her house, her unsuspecting comrades, Godefroi and Orlan, and the wonderful, carefree thespers who played like children.

She was especially kind to Klyffaude in the days after Midsummer. She no longer wished to humble him, for she'd been humbled herself and cruelty had ceased to be an amusement. When they spoke, Laurel was simply courteous and she puzzled the young thesper more than when she teased.

A feast was set on the thesper's last night at Wizardes Cliff. The troupe was merry as always, excited by the prospect of travel, eager to present their new productions. The conversation at the table bubbled with laughter, but Laurel had no appetite. After the dessert was brought in, she slipped away to the roof.

Only the crash of waves against the cliffs and the rattle and murmur of servants clearing the remnants of the meal in the hall below disturbed her reverie. The waning moon shone and the sea glittered bright. The towers about her were ghostly, made more of dream than solid stone. On another night such as this, not so long ago, she'd tried to touch all of the universe and join herself with it. That communion had seemed desirable; she'd imagined that the union of body and mind, soul, material and ethereal would enhance her powers. She would know all secrets by being one with them. Now, she knew the secrets: All that lay beyond this little world was a measureless void that waited to engulf her. Union was oblivion. She, Laurel Windswift, magician, maiden, child of Earth, would cease to be. If the power she contained, once free of the frail body and being which housed it, was great enough to survive, it entered that space between where the guardians set their bastions against the Outside, undying, without joy or light or hope of ultimate triumph. This was what she had read and not understood in Uillod of Orkeney's text: *We become as angels.* In the greater realm, the battle went on forever.

The door behind her creaked open and she turned to find Klyffaude at the low doorway beneath the turret. He ducked and stepped through. "I didn't mean to intrude," he said softly. "You were missed downstairs."

"I came here." She knew this was a silly statement, but she didn't wish to drive him away.

"'Tis a beautiful night," he said. "I can't fault you for choosing this solitude. I don't much like being alone myself, but I know that magicians prefer it so. And if one must be alone–" He stood against the parapet, arms flung wide to embrace all the night with a gesture. "Do you know, I think this castle is the most wondrous place I've ever seen."

"I do too," said Laurel. "'Tis suited for study and contemplation."

"What is it you contemplate now?"

"Magical matters." When she looked up, his eyes were solemn upon her.

"You are troubled."

"Yes," she confessed. "I vow to you, Klyffaude, if you dare make jests about Olyr–"

"I would not," Klyffaude protested, startled by her vehemence. "But what does trouble you? Can you say?"

"You wouldn't understand."

"Laurel, I am not so dim-witted," he answered. "You think me an empty-headed oaf."

She was surprised, and slightly ashamed, at this accusation. "I do not."

"You do," he insisted. "I know you think me a lackadaisy. Fair—I do not pretend to be a great scholar or philosopher, but I am a friend. I've thought us friendly. I hoped you enjoyed my company, even if you jested. If you permit, I may prove myself more useful than most fools." He smiled. "You think me impudent to speak so boldly?"

"No, I do not," said Laurel. "I rather like your boldness. You have freedom with your words. Thespers are always so full of laughter. So free."

"'Tis why we are called Free Folk."

"You have no responsibilities."

"What responsibilities do you have, Damosel?"

"I shall take up the weight of the world. Wizards are not free, Klyffaude." She shut her mouth, for she would say too much if she let herself.

"You won't be a wizard for many years," the boy replied. "'Tis silly to fret over troubles—whatever they may be—long before they are upon you."

Laurel smiled. It was a thesper's good fortune to never think of the future. "You can't understand."

"You haven't told me all."

"I cannot. Not because I think you stupid, for I do not. 'Tis simply a wizard's secret."

"The secrets that My Lord Redmantyl always keeps from Teddy to vex her?"

"Yes, but it isn't meant to vex. Wizards aren't meant to tell their secrets to anyone."

"I thought you weren't meant to know of such things yourself?"

"I do, nevertheless— Oh, Klyffaude, let's talk of something else. There's nothing you or I can do. No more of magic, I pray! Anything else! If you offer comfort for my troubles, you will help me forget them."

Klyffaude searched for some topic. "Poetry?" he suggested at last. "I don't imagine you are much fond of poetics, but a pretty verse is pleasant enough to ease the mind. Do you recall the poem I taught you?"

"'The colors of my love'?"

"That exactly. Do you know, I chose it for you? I think of you upon its recitation, whenever we perform. I know—'Tis not like you at all. Oh, the snowy fairness is like, but you've nothing of gold nor ruby-red about you. Is it magic which makes you and your kindred so fair? In truth, you are the most passing strange family I've seen!" His grin flashed. "But not ugly for it. No, rather the opposite. Shall I divert you more, Damosel? It will amuse. Shall I tell you how I delight in our visits here? When we travel elsewhere, I think how glad I would be to hear your voice again, calling me a liar and pert knave and a fool. I would have no one else speak so to me."

He spoke playfully, but there was more than play in his words. She wasn't surprised by what followed. "I do love you, Laurel. I speak not in jest. 'Tis not deceit."

"I believe you."

"You are amused? It is laughable, is it not? The maiden I care best for is she who scorns me."

"No," but she did laugh.

"I have made you forget your trouble?"

"By gods, yes!"

But he may have begun another. Klyffaude had always been a playmate, a boy she made jest of and occasionally wanted to strike, but not a lover. They were not gentle together; she'd never thought his extravagances were uttered in earnest. She'd cut him at every opportunity, exposed his flattery, mocked his vexation, struck down his impertinence, and had somehow unintentionally stabbed through to the heart. His heart. Klyffaude wasn't playing anymore. The time for games had ended.

She'd almost forgotten what it was like to have a boy's eyes shining so intently into hers. And there were more words: Klyffaude was saying wonderful things to her, about her. On and on, he spoke hastily, as if expecting her to stop his mouth at any moment, but Laurel didn't stop him. She delighted in it, even as she knew that she ought not listen.

"Laurel? You've not said—"

"What will you have me say?" she replied. "You weave lovesome words so easily. I never can. Ask, so that I may answer."

"I have spoken my heart, but yours remains secret. You are not entirely displeased—I see that plainly—but I cannot know if I only amuse you, or if there is more. If you will tell me—" Words left him. "Do you? Can you?"

Laurel did not reply immediately. What might she say? She couldn't speak her heart. She did not know it. Love him? She liked him. His company was entertaining. His pretty words were a pleasure to hear. He'd been her friend. But even when she'd resolved to be kinder to Klyffaude, even as she'd heard him speak of love, she hadn't intended that they should approach such intimacy. She hadn't wanted to love him, but she'd won his love and she felt the weight of that responsibility. He was vulnerable to her scorn as he'd never been before. Encouraged by her silence, he'd surrendered all his most tender feelings and she'd given nothing in return, not the smallest word. She might have stopped this, protested at the first confession that she didn't care, but it was too late for that now. She'd let Klyffaude go so far unchecked and she must answer for it. But how could she answer those blue eyes, hopeful, waiting?

She'd lied to Olyr and said that she would remember him when she hadn't known surely that she would. Could she lie to Klyffaude as well? Deceit was abhorrent to her when she had no good reason to conceal the truth. She protected nothing here but Klyffaude's feelings and, truth or lie, she must hurt him eventually.

"Klyffaude, I cannot say."

"You mean to tease me still?"

"No, I—" Pain would come certainly, in the end, but she could not hurt him now. He wanted to believe her. He would.

She kissed him.

At dawn, they were still there, clinging to each other as if the wonder of this night would end once they parted. Laurel didn't know what had happened, but she wasn't sorry. When she would let him be gentle, he responded with such unexpected tenderness that she was overwhelmed.

She could only answer in kind. They'd talked for hours, until their voices were hoarse and there was nothing more to be said. They shared all that they could. Then Klyffaude had held her and, his arms about her and him in her embrace, they enclosed themselves together. In madness and darkness, she'd found sanctuary. Warmth quickened in her veins, sang in her ears, trembled through her innards. A wonderful, heady thrill made her dizzy at each touch of his lips. Her blood could not be cold, nor her mind impartial. She was thankful for Klyffaude, for having this peace with him, if only for a little while.

Perhaps she did not lie. Love or not, this feeling was pleasant and she was reluctant to lose it so soon.

"You'll go today," she said.

"You might come with us. Laurel, join the troupe!" When she looked up, surprised, he continued earnestly. "Come along! Surely Teddy will make you welcome if My Lord does not object."

"He will," she sighed. "And rightly so. Klyffaude, I can't leave. Don't you see? I'm no thesper. I shall be a wizard. I must be."

"I understand." He shook his head. "Wizards. You know, you may be a great lordling one day, and if I travel as a thespian we may truly be like My Lord and Tedora. You won't go and I can't stay."

Laurel sank against the parapet and, head pillowed upon her arms, slipped into drowsy dreams. She saw a tall figure, red-robed and silver-haired—but herself, not her uncle. Wizardes Cliff was hers, her pale walls silent and cold, her great books filled with arcane knowledge and all the wonders of magic. She was supreme, Layn Redmantyl, guardian of the gateway and destroyer of lesser magicians, but she was alone. The troupe came and, with them, Klyffaude. They had nights such as this, one night at a time, then he was gone. That was the way it must be for great wizards and their lovers; Lord Redmantyl lived so alone and Tedora came to him. For a time, they were together, but she wouldn't stay and he could not leave his place for her. Yet, he continued to wait and she returned to him. Were they happy? Would she be?

"Laurel, you must come!" Klyffaude's plea woke her.

"I can't."

"You'd like to. I see it in your wondrous eyes. You want to get away from– Whatever. It matters not. The desire is there."

"I cannot escape what I am." She rested her head. "I am a magician."

After breakfast, Klyffaude went to pack his things and Redmantyl

Kathryn L. Ramage

summoned Laurel to his chambers. "We must speak, Niece. I've been told that you and Klyffaude were together all this night past. Is it true?"

"Yes." She felt his eyes cut into hers and touch her mind, seeking the answer to an unasked question. Laurel didn't try to conceal any secrets from him, for that would be useless.

Redmantyl became solemn. "Laurel, this must cease."

"No," she protested. "I am past sixteen and you cannot tell me who I must and must not choose."

"An ordinary lass has the right to choose her suitors and no one may speak against her," he agreed. "But I shall speak, for you are no ordinary young woman. Laurel, though I call you wizard, you must yet become a mage. You are aware of the vows you take upon completion of your apprenticeship—throughout the five years of magedom you must never taste bloodied meats, sweets nor salt, nor spirits. You must keep vigil on the nights of Wizard's Keep and you must remain chaste. One lapse will bring about your ruin. Your magic is lost if you fail. You know the reasons for this perfect self-command better than any apprentice ought."

"But I shan't fail!"

"You mustn't fail. So, as I cautioned Olyr when he grew too fond of you, I must warn you against falling in too close with Klyffaude." He studied her again. "If you have not fallen too close already. Laurel, he is a danger to you if you wish to maintain your place as a wizard."

"I do."

"Then this must end. Love is ruinous to a young magician. You are not in command of your heart and apt to think that this lad is all to you. You will forget—not at all times, but at little times—that you have higher responsibilities. Your magic must be first, or it is nothing."

"I've heard this before," said Laurel. "It sounds so unfeeling."

He sighed. "Child, it is not for all your life. When you are a true wizard before all, you may have Klyffaude or Olyr, or any lover you wish. You may wed if you do not impede your ability. You may have wine and roast beef, and love—but as pleasures, not necessities. A girl of twenty does not have sufficient command to guard herself against uncontrolled desires, and I have hoped too much for you to see you ruined by a pretty thesper."

"You have your own pretty thesper, Uncle," she retorted.

Redmantyl gave her a single, cutting glance of reproach. "If I believed my love for her compromised my magic, I would abandon it."

136

Laurel doubted he could cast Tedora away so easily; she knew, now more than ever, what the headethesper meant to him. "You could?"

"I do not say it would cause me no pain to do so," he admitted. "But I would. I would be able to. I have such command, Laurel. I may abandon all things in a moment if I must for magic's sake. That is why I am who I am. This, also, is a place you are fit for if you do not forget what you are."

"I could never forget, even if I wanted to."

"You know as well as I that this is best, and you will not endanger yourself simply to be contrary."

"Yes, Uncle," Laurel consented at last. "I shan't think of him again."

She knew that everything Lord Redmantyl had said was for her own good; she'd known before the first words were spoken. Something had awakened within her last night and she felt that she might easily give too much of herself to this exciting new sensation and lose the careful control that she'd given so much effort to maintain. Love or not, it *was* a danger. The possibility of failure lay before her; she might fall if she let herself, and Klyffaude was not worth the lapse. He was a brief pleasure, an amusement, a pretty piece of romance. It would be a mistake to think him more.

Knowing this, however, didn't belay her resentment. It wasn't fair! If she were an ordinary young woman, she might do as she pleased. She might love Klyffaude as much or as little as she chose. She would not always have to be mindful of her responsibilities and maintain such strict self-command. She could forget the evil that waited hungrily for her and simply have her fun as other girls did. The housemaids flirted with the man-servants; the daughters of the Lyges tradesfolk had their cowherd lovers. They did as they pleased without a thought to higher duties. How wonderful it would be to remain so blissfully unknowing!

But she was not like ordinary girls. She knew. She had her duties. She was like her uncle and, truthfully, that was what she wanted most to be. She intended to be Redmantyl herself and that meant that certain delights of youth must be put away from her. Careless, innocent freedom was not hers.

Before midday, she met with Klyffaude to make her farewells. He took her hands and looked into her eyes; in his, she saw more love than she thought he could possibly feel. She wanted to meet that emotion, match it, join with it, but she did not lose herself in this newborn passion.

"Laurel, you will not come?"

"I cannot. You'll return again in three or four months, and I shall be here," she promised. "We'll see each other again."

"That's much too long to be apart!"

"The time will pass. You'll hardly notice it." Laurel smiled. "Fare ye well, Klyffaude." With one quick kiss, she let him go.

Atop the Shadu Hall, Laurel watched the troupe depart with the same sense of doom she'd felt when Olyr had left: When she saw Klyffaude again it wouldn't be the same. He would not change, but she would.

In the weeks that followed, she began to forget him. His face blurred in her memory; the thrill of his recalled kisses dulled. The brief sanctuary she'd found with him was shut forever. But the loss could be endrured. When the troupe returned, she would meet Klyffaude with her old, easy playfulness. She would treat that one night and day as a game, no different from the other games they'd played. If they spoke, if he still spoke of love, she wouldn't offer encouragement. She would not open her heart to him again. He could be nothing to her, not now. There truly was no choice; she must be a magician, before all else.

To abandon all for magic, she gave herself to intense training. She endeavored to become cold as ice, unyielding as steel, quick as lightening—all that was best in her uncle's powers and all that hers should be if she would follow him successfully. Laurel set her powers against his and fought as if her life were forfeit. In the Daune Tower room, she wove spells about herself and Lord Redmantyl assaulted these defenses. He broke them more easily, and more often, than he liked, then the spells were reset and the battle began anew. She dreaded the chilling blast that announced the breach of her wards and meant that she had lost again.

"Must it be so harsh, Uncle?" she wondered after a particular rigorous session. Her head throbbed and her hands trembled with fatigue and impotent outrage at her last humiliation.

"A wizard must be invulnerable," he answered simply.

"You are even more harsh in your treatment of Orlan and Godefroi." She'd seen the nettle burns upon their backs and arms, evidence of some test she'd never endured. She felt the tears they suppressed.

"Both lads are too tender. They leave themselves more exposed than a good magician ought. If I have been harsh, it is for their benefit. If I am hard upon you, Niece, it is for the same reason although my methods differ. You are not made of that same softness. Your will is already formed by nature against the influences which Orlan and Godefroi are prey to. Were I to strike you, Laurel, would you weep?"

"I never weep!" she shot back.

"You are not sensitive to physical discomforts," Redmantyl said. "I do not call upon you to stand against pain, nor hunger, for such exercises are no test of your will."

This was true; the exercises which reduced her fellow apprentices to tears were no challenge to her. She'd never been faint during days of fast or hours of sleeplessness and she did not flinch at any blow. "Yet I am vulnerable," she said, and destroyed the chalky traces of the useless pentagram drawn on the floor around her.

"You are," he agreed. "If I understand your temper rightly, you are too quick to anger and too much afraid of defeat. These passions mislead you. Yet I cannot fault you for them, for they are my own."

"I cannot cease to feel, Uncle."

"You misunderstand. Emotions themselves are not wrong. It is their overindulgence which distorts your perception and leads you to error. You need not turn yourself to stone, Child. Laugh as you will, but do not be so merry that you disregard a true threat. Weep if you are sorely grieved, but never become incapacitated by sorrow. Anger is not always a distraction. If you recall, you were first brought to your powers through vexation. But it must empower your magic, not burn it away or misdirect it. Do you see?"

Laurel nodded. "What must I do?"

"You must learn to think, first, and not act upon impulse. Magic is directed by the mind—remember! Without that, it is no more than an uncontrolled burst of energy and no use to any magician. We shall work to that purpose. I will guide you but, ultimately, command lies with you."

The hours of practice became longer and more intense. Laurel set her spells and battled morning and night until she employed all her will not to fall into weary stupor. But she was made strong. She wouldn't let herself become indignant when she fought, for she realized that rage only undermined her defense. If she flew furiously to guard one weak spot, her uncle easily breached another, forgotten vulnerability; with a cooler head, she could defend both spells. When she fretted at a mistake and anticipated failure, her resolve dwindled and she hesitated at the most crucial moments; she learned not to think of defeat and to correct her errors before he could strike through them. He still broke her spells, but they held against assault for greater periods. More than once, he surrendered, claiming that he could not defeat her without raising their mock battles to the level of true wizard-war. Her defense remained imperfect, but she was able to withstand the force of rival powers.

Maryemas passed quietly.

Lord Redmantyl called her to his sitting room one day after the Keep. "Laurel, I must ask you to go to New York."

Sent away! "What have I done, Uncle? Is it my fault?" But Laurel knew that it was: her infatuation with Klyffaude, her intrusion upon the Keep. She'd been too troublesome. In spite of her efforts, she hadn't attained a magical perfection and Redmantyl must despair of her. "I shan't meddle again, if you will have me stay. I shan't cause you trouble. I promise to be good."

He smiled at her gently. "It's not your fault, Child. You've done remarkably well considering what you must endure."

"But you send me away?"

"I have an errand for you. Of recent, I have sensed something in New York."

"Not–?"

He understood her horror. "No, certainly not. It is a thing I do not entirely understand at present but it deserves my attention. A disturbance in the fabric of living energies. I felt it first some months ago, near Storm Port, but disregarded it. Such anomalies occur in nature. The radiant forces in inanimate objects, certain rocks, star material which has fallen to earth, may have strange effects on the lifeforce. I imagined this to be so. But when it moved suddenly, miles south to New York, I knew that it lived."

"It is human?" Laurel wondered.

"I cannot determine. There is nothing in my experience quite like it."

"Is it dangerous?"

"I think not. I do not say that it is a threat to us, but it is an oddity. It must be examined. Perhaps it is nothing. I need an agent to observe the town more closely."

Laurel was intrigued by this vague description. She, too, wanted to discover what aberration had occurred. She was proud that he'd asked this of her, and she was ready to go in his service. But she sensed that he hadn't told her all. "You will send me?" she asked. "Why?"

"I cannot go myself," Lord Redmantyl answered. "I am too prominent and my presence will put up guards everywhere, mortal and otherwise. There is no lesser magician I might trust with this service. Olyr is too far away to be readily summoned and the other apprentices are unprepared. You are capable, Niece. Also, you are of New York. I've received messages from your Aunt Kaiese of late. She tells me that if you do not set fires and are able to keep your temper civilly, she will have you return. I believe she has learned of your apprenticeship and disapproves."

"Who would have–" Laurel cried in astonishment. "Io! The imp!"

"Likely," he agreed.

"But why does my aunt wish me to return? There is no love between us. She was glad enough to see me go. Surely it's absurd that she calls me now, as I am nearly one and twenty."

Redmantyl shrugged. "It matters not. I would contest her claim upon you but, in these circumstances, it is advantageous that I seem to surrender. I ask you to return to her home for a time. You will not be conspicuous. Your return will not draw remark, as the arrival of a strange magician might. In New York, you will seek this anomaly. Find it. Watch it, unnoticed if you are able, and discover its nature. Inform me. If the situation is more perilous than I anticipate, I will assist you. I will give you spells necessary for your protection. Do you consent?"

Laurel nodded. "When must I go?" she asked.

"Soon. It would be foolish to tarry."

The household flew into commotion at the news of Laurel's departure. Servants she barely knew now said they would miss her terribly. Dulsye wept. Simon plainly disapproved of the arrangements and said so frequently: Dam'sel had no business traipsing halfway down the Northlands and the master had no reason to let her go; her place was here, with them. Orlan and Godefroi grieved; incomplete apprenticeship was inconceivable to both boys and they stayed at Laurel's side, perplexed, through her last days at Wizardes Cliff. They'd wanted to ride with her out of the castle, but Lord Redmantyl forbade it. All teary farewells were made within Wizardes Cliff and the wizard and his niece departed. Alfryda, who would accompany Laurel through her journey, followed at a discreet distance.

"You must not forget," said the wizard, "though you are a

magician of no little power, you are not prepared for all the hazards a true wizard may encounter. I have given you what lessons I can in so short a time. The rest must be learned through experience. Guard yourself well. Remain vigilant on the nights of Wizard's Keep, as I have taught you, and keep your eyes open."

"I shall, Uncle." Tears blurred her sight as she thought of how she loved him—not with the awed, fervent adoration of Godefroi, Orlan, and Andemyon, but surely so deeply. She touched the newly engraved silver amulet tied by its scarlet ribbon about her throat. He'd given it to her this morning.

"*We are bonded by our blood*," he had explained, "*but this spell will enhance that bond. You will be able to communicate with me. If you call, I shall hear you.*"

She felt the power of the spell. She knew him best now, at their parting. Lord Redmantyl loved her too. It hurt him terribly to let her go, even as he sent her. She felt his sorrow; it ached within her breast, no lesser pain than her own. He would weep, too, if he allowed himself.

"I'll do my best for you, Uncle," she promised. "I'll return so soon as I am able. My home is here. There's never, truly, been anyone except you. I have had no mother or father—only you of my blood." Laurel turned in her saddle, surprised, for she suddenly sensed something more than grief: his heart had began to beat rapidly at her words. "My father?" she guessed. "You– Do you know who he is?"

"I vowed I would not tell you," Redmantyl answered.

"You do know then?" she pursued.

"I know."

"But you won't say?"

"I cannot."

"Does my Aunt Kaiese know?"

"Yes, but she will not tell you either. Your father is no man to concern you, Maiden. Think on him no more."

Laurel puzzled at this astonishing information, but it was useless to demand more. The bond had been deliberately dissolved; Redmantyl had assumed an unbreachable silence. His mind was closed to her.

At Grynlet, they stopped to water the horses. Laurel would ride on until nightfall, but Redmantyl would go no further. He embraced her before he sent her on her way.

"Good luck, Child."

"I'll return soon, Uncle," Laurel promised again, more urgently than before. "This won't take very long!"

Laurel

New York
1949

sen

Laurel did not return to Wizardes Cliff in November. Before autumn was ended, bitter cold and heavy snows foretold that the Northlands faced the worst winter seen in many years. It would be suicidal folly to leave New York. The town was trapped. Snowfall upon snowfall accumulated in the streets and buried the countryside. Drifts piled high against every wall, shutting doors, blocking windows, crushing roofs, weighting trees until the branches snapped. The Coast Road lay frozen.

Those caught unprepared by the chilling weather suffered most. Shops closed. Woodpiles dwindled. Larders emptied, and the poorer folk went hungry; if they kept beasts, they killed them. Farms beyond the town were lost in smothering white and unfortunate peasants and yeoman, homes uninhabitable, supplies depleted, livestock destroyed, made their way to town. Many who couldn't afford rooms at an inn turned to the charity of the Church and slept in chapel pews.

The great merchant houses also felt the difficulties of a long and violent winter, but they suffered less. So long as the port remained open, their livelihood was not threatened and their business went on. Income secure, they were assured of whatever food and fuel was available. Laurel's Uncle Nikholas worried more than his fellow merchants for, as Mayor, he was given to protect the town and provide for all its citizens in times of emergency. He had the responsibility of the beggars, farmers, and shopkeepers until a thaw allowed them to return to their livings. With the Sheriff, Portreeve, and parish clergy, he arranged the gathering and distribution of incoming supplies and prevented the looting of abandoned shops and dockside warehouses. Constables, garrison guards, and fit volunteers patrolled the streets at all hours, inspecting the locks on exposed doors and windows, chasing off thieves, enquiring at any household where no smoke rose from the chimneys, and bringing indigents to safe lodging. No one must starve or freeze. Any found dead were quietly taken to the churchyard gates to await burial.

Nikholas shut himself in his office for days together, or went through the snowy streets to seek the council of his administrators. He rarely attended the evening table and he slept at his desk more often than in his bed. He vowed aloud that he wouldn't seek reelection at the summer, when his seven years ended; he called his mayoralty more trouble in four months than in all the time before.

The Mayor's family didn't worry at the crisis. Kaiese and her daughters had nothing to fear; the winter's chill never reached them. As Nikholas had an office for his business, so Kaiese had hers, a private parlor at the back of the Mayor's Hall. Here, a fire blazed and the tall windows were draped with soft tapestry against the icy drafts. Chairs, coucheries, windowseats, and tuffets were all plumped with cushions; no guest was ever required to rest against hard, cold wood. In this comfortable room, Kaiese reigned, directed her household, kept her account books, educated her daughters, and received visitors. If she felt Nikholas's absence, she did not mention it.

The situation at the Hall was not intolerable; rather, Laurel was intrigued, for it seemed at first that her aunt courted a new husband in spite of the fact that Nikholas was in excellent health. Men of local merchant families visited the Mayor's Hall that winter, and Kaiese welcomed several noble guests before the town closed against the weather: Some were of her own age, but others were distressingly young to pay court to a woman in her fifties; some came only once and others were at the house regularly. They sat with the Lady in her parlor and she served wine and dainties while her daughters sat and smiled.

It didn't take long for Laurel to understand that the young men came to see Igren. This struck her as perfectly right—no surprise that a pretty maid should have admirers—though the mode of their admiration seemed so oddly disinterested. One pretty young Lordling, a frequent visitor, rarely addressed anyone save Kaiese; Laurel didn't feel foolish that she'd mistaken this boy her own age for her aunt's suitor. Other visitors continued to perplex, for some never once blinked at her beautiful cousin.

One afternoon, Kaiese received a wealthy merchant who had traveled from Storm Port. At least, Laurel thought he must be: A large man, bald-pated and grey-bearded, past sixty, he wore the dusty gray and pale blue of a merchant, but in cloth of the finest soft wools and shining velvets, richly embroidered with thread of gold and clasped by looping golden frogs. A heavy gold chain hung upon his chest and a jeweled ring weighted his middle finger, but neither was seal nor signet of office. He was no mayor nor Duke's minister, nor even city reeve. Kaiese welcomed him as if he were a great Lord and he seemed to take her flattery as his rightful due. Laurel didn't know him, but Igren said she'd seen him before. With uncharacteristic vehemence, she also called him horrible. Both maids sat in silent attendance, though they would rather have been elsewhere.

"Wicked bloody weather," said the visitor between bites of honey-cake. "Storm Port's a white hell. My coach-horse broke a leg on the ice 'tween here and there and had to be left on the road. Bloody waste."

"I would not dare go beyond our town walls," Kaiese answered. "You must be courageous indeed to journey so far."

"Business obligations," he replied. Laurel gathered from subsequent remarks that the Storm Port harbor was blocked by ice and his cargo had been sent here. Kaiese's company was usually dull, but this guest was an outright bore. He spoke nothing that was not self-interested: he complained of the inconvenience in his travels, the wretched snow, the negligence of the servants who attended him at the inn, the stupidity of the Portreeve who had charged him a higher tariff than he was accustomed to pay at his home port. Yet Kaiese hung upon his words as if he spoke most lovingly. As he never once glanced at Igren, Laurel assumed that he must be a business acquaintance of Nikholas's and that Kaiese attended to him—as she attended to all her husband's trade interests—while the Mayor was busy elsewhere. The girl drifted to her own thoughts, far from the warm little room, and her cousin, beside her, worked quietly, painstakingly, at a piece of embroidery.

"I do not know your name, Maid." Suddenly, he addressed her.

"'Tis Laurel, Syre."

"Yes!" he cried with surprised interest. "I've heard of you. My Lady's niece. You've been away." He stared intensely. "Your mother was a soldier? Swordsmaid, I believe My Lady said."

"Yes, Syre."

"You have your aunt's height." Eyes ran up and down her frame, appraising critically. He nodded. "She might go for Captain of the Guard and make a deuced good job of it. Do you shoot, Maid? Ride? Fence?"

"I am a swordswoman myself."

"Ah!" he cried again, much satisfied with this answer. "You have a horse?"

Laurel wondered if he wanted it for his coach, but she answered simply, "Yes, Syre. A palfrey."

Kaiese volunteered that Igren rode far better than Laurel. Her visitor ignored this.

"Bloody waste to leave a healthy maiden always sitting. 'Tis done your cousins no good."

Igren's needle paused, half piercing the taut linen, but she did not lift her head.

"I'll have none of weaklings," he told Kaiese. "My wife was a mousy little thing. Shivered at every chill wind, she did. This blasted winter would freeze her through if she'd lived to see it. No, give me good, solid, strong folk about me."

The lyric of his complaint changed, but the old song went on and on. He spoke of his sickly wife and of the wife before her, of the tiresome sound of a weak woman's whine and of babes born cold and silent, all without grief. Whether he talked of his injured horse or his belated wives, his tone remained that of a man cheated; so far as he could see, all was done to vex and thwart him.

Laurel must agree; he was horrible. She couldn't imagine why Kaiese found him attractive.

"Who was that man?" Laurel asked after the guest had departed.

"The Goldsmith?" replied Igren. "He is a moneylender of Storm Port. He was here last summer, before you returned."

"And why does my aunt fawn upon him so? Is she in his debt?"

"I don't think so," Igren said vaguely. "He— He comes to pay his court."

Laurel was baffled. "For my aunt?"

"No."

That was sufficient answer. "Oh. Igren, you— Why didn't you tell me of this?"

"What was I to say?" Igren enquired. "You saw for yourself."

"I saw that the young men came to gape at you. I didn't know how my Aunt Kaiese brought you to her parlor like a piece of expensive goods to be looked over and bid for by this repulsive old devil! 'Tis twice more horrible than anything I imagined! Surely you wouldn't accept such a man?"

Igren's complexion went pink and she turned her head. "I hope Mama will choose another."

"Such as Rosandre of Daubenai?"

"He is sweet. Imagine, an entire country of people who speak so beautifully. But I think he prefers Iobethe."

"Little Io! Horns of Osiris!" Laurel swore in amazement. "Io's but a child."

"She'll be sixteen at Michaelestide."

Laurel was shocked. It was not inconceivable that the merchant youths might come to gape at Iobethe as well as Igren. Both were pretty maids; it was natural. It was even possible that men twice and thrice their age might make offers. But Igren was only nineteen and young yet for marriage. Certainly, Iobethe was far too young. It was grotesque to think that thin little child a wife! It was beyond belief that Kaiese would court the Goldsmith for either maiden.

Yet Laurel did believe it was so. There were calculations behind it: Kaiese was anxious to see her daughters married well and she'd taken advantage of Nikholas's position while she had the opportunity; if Nikholas fulfilled this winter's oaths, he wouldn't seek reelection and the family would lose their prominence among the merchants with their own daughters to wed. Kaiese meant to use the time available to draw the most promising bachelors, even if Igren and Iobethe were too young to sign a marriage contract.

"My Lord Rosandre is not yet of age himself, so they must wait at least a year," Igren continued. "But Mama will consent."

"For a price."

"That's unkind, Laurel."

"'Tis true," Laurel insisted. "She means to sell you off to the highest bidder regardless if it is pretty Rosandre or this Goldsmith fellow or one of that wretched lot of town-bred boys. Igren, you won't marry, not so soon?"

"I haven't seen anyone I would like to wed," said Igren. "When I think of husbands, it is someone different..." She fell silent. "Do you remember that thesper-lad at Wizardes Cliff? The red-haired boy. He was so free and bold, yet kind. I could not be afraid of him."

Laurel did not like the turn of this conversation. "He meant so much to you?"

"No." Igren shook her head. "If I met with another so bold, in a position to choose a wife, perhaps— But Mama would not approve. If another I did not like so much spoke for me and she thought him suitable.... It is her choice."

"And what if you are made wretched for her choice?"

"I must marry," Igren answered simply. "Mama wants what is

right for me. She says that it is a girl's good fortune to make a prudent match young. She wouldn't choose wrongly in a thing so important."

"Do you truly believe that, Cos?"

Igren did not reply.

Rosandre, Lord St. Elise, was the youngest son of Giselle of Daubenai, a minister at the Paris court. Her uncle was Bishop of Kallaykirke, the see across the river from New York, and the boy had been sent to finish his education in the cleric's house. A fair-haired youth, just twenty, Rosandre was at the Mayor's Hall more frequently than any other suitor.

On Sunday, he accompanied his granduncle to Mass, but contrived to escape the Bishop after the service and escort Kaiese and her daughters. As always, he was dressed in perfect Parisian fashion: fox fur cape, which he generously offered to each lady; bright blue hat like a round, plump pillow with white feathers jutting up at the back; velvet sleeves slashed open to reveal rows of silver lace sewn beneath. Nikholas called him ridiculously pretty, but Kaiese had the highest praise for this youth and, from bedchamber gossip, Laurel knew her cousins found him splendidly exotic.

When they reached the Hall, Kaiese asked Rosandre in. "You must take something to warm you," the Lady insisted and offered the youth her arm. The girls followed them to the parlor. "Surely your Excellent Uncle could not object if you remain with us this morning? He is most generous with your time, My Lord."

Rosandre smiled beautifully. "He could not help but be so, when I am made welcome by so gracious a host."

Kaiese sent to the kitchens for refreshments and brought the youth to a tuffet before the fire. Igren and Iobethe sat opposite him by the half-circle hearth. "Will you be at Kallaykirke much longer?"

"I am not meant to stay in the Northlands," he replied. "Mother intends me to serve My Lord Kharles and writes that I must take my place at court so soon as I am fit. She expects that will not be many months from now."

"She has grand plans for you," Kaiese said warmly.

"But I should be content here forever," the boy replied in earnest. "I have been most happy."

"'Tis kind of you to say so, My Lord."

"Not so kind as you have been, Dearest Lady. I call your house best of all I have been in and I call you the most wondrous people of all I know. My Lady Kaiese's kindness is praised throughout all the land."

The words might have sounded unnaturally formal and exaggerated upon other lips, but the young Lord spoke as if every politeness were a sincere thought. Rosandre had been brought up from infancy to affect perfect manners and it wasn't possible for him to speak any other way. He possessed the elegant mind of a courtier. Regardless of his purpose, the boy was a delight to listen to. When the snow had been at its worst and the occupants of the Mayor's Hall had no other company for a fortnight and more, Rosandre had come to brighten the dreary situation.

"'Twould be wretched if I must always stay at my Granduncle Lucian's side and recite his lessons," he confided. "It is too much like the Abbey at Chartres, where Mother kept me when I was small." This was not unusual; although religious houses were havens for the orphaned, illegitimate, and abandoned, many noble families gave their children to the care and education of the Church as well. "But you have seen yourself how it is."

"No," Kaiese answered regretfully. "I was never at an Abbey, nor have I sent my daughters."

Rosandre refused to believe this. "Impossible!" he cried. "Maidens who are brought up in an Abbey possess a certain air—how may I say?—a gentleness. The holy Sisters impart a wonderful finesse. No! I tell you, Dearest Lady, I would know such a maiden anywhere, even if she were a mere serving-girl. Surely a Lady so elegant– Surely the damosels– No, it is impossible! No one could grow to such grace outside the holy Sisters' care. Angels must have tended them."

"Would I had sent my darlings to the Abbey of St. Samandra or Maryesfont," Kaiese said. "Their education has suffered, but I feared more for their health than their learning. Rather a girl has a bright bloom to her cheeks than a thorough understanding of letters—Do you not agree, My Lord?"

"Oh, certainly!"

"I think my efforts have repaid me well. You wouldn't know now, to see her, that Igren was a delicate child in her infancy. I could never bear to send her away from her home, save in times of plague."

"Indeed, My Lady," Rosandre agreed generously. "You've done all that the Sisters might strive for, and more still. I commend you."

The pleasantries had scarcely begun when the porter admitted another youth, Martin Sheriffson, with a message for Nikholas. Like other half-grown offspring of the town merchants and the Council, Martin ran errands to the Mayor's office so that he might become familiar with his family's business, or with Nikholas's.

A number of merchant youths had been sent to court Igren; the prize of a girl so lovely, so sweet, so placid of temper, and generally acknowledged to be uninterested in her father's lucrative wineries, which she would inherit, was considered well worth winning. It was understood that her husband would take up her business concerns for her, and younger sons with little hope of receiving an important part of their own family trade had come to offer themselves as earnestly for wine as for love. Most were dismissed quickly—Kaiese aimed higher—and the few who persisted were made welcome, but not encouraged.

Martin's commission was brief this day and he soon found his way to the parlor. "M'Lady," he first bowed to Kaiese. "M'Lord Rosandre, Dam'sels Igren, Iobethe." Martin smiled on the girls, then his eyes passed to her. "Laurel."

"Martin," she answered. He might be twenty-two and ready to give himself in marriage to a former playmate, but Laurel only saw the little brat who had tormented her in childhood. She hadn't forgotten.

"Will you take some refreshment with us, Martin?" Kaiese invited. "You are not required elsewhere?"

"No, M'Lady." He took a seat and looked about for the refreshments, which had not yet arrived. "But you may as well hear the worst of it. Father agrees with His Mayorship that there be no Fat Tuesday festival this year."

A noise of disappointment went up about the room. The girls looked dismayed and Iobethe was moved to complain, for she'd been promised that she might join the grown folk at the spring celebrations.

"I imagine it's all for the best," Kaiese ended the lamentations. "Hush, Io. How can one dance in the Square when the snow is up to the eaves? Hush, I pray you. There'll be opportunities later, when things are right again. We'll have festivals so fine as last year. Do you recall, My Lord Rosandre, our last autumn festival? Now, which was it? 'Twas in November, I think. We had only a dusting of snow then."

"'Twas Celiamas," Laurel reminded her.

"'Twas the St. Celia holiday, My Lady," Rosandre agreed.

"Yes," Kaiese said. "We've not many so grand as that! 'Tis a shame it must come so late—the Blessed Saint of Music might reasonably have her day earlier in the year. Do you know, I met my Nikholas at Celiamas many years' past? I was no one to the town then, but he was most kind. He would dance with no one else that night."

"You must have been a most passing fair maid, Dearest Lady."

She smiled. "Not so fair as my daughters have become, I assure you. If you recall, My Lord, you were first made acquainted with our household at the festival circle."

"I remember it well," the youth assured her.

"How gracefully you danced when you took Igren in hand! 'Twas very pretty, the pair of you."

"Pretty indeed," Martin said with a touch of masculine contempt.

Rosandre did the only courteous thing to be done; he snubbed his rival by deliberately misunderstanding the insult. "Gramercies, young Syre. Surely you might do as well with the honor of a maiden's company. I should be so enraptured again if Damosel Igren would condescend to me." He bowed his head to Igren, who gave him a shy smile. "Perhaps Damosel Iobethe will be generous as well this Whitsuntide?"

Iobethe looked earnestly to her mother, who answered: "She is not yet sixteen, My Lord, but perhaps we might make certain allowances."

"Delightful of you, Dearest Lady!" Rosandre cried. "I await the day with impatience." Martin may have sought to win hearts here, but he was simply unable to compete with these persuasive courtesies.

"And you, My Damosel?" Rosandre had turned to Laurel.

Martin grinned. "Laurel can't dance a step for her life."

"I am not so graceful," she replied, ignored the jibe. "But I have danced. At my Uncle Redmantyl's house, we had grand balls on the courtyards every summer and danced for hours."

"I never seen you at a figure last autumn," Martin accused.

"No one asked me."

"Shall I ask, My Damosel?" Rosandre offered gallantly.

"My Lord, 'twould be an honor, if my Aunt permits."

Laurel had no intention of remaining in New York to see Easter, let alone Whitsunday, but she couldn't resist stinging her aunt. Already, Kaiese found it unbearable that Rosandre should give attention to her niece. With deft abruptness, she turned the conversation to holidays past, of sprightly music and clear, warm nights, of how beautiful Igren had looked in this dancing figure or that. The visitors were successfully diverted; Martin turned occasionally to tease Laurel and Rosandre addressed her because it would be discourteous to ignore her after speaking once, but their attention was upon Kaiese. As Mayor's Lady, she had the privilege of choosing what amusements the town would receive once the winter emergency was ended and all citizens and visitors had time to play.

Kaiese had determined that the snow would not dare remain past Lent and there would be fair nights at Whitsuntide, when her plans were cut short by a commotion at the front door: the rising voice of the porter carried from the entryway, struggling against the harsh tones of a stranger.

"Niece, go and see what the trouble is," Kaiese directed without looking at her.

Laurel left her place in the corner. The source of the disturbance was a blue-robed youth, not thirty, his wild red hair in a long tangle and his complexion burnished to copper by winter winds. In spite of the young noble's threats, the porter stood his ground as bravely as a soldier at a fortress gate and shouted back, as loud, that no madman would get into the Mayor's Hall unless he gave a proper name.

"What is it?" Laurel demanded through the uproar.

"I am Geyraulte, Earl of Oerykeshire," the intruder replied, as if this were sufficient explanation.

It was. The Earl of Oerykeshire was Nikholas's liege. Laurel had heard much of this nobleman during her uncle's term of office, but Geyraulte had never before come to town. His seat was at Oerykton, far to the north, and the young Earl was not famous for his travels. For the last seven years, Nikholas had governed independently; Geyraulte had not shown even an obligatory interest in his southern port, so long as New York sent the requisite share of revenues and guards to serve at Oerykton. Were it not for the occasional gossip carried down from the wild north, New York might forget it had such a Lord. However, he was here now.

"Earl or no, he's got no right to come in without giving his business," the porter protested. "Pushes in as if he owns the lot of us. Pushed me down, he did!"

Geyraulte glared as if he would like to push him down again.

"Enough," Laurel said before a fistfight ensued. "Return to your place, Jemrye."

"Flog the wretch!" Geyraulte snorted. "I never met such bold manners from a doorkeep. I'll have the skin from him myself!" He flung his fur cloak to the floor and kicked it after the retreating servant. "Flog your master too, for barring his door against me."

"You've not visited before, My Lord," Laurel addressed the angry Earl with as much courtesy as she could employ. "We didn't know you."

"You ought to." He tried to glare her down, but Laurel wouldn't be bullied. The Earl was in a fierce rage, but she had her own powers, greater than his. Geyraulte could only meet her eyes for so many seconds before he faltered.

At last, he asked, "Who are you, Maiden?"

"I am Laurel, the Mayor's niece."

He looked her over quickly. "Yes. I came to see the maid I saw at Mass—one such as you, fair, but littler and more pretty. They say she is the Mayor's daughter and I would meet her."

Laurel grinned. "My cousin Igren. Will you come in? She sits at the parlor with her mother." The young man consented to follow her.

"It is our Liege Lord Geyraulte, Aunt!" she announced at the parlor door, and stepped aside as he brushed past her.

Kaiese quickly dropped into a deep curtsey. "Welcome, My Lord."

Geyraulte bent his head in brief acknowledgment. His eyes darted about the room, sought, and found Igren. "I've come to see your daughter, M'Lady."

Igren, seated, could not curtsey as her mother presented her. She would have fallen to her knees had she tried to rise; Laurel saw how she trembled.

Geyraulte gave his hand. "An honor, Dam'sel."

"You must forgive our unreadiness, My Lord," Kaiese apologized. "We hadn't heard you were in the town."

"I arrived only this Friday night," he answered as he took the nearest seat, on the coucherie next to Martin, and enjoyed the exclamations of astonishment about him.

"How came you in such weather?" Kaiese asked.

"Because of such weather, M'Lady," he replied, still grinning. "Storm Port is frozen."

"We've heard tales of the disastrous happenings there," said Martin.

"You must believe 'em, Lad. Our ship was turned from the harbor and we had to take port here. But I'm not sorry." He looked pointedly at Igren. She didn't meet his gaze. "I've not been down to the Suthing much before this, but I'll have to tend to my duties here more often."

"Were you abroad very long, My Lord?"

"I wintered in France. My sister wed the Count of Flaunders at Christmas, you've heard, and she would have me with her as our mother couldn't go."

"What a splendid ceremony it must have been," Kaiese murmured.

"Ah," said the young Earl with indifference. "'Twas like any other wedding, all candles and songs. But the Count, now my brother, made a proper show of it."

"Did you travel much, My Lord?"

"We went about to the border counties and met some of my

brother's kin at Brabant and Lorraine, but I stopped mostly at Paris."

"How wonderful!" the Lady exclaimed. "We've heard so much of the Paris court," with a smile to Rosandre. "They say 'tis far more fine than Pendaunzel. I pray you, tell us."

Geyraulte made a noise of disgust. "'Twas no delight, Lady. Oh, I'd heard as well as you the wonders of France and I had fancy to go and see for myself, but I found not much to my liking in those Frankish courts. There's nothing to our own Oerykeshire! Their wines are weak as water, and their maidens so false as painted cats and the men little different."

"France is my homeland, My Lord," Rosandre said gently.

The Earl nodded. "Aye, I well believe that."

Rosandre was too well-bred for bristling offense and he directed his attention elsewhere. Geyraulte didn't mind. He cared little for parlor conversation; he was obviously unaccustomed to such formalities, openly impatient, and he looked as if he would have the Lady Kaiese, Martin, and the Frankish fop disappear so that he and Igren might speak together plainly.

"Some redberry tea?" Kaiese offered as a maid-servant brought in a tray heavy with tiny porcelain bowls, a steaming pot, and plates piled with hot-cross buns. To smooth things among the guests, the Lady dispensed the warming drink and enquired after the health and doings of Martin's mother and father, whom she knew well, and the health and doings of Rosandre's mother and Geyraulte's mother and grandmother, whom she had never seen. Rosandre's replies were beautifully eloquent; Geyraulte barely answered, and Martin popped in a word or two whenever he could before Nikholas summoned him away.

When the Earl wearied of so much polite talk, he rose abruptly. "Gramercy, M'Lady. I must go." With one last glance at Igren, he took himself out.

"What an odd man!" Iobethe laughed in spite of her mother's look of reproach; their last guest had not yet departed, but Rosandre was amused, not offended, at this outburst. "Oh, Mama, I'm sorry, but he is, truly! Laurel, don't you think? Do you suppose he'll be back to ask for Igren's hand tomorrow?"

"Hush such nonsense, Child," Kaiese said, but her thoughtful expression might be interpreted as if she did not think the idea so silly after all.

There was a thaw at the end of January. Snow slid from the shingles with a whispery rush and tinkling crash. Icy sheaths about bare tree branches dropped away and icicles fell from the eaves to stab the piled drifts beneath. Blasting winds no longer tore through the thickest clothing and burned exposed flesh. The snow lay deep, but New York was no longer in a state of desperation. Shopkeepers reopened their doors. Farm folk returned to their abandoned homes with fresh supplies and began to repair the blizzard damage. Beggars reappeared in the doorways and those who could afford to be were more generous than usual. Some simply went out into the streets because they'd been shut up for so long. Thanksgiving masses were held in all thirteen churches and, across the river, the bells of the Kallaykirke cathedral chimed. Constables went more leisurely on their patrols and dockyard guards, free of thieves, relaxed their vigilance. The townsfolk talked of celebrating Grande Tuesday, with or without the Mayor's leave; they felt they deserved a good holiday after this rough, cold season.

On the eve of Ash Wednesday, the best merchant families were invited to a ball at the Sheriff's house. Little Iobethe had her first dances that night and she was enormously happy though Rosandre wasn't there. Igren was named a beauty, and younger sons offered themselves for each dance. The maiden was oddly confident, for she gave her hand readily to any youth who asked, without her mother's urging, and her dancing steps were free from her usual careful self-awareness; her thoughts went beyond the festival hall and now and again a little smile touched her lips, but not for any of her partners. Afterwards, the young folk took up their festival cloaks and masques and ran out into the streets to knock on doors and smash crockery on the doorsteps in the Festival of Dreams.

Laurel wasn't invited to the ball and so stayed home and assisted her uncle. In all New York, Nikholas was the only official to remain at his desk. Spring had not yet come and he had the town's recovery to plan.

Throughout the winter, Laurel had served as an auxiliary to the constables. There had been some objections from the town council when she volunteered, but her uncle Nikholas welcomed any help and Laurel was well-adapted to the duty. Her skill with a sword had attached her to the garrison in defense of the port and closed shops and her strict self-discipline enabled her to patrol the streets from dark to dawn without fatigue. Her magic, surreptitiously used in emergencies, had thawed more than one half-frozen victim.

She was called out less often once the winter danger had passed, but on Wednesday morning, while the more pious citizens of New York were at Mass, the constabulary and garrison were summoned to clear away the aftermath of the night's revelry. The Festival of Dreams had become unrestrained after midnight, and more than old pots and jars were smashed. Bricks had been lobbed through shop windows. Porch railings were torn away. Signs had been taken down and exchanged: a cobbler's shoe hung over the butcher's door; an ink and dye vendor had become *The Three Trees* tavern.

Laurel worked past midday then, dismissed, went to a tavern below the east gate for hot cinnamon cider. Warm clay mug cradled between achingly cold fingers, she took a stool by the fire, stretched her muddy boots to the hearth and spread her cloak out to dry. She didn't often visit such places, save at the invitation of older guards who remembered her mother with some fondness and were ready to tell tales of that strange, wild swordswoman. She hadn't been in here before, but she recalled that the alekeeper's storehouse had been raided not too many weeks ago and she'd taken part in driving the looters away from the mews behind the house. The room was crowded with townsfolk escaping their homes for a little time in spite of the Lententide strictures. No dicing. No music. More cider and tea were sold than beer. Last night had been their release; today, the people came simply to be out again.

Laurel turned her back upon the laughing, chattering crowd and ignored them. Though she lingered to avoid her inevitable return to the Mayor's Hall, she didn't seek companionship nor amusement among these people. As she distinguished a familiar face here and there, recognized the voices of individuals in the babble, she knew she would not be welcome.

Fragments of a conversation at one table began to reach her ears:

"...since *she's* returned. Blessed riddance..."

"...don't know why they allowed *her*..."

"...her uncle...Mayor's defended her, even against Father's advice."

"'Tis disgraceful the way she runs about."

"The Devil's own."

"Wicked thing."

Not all maidens were so carefully sheltered as Igren and Iobethe. Many daughters of the great merchant houses were left to run with their brothers. A group had gathered here, street-wise youths and girls: Martin Sheriffson, his elder brother Peter, the Dyemerchant's daughter Amabel, Portia Paperpresser, her sister Rosalynde. They were a well-brought-up, well-dressed lot, well on their way to becoming rapacious dealers in their family trades. Laurel met them rarely in the months since her return to New York; she had, in fact, avoided them whenever possible. These were the enemies of her childhood.

One of them alone was unpleasant, but easy to disregard. When they gathered together against a common foe, they were relentlessly cruel as only children raised in comfort and overweening courtesy could be: Where the common lads had hurled stones, the merchant children had chosen spiteful words and suggestive snubs as their weaponry. The old game hadn't changed.

"She's out at all hours," Martin told his companions, raising his voice to ensure that Laurel overheard. "I have the news from the Mayor's own porter. She comes in at dawn after merciful Christ knows what mischief."

For a moment, Laurel shied. She was on the tangled streets of her childhood, steeling herself against their scorn and insult. At their laughter, she remembered the sting of long-ago humiliation. She felt the shame of an outcast, the hurt of a little girl despised for her strangeness. Then she recalled herself. She was no little girl. Not small. Not without defenses. Not ashamed of her strangeness. Not afraid.

"I have given fair duty to a town I would as well see under ice 'til July," she said as she turned to them. "What have you done this winter?"

The laughter was hushed at this unexpected rise to the bait.

"I have been at home, as a decent maid should be," Portia made her smug reply. Her sister giggled.

"And you, Sheriffsons?" Laurel asked. "Were you also snugly kept at home?"

The ancient codes of chivalry had long since been debased, yet there was one tenet, translated into common law, which all Norman citizens understood: in times of common need, everyone must give aid. For fit youths, this usually meant armed defense. It was as near true warfare as any might hope to see in these peaceable days, and as honorable to swear allegiance to one's liege in the town as on a battlefield. Though some merchant families were generous with their supplies and a few even sent their sons or servants to assist in emergencies at Nikholas's request, Laurel knew that these two had never once acted in the town's behalf except as messengers for their father. In the same months, she had fought for the safety of the town a half-dozen times. She'd served while they shirked a traditional obligation—as grown sons of the Sheriff, chief of the local constabulary, they were especially lax. As a guardian, she had proved herself ten times their worth. The damosels might look upon such duties as unseemly for maidens, but the boys would feel the implied charge of cowardice.

"I have been out—" Martin countered her insinuation.

"Brave lad! To risk catching chill!"

"'Tis your witchery that's caused this unnatural snow," said Peter. "We had no such trouble 'til *you* returned."

"Years of peacability," added Rosalynde helpfully.

"Mayor Nikholas should have barred you from our town hereafter."

"I weary of these games," Laurel cut through the taunts. "You insult my uncle Nikholas. You insult a profession who protects your precious family wares while you sit idle. You insult the ranks of wizardry."

"The spawn of demons," proclaimed Portia.

"Satan himself fathered you!" Martin shouted. "Called up by your mother on All Hallows!"

"I think you ought to apologize," Laurel answered softly, menacingly. She met the eyes of each in turn until the merchant-youths grew unsure of themselves and were forced to look away. There was a tense and unpleasant silence as they understood that their intended quarry was not going to flee. *Elf, changeling, imp, demon*—Laurel had heard the words flung at her often enough by these same children. They called her unnatural and evil for her magic but now, for the first time, they began to realize the significance of their accusations. A magician was a dangerous thing to meddle with. They had blundered recklessly into peril. She saw doubt creep into their eyes: had they begun a game they could not win?

But a persecution of such long standing could not crumble so swiftly. They'd known Laurel too long to fear her as a true spellcaster. Amabel, who had been quiet since Laurel had turned, was the one to pick up the gauntlet.

"Not to you."

This show of daring spurred Martin to a bravery he did not feel. "Wh-what will you do," he retorted. "Curse me? Blast me to ashes?"

"You know I could, yet you will insist in drawing my wrath," she warned. The tables around the room trembled. "Have a care, children. If the Devil has fathered me, he has taught me my birthright well."

Lord Redmantyl had warned her against ostentatious displays of magic. With her temper, it was too easy to lose control. Already, the patrons nearest them had abandoned their tables and benches; some left the tavern, while others inched back against the walls to get away from the imminent brawl. In another moment, she would go too far. But this was a rare opportunity for revenge and she would not surrender it so easily. Scorn her, would they? Prattling puppies! She wanted to shake them to the ground. If they looked for sorcery, they would see it!

The mug in Peter's hand shattered; the intact curve of the handle dropped as cider sprayed over his yelping companions. "Witch!"

Laurel was on her feet. "Will you burn me on the church green? You may try. I'll burn the town with me! I've no love for you any more than you have for me, and more reason to see you in flames." Dust motes in the air popped and shimmered. With the fire behind her, casting burnished lights upon her hair, glowing through her paisley-lined cloak, touching the glamour about her with reddish glints and throwing her face into shadow, she looked mysterious, larger than mortal, dangerous. She blazed. "Only the foolish and the dead make enemies of wizards. Which are you?"

"Magician." The tavernkeeper was at her side, pale as her former tormentors. "This is a quiet place," he said. "Whatever quarrel ye have with the lads, it's no reason to harm my house. Ye'd best be out of here. All of ye."

"Gladly." At the doorway, she paused to see if the youths were prepared to carry on their challenge outside. Not one of them appeared eager. In triumph, she exited.

Nikholas summoned her to his office before dinner; news of her conduct had traveled swiftly. As Laurel went up, her aunt waited at the doorway, angry and frosty.

"Husband," said the Lady, and Nikholas, at his desk, looked up as if he'd forgotten she was there.

"Yes," he agreed to nothing in particular. "Laurel, I've been told that you misbehave yourself in my town."

Laurel feigned innocence. "How, Uncle?"

He chuckled. "How indeed, Niece. Sheriff John's come to me to demand protection for poor Peter and Martin against you. If you will take down the lads, I daresay they asked you to, but I can't have you smash up a good alekeeper's crockery. You must behave yourself better."

"Yes, Uncle."

"And no fires. It makes a tavern inhospitable."

She smiled at this indifferent scolding. "I set no fires. I've outgrown that long ago, I promise you. If there is spell-casting, it is only what I wish to do."

"See that you don't wish to do much. It isn't fitting for my own household to disturb the peace, you know. It causes talk."

"Yes, Uncle."

Nikholas was satisfied. "Well, that's done." He dipped his pen in the inkwell and resumed his writing as if he were already alone.

Kaiese had expected more. "That's all you have to say to her?"

"I can't have the girl arrested," he answered, not looking up. "She is our niece, My Lady, and she's been of service to the town this winter."

"But her unmaidenly conduct! Brawling in an alehouse! And magic!"

"Now, my dear, that's your concern. It's not my place to teach a maid better manners." Nikholas waved them both away. "Leave me, I pray."

Her apprenticeship was lapsed, but her studies were not abandoned. She worked as best she could in the winter-confined mercantile town, far from any font of magical learning. She read and reread the copybooks she'd brought from Wizardes Cliff until she could recite them, and wished she'd been able to bring more, for books—any books—were nearly impossible to obtain.

Few could read in New York and few wanted to. Why read when the process of writing out and binding books by hand was so lengthy, difficult, and expensive, and the opportunities for common folk to possess them, even briefly, rare? No merchant house kept more than its own accounting ledgers. Nikholas owned a set of heavy, wood-bound and tatter-leafed books of the Northlands law, passed from mayor to mayor for the past three hundred years and appended at intervals, but they were unused by him and useless to her. Likewise, the churches kept jealously protected Bibles and the Bishop's Palace at Kallaykirke was reputed to hold a good-sized collection of religious addenda; with Nikholas's authority, Laurel might be allowed access to this private library if she chose to ask. She did not. Her Latin was as good as any clerics—better than many—but she doubted she would find much comfort in Church dogma. The books that would allay her unease, the writings of great magicians on their efforts to understand the power they possessed and the spells they found most successful, were unavailable.

She practiced the spells she knew and wove protective wards as she had in her frantic mock battles but she didn't know how these would stand against a true assault. At All Hallows, Midwinter, and Candlemas, Laurel enacted the ceremonies of Wizard's Keep exactly as Lord Redmantyl had taught her, but each night's vigil passed without incident. They had overlooked her.

Were her spells effective? Was she a magician full capable of defending herself? If called to fight at the Equinox, would she be ready? If she faced some danger here in the city, would she be prepared? These questions remained unanswered.

As to the reason her uncle had sent her here, she occasionally *felt* danger around her, nearby, but she couldn't say what it was. The anomaly Redmantyl had sensed was present, but it remained mysterious. Nothing had happened in all her months in New York; she'd seen no sign of strange creatures or strange events beyond the winter itself, and she couldn't intervene in that. She sent frustrated messages at the first deep snows, asking if she might come home, but Redmantyl's reply was unchanged: *No, stay. It is not finished.*

She was certain he must be mistaken. It had not begun. Throughout the long winter and during the first days of thaw, Laurel looked impatiently at the snow and wished it might disappear. She was bored, impatient to leave New York, ready to depart with or without Redmantyl's permission. One thought turned over and over restlessly in her head: *Out. I have to get out.* She despised this dreary town. Her mission here had come to nothing. What reason did she have to remain? She was a spy with nothing to spy upon. She wanted to go home.

When the road from New York to Storm Port opened, travelers trapped by the winter finally made their way home: the Goldsmith departed; Geyraulte stayed on. Others, barred from the town, were able to return.

"Daughters, be quick!" Kaiese summoned Igren and Iobethe. "My Lord Ambris is here! Your father has met him in the Square and invited him to dine with us." She threw a furious look over her shoulder at her amused husband, still shedding his wraps at the front door. "He will come at any moment!"

"I thought so long as I was able to join you at dinner, my dear, we might have some good company," said Nikholas. "You've always been pleased to see Ambris before."

"But tonight–!" She whirled back to the girls. "Upstairs, and quickly! Your best garments!"

The Mayor's Hall, which had hitherto been a house of comfort, was discovered now to be unsatisfactory. The rooms were chilly. Dust lay everywhere. Not one of them was decently dressed to receive a guest. Floors must be swept. Fires must blaze in every grate. The dinner, brewing all afternoon and nearly ready for the table, wasn't fit for Lord Ambris and must be augmented with sauces and sweets and a course of fish or squab. Kaiese drove her household into a flurry of motion; in the kitchens, the parlor, the dining hall, the rooms above, everyone from Nikholas to the scullions was spurred to activity.

Laurel remained in the lower hall, where she'd been when her uncle had come in. She'd never seen her aunt create such a fuss, not even for the most prominent merchant acquaintances nor the most prestigious suitors. This guest must be one of the noble visitors who had come to the house last autumn; Kaiese had taken to dropping their names to the point where Laurel ceased to notice. Certainly, thought Laurel, she'd heard this Lordling's name before, but she couldn't recall any face to match it.

Kaiese, flying down the stairs, found her idle. "Laurel, go and assist your cousins."

"Am I not to sit to dinner too, Aunt?"

Kaiese scowled. "If you are not pert, you may join us at the table. Be quick now! There is so little time." She swept down the corridor to the kitchens, directing servants left and right as she passed.

Laurel followed her cousins up to their chambers. Woolens and velvets of pale blue and gray lay scattered on the floor and bed and wardrobe chests. Igren, silvery hair tumbled about her bare arms, white stockings loose about her knees, petticoats frothed at her waist, struggled to fix all three without assistance. Iobethe pettishly threw aside lacy blouses and bewailed her short, childish skirts. She could not assume the long skirts of a mature maiden until she reached her sixteenth birthday; her finery wasn't so fine as her sister's and she was openly jealous of Igren's wardrobe.

Laurel hushed the younger girl and helped the elder, tying strings and silk ribbons and locating combs and shoes as they were called for. "Who is this Lord Ambris?" she asked as she knotted the lacings of Igren's best velvet bodice. "Another suitor?"

Igren blushed. "He is Earl of Eadeshire. Father's friend. He stops with us now and again when he travels to the court at Pendaunzel. A suitor? I had not thought.... He was wed."

"But his wife died," Iobethe said. "He was here often before that, but not so much since he put on mourning. Oh, Igren, think–!"

"I won't think of it," Igren answered simply. Kaiese's gentyl-maid came to dress the girls' hair and Laurel, no longer needed, left. She did not care to change her own clothes. Her beribboned breeches met her aunt's disapproval, and so she wore them daily. She was no pretty prize to be won in these elaborate marriage games and she thought it pointless to make herself presentable to her cousin's suitors.

There was a knock at the front door as she descended to the hall. The porter had gone from his place on a last-minute errand and Laurel went down to answer.

"Laurel!"

She didn't recognize him immediately; her first thought was that it was fortunate for Igren and little Iobethe that the Earl of Eadeshire was not so old as the Goldsmith. Oh, he was perhaps forty, but she'd imagined that this widower, her uncle's friend, must be ancient and withered. His face was square and broad, oddly familiar, unlined, his hair dark and curly, streaked with rich reddish tones, his eyes nearly black beneath raven brows, his complexion toned olive, like an Italian or Spaniard. A quiet-looking, middle-aged nobleman—nothing *here* to cause such uproar. Then she saw the golden lions on the sash across his chest and knew that she'd met him before.

"I didn't know–" Ambris began. "I had not heard you'd returned to New York."

"I've not been home many months, My Lord. You recall my departure? I barely spoke to you that day." She stood in the doorway, blocking his entrance, and stepped back quickly. "My aunt and my cousins make themselves ready. Will you sit and talk with me while you await them?"

The parlor had been vacated by scurrying maids only seconds before. Cushions were plumped to mountainous heights—feathers still floated down to the carpets—and fresh wood filled the grate. Ambris stood before the roaring fire. "You were no more than a child when I saw you last, but you are quite a young woman now. How are you, Maiden? Will you stay here?"

"I hope I shan't," she answered. "I plan to return to my home with my Uncle Redmantyl soon." She glanced out the window at the tall piles of snow sliding into puddles in the garden. "I have been 'prenticed to him these last four years. He tells me I shall be a great wizard one day."

"I do not doubt it."

"Shall I show you some trick I have learned?" she asked, encouraged. She was about to when she heard Kaiese and her cousins on the stairs, and instead rose to make herself inconspicuous.

Mother and daughters entered with fair plaits smooth and velvets unwrinkled, cool of face and calm of manner, as if they hadn't troubled at all. Kaiese curtseyed and Ambris offered his brow to her hands, the proper gesture of respect to greet one's host. This little ceremony completed, Igren and Iobethe were brought forward. The Earl made polite remarks on how they'd grown since he had last seen them—indeed, he barely knew Iobethe now.

As they seated themselves about the hearth, the conversation moved from courtesies to informal chat. Kaiese, laughing, told Ambris how he had caught them by surprise and promised that Nikholas would be down to join them shortly. She apologized for the scant table, but trusted that My Lord would understand the hardships they'd faced in this winter now thankfully past. She hoped it had not been so miserable at Pendaunzel; when assured that it had not, Kaiese announced she thought to visit the city herself at summer. Her family hadn't heard this plan before and Igren looked alarmed as the Lady elaborated: If the Gracious Lord Dafythe called a Mayor's Council before the end of Nikholas's term, they absolutely must go. She looked forward to it on her daughters' behalf. How thrilling they would find the court! What splendid folk they would meet! Perhaps they would be presented to the Duke.

"You might present them yourself, My Lord."

"'Twould be no small pleasure," Ambris assured her. "Your daughters would bring a new brightness to the old halls, and I don't doubt that Igren will have her share of admirers." This was said with avuncular affection and Igren didn't blush so deeply as she might. "I should be proud to present them, but I fear I shan't be at court this summer. I've been too long absent from Eadeshire and my attention is required there."

"Your father must feel your absence dreadfully."

"I daresay, Lady Kaiese, but my shire must feel it more after these months. My father will have to do without me 'til after the harvests."

Laurel puzzled at this exchange, recalled gossip she'd overheard but never given attention to, blinked at Ambris's lions, and burst with the question: "The Duke is your father?"

Kaiese scowled, ashamed by her ignorance and her bad manners to advertise it aloud, but the guest smiled.

"I beg your pardon, My Lord," Laurel offered. "I knew that there was such a one—I didn't know it was you."

Now, she understood her aunt's particular interest in this nobleman. He *was* a magnificent catch, greater than any other man who had visited the Hall. For what were a wealthy merchant, a pretty

French courtier, and a rough, countrified Earl together compared with the Duke's bastard son, the Emperor's cousin? Ambris might have come as a family friend, but Kaiese desired a connection more close than friendship. It would be a triumph past the Lady's highest expectations if he offered for Igren.

Despite this, dinner was pleasant; Ambris brought tales of Duke Dafythe's court, and more. The Mayor's household was hungry for news from beyond the snow-piled walls of the town, and the Earl was an excellent reporter. He knew everything worth hearing: as his father's councilor, he was one of the inner circle of the Northlands's government and, along with local scandals—who was to marry, who had died, who had received appointments—and stories he had gathered at Maryesfont and Storm Port on his travels homeward, he brought them the latest information from Europe. He could give particulars of trade agreements with the Italian kingdoms and the Holy Roman Empire and tell of the Emperor's doings in London and Paris with more accuracy and detail than Rosandre or Geyraulte had been able to provide. The Mayor's family were the first in New York to hear of the uprisings in Navarre and the strained diplomatic relations between the Empire and Spain; they were the first to discuss the possibility of war. Not once did the table talk take up the tones of a parlor courtship.

Kaiese might design to match a daughter to this Plantagenet, but Ambris wasn't interested in either young girl. He hadn't come as a suitor, but as a traveler who sought rest and comfort amid old acquaintances. He made this plain: his chief conversation was with Nikholas upon their mutual interests. He addressed the girls with the familiar kindness which adults reserved for the half-grown children of their friends and met the Lady's unmistakable hints with courteous incomprehension, and Laurel liked him for that.

"Have you made up your mind yet?" Nikholas asked after dinner.

"Mayor?"

"How long you shall stay with us in New York?" the Mayor explained, pleased with his wife's mortification. "'Tis a rare pleasure to see you."

"I must go on to Eadeshire if the roads are passable," Ambris answered. "But I shall stop again when I find myself in your charming town."

Kaiese invited Ambris to stay awhile, but the Earl pled weariness. The rest of the household did not insist on keeping him. The hour was late; Iobethe was nodding with sleep and Nikholas, though glad to have guests, was equally glad to have his house quiet after the guests had gone.

Feather-light snow fell as they showed Ambris to the door. No lamplighter nor constable was in the dark street and the porter looked fretful at the prospect of going out as he helped the nobleman with his furry wraps.

Laurel took up a cloak and threw it about her shoulders. "I'll go."

Ambris protested. "I couldn't ask a maiden to guide me on such a snowy night."

"'Tis no trouble," she answered. "I've stood in the service before." She lit a torch from the porter's lamp and went out.

"Niece–!" Kaiese began.

"Oh, have her go," said Nikholas. "She knows the streets well enough."

Ambris looked at him, then at the young woman descending the outer stairs, and he followed her down.

"You mustn't fret for me, My Lord," Laurel told him. "My uncle is right—I know the streets far better than little Jemrye. I shan't be lost. You, however..."

"Do you often act as servant, Maiden?" he asked.

"When I must. In the worst weather, I was out often. I walked with the constables to search for poor lost beggars in the snow and drove thieves from the empty shops. Once, I stood all night to secure the ports."

"But you are the Mayor's niece."

Laurel shrugged. "'Tis better than sitting still. We've all been called to unusual service this winter."

"True," Ambris agreed. "Many of the nobility have felt the obligations of their position for the first time in this crisis. We are called to provide and protect for our people, you know, only our protection is not much required these days. The common folk are able to go about their business without fear, and young maidens are too frequently capable of defending themselves." He smiled at her. "At Pendaunzel, half the women dress like the castle guard. My sister has made warrior-maids fashionable again."

"Your sister?" Laurel echoed, uncomprehending. Then she laughed. "Prince Margueryt."

"Yes."

Laurel picked her way between the high drifts and around the dark patches of ice; Ambris watched her move ahead of him, leaping puddles and turning to point out especial dangers in the path with more nimble grace than the average attendant. Once, when he slipped, she leapt back to catch his arm and help him regain his feet. They crossed the empty marketplace and arrived at the door to the inn where Ambris had taken rooms.

He paused there, as if he would stand and talk in the falling snow, but he only said, "I bid you a pleasant night, Laurel."

"And you, My Lord."

He went in. She doused her torch in the slush-filed gutter. The moon shone through a gap in the clouds; snowflakes fluttered about her like near stars and ice glittered in bright liquid paths through the streets. With this light, she saw herself home.

heyghte

The thaw continued through February. Despite the change in the weather, the town kept its isolation and its citizens remained indoors. The snow melted rapidly, too rapidly; the river overflowed and the water, having nowhere to drain itself off, flooded New York and Kallaykirke. Streams banked by slabs of mud and ice flowed through the streets and dirty water filled all underground chambers. An inch of water stood in the kitchen of the Mayor's Hall and the pantry and wine cellars beneath the house were filled to the beams. Servants had hurried to save the household stores and Nikholas' livelihood; kegs, barrels and jars of preserves crowded the corners of the scullery and piled high in unused rooms. Shopkeepers brought their damaged merchandise up onto their porches to sell at ridiculously low prices. Horses and cartwheels were caught by the deep muck, and foot-travelers fell if they didn't step carefully. The dockyards remained open even though the southward piers were under water and the rest of the wharf always in danger. Regular business was impossible. But Laurel braved the flood that morning, for Leobolde Goldsmith had returned and visited the Mayor's Hall.

She picked her way down the Parade from doorstep to doorstep, wading the icy waters where she couldn't leap. Her boots were soggy when she reached the market square, now a shallow pond. Ducks and geese sunned themselves at the base of the market cross and swam freely amid abandoned stalls crushed by heavy snows and blown down by fierce winds, and squabbled greedily over the scraps children threw from the steps of the surrounding shops. The children themselves fought over who should have the privilege of tossing this burnt crust or loaf-heel; the braver waded into the water to retrieve soggy fragments and feed the birds by hand.

A pair of older boys in fur cloaks stood on the porch of the Goldbell Inn, laughing at the sport. A tall man in noble blue traveling robes emerged behind them.

Laurel called to him. "My Lord Ambris!"

He looked up, surprised, then went down the steps and made his way around the square; the boys leapt after him but hesitated at the deeper currents along Market Street. Ambris splashed through with confident strides. "I didn't hope you would still be here, dear maid."

"I cannot yet leave the town, My Lord. You return to Pendaunzel? You were there not a month ago."

"The boys are to serve as squires to my sister Mara." He turned to where the pair stood waiting. "Laurel, my sons, Eadrik, Lord Ellsrood, and Eduarde, Lord Laufegcrike." At his broad gesture, both boys bowed with some confusion and pushed tousled, dark locks from dark eyes to blink at her. "I meant my steward to accompany them to the port here, but at the last I thought it better to bring them myself. Are you on an errand, Maiden? I have been told it is not safe to go about the town."

"It's not," Laurel agreed, "for fools and cowards. But 'tis simple enough if you keep care of your steps and aren't afraid you might slip in the mud and spoil your finery, My Lord. *I* know how to get about."

Ambris smiled. "May I walk with you?"

"If you like." In truth, she was glad of the company. With the streets deep with water, she had few places to go; before she'd seen Ambris, she was not at all hopeful of finding a way to occupy the hours until she could safely return to the Hall.

Ambris crossed the flooded square and spoke briefly with his sons, then returned to take her arm. They walked to the little hill before St. Matthieu's, a muddy, common green above the water.

"How many children have you, My Lord?"

"Seven."

"Tell me of them, all of them." She recalled that he'd mentioned a family, but she hadn't imagined so many children, nor children so well-grown. Eadrik must be fifteen or sixteen, Eduarde perhaps a year younger. They were Iobethe's age and not much younger than herself. "What are their names? Do they all bear titles?"

"No. In ordinary circumstances, Eadeshire is obscure. Ellsrood is the traditional name for the firstborn, but Father created Laufegcrike for Eduarde. My next boy, Arthur, will be twelve at Lammas and Father plans to title him upon his confirmation."

"And after Arthur?"

"Bertrande is ten, Marcius seven, Mathilde—my girl—six, and the baby, Guylliame, is three."

"Are the little ones at Eadbury?"

"For now. I think to send all but Gilly and perhaps Mathilde to the Sisters of Samandra when the roads are more easily traveled. I am not always able to see to them myself and My Lady Margaude, you know, is dead." He looked around to find his sons; the younger had joined the neighborhood children around the pond, and the elder boy was not in sight. "Her illness came swiftly and took her before I was aware of the danger. She insisted that she was well. I had no reason for worry, 'til it was too late. We– I could do nothing for her. Gilly wept so for his mother and asked where she had gone. The older lads wept too. Oh, they kept to their rooms so they wouldn't show themselves weak and childish, but I knew. And now, I must find proper places for all of them. I can't leave them at Eadbury in the care of servants any longer." Laurel leading, they crossed the Matthieu parvis and passed through the alley between the church and rectory. "Where are we going?"

"Up to the walls."

"You are permitted to do this?"

"My Uncle Nikholas does not protest and the guards know me," she answered as they went up the narrow, steep steps to the rampart. "As I have been of service this winter, I come and go as I will." The guards did know Laurel; some offered greetings, others watched with wary eyes and crossed themselves behind her. One guard, recognizing her companion, bowed deeply. "I expect they are more surprised at you, My Lord. I am rarely in anyone's company."

"Do you know, Laurel, that in the early days of the Empire a young maiden as you are wouldn't go about alone?" he told her. "Likely, you would have been kept so carefully as if you were meant for the Sisters from birth. In some parts of the world, it is so today. In Venice, Rome, Spain, respectable maidens will not venture out without a gentyl or duenna for their protection. I daresay many a good Norman matron would still call you scandalous."

Laurel laughed in disbelief. "'Tis wonder such maids know men exist."

"Suitors are introduced when they are of an age to marry," he answered.

"Why, as my Aunt Kaiese does! She has matchworthy men to sit and stare at my cousin Igren while she asks after their families. You were there yourself, My Lord. You saw how it was."

"Yes," said Ambris. "I did perceive that Damosel Igren was being presented to me."

"But you wouldn't–?"

"Not little Igren. She's become quite a lovely maiden, yet I cannot look upon her and but recall that wordless child I first met at Mayor Nikholas's house. That wasn't so many years past."

"Had I been brought up as a marriageable maiden, I might be so dainty and timid as Igren," Laurel said thoughtfully. "But no one taught me to think myself so. I've been left alone for too long and, in truth, I've come to like it. 'Tis far better than being shut into the parlor to wait for a husband. Let them call me bold, the gossips! I wouldn't know how to be anything else."

"I shouldn't like to see you as anything else, dear maid. Were you taught gentleness, I would believe a most remarkable creature had been lost. When we first met I wondered at you—at what you might become."

"Have you been a friend to my Uncle Nikholas very long?" she asked. "I don't recall seeing you at the Hall before."

"I didn't meet your uncle 'til after you had gone."

"Yet you know so much about me."

"Maiden, that could not be avoided. Your aunt and uncle speak often of you."

As they passed the next guardspost, a little squire smiled at them with knowing malevolence. Laurel shuddered and stepped away quickly.

"Do you know her?" Ambris asked as he followed.

"I've never seen her before," Laurel answered. "Not to recall. But some of the townsfolk have never liked me." She maintained her swift pace until a turn of the wall put the guardspost out of sight. "Shall I show you the town, My Lord?"

From their vantage point above the floodwaters, Laurel pointed out landmarks and features both within and without the town. She knew that Ambris must be nearly as familiar with New York as she was herself, but he expressed a courteous interest in each little chapel, courtyard, and cluster of trees where she and Igren had played as children, and encouraged her to go on as if he were a stranger here. At the Kalligate, which opened onto the bridge that crossed the River Froth and led into Kallaykirke, they returned to the street. They crossed the shop-heavy bridge over the river, which surged dangerously against the bridge's underpinnings.

Ambris told her of his troubles at Eadbury, of the siege his town had faced this winter, of thieves who had been raiding isolated farms and manors and were now held in prison until he could hear the case against them. He bemoaned the lawlessness that disaster brought and wondered at why the worst emerged in some folk when their very best was needed. It was most unchristian and unnorman to take advantage of weaker persons. He spoke of his cousin Katheryne, as the family was unable to find her a suitable match. The Irish Prince was an especially troublesome problem, for she'd come to the Northlands as a small child and been adopted as Dafythe's daughter, but now that she was a grown woman she had no right place within the dukedom or in her homeland.

"It is improbable she will return to Eirelande," Ambris confided. "She is a stranger there and the Irish do not welcome foreign governors. They are peaceable enough with her father's regency."

Laurel had never been interested in such news—what did it matter to her if thieves were hung or the Irish Prince wed?—but now she gave attention. Her ignorance had embarrassed her once before this man, and she didn't want to be caught out again.

"I don't know much of Eadeshire," she confessed. "'Tis all wood and farm, isn't it? Not a land of great wealth."

Ambris smiled. "You speak like my sister. She calls Eadeshire 'a haven for farm-folk,' and takes no interest in its doings though she is its governor by right. But she is Prince of Gossunge and will come to greater than one little shire, to all of the Northlands and perhaps more."

"How came it to you, My Lord? Was it your mother's?"

He shook his head. "Not my mother's. The last Earl Gillefleure was my father's wife. Margueryt is her one child, but upon her death I was given to her land. 'Tis not much, I grant, but it has given me an opportunity to see how I might fare as governor. Indeed, the endeavor has impoverished me. Eadeshire is not wealthy, as you say. A magistrate of Pendaunzel receives greater income than a provincial noble who cannot tax his farmers overmuch."

"But you own Eadeshire."

"I do not."

"You do!" Laurel insisted. "You are its Earl?"

"I was given to keep care of the land by my father."

"Then it is his? He owns the Northlands."

"No."

"The Emperor then?" And when Ambris shook his head: "Well, *who*?"

"No one, Maid. How can land be owned? It isn't a horse or coach or a bag of gold coins—It is the Earth beneath us. I own Castle Ellsrood, but not Eadeshire. Do you see that, Laurel? The Emperor is given to govern the Norman peoples and to protect the land they live upon by Grace of God, and he shares this great responsibility with his chosen governors. When he has children, they will also take their places as governors. Princes, Regents, Earls, all—we are the Lords and protectors. To neglect that which we are given to before Our Almighty Lord is no less than suicide. I believe this is why neither nobles nor common folk are much fond of merchants: they do not understand that land is the substance of life. The merchants remove themselves from it here in the cities. They never see the fallow fields, the growth, the harvest, only the profit of it at market. My father says that the most dangerous thing the nobility can do is forget its obligations to the land and the people who live upon it."

"I expect that my Uncle Nikholas has never walked the yards where his wines are pressed," Laurel said. "Perhaps it is so for all merchants. Have you heard the saying—that merchants have the manners of peasants and the snobbery of nobility? Pardon, My Lord, but 'tis said." Ambris did not look offended, so she went on. "My aunt and my uncle—Lord Redmantyl, not Nikholas—are born of simple folk, even if they carry themselves better these days. They may remember how it was."

They'd gone the length of New York and around Kallaykirke, which was little more than a village surrounding the cathedral and Bishops' Palace, then back across the bridge again. By this time, they'd returned to the shallow streams of the Market Street.

"Shall I ask you to dinner, My Lord?" Laurel offered, reluctant to have the conversation end. "My aunt would not object to such presumption on my part."

"Gramercy," Ambris answered. "But I must refuse. The lads haven't ever been so far from home and the journey from Eadeshire was more for them than I thought. We plan to leave tomorrow morning and must be at the dockyards for the first ships. You will not say we are here? It would seem an insult to your gracious aunt."

"I shan't betray you," she promised, and left him on the square.

When she returned to the Mayor's Hall, Rosandre loitered at the doorstep.

"You might have gone in," she said. "You need only knock. The porter knows you."

"I did not dare, My Damosel." The boy ducked his head, as if to confess some grave misconduct. "'Tis late for a call. I must beg your pardon, but I was allowed no better opportunity to slip from beneath my granduncle's eyes and, had I waited, all must be lost."

She sent Jemrye up with a message to her cousins and escorted Rosandre to the parlor. She hadn't been alone with the young Lordling before, and he now regarded her with polite curiosity. Laurel knew that he must wonder at her place in this household. He could see that she was kin to the Mayor's family; he'd seen for himself that she sat their table and lounged in the corners of the parlor while Kaiese held audience, but he must also have observed that she was given no deference of address and she dressed like a far-riding courier or wandering minstrel. He must wonder, but he was too well-bred to remark. He persisted in speaking to her in the most polite terms as if she were no different from the more delicate maidens of his acquaintance.

"My Damosel Laurel," he began tentatively. "We do not know each other so well, but we are of an age and I am made welcome in your aunt's house. You know no wrong of me. May we speak as friends?"

"Certainly, My Lord Rosandre."

He smiled. "You may know, My Damosel, what reason I have to visit My Lady Kaiese's parlor so often."

"It hasn't gone unnoticed."

"Ah, it is too obvious! She is most fair, is she not?"

"Igren, My Lord?" Laurel guessed.

Rosandre blushed. "No."

"Io is fair too," she agreed. "But you don't care for my cousin Igren? Many call her a most beauteous maid."

"Damosel Igren is lovely past all compare," the boy replied. "A man must be mad to think otherwise, but she is beyond my dreams of happiness. You will understand, Damosel Laurel, and not be struck with offense? When I am here before My Lady, you at one elbow and Damosel Igren at the other, it is as if I kneel before Hera, Athene, and Aphrodite like poor Paris, but unable to judge. I cannot think but to admire. I am humbled. You are not– You cannot be as ordinary women."

"And Io is an ordinary maid?"

"She is above all ordinary maidens!" Rosandre insisted. "She is a muse that I may embolden myself to adore and perhaps coax from the heights."

Of course, he spoke nonsense, but it was beautiful nonsense. Laurel didn't mind listening. She was amused, yet touched, by this youth so earnestly in love with little Iobethe. It was a pretty, innocent thing. "Why can you never speak so to her?" she asked.

"I dare not. It is not done. 'Tis too forward for a youth to pay his court without invitation. The mother first, 'tis said. Win her heart, then the maid's hand. My own mama would think me knavish to behave otherwise. What would My Lady think! And Damosel Io– No, it is too terrible to contemplate how I must sink in her eyes if I make myself too bold!"

"Yet you speak freely to me, My Lord," Laurel murmured playfully.

The youth was immediately crestfallen. "I have given you insult."

"No, My Lord. You are perfectly charming."

"Does she speak of me?" he asked. "What does she say? I cannot hope I have been noticed. So many might offer more. My Lord of Eadeshire, they say, is here whenever he passes the town."

Laurel smiled. "I would not fret over such tales. You are noticed, I promise you! My cousins, both, speak highly of your manners and your looks. They do like you."

He brightened hopefully. "Do you think she will have me, Damosel, if My Lady gives consent?"

"Yes, certainly, if my aunt consents," Laurel answered with a touch of sarcasm which was lost on the heart-struck boy. "My uncle may have you wait a year or two–"

"Oh, but he could not be so cruel!" the young Lord cried. "Mayor Nikholas does not speak of it, I am sure. `Tis all to the mothers to decide, Mama and the fair Lady. Fathers are nothing to a marriage. They see to the contract and–" he waved a hand. "They think no more of it! It was so when my mother chose wives for my brothers Noel and Fabris. Papa said that she would please not find them ugly wives and left her to her business. But of course," Rosandre added, "he is not their father and does not have to settle his estate upon them."

"Does your mother know of your love?" Laurel asked.

He shook his head. "But she will understand. Mama was not eighteen at her first marriage. I would die if my love's heart were not mine."

There was a sharp whisper and a rustle of skirts in the corridor, and the youth rose as Kaiese entered her parlor. Iobethe followed, face bright. "My Lord!" the Lady greeted her guest, and Rosandre turned his pretty pleasantries to her. Laurel retreated to her seat at the window.

Rosandre made his excuses and departed for Kallaykirke before he was missed at Evensong, and Leobolde Goldsmith returned for dinner. Laurel was asked to join her family at the table. She found the Goldsmith no less repulsive than she had at his last visit, but she was relieved to see that Kaiese didn't give him serious consideration as a suitor. Igren wasn't pushed at him as she'd been pushed at more likely prospects, and Laurel took comfort at this for her cousin's sake. She'd been afraid: Surely to surrender gentle Igren or little Iobethe to this man would be like giving over lambs to a hungry wolf!

Nikholas, in jesting mood, took command the dinner conversation and entertained the visitor by trading success stories and telling tales of his good fortune in finding such a rare and wondrous creature as the Lady Kaiese. The Goldsmith must wonder at that.

"She trapped me with magic," he explained solemnly. "'Twas that strange, silvery fairness—I thought myself under a spell. You cannot see it so, with the four of them about the table, Syre, but if you had seen her then! You ought to have seen her. In my mind, she was after the likeness of my niece. Yes, quite like Laurel in those days, but not so wild."

Kaiese opened her mouth, then reconsidered and kept her peace. The Goldsmith fixed his eyes upon Laurel.

"There's a hardness to that race," Nikholas said. "Her sister had it too, and her cousin, Lord Redmantyl." He was aware of his wife's discomfiture, but enjoyed it with the length of the table safely between them. "In spite of their looks, the girls take after my own family—a feeble lot. I was alone in the world at twelve, not aunt, uncle, nor cousin left, and the whole of our trade given to me. Twelve, Syre! The lawyers had to look after the mess 'til I came of age."

"Lawyers? Blood-sucking thieves!" the Goldsmith proclaimed. "'Tis fortunate you weren't beggared by them, Mayor." He took up his drink. "My father lived too blasted long to suit me. One hundred and sixteen years."

"You haven't suffered for it."

The Goldsmith grunted in disagreement. Kaiese offered more wine.

"Poor little things," Nikholas continued once they'd retreated to the parlor for brandy and cakes. "We fret for them still, don't we, My Lady? I'd have a good merchant ask after them—the local lads have been buzzing about and there's one or two I wouldn't mind taking into my concerns, but My Lady's set their hearts after noblemen, and damn me if the nobles haven't obliged! We may well wonder if 'tis for my Igren's beauty or if the Lady's cast her own spells. She won't tell, will you, Dearest? But the lordlings we see at this house—My Lord Rosandre, My Lord Geyraulte, My Lord Ambris. I can't think which we'll choose. Which d'you like best, Daughter," he addressed Igren, "the pretty one, the loud one, or the royal one?"

Igren didn't answer.

"I'd like the pretty one, if you please, Father," Iobethe piped up.

Nikholas turned to her. "A taste for Frankish silks, and at your age! Fancy the stuff your mother's put into your head! What will you do with such a husband, my little one?"

"I'll go to the court at Paris," the girl answered sincerely. "I'll wear the grandest velvets and gems as ever were seen. I shan't have to mind my bedtime and I'll dance 'til dawn at every ball, and even with My Lord Kharles if he asks."

"And what if My Lord Rosandre doesn't ask after you? There are some that come to gape at your sister, you know. This boy may be one of that lot."

"He isn't," Iobethe replied with confidence. "Besides, Igren has so many boys, she mustn't mind sharing one."

Igren turned pink, but her father and the Goldsmith laughed. "No, she certainly mustn't," Nikholas agreed. "Little Maid, my apologies. You are far more your mother's child than I suspected. If the Frankish lad comes by again, I'm quite sure you'll have him and with my blessings."

Upstairs, after the Goldsmith had gone, the girls prepared for bed. Velvet bodices were unlaced, heavy skirts dropped on the floor and kicked away, silver plaits combed and braided, flannel nightgowns and robes pulled on, gentyl-maids dismissed.

"Iobethe, how could you?" Igren said once they were alone.

"Why shouldn't I?" the younger girl retorted. "'Tis true. I heard Rosandre—he said so much to Laurel before we went into the parlor."

"Oh, Io, you didn't!"

"I only wanted to know. We've always wondered who My Lord Rosandre came for, as he never said a word to Mama if he liked you or me best. And he likes me! I didn't hope– But 'tis most wonderful this way, that he wants to marry me instead of you. You don't like him so much, Igren."

"I do," Igren responded. "He's lovely."

"You don't like as much as I do. Igren, promise you won't have him, even if Mama says you must? I think he's the prettiest of the lot. And I should love so dearly to see Paris! If I don't take him, Mama will push me at My Lord of Eadeshire and he's so horribly old!"

"My Lord Ambris is not old, Imp," Laurel said indulgently. Kaiese had filled the child's head with ideas of spectacular marriages and Iobethe seemed so ready to be admired that Laurel sometimes believed the girl might fly at the first suitor before she knew what marriage truly meant. Iobethe spoke of parties and pretty clothes, but it was obvious she knew nothing of what it was to be a wife. She'd never imagined a kiss, or the activities of the bedchamber, or childbirth. At fifteen, she was too young to know. If Iobethe must marry as a child, then marriage to another child was preferable to marriage to a mature man. Rosandre was as innocent as she.

"You might have worse," Laurel told the girl. "My aunt might push you at the Goldsmith. He's far older."

"*I'm* not who he'll ask for," Iobethe answered.

"Io, hush!" Igren said softly, urgently. "I would like better not to think of it so much."

"Don't you want to marry?" Iobethe asked in amazement.

"Oh, of course." Igren stretched out across the foot of the bed, arms and toes dangling.

"Mama says it's best that maids as we are marry well and young."

"Yes," she agreed vaguely. "If only..." Her eyes turned to Laurel and a little smile touched her lips. "You never think of such things, do you?"

Laurel laughed. "I? No, Cos. Wizards never marry if they are truly wise, only take lovers."

"Laurel, you mustn't say such wicked things in front of Io. Mama wouldn't like it."

"If my aunt thinks this little thing fit to wed, she must think her fit to know that women do take lovers from time to time."

"It isn't fit," Igren answered.

"I won't tell," Iobethe said eagerly. "I won't! I swear it! Tell me of lovers, Laurel. Do you have one? Tell, please?"

"Of course not," Laurel responded.

"There is no one?" Iobethe was disappointed.

"No, not now."

Igren looked up, curious, but Laurel went up into her own little cubby above her cousins' rooms.

She hadn't thought of love since she'd bid farewell to Klyffaude. She, too, was fond of Rosandre and didn't mind any more than her cousins when he paid his charming compliments. If he'd spoken of her as he had of Io...

On occasion, Rosandre reminded her of Klyffaude. Nothing of their physical features were like: one was tall, the other smaller; one red-headed, the other ginger-fair; one common, the other noble. Where Rosandre was the quintessential courtier, bound by every social custom created through the civilized centuries, Klyffaude mimicked the courtly style but remained free of its rigorous codes of conduct. Where one boy was solemn, the other always spoke with bright humor. Yet, there was a similarity in their fanciful dress and manner. When this pretty French Lordling spoke, she thought of the thesper. She wondered what Klyffaude had felt when he had returned to Wizardes Cliff last autumn and found her gone. Had she hurt him very much? At times, she wished he might come to New York to see her, so that she had a chance to explain.

But that would be magnificent folly. She couldn't see Klyffaude. She couldn't remember. Love was impossible. It had cost her great efforts of will to shut away the growing passions of a healthy young woman, and she had no reason to open that door again, even the least little crack. Not now.

It was a matter of self-command. She mustn't allow herself to give in to her weaknesses, not even after she'd achieved mastery over her powers. Full wizards, it was said, could enjoy wine with dinner, but not too often. For the magical, any self-indulgence which might become habit must be abandoned. The inability to cast its influence aside was the mark of weak wizard, and weak wizards toppled easily. Laurel was determined that this would not be her. When she came fully to her powers and self-command, there would be opportunities to play and give her heart—just a little. She could never give more.

"Will you stay at Pendaunzel now, My Lord?"

"No," Ambris answered. "I'm needed at Eadeshire. I shall return to New York within the fortnight."

"I didn't think it possible to go to and fro at such speeds."

"Ships may go swiftly under fortunate winds," he answered vaguely. "I expect you'll be gone before then?"

"No, I'll be here," Laurel replied. "But I don't plan to stay much afterwards."

They stood on the porch of the inn, well above the flooded square; Ambris's sons had accompanied the grooms to fetch the horses to convey their baggage to the docks. Laurel had left the Mayor's Hall in the earliest light, hoping that Ambris was not yet gone. It was a foolish, impulsive thing to do, she knew, but it had pained her to think she might not see him again. He reminded her of Lord Redmantyl, whom she missed terribly; it was a comfort to be with this man who seemed so much older and wiser than herself. Some of his high talk confused her, but she believed he was accustomed to speak so and she was ready to admire him for it.

She marveled at him. Were there such people who believed every fine idea they expressed? Ambris seemed to. She didn't doubt that he acted according to his sense of honor and sense of purpose. Even now, he dwelt on the responsibilities which awaited him: his land, his tenants, his castle, his children.

Ambris had been surprised to see her, but he seemed to understand that she'd taken some trouble to be out so early and he wasn't displeased.

"Will you visit the Mayor's Hall on your return?" she asked. "You know my aunt will fret if she learns you've neglected her, no matter how your Eadeshire fields call you away."

He smiled. "I'll visit and make my apologies, but I pray My Lady Kaiese will not expect me to stop for more than a day. Jest if you will, but I have let my shire go too long untended and my steward cannot take all duties upon himself indefinitely."

With a splash, a creak of cartwheels, and a clatter of iron-shod hooves, the horses arrived. Eadrik and Eduarde climbed up behind, shouting joyfully as the porters threw down parcels from the porch of the inn and grooms scrambled to pile up the baggage.

"We must make our farewells," Ambris took her hand and kissed the cold palm, as courtly a gesture as Rosandre had ever made. "I am glad to have seen you again, dear maid. I shall listen for tales of your wizardly adventures." His sons called for him, and he went down to the cart.

Laurel waited until the guards at the Kalligate blew their trumpets to warn all travelers that sunset was nigh and pulled up the iron pegs which held the great doors open through the day; she exited as the doors swung shut. She crossed the bridge into Frankeshire. Instead of entering Kallaykirke, she chose a path along the river, even though it was thick with mud. Laurel struggled through the ankle-deep muck and cursed furiously at each step. The walls of Kallaykirke loomed over her and the pale towers of the Bishop's Palace and the cathedral, one at each end of the small city, reached up into the deepening twilight like huge, ghostly claws. The sky was heavy with clouds and wind blustered past her ears, but she didn't have far to go. Once she was past the city, Laurel left the path and crossed meadows and untilled fields to reach the woods.

It was St. Benedict's Eve, the night of the spring Equinox. Laurel was shivering when she found the clearing in the wet woods where she'd made her last vigil. According to the ritual, she must eschew all mortal habitations—towns, especially, but farms, Free Folk encampments, even lone travelers who sought shelter beside the roadways were to be avoided. Wizard's Keep required that she draw the danger to herself, not to the living energies of other, more vulnerable, beings nearby. She'd spent much of her childhood in these woods and it hadn't taken her long to locate an appropriate place within walking distance of New York.

The little clearing was as muddy as the road, but it must be cleared before she could begin the rites of the Keep. She was unsure of the exact time: a crescent moon appeared infrequently between the drifting clouds and little of the firmament showed to identify the stars. Quickly, she pushed aside the fallen branches and kicked away the leaves. The ground beneath was cold and slick; Laurel crafted her best spells of protection on the damp earth and fixed the rim of her pentacle with a psychic barrier. No harm could come to her within the circle. Goblet set before her folded legs, she poured the contents of the linen packets—herbs, incense, powdered metals—she spilled three drops of wine and, knife at her wrist, eyes shut tightly, she waited.

Her breath quickened. Her mind opened to the night beyond the close-set trees, the enshrouding mist, the cloud-covered sky. The heavens unfolded before her. No curved ceiling of firmament, this; space stretched on and on, past scope or understanding. She sought the depths of the ether, but her mind couldn't reach so far. There was always more, beyond her grasp. Distant planets, comets, blazing white stars wound their great circuits in countless variations of pattern. The bulk of the earth tilted in its ecliptic plane, shifted toward the moment of equinox. She was aware of the motion. When the orbits arrived at a certain alignment, the Gateway would open and They would have their opportunity. She must distract Them, entice Them with the promise of her magic, yet keep Them from taking her until the way was shut and their time was lost again.

Such was the duty of a wizard. All her discipline, all her education, came to this. She had fasted through three days and meditated through two nights. Her will was strong, her spells impregnable. She was empowered for battle, though she hoped she wouldn't be tested tonight. Engaged in this void, Laurel felt herself so small, so young, so fragile. Her life was no more than the faintest spark in a chasm where night reigned and devoured all eventually. Yet, she was desirable. Trapped in their ethereal sphere, the Outsiders wanted to extend their influence into the material. One mortal life was insubstantial, but a billion lives together glowed irresistibly and drew Them again and again. They envied the light and the pleasures of the senses. They despised the freedom of the mortal creatures who remained pitifully ignorant of the danger they tempted in their conspicuous place. They desired, hated, sought to corrupt. They wanted to touch her world. They wanted power here. She, and others of her kind, had power—power slight when compared to theirs, but part of this world and therefore of use. A magician in their grasp would be an effective tool. Capable of bearing inhuman magic, exerting forces of its own, it would be a focus for Them to work through. She knew that her own talent was remarkable. And They knew of it, knew that she had great potential and, immature and incompletely trained, was more vulnerable than a grown wizard. If They came, They would come to her. If she lost–! No, she would think no more of that; capture was worse to contemplate than death.

The cosmos turned. The earth tipped in its place. She pressed the little blade against her wrist, ready to cut. Magician's blood, a few drops, would bring the potion before her to life. With this spell, she exposed the essence of her self, as if to cry *Here I am*. She became a beacon.

Time.

But the crucial moment did not arrive. Much of the heavenly configuration was far beyond her perception, but Laurel knew that it was not precise; something did not happen. She felt nothing. If the Gateway opened, They did not come through. No blood was drawn.

Her wrists were not yet scarred, for the previous nights of vigilance had been the same. She sat, awaiting a battle that was never joined.

Redmantyl had told her that the heavens came close to this precarious alignment eight nights of each year, but the Others didn't always attempt to make their escape. Laurel thought that this was too simple an answer. If They were so desperate as she knew Them to be— They had *touched* her; she had felt their manic glee at her prospective capture—why did They not hang at the door, ready for any opening? Did the opportunity not come so often as the custom of Wizard's Keep indicated? Was there some cosmic element in the arrangement of the Gateway which she didn't understand? Did They reach into other spheres she didn't know of and conquer there? References to their activities were so obscure and confounded by myth that she remained ignorant.

What were They, exactly? She remembered Redmantyl's scholarly exercise, his collection of tales on the origins of evil. Some legends claimed They were outcast servants of a Most High. Others implied that, though humanity had existed a mere six thousand years, the earth was far older and They had battled for its possession in those immeasurable eons. Were They demons? Lucifer and the fallen angels? Furies released from Pandora's box as punishment for Prometheus's theft? Decayed antediluvian gods? The malign spirits of a hundred folklores? The unleashed minions of a Dark God's ambitious apprentice, who stole some object of great power and cast darkness upon the earth? She felt the horror of an essential truth that lay behind the remote symbolism. She understood that Redmantyl had gathered these tales to find an answer. He didn't know either.

She would have liked Lord Redmantyl here with her now. Even if he didn't answer her questions, he would quiet her apprehension. His power had shielded her; she knew that when danger came, he would fight for her as he had on that last, horrid Midsummer eve when she'd followed him to his Wizard's Keep.

She wished now that she'd never done it. Redmantyl had warned her time and again: An apprentice had no business meddling in the affairs of wizards and pursuing knowledge she was unready to support. He had urged her to wait, but she couldn't listen. She'd been too curious, too impatient to learn everything at once, too confident in her ability to cope with all the responsibilities of a grown magician. Her uncle, she imagined, had thwarted her; he thought her too young and careless. She'd been anxious to prove him wrong. Frustration had made her more keen to discover his secrets. She simply hadn't believed that the ceremonies of Wizard's Keep concealed so enormous and hideous a truth and so she had followed him. That night, innocence and peace had ended. She paid for her curiosity.

Laurel knew that she should not be here tonight. She shouldn't bear the burden of this knowledge, shouldn't need to place herself in such peril, for another ten years. As a grown wizard, she might do battle without fear. The proper training of a young magician would have equipped her: seven years of apprenticeship taught the novice the importance of perfect self-command and the exercise of magic in spellcraft; five years of magedom steeled the potential magician to an impervious will and constant vigilance. Only at the completion of their final tests did wizards learn the reasons for their intense discipline; all secrets were revealed when the magician proved capable of bearing the responsibility. Many failed. Many were cast from the ranks of magical. Many fallen magicians were destroyed. None who showed themselves unfit were permitted to take up the duties of a guardian, lest the Outsiders discover them and take advantage of their weakness.

She had brought this upon herself. Due to her folly, They knew of her. They would seek her out. She had drawn attention to her magic and, ready or no, she must defend it.

The night sky turned above her. Hidden by clouds, the moon set. A light rain began to fall. At last, Laurel rose, limbs stiff, clothes sodden and nose running. She trembled, though not entirely from the cold. Wizard's Keep had passed. She was safe until May Night.

When the gates opened at drizzling dawn, Laurel entered the town. She trudged through quiet streets and alleys to the stable-yard and scullery door of the Mayor's Hall. The cook gave her toasted bread, warm honeymead, and a bowl of steaming hot broth and fussed at her bedraggled condition.

Laurel paused on the little landing between the kitchen, the servants' stairs and the corridor which led to Kaiese's parlor and the dining hall and listened to the voices of her aunt and uncle in ordinary morning conversation. Then she crept up to her chamber, shed her muddy clothes and bathed without interruption, then curled gratefully beneath her down comforters. It would not be often, she knew, that hot broth and a soft bed would be available after such miserable nights.

She was near sleep when Igren returned from her breakfast. "Laurel," her cousin whispered. "I told Mama you were too ill to come down."

"'Tis true."

"Where have you been?"

"I couldn't tell you."

Her cousin made a soft, shocked noise.

"Oh, nothing of that sort, Cos! Who among the wretched boys in this town would I stand in the rain all night over?"

"You've done this before," Igren observed softly. "Mama's asked if I knew what mischief you were at. I said I didn't know but, Laurel, I do wonder. I can't help it if I worry for you."

Laurel lifted her head from beneath the blanket. "'Tis nothing, Igren. Nothing to worry for. Let me sleep."

She belonged less to this town, these people, than she ever had. In her childhood, she'd felt an innocent's sense of misplacement; she had been wrong, but she didn't know how. Now, she understood.

Never subtle nor given to introspection, Laurel was forced by meditation to gather her thoughts. More than her magic or her boldness, her knowledge of what the world was truly like set her apart from ordinary folk. Their amusements, their business, their religion baffled her. She watched the daily conduct of their lives: the merchants scraping pennies at their shops, Kaiese and her matchmaking schemes, Uncle Nikholas in his office with his scribe, youths her own age laughing as they pursued careless sport, little maidens sighing after the youths. It jolted her senses to move so abruptly from the depths of infinite space to the courtesies of Kaiese's plush parlor. Sometimes, distant stars burned bright in her mind while the velvets and tapestries grew insubstantial before her. One seemed far more real than other.

She heard the music of spheres ringing and she ached to speak: How could they care for such trivialities? Didn't they see what passed just beyond their noses? Why should she sacrifice herself to preserve this pointless way of living? But, no, she couldn't tell them. They wouldn't believe her if she tried. To hint at her knowledge would only make her more strange to them, and they eschewed her as fantastical and even sinister now. She didn't belong in New York, but she could not yet leave. And Wizardes Cliff was so far away.

She was out of place in their Church. In her childhood, the ceremonies of Christianity had been alien and incomprehensible; now, they were actively hostile. If she attended Mass these days, it was at her aunt's insistence. It was easier to sit in the Mayor's pew behind her cousins, teeth clenched and fists tight against her belly, enduring until she was set free, rather than fire up unwanted battles with Kaiese by refusing. The priests had set their own magic on their temples and cast out magicians who professed to serve no higher power. Pagan, atheist, agnostic—they made no distinction. She was a heretic and she was not welcome.

This was more than estrangement from Christianity: Wizards were not meant to give themselves to the service of any gods. Lord Redmantyl had taught her that faith distorted perception. The lessons of wizardry and the tenets of the Church contradicted each other; to maintain her power in one, she must disregard the other. The distraction of serving two practices would be her downfall. She mustn't involve herself in the rituals of any religion—observe, perhaps, but never participate. So, Laurel went to St. Matthieu's, but she didn't go to confession. She did not receive the Host.

No renouncement here: Laurel had left the Church long before apprenticeship. Its teachings of passivity, suffering, and unquestioning obedience were meaningless to her. Christianity explained itself: *It is this way because God wishes it so.* It gave her select information and said she must be content. But Laurel couldn't help her dissatisfaction. There were questions she needed answered. If there were truly an omnipotent being, how could it allow these Others to toy with her world? How could the Creator of the Heavens design that celestial doorway to permit their escape? Why create evil beings at all?

What was God? There were certainly greater-than-human forces, creatures of vast supernatural power, some benign, some malevolent, which had been deified over the millennia. People had made gods of the sun and moon, rain, river, and harvest. The Others, too, were called gods by some.

Her education had left many questions unanswered, but it satisfied her more than Church dogma.

Laurel did believe in a god—a Most High—but she suspected that this force was above the struggles of lesser beings: mortals, wizards, and Others. She knew that the universe was not as Church science would have it. Her uncle's books often depicted the orthodox diagram of an Earth-centered universe with the sun and moon and seven planets in subordinate orbits, but wizards didn't describe it so. Her own observations were likewise contradictory. She had touched only a fraction of the cosmos, yet she knew that it was far more complex. A god who had created the clockwork cycles of Ptolemy was a comprehensible thing; a god who designed the vast whirling glory of unbearable hot and cold she had glimpsed was far too strange to be understood. If it existed, it would no more interfere in their affairs than in the everyday doings of insects or mice or wildflowers. Therefore, belief contained no comfort. Why fall prostrate to a force that created and moved on, indifferent to its creation? It had banished the Others, but didn't act to prevent their return. It would not intervene for the protection of humanity. It would not help her.

She was an independent agent; enemies were everywhere. Ordinary folk spurned her. The Church had closed its doors against her kind. Other wizards were rivals; they did more than test each other for weakness in battle, she was certain. Western wizards were as jealous and vengeful as mortal warriors. Outside lay the worst of all.

As a wizard, she would always be alone. That was the nature of the magical: They set themselves apart, eschewing emotional bonds which might entangle and deter them from their purpose. She couldn't depend on any external strengths to bolster her. The only faith she could call hers was faith in the power she possessed. She must rely on that.

* * *

Some days after the Equinox, Laurel walked through the town with a familiar sensation of danger buzzing in her ears. It was nearby. Behind her– She turned in alarm. Nothing. No, wait. It *was* there.

A little guard marched past, a maiden smaller than regulation allowed and younger too, a child in her mother's uniform. Their eyes met. Laurel recoiled. The girl ascended to the guardspost above the gate without another glance; Laurel stared after her, heart thumping wildly. For a moment, she was frozen. Then, courage redoubled, she followed and sought one of the guards she knew.

"Who is that little girl?"

"Alys, Dam'sel?" The guard shrugged. "She's the sergeant's squire, come down from Storm Port."

"When?"

"Oh, months ago now."

"She's been here since last summer?" Laurel pressed.

The guard thought. "I didn't notice her myself, 'til them in the women's quarters began to talk. Wouldn't have her, but I couldn't tell ye why. She's a quiet lass. Not what I'd call a goodly-built guardsmaid, understand ye, Dam'sel—a little chit like that!—but she does as she's bid. Sergeant's made a pet of her. Promoted her proper into service, he did, when we had need of more hands at the winter."

"Alys," Laurel said. From Storm Port. A young maid, half her size, tawny cheeks and chin still round with childhood, not notably pretty, not especially plain. No one she might notice in a crowd. What more had she expected to discover? What, indeed.

This Alys had done nothing, said nothing. Honest folk would laugh to call her sinister. What crime was committed? What evil had the girl done? Was she murderous? Wanton? Cruel? Deceitful? Was she given to necromancy? She did not glow with magic. Rather, she was its opposite; she lacked even the natural energies of the magicless.

Laurel sought the sergeant next. A man who looked as if he had recently suffered an illness, he was immediately wary when she mentioned the girl. "My Alys? What d'ye want to say she's done now?"

"Nothing," Laurel explained. "I simply wondered. She seems so young to be in the guards–"

"Oh, I know how they talk," he interrupted as if she had not spoken. "I know how they whisper after her. Filthy-minded beggars! She's a good girl—I tell you that." He looked up; from the top of the gate, Alys smiled down at them. The sergeant's expression was disturbing, like a hopeless lover desperately seeking to please his unyielding beloved. "A good girl. I won't hear no wicked lies against her."

There was no evidence of evil, yet Laurel *felt* it. That absence of living energy concealed something grotesque. She shuddered when she met those night eyes, repulsed as she might be by a dead mouse accidentally trod underfoot or a cold, scaly water-thing brushing against her body in a stream. Her nerves thrilled with danger. She'd seen this girl before, watching and smiling secretly. She'd sensed this presence months ago, though she hadn't understood until now what it was. *This* was why she had come to New York.

nyne

Geyraulte came unexpectedly to the Mayor's Hall the next afternoon. Since he'd first breached Kaiese's parlor, he visited whenever he chose—after breakfast, long after dinner, any hour between. He made no excuse; he plainly came to gaze upon Igren. Laurel was entertained by these visits. Kaiese, she believed, wouldn't endure him in her house if he were not Nikholas's liege lord and Geyraulte, in return, was barely courteous to the Lady. The young nobleman was arrogant, rustic, brisk and impatient, outspoken when a more urbane man might keep his tongue. He was unaccustomed to courtship games. Kaiese's parlor refinements infuriated him. He could not woo with polite, useless words to a protective mother and competing suitors and no words of true heart to the maid he wished to win. He endured this foolishness to be near Igren. When he came, he would sit and stare at the maiden for hours, then leave as abruptly as he had arrived.

Nikholas also observed the courtship with amusement. "I should ask his intentions toward the lass, if I weren't so afraid of him," he declared, then left his wife to arrange matters with the lovestruck youth. But Kaiese was so anxious to be away from Geyraulte herself that she relaxed her proprieties and suggested that his Lordship might enjoy the Hall garden, a little patch of green between ivy-covered walls.

The breeze was chilly but the sun bright. The poplar trees, which blocked the scullery door and stable alley, unfolded their first leaflets and the first flowers pushed up from repaired beds. After icy months of winter, it seemed as if spring were finally upon them.

Geyraulte, given the opportunity to converse freely with his beloved, was suddenly lost for words. Boldness checked, he wandered the pebble paths at Igren's side. The unenvied task of chaperonage was left to Laurel. From her own romances, she knew that the duty consisted of staying in sight of the courting couple and reminding them to keep their behavior proper. This was absurd for Igren, who couldn't be improper even in private, but customs must be observed. Laurel stayed inconspicuously near the pair. Iobethe capered about on the slick grass; her little boots plunged through muddy puddles, splashing the new flowers and hedges. Laurel threw warning glances, but the girl was in high spirits, happy to be out in sunlight again and ready to brave her cousin's displeasure. Daring, she flung her cloak into the straggling survivors of last year's herbarium.

"Io, put that on!" Laurel scolded.

"But 'tis so fine out," the girl protested. "I'm not at all cold."

"It's not so warm as it seems. Have a care for yourself—I won't be blamed if you fall ill. Grown maids don't behave so babyishly."

Iobethe made a face, but she shook out the cloak and swung it over her shoulders.

In truth, Laurel was ready to cast aside her own cloak. The promise of this day made her impatient. Long winter, stifling her with merchant prejudices and parlor proprieties and months of waiting, was nearly at an end. She had found Alys; she could watch the girl, learn what she was, determine if there was truly any threat, and then her duty here was done. Soon, she would be able to leave New York. She would go home.

"Laurel, will you do something magical?" asked Io.

"Not for you," she refused bluntly. "After you carried tales of my apprenticeship, wicked little imp."

"I didn't, Laurel. Honestly."

Laurel glanced at Igren. "Who then?" Certainly, the girl must confess before leaving the blame to her sister.

But Iobethe shook her head, eyes wide and innocent. "I never said a word. Mama knew. She would have you return."

"She must know she can't keep me," said Laurel. "I chose to come and I shall leave whenever I wish." Kaiese watched from the parlor windows; she couldn't hear their words, but her eyes were upon them. "Very well, Cos." Laurel clapped her hands: bright lights burst around her, showering upwards and scattering the songbirds in the nearest trees. Iobethe laughed.

Geyraulte's eyes were large. "What manner of witchery is that?"

"It is no witchery," Igren answered. "My cousin is a magician. She is 'prenticed to our uncle, Lord Redmantyl."

"Good Lord's Mercy." The young Earl crossed himself.

"Tell me of the Northing, I pray you, My Lord," Igren said, placating. "I should like to visit one day."

"Would you?" He beamed at her, distracted.

"I have heard it is lovely."

"Ah, lovely!" Geyraulte dismissed the word. "Not so pretty as this." He waved a hand at the soggy garden. "'Tis hills and mountains and woodland, not thick with flowers. I daresay you'd call it rough."

With a gentle hand, Igren turned his attention away from her cousin's conjurings.

Sparks hissed on the wet grass.

"I should like to be a wizard," Iobethe said wistfully. "You can do such wondrous magic and blast everyone who's been mean to you with lightning, and you stay out all night if you want."

"Hush," Laurel answered this last. "I won't have you carry *that* tale either, Imp."

Iobethe pouted. "Laurel, I *didn't*–" but Laurel walked away. The spell-casting had not relieved her; rather, she felt all the more how she was caught here. Soon, she promised herself. Soon.

From the bower at the bottom of the garden, Geyraulte's voice rose earnestly. Once encouraged, he spoke well enough.

"–filthy pile. I don't care much for the cities nor the city-folk, Dam'sel. I've seen 'em and I prefer my own people. We don't have these dances and festivals every other day as you do here. No, our ladies like a modest amusement. My mother's most particular to the needlecrafts. I see that you like that sort of task yourself, Dam'sel. You're always at something fancy. Most pretty, I call it. A Lady's proper work. My gran'ther's made a garden about our Isolde Chapel— the ladies of Oerykton have their chapel outside the castle and Gran'ther's planted the yard with willows and roses. 'Twas before I was born, and the trees are all big now. She calls it a fitting place for prayer, and you might think so too if you saw it, if you wish to."

Igren would not meet his eyes.

The girls went upstairs to dress for dinner. When they returned, the parlor door was shut and murmuring beyond told that Kaiese was at last in conference with their guest. Suddenly, Geyraulte roared: "What do you mean, Lady?"

Kaiese's reply was too soft to be distinguished. Igren took her cousin's arm.

In the parlor, Geyraulte's voice rose again in oaths of disgust. The door snapped open and the young Earl burst out. He met Igren's eyes, outraged, desperate, and opened his mouth as if he would speak, but Kaiese came to the doorway behind him and he turned away and left the house without a farewell.

The Lady blazed as Laurel did in her worst tempers. "Igren, you are to have no more to do with that man," she said, "unless he offers for you properly."

Igren's eyes filled with tears and her fingers on Laurel's arm tightened. "You told me I could not hope to do better, Mama."

"I erred then, my pet. Perhaps you may. We mustn't give away the game too quickly. If he imagines he may have you as he will because you are a merchant-daughter and child of his vassal, he thinks wrongly." She patted the girl's cheek gently. "Hush now, Daughter. Don't fret for that one. If he's worthy of you, he'll return. If not, there are others. Think of them!"

Once she had discovered the anomaly of Alys, Laurel pursued her mission zealously, but unobtrusively. Though she no longer served as an auxiliary, she frequented the garrison and visited the guardians' favored haunts, initiating casual chats with whomever she could. She listened to gossip. She eavesdropped. She observed. She loitered at the gateposts and patrolled the streets and wandered the walls, hoping to catch sight of that little squire in outsized soldier's garb.

She rarely asked a direct question, for the guards were ready to discuss any oddity in their ranks with little encouragement. The girl the sergeant had taken in was a persistent topic. Rumors were fantastic and contradictory. Within a week, Laurel had learned that Alys was the sergeant's kin and ward, that she was his minion, that she had seduced the unwary male, young maid as she was, that she had witched him, that she had been a Storm Port barmaid, that she had simply appeared in the garrison one day, in uniform, without training, that she never spoke of her life before New York, that she could foretell the future, that none of the other guardswomen would lodge with her, that she was sneaky, that she was a cool little liar, that she put curses on her enemies, that she was always missing on the nights of witches' sabbats, that she was wickedness itself, though no one could point to a specific example of depravity.

The sergeant-at-arms himself was protective of the girl, as if he had found a rare treasure. His Alys was a poor foundling, he insisted, so small, so fragile, so helpless alone—how could his fellow guards make up such horrid lies about his sweet child? Laurel wondered what the true bond lay between this man and that odd little maid. The haunted, haggard look she'd first observed persisted, as if his illness had begun to eat him away from the inside.

Laurel heard all this, and didn't know what to believe. There was no reliable source of information, except for the object of her investigation. It was time for a confrontation.

But Alys remained maddeningly elusive, as if she knew she was hunted and so made herself unseen. She wasn't at her post. She wasn't at the garrison hall. She'd been in the tavern, but departed minutes before Laurel arrived. There were glimpses, no more, and the girl was gone.

Nevertheless, Laurel chased the mystery undaunted. This was the reason her uncle had sent her to New York. She must learn everything she could of Alys. She tried to comprehend the phenomenon of this strange child. When she'd left Wizardes Cliff on her inexact quest, she'd imagined she sought some creature, misshaped and monstrous, spawn of the Outside, which hid in the back streets and alleys and preyed upon innocent citizens. It had been a surprise to discover an ordinary little maiden, not a monster, was the source of Redmantyl's disquiet. But was Alys an ordinary maiden? Why, then, was there this feeling of danger? Why did she shudder at the sight of the girl? What was the meaning of the unnatural, inexplicable nullity which cloaked her? Since she'd become aware of Alys, Laurel imagined that the girl must have obtained a piece of stellar material. She had read that stones and metals which fell from the skies were possessed of peculiar properties unlike anything known on earth; perhaps Alys had picked up such a heaven-born meteorite as a curiosity and wore it as an amulet, and so it had gained some aberrant influence over her.

She didn't think the girl was a magician. Laurel knew she would have sensed a magical presence if one had existed so near her. She saw the glamour about her aunt and cousin, disused as their magic was; when she bothered to cast her senses in search of them, they were easy to locate. She *felt* her uncle, the bright aura of his power, hundreds of miles away. Alys, however, had no such glamour. She was dead of light, as dark to the psychic senses as unliving mass– No, more than unliving mass. An absence of all energies. It was as if she wasn't there, a tiny speck like the void between the stars. Laurel didn't wonder that the girl had gone undetected for so long. It was more strange that she should suddenly burst through, boldly revealed. Had Alys deliberately made herself known? If so, then why did she continue to hide? Alys alone knew the answers to these questions. She must be found.

Laurel began to believe it a hopeless task: Alys's lack of living energies made her difficult to detect, impossible to seek within the teems of humanity in the town. Alys had hidden from her for months and might hide for months more. The girl might leave town unnoticed. She might have already gone. Laurel was prepared to report all she'd learned to her uncle and relinquish her charge. She'd done what was expected. What more could Lord Redmantyl ask?

Then she felt that thrill of danger and knew that her quarry was nearby.

She stopped in the Mayor's Parade and turned swiftly; there was no sign of Alys behind her. But she wasn't far away. Laurel was certain of it. She ran around a corner, to the end of the street before the Matthieu parvis. Across the green, a small figure just passed from the shadow of the church, exiting the passageway behind. The little squire didn't look up, nor even glance over her shoulder to acknowledge her adversary, but Laurel felt that Alys was aware of her. It was as if she had been called.

She ran to catch her. Alys walked briskly down toward the Kalligate and the river, in the direction of the women's quarters. Too many people crowded the wide street. The small body slipped through easily. Laurel pushed and leapt, ignoring the indignant looks and shouts of the commonfolk as she passed. She couldn't let this chance slip away. Alys was still so far ahead. She was losing the sense of her. She was about to lose sight of her. The dark little figure turned into one of the narrow streets before the gate, the oldest part of town where the gables of ancient houses met overhead. The Tunnels.

Laurel struggled to that side of the broad street and slipped along, against the shop doorways, to reach the passageway where the girl had disappeared. Patches of dark and light dappled the length of the enclosed lane. Alys was at the far end, back to her, walking away.

"Guardsmaid!" she shouted.

Alys stopped and waited.

For the first time, they met face to face. The girl was even more childlike at close examination: body undeveloped, limbs thin and bony, face babyish. She didn't come up to Laurel's breastbone.

"Who are you?" Laurel asked.

"Alys of Lyngreen, an it please ye." The voice was girlish, guileless, even timid, but the eyes laughed.

"Lyngreen was burned." Laurel recalled Klyffaude's words: *Not a house left standing. They say a child caused it.* At the time, she'd imagined some carelessness, an accident at the hearth, but when she met those mocking night eyes she knew that it wasn't so. Every evil thing she had imagined of Alys was true.

"Yes, long ago."

"What are you?" she whispered.

"You know."

"No, I don't. Tell me. I must know."

"I am like you."

"Are you a magician?"

The girl laughed. "No. I'd like to be."

She walked on to the next narrow street, into long shadows. Laurel kept at her side, stealing perplexed glances. There was no amulet about Alys's throat nor dangling at her leathern belt. She could discern no spell. Yet the void encloaked the child entirely. Laurel saw her, heard her voice and the click of her boots on the cobbles. If she touched her, she knew she would find a creature of flesh and blood. But she sensed no heartbeat, no thought nor emotion, no living essence. She might almost believe that she faced nothing more substantial than mist. "Why have you come here?" she asked.

"To find you."

This reply jarred: Alys had come to New York before her.

"You know who I am?"

"I do," Alys answered. "You're the white knight with sword of flame. I've dreamt of you. I knew you'd come. I waited for you." At the end of the Tunnels, a shaft of afternoon light fell over the roofs of the warehouses and into the work-yard above the town's docks. "I watched you," said Alys. "When you first came to the town. They said I must be on my guard. You meant me harm."

"Who said this?"

Alys smiled up at her with something that looked like honest, youthful admiration. "But I'm not afraid of you. I wanted to meet you."

"For what reason?"

"You know. 'Tis why you've come too." Alys gathered up the hems of her too-long cloak and ran across the yard.

She knew what Alys was.

Laurel, shivering, paced the floor of her darkened room that night. For hours, that enigmatic conversation had puzzled her. What could it mean? Was Alys only playing with her odd replies? Was the concealment of her own making, or was it beyond her control? Had she foreseen Laurel's arrival as she claimed, in her dreams, even before Laurel had been sent to New York? How could she know? The powers of prescience were not possessed by ordinary folk. Alys was not a magician. Was she? Laurel had spent hours trying to untangle candor and evasion from deliberate lie. Now, she understood.

Lord Redmantyl had explained to her what the Others sought: *They will take a soul for their purposes, if the soul is weak or willing.* They sought to extend their power into this sphere through a mortal captured or one who offered itself. Alys was such a soul. Worse, she might be a renegade magician. Through her, They would gain their foothold. Her concealment was to that purpose: She hid her magic, hid her thoughts, hid her existence, hid her purpose from the psychic gaze of wizards who would try to stop her and destroy her. Somehow, she'd learned of inhuman powers which sought human service. If rumor was truth, she attended the nights of Wizard's Keep. She awaited the opportunity to be taken.

This was unimaginable horror to Laurel, though she knew from her studies that it had been sought by others before. It was madness, but to what end? Why?

What must it be like to be a puppet dangling at a master's strings? Was there security in knowing that the worst had already happened? That the soul was destroyed but, somehow, the body went on? In their grip, Alys would be protected from lesser injury. Nothing could harm her. She needn't worry what fate awaited; that was sealed for eternity. One who gave herself to such vast forces would likewise possess power, not her own, at her own command to employ as she chose, but power beyond that any mortal magician wielded. What could such a servant do at their bidding! What destruction might that little maiden unleash! There were people lost and angry who hated humanity and yearned to shake it from its complacency. There were those refused by the ranks of wizardry who sought revenge. There were those mad. *They* would find this prospect attractive. They would glory in the ruin. To be the agency of destruction was more desirable than to be one of the defenders who fought to keep chaos at bay.

This was more than Laurel was ready to cope with alone. Her uncle wouldn't have her face down a mortal enemy so soon; he'd promised that she was meant only to observe and report and that he would come to her if she needed him.

At the edge of her bed, amulet clenched between her hands and pressed to her brow, eyes squeezed shut, Laurel called out to Wizardes Cliff. She sent an urgent message, a mixture of words, images, sensations that summarized her problem. Lord Redmantyl would know what to do.

The reply was only the most vague instruction, but Laurel understood. The responsibility was hers. Alys mustn't have the opportunity to give herself over at May Night. Laurel saw that she must use whatever means were available to prevent it.

She returned to her bed but she didn't sleep.

***

When Ambris returned to New York, he was at the Mayor's Hall as often as Rosandre. No longer eager to return to Eadeshire, he lingered in town for more than a week with no sign of hasty departure. He sent instructions to his steward, but didn't speak of following them. It didn't escape Laurel's notice that he sought her out especially. She was pleased that he'd chosen to befriend her; through his words, she was admitted to worlds she longed to see once she had escaped New York and completed her education. Ambris had traveled as much as Lord Redmantyl. He knew as much of London and Paris and Rome. But where Redmantyl spoke of alchemical laboratories in Malta and mountain strongholds of ancient Asian magicians, of Stonehenge and Tianhuanaco, Ambris spoke of grand palaces and courtly intrigues and monarchs he called Cousin. He told her of baby elephants in the royal gardens of Dongola, of winter balls at Kiev, of missives to the Pope. He'd spent his childhood at the court of his uncle, Kharles IV, and later, as a young lawyer, had traveled on diplomatic journeys in the Emperor's service. He had served as adjutant to the Royal Ambassador at Venice and stayed in the Grand Doge's Palace—the Doge was a cousin—then acted as special emissary to the Dowager Empress Marianne and her son, Prince Juan Maria of Navarre. Before he was twenty-eight, his career had been spectacular; upon his marriage, he had been granted Eadeshire.

"My father and uncle brought me forward as if I were a rightborn Prince," he told her. "Indeed, there was a time of my childhood that I imagined... I didn't truly understand 'til Mara was born that I would not be Duke."

They had stopped at a tavern during a chilly walk. The only customers at midday, Laurel sat on a table, legs folded beneath her, and Ambris, encouraged by her informality, leaned against the bar.

"You don't bear resentment?" she asked.

"Against whom?"

"Your father."

"He has done all he can for me," Ambris answered. "He's never treated me as less than his child. Few men can be said to do so much for their bastards. We have our obligations and loyalties as any father and son."

"I wouldn't know duty nor loyalty to a father," said Laurel. "What of Margueryt?"

"When she is Duke, I shall give her my allegiance."

"What of your mother?" she pressed, doubting his impartiality. In his situation, she was certain she would feel cheated. "You never speak of her, My Lord. Who was she?"

These were impertinent, prying questions, but Laurel thought she might ask them. Though she'd been brought up to respect and fear the nobility, it was impossible to fear for offending Ambris. She realized that she was sometimes unabashedly rude to him, but he didn't freeze into injured dignity. If he scolded, it was with playfulness. He wasn't as she imagined the Duke's son ought to be—haughty, self-important, and supercilious. Instead, his manner was inviting and confidential. He would tell her, if she wished to know.

"My mother?" said Ambris. "I thought that tale was well-known, but the time is nearly fifty years past and you are young, Maiden, and astonishingly ignorant of courtly matters."

Laurel grinned. "I could never care for it, My Lord. 'Twas no one I knew."

"Well, my mother was a gentyl-maid of my grandfather's last wife, the Infanta Marianne, and came with her from Navarre."

"A Spaniard?" Laurel spoke with the usual Norman horror at the mention of Spain. So this was the explanation for Ambris's Mediterranean complexion!

"A maid of Pamplona, of common birth. No one. The Redlyon would not consent to their marriage, of course. He had hopes of a better match for his Prince of the Northlands and so sent her from the court before the love-affair became a scandal. There are rumors: she returned to her homeland, she went to a nunnery, she wed another man, she became a dancer in a traveling troupe. I know not if any tale is true. After the Redlyon's death, she came to Pendaunzel and my father was beloved of her again as if they'd never been parted. He spoke of betrothal, but she refused him that honor. Then, she was gone. He heard nothing from her for more than a year, until at last the priests at Belminstre sent news to him. I had been left there, with a note and a ring which he'd given her. Father came to be assured that I was truly his and he brought me to Pendaunzel."

"I have heard this tale," Laurel said. "'Tis a ballad played by the minstrels, but there are no names to it." As if to prove it, she sang a few lines:

"My Lord's Love has gone again.
O where is she now? O where has she gone?
She's left My Lord heartsore and all forlorn.
O whither she? Whither she? Who?

"What became of her? Do you know, My Lord?"

"I've seen her," Ambris answered. "She visited me once at Oxford when I read for the law, and she came to Eadbury a few years ago to see the children. Where she lives otherwise, I cannot say. I've never cared to know." At Laurel's surprise, he explained: "She is the woman who birthed me, but I am not obliged to love her. My Layn Gillefleure and the Empress Penelope were always more motherly to me."

"I should have liked to know my mother," said Laurel. "She left me too, when I was small. They say that she was a wicked woman."

"Wanton?"

"Yes, *that*, but more too, I think. Perhaps witchery. The old guards who remember her say that she knew something of spellcraft. She wasn't magical, but hedge-witches don't need to be. I don't want to imagine what mischief she might have been up to. The Council sent her from the garrison to be rid of her."

"She died in the Marches."

"My aunt speaks of her to everyone, except to me," Laurel observed dryly. "I've only my own memories of her, and no father at all. I might so easily have been left by the pixies."

Ambris laughed. The alekeeper's maid glanced up at him, then returned to her sweeping the spaces between the empty tables.

"Why do you imagine she didn't wed him?" Laurel wondered. "Your mother. She might've been Duquinge of the Northlands and you rightfully My Gracious Lord's heir."

"Perhaps some impediment kept her from it," he answered. "She may have acted for *his* good. A Norman Prince cannot marry a Spanish peasant without some ramifications. Perhaps my father's station meant nothing to her. You, Maid, would not yourself wed merely for the distinction of a match with a Plantagenet."

"Yes, but if I had a child I think I should readily move the Heavens for his betterment. I should marry regardless of my feelings, or lie to my lover if I were already wed elsewhere. At least, I would stand by my child to protect him. She might've done as much for you. Yet you do not bear grudge against her?"

"What would that accomplish?" Ambris asked. "All has passed, years ago. I do not dislike my mother and I am able to do her the justice to think that she has reasons, untold, for what she's done. What benefit to me if I wish it had been different? I am content with my place. It is not so miserable a thing to be known as a just magistrate, trustworthy councilor, and loyal son."

"You are all of those, truly," Laurel said. "Everyone speaks of you with highest praise. But you might have had so much more."

"I was not made for a higher place."

"No, your proper place is Eadeshire."

"If I were meant for more, I should have it. But I am not. I am meant by my nature to give myself to the service of my family, as Mara is meant to be Duke. We have our proper places. If we are not born there, we seek it. That is the stability of the Empire. Imagine—if those common-born but especially clever are left to drudge all their lives with no hope of employing their talents, their discontent will make them rebellious. And if the mean and stupid are given positions of power, it is disastrous. It is the duty of all Norman citizens to cry against an unfit governor."

Laurel thought this sounded subversive. "So, if our Kharles were–"

"I speak theoretically," Ambris answered abruptly. "It is unwise to name a living Emperor unfit without good reason."

The young woman was silenced for only a moment. "What of those who are not proper anywhere?" she began again.

"If they are fit for no part in Norman society, they go to the Free Folk. That is what Free Folk are—those who do not belong elsewhere. The thespers and carnival troupes are more organized than most, though they have odd fellows and rogues in their company too. Or such people travel to the wilderness or go to sea until they find their right place in the greater world. Everyone has a place if they are permitted to find it. You've said as much yourself, my dear girl—My Lady Kaiese and My Lord Redmantyl were born of simple folk."

"A milling family," Laurel provided what little she knew of her family's history.

"Yet they are not millers now. Think what two such formidable creatures would be if they remained so against their inclination and abilities."

"Uncle Redmantyl would be miserable," she agreed. "He says that if you are magical, responsibility for that power cannot be escaped. You can never be content with any other lot. I know for myself that I couldn't wish to be anything save a wizard. Yet we are all magical, My Lord. My aunt has some talent, but she will not use it."

"'Tis pity," said Ambris. "I think she would be a woman more at ease if she did."

This was a new idea for Laurel. She'd always imagined that Kaiese was angry and officious because she was– Well, because she was Kaiese and therefore possessed these qualities. Laurel had never considered that there might be a reason. "I think that if I were her, I should go mad," she said.

Ambris seemed to understand. "You shan't be here much longer, Laurel," he said with some sympathy. "And, when you go, I shall miss you."

She smiled at him. "Surely you'll remain my friend?"

"Of course. If you wish."

With warmer weather, the prominent dames of New York and Kallaykirke went abroad again, braving the mud to visit and to share the news they had kept through the snowy months. They called upon Kaiese as the Mayor's Lady, but they didn't receive her as one of their own. Beneath centuries of proper, codified Norman manners, they despised her as deeply as their children scorned her niece. From her seat at the parlor window, Laurel observed. She imagined she'd been witness to such scenes since her childhood, but had been too lost in her own hurt at each snub to see that it was not her alone: it was all her family, herself, her aunt, her long-dead mother, even Igren—if any could truly treat Igren with contempt. The guests addressed the gentle maid as *Uindaughter* rather than *Damosel*.

Perhaps, Laurel thought, this dislike had begun long before her birth. She'd heard the story often enough: Thirty years ago, Nikholas Uinmerchant had been a wealthy young man, sole heir to his family's fortune and naturally a marriage prize to the daughters of the town's great merchant houses. Many of the staid matrons in this room, then hopeful maidens, had paid coy court to the eligible youth but none had taken him. Then, Kaiese had come to visit her sister Tomasin in the garrison and met Nikholas. She immediately succeeded where all others had failed. It still stung that this newcomer to the town, a miller's daughter, had snatched the Uinmerchant from their midst. The dames attributed Kaiese's success to magic. They pointed to the success of all her husband's ventures. They whispered of her cousin, Lord Redmantyl, and her wild sister behind her back. Nikholas too spoke of how Kaiese had ensorcelled him—a cynical jest, but Laurel wondered if it were, indeed, true.

Kaiese was snubbed for her magical connections, her low birth, her wild sister, and her own strange fairness. She didn't have the decency to behave as a proper merchantwoman. She didn't disguise her ambition and held herself with a subtle aloofness which implied that she was their superior and deserved better things. She welcomed noble visitors as no other Mayor possessed the conceit to invite, and made efforts for her daughters above their own matchworthy boys. As if proud of her alien appearance, she refused to cover her head with veil and wimple in the manner of well-bred dames, but braided and piled her long silver plaits into a glorious crown. Men found her overwhelmingly attractive; they admired Kaiese and envied Nikholas his good fortune. To the Dame Cornmerchants, Furriers, other Uinmerchants, this was unforgivable.

Laurel did, decidedly, pity her aunt. How could Kaiese bear these dagger-laden smiles and insult-shaded courtesies? The dames chattered endlessly—who had brought their prices up by two-pence, whose daughters would soon be betrothed, how delightful the tea-cakes were, how much they spent on repairing their gardens or purchasing new draperies—with avarice unconcealed. After these long months, Laurel found it intolerable. Kaiese had lived amidst it for years. She might've had so much more if she hadn't refused her magic and taken up a way of life which a true magician must despise. All was done of her own choice, her design, but did that misused talent urge her to discontent? Did she feel her mistake?

This afternoon, the parlor was crowded. The Sheriff's wife with her younger son and unmarried daughters had descended upon Kaiese's hospitality and brought with them that intertwining of cousins and associates which made up the best society of the town. No seat was unoccupied. Serving-girls brought in tray after tray of dainties and darted in and out to bring in fresh brandywine and new pots of hot tea and the hostess dispensed these refreshments as graciously as she might to welcome friends. No one spoke above a murmur, but the combined effect was clamorous. Councillor Jehane and Portia Paperpresser whispered poisonously in the corner. Rosandre wandered, charming as always with his Frankish "My Dames" and "My Damosels" as he gave polite attention to the merchant-wives and daughters and left each one smiling after him. Martin abandoned his mother at the hearth to pay court to Igren, but the maiden was no more than civil to him. These rebuffed efforts particularly amused Laurel. Igren did not tease; she was simply indifferent and her thoughts lay elsewhere. Geyraulte had not been to the Mayor's Hall in a fortnight.

Martin, aware of her smirk, turned from his attempts to draw Igren into conversation to seek revenge. "Do you know, Laurel, how I fretted for your pretty cousin? That Goldsmith of Storm Port calls so often I feared she would be given to the old wreck. 'Twas pleasure to hear that he comes for you."

"He hasn't!"

Martin only laughed in reply.

"Liar!" she hissed after him, then spoke to her cousin. "What a horror he is! Did you hear?"

Igren had, and ducked her head.

"Igren, it is a lie?" But she knew that it was not. "Why didn't you tell me?"

"I– I never knew surely–"

"But you might've spoken!" Laurel's voice was rising.

"I thought you must see for yourself," the girl continued through this outburst.

Kaiese, at her tea-table, lifted her eyes in a brief, chilling stare. Laurel glared back, but she could not speak. Others, nearby, glanced up in disapproval. From his place at his mother's shoulder, Martin was grinning. She left the room.

She sought her uncle in his office.

"Is it true? The Goldsmith?"

Nikholas blinked at the interruption. "I know that he likes the look of you, but he's not made an offer," he answered. "But I daresay if your aunt wants him to, he will. He's returned to our town today. Perhaps it's for that reason. Ought I give my blessings?"

"Not to that wicked old thing!"

"Ah, you object?"

"I bloody well do!"

"Have a care with your language, Niece. Well, if you don't like it, take it up with your aunt. `Tis her matchmaking and if you aren't quick to stop her, she'll be about ordering the wedding clothes. Are you certain you won't have him? He's not a sensible man, I think, but I can't fault him for it. He'd be fool enough to ask for My Lady herself and bargain for more than he thinks to gain."

"He's so old."

"Many men are a bit older than their brides."

"He's older than you, Uncle!"

"All the better, I'd think. A young girl as you are might wed the old raise-hell and be widowed quick enough, and have the Goldsmith's gold without the fuss of him about the house," Nikholas answered. "Most women would consider that reason enough to marry, you know. But if it's not to your liking, you must go to your aunt. `Tis her arrangement and no concern to me one way or the other." He picked up his pen. "Do as you will."

It was Kaiese's arrangement; she must confront her aunt. Nikholas was indifferent. Even if he cared, he wouldn't intervene against his wife's wishes. Laurel sat at the top of the stairs and waited, watching as one guest after another departed and, at last, Kaiese stood alone in the entrance hall.

"I hear that the Goldsmith has returned to town," she spoke.

The Lady looked up. Her lips pressed tightly together.

"Did you invite him? To ask for me? Aunt Kaiese, if you imagine I will agree to such an arrangement, you are past madness."

"Do not shout through my house," Kaiese replied frostily. "I will have no insolence from you, Girl." She turned and swept back to her parlor. The housemaids who had come to clean up were startled by her unexpected return, but at her command, "go now," they fled. Laurel came to the doorway.

"You haven't yet, but you will. The Goldsmith, Aunt?"

Kaiese's mouth turned down at one corner. "Do you think I act to spite you? The match is all to your advantage. The Goldsmith has a great name in Storm Port and wealth to give a wife the luxuries of a noblewoman. And what will he receive in return? You! Nameless, dowerless, willful and ill-behaved. Who are you to be proud and refuse?"

"Who am I to be given? I have no part in your schemes. Can you not bear to surrender Igren to that man and his advantages, or will he not have her?"

This was nothing more than an angry snap; Laurel had spoken without any thought but insult, but Kaiese's singular reply—"Be silent, Brat!"—told her she had stung more deeply. The Goldsmith did prefer her; Kaiese was sore for that, but she was ready to make the best of the situation.

But what reason could Leobolde Goldsmith have for wanting her? Not greed nor lust; Igren was both more wealthy and more attractive than herself. Igren was also more compliant. Any man who liked a peaceful home would choose a wife he could command. Certainly, this man would demand it. Laurel could think of only one reason why the Goldsmith should prefer her to her pretty, wealthy, docile cousin: she was in vigorous health while Igren was frail.

She asked as much, and Kaiese answered frankly.

"Your cousins are not strong girls. If either had such wit or will as yours—perversely misused as they are—what might be done with them! But they are silly, gentle creatures. I am left to do my best to find them suitable husbands. Good Lord be praised that men are so foolish to see only beauty and nothing of substance." The Lady, however, would not forget her point. "The Goldsmith is a marvelous opportunity," she persisted. "Think, Child! He would care for a wife splendidly. You'd have a grand house of your own and more wealth than any common-born Northlander can claim. Carriages, servants, a place in Storm Port akin to Lady. You might have all the city at your feet. I have asked the Goldsmith to our house tomorrow. Show some appreciation for your own best interests and welcome him. Don't make a fool of yourself—or me!"

"Would you have him, Aunt?"

"I would."

Laurel knew that she spoke the truth. Kaiese's ambition for her relations was only a step behind her ambitions for herself. It didn't matter that Leobolde Goldsmith was past sixty, that his words revealed his cold-blooded heart and his eyes told of deeper cruelty. Kaiese would marry him. She sought to take through marriage the greater realm which she might have rightfully taken for herself. As she sought to rule New York, so she might have ruled Storm Port. She expected that no reasonable woman would behave differently.

"I would rather have that for Igren—I cannot lie—but *you* rather than some greedy little vixen of no connection to me."

"I won't marry anyone, *ever*," Laurel answered. "If I desire riches, I can take them as a lordling in my own right once I am a wizard like my Uncle Redmantyl. *He* commands far more than Storm Port. It is far better to be a wizard than a merchant's wife."

"Little fool! Do you know what you say? Magic may make you a lordling, but only after years of danger and sure corruption to the soul. You'd live on the road like a beggar and fight for your life at every turn. A husband will give you position the moment you are wed. Thankless, *thankless* brat!" she spat. "You are ungrateful for everything I've done if you abandon all you might have for that taint of our blood."

"I have heard that same cry of my ingratitude for all my life and I am weary of it!" Laurel shot back. "What have you ever done for my sake? You treat me as if I were no blood of yours and a burden upon your charity! You bully me because I will not bend to your will, then try to sell me off to whatever wealthy old letch might grasp when 'tis to your profit, and for this I must express unending gratitude! No more! I owe you nothing!"

"I might have left you to the streets or sent you to the Sisters where they deal most harshly with *our* kind. Instead, I took you in. I brought you away from that mother of yours—'tis pain to speak so of my own sister, but she was wicked! Unnatural. She sought things abominable. What she did– No, I will not tell you. Our kind has no right place. We are chidden of God. I tried to save you from that, but you are tainted with that same corruption that destroyed her. Already you meddle in affairs no mortal ought to. Oh, I know what you are about on the witches' sabbats. You are damned if you follow that path. Know it, Girl! Know well what you do!"

An unpleasant scent of scorched fabric rose from the walls and floor as their furies met. Then Laurel remembered her pity. If she cast aside her abilities as Kaiese had done, she would feel crippled, as if she were only half of what she ought to be. Kaiese might've had all the power she desired, and more, if she hadn't been afraid. Wizardry had its dangers, true, but Laurel knew it was better to fly as an eagle and fight other eagles than to always remain on the ground and pretend to be one of the barnyard fowl. Kaiese had chosen the latter; Laurel might despise cowardice, but this was truly more pathetic than despicable.

She spoke more calmly. "I am not like you, Aunt. My ambition lies elsewhere. I am not afraid of my power and I will not refuse it even if it holds danger. I will have nothing to do with your Goldsmith. I pray you, do not encourage him. Do not invite him here."

"You forbid me guests to my own house?"

"If he comes again, I will leave."

"Prideful little wretch. Lucifer's fall, and be damned." Kaiese shook her head. "Go then! Seek your doom, and blessed riddance if you find it."

Kaiese and Nikholas had had seven children together. Laurel remembered a boy older than Igren and a baby girl born the year before Iobethe. Sarellen, younger than Io, had died at the age of eight. All were buried in the St. Matthieu churchyard with two elder children Laurel hadn't known. She and Igren used to gather flowers to place on the lengthening row of little graves and read the names inscribed there: Uaine, Elsabethe, Arian, Lyde.

It was tragic, yes, to lose five children but not unusual. Many families—merchant, noble, and common—were so stricken. The great houses customarily celebrated a child's seventh birthday, for one who survived infancy might well live to maturity. The seventh birthday was an event only less important than the fourteenth, when a child was confirmed, or the twenty-first, when a child came of age.

Nikholas acknowledged that he was of a weak bloodline; he'd been the only child of the Uinmerchants to thrive and his children were notoriously vulnerable. They caught cold easily. Fevers and chills came upon them without warning. Laurel recalled how her aunt had worried over Igren's delicate health and fretted at every cough of Iobethe. There had never been such fussing for her.

Laurel hadn't considered herself a part of Kaiese's matchmaking. She had no dowry; she was too tall and robust to be comely and too outspoken and forward in her manner to be pleasing to gentle folk; her mother was unimportant and her father unknown; her more reputable aunt and uncle did not favor her. While rumor might whisper of the advantages of receiving a magician-lover, wizards were not reputed to make good wives. She was never encouraged to think herself a marriageable maiden and had never been pushed at prospective suitors as Igren and Iobethe were. No one had given her more than polite attention and if there was too much of that, Kaiese distracted the young men with references to Igren's charms. Laurel had noticed that the Goldsmith took an unseemly interest in her, but she imagined that Kaiese intended him for Igren or wanted him simply for the prestige his company brought to their house. She knew, too, that he was fascinated by Kaiese's exotic fairness and admired her personal power; he may have come to win the Lady's favor. Regardless of Kaiese's reasons for having him visit so often, Laurel hadn't thought that her aunt encouraged the Goldsmith for her. But, as Kaiese had honestly answered, better her than no one. *She* could give her aunt an alliance to this wealthy merchant, and give him what he wanted in the bargain.

The reference to strength was well understood. Leobolde Goldsmith was an aging man with enormous wealth and no heir. He had stated quite openly in parlor conversation that he had married twice and fathered no living child and it was obvious, even if he didn't say so, that he blamed his wives for this. If he wed again, he desired a wife in the best health.

She suspected that her aunt had called her from Wizardes Cliff for this reason. Her magic was not at issue. Kaiese rarely mentioned her apprenticeship and, when she did, it wasn't to scold. So long as Laurel kept control of her temper and didn't set fire to the drapes, the Lady didn't care what talents she employed or concealed. Laurel could even imagine Kaiese presenting her daughters to the Goldsmith, who dismissed them as unpromising, and Kaiese, not anxious to lose such an opportunity, recalling that she had a niece.

Laurel left the Mayor's Hall. Though it was dusk, she was ready to take her palfrey from the stable and fly immediately. She must get away from here, quickly, before she became entangled in her aunt's schemes. She walked, thoughts turning wildly, until she waded into the muddy pond of the market square. In the fading twilight, the torches of the Goldbell Inn, where Ambris stayed, glowed invitingly. She splashed her way to the porch; the innkeeper directed her to the common room.

She brushed down the unlit corridor to the room above the kitchen, then paused. Ambris was singing softly, thoughtfully, verses to the song about his mother:

> *Has she gone to the Sisters to pray to the saint?*
> *O where is she now? O where has she gone?*
> *Our Lady forgives what My Lord mayn't.*
> *O whither she? Whither she? Who?*

> *Has she gone to thespers to join in their dance?*
> *O where is she now? O where had she gone?*
> *Embracing the rushlight of fancied romance.*
> *O whither she? Whither she? Who?*

Laurel stepped to the doorway. A minstrel who had been in town throughout the winter sat at the hearth, fingers light on the lutestrings. Ambris stood at the windows, smiling as if well aware of his absurdity. Imagine, noble liege singing for the entertainment of troubadour! The minstrel joined in the chorus:

> *"My Lord's Love has gone again.*
> *O where is she now? O where has she gone?*
> *She's left My Lord heartsore and all forlorn.*
> *O whither she? Whither she? Who?*

> *Has she sailed to her homeland far o'er the sea?*
> *O where is she now? O where has she gone?*
> *For a Spaniard's heart 'tis won and lost easily.*
> *O whither she? Whither she? Who?*

> *Will she return to him, My Lord's Love?*
> *O where is she now? O where has she gone?*
> *Will he embrace her–"*

He turned and saw her. "Laurel." He smiled, then observed her expression of pain and outrage. "Laurel, what is it?"

The minstrel discreetly left them.

"My Lord, I am come to bid you farewell."

"You leave?"

"Tomorrow," her voice shook slightly.

"Alone? Laurel, you cannot. I have seen the road to Storm Port and it is no place for a lone traveler. Only think how the Greenwaters Island roads will be, for they are dirty little paths even in the best weather. Your palfrey is a delicate beast, meant for a maiden's ride. 'Twould be more safe to walk yourself."

"Then I shall! I must go! I cannot bear the Mayor's Hall another day."

"What's happened?"

"My aunt has been courting Leobolde Goldsmith for me."

"The moneylender from Storm Port?"

"Odious old wretch! But she thinks him a splendid match." Laurel lifted her chin imperiously, in a fair imitation of Kaiese. "It is impossible that any maid of good sense—and no dowry—would refuse such opportunity. He comes to the Mayor's Hall tomorrow. If the lecherous beast dares lay a paw on me, I'll run him through!"

She lay a hand at her hip as if she sought the hilt of her sword, but it wasn't there. "Damn him to hellfire!" She twisted in unspent rage and slammed her arm against the mantelpiece.

Ambris watched her fury and distress, then rose from his seat, resolved. "Will you receive advice?" he offered.

"What advice do you have to give?" Laurel shot back.

"Only this, Maiden: it is not good to act on the impulse."

"But I must go!"

"Perhaps, but not as you plan to fly now, unprepared." He took her shoulders and gently brushed the sweep of a white tress from her face. "Be calm. I think you are in no immediate danger." He smiled. "My Lady has not accepted the moneylender?"

"No," Laurel agreed. "She cannot. I am no little maid to be given against her will!"

"Indeed you are not. Return to the Mayor's Hall, Laurel, and sleep. You may think better of this in the morning."

Laurel was angry, but she knew he was right. It was advice Lord Redmantyl might have given. To leave New York now would be the gravest error. Alys was still free and May Night approached. Redmantyl had given her the responsibility to act for him in this important matter and all the evil that followed would be of her own making if she failed. Duty held her a little longer.

"Will you go home and reconsider?" Ambris asked.

"I will," she answered.

The Goldsmith arrived at the Mayor's Hall late the next morning and Kaiese welcomed him to her parlor. Nikholas hid in his office until he might be called to act on his duties as head of the household. Laurel was summoned to the parlor soon after the guest had been received. She went, tensed and ready for battle.

If Kaiese continued to insist on this match, Laurel planned to fight until her aunt understood that she no intention of marrying anyone, least of all the Goldsmith. She wasn't afraid. After all, what could Kaiese do? The Northlands was a free land; no woman could be forced to wed against her will. Laurel had grown up intimidated by her formidable aunt, but *she* was grown now too and in possession of her own will, as strong. She would hold firm so long as her aunt persisted in this foolish matchmaking scheme. And if the Goldsmith was encouraged to make his offers, she would tell him distinctly why she refused. Last night she had fretted. Today, she looked forward to the confrontation.

She sat on the coucherie facing the Goldsmith as Kaiese fed him honeyed tea and raisin-cakes. No word of intent had yet been spoken: the guest talked of his business interests and Kaiese asked appropriate and flattering questions at intervals. Neither addressed Laurel. If the young woman hadn't been forewarned, she would not have guessed why her aunt required her presence. Even knowing, she felt as if she were intruding on someone else's courtship.

That was the ultimate insult in this. The Goldsmith didn't even want *her* to play the role of useful wife and heir-bearer; he wanted Kaiese. The Lady's principles, however, wouldn't allow her to abandon Nikholas. Though she might be willing to wed the Goldsmith if she were free, infidelity was a direct contradiction to Kaiese's sense of virtue and her aspirations. Yet she could not entirely dismiss this wealthy and influential suitor. Laurel was offered as a substitute.

The Goldsmith didn't know anything about his intended bride. He didn't perceive *her*. She was simply a healthy young woman who looked something like the Lady he desired. He wanted Kaiese, but Laurel would do.

"You must know, My Lady, that I've returned to your town for reasons other than my usual business." The Goldsmith glanced across the tea-table at her. Laurel was immediately *en garde*.

"I had guessed as much, Syre," Kaiese replied. "If I may say, your interest has not passed without notice."

"I guessed as much myself," said the Goldsmith. "Are things settled then?"

"You may speak to my husband Nikholas." The Lady rose from her seat. "And, of course," with a warning glance at Laurel, who glared back, "I pray you pardon my absence–"

During this exchange, there had been noises outside the parlor: a knock at the front door, the porter's footsteps, a hushed conversation in the entry hall. Now, as Kaiese began to make her exit, Jemrye tentatively approached the parlor door.

"'Tis Lord Ambris of Eadeshire, Lady. He asks to speak with you."

"Lord Ambris?" the Goldsmith wondered aloud.

"The Duke's son," Kaiese answered modestly, as if it were nothing to have this opportunity to display her household's importance before her guest. The Goldsmith did appear impressed. "Jemrye, escort him in."

"My Lady, he asks for private conversation."

Kaiese was obviously baffled by this strange request. What personal business could Ambris have with her? She turned back to the Goldsmith, smiling to hide her momentary confusion. It would be an act of unforgivable discourtesy to abandon her guest because one of greater rank had come to the door. How to make her excuse? Then her expression brightened. She had been about to leave the Goldsmith alone with Laurel before Ambris had asked to see her.

"Syre, pardon me."

"Certainly."

Once the Lady had gone he turned to Laurel, but she had also risen from her seat. "Syre, you must pardon me as well. Please, take whatever refreshments you will in our absence."

The Goldsmith took a raisin-cake from the plate she offered. "I'd like to meet this Lord Ambris myself," he said.

"Perhaps later," she answered, and followed her aunt out.

Ambris was in the front hall with Kaiese. Nikholas had emerged from his office and stood on the stairs above them. The nobleman looked somewhat embarrassed, conscious of his breach of established courtesy by summoning the Mayor and his Lady here so mysteriously and abruptly. He explained himself: "I come, My Lady, to speak for your niece in her difficulty with the Goldsmith."

"My Lord, respectfully, but it is not your concern," Kaiese replied with cool formality. She glanced back in the direction of the parlor, saw Laurel in the corridor, and scowled. "The private affairs of

213

merchant families are not subject to noble approval. My niece's betrothal does not require your consent."

"It requires mine," said Laurel.

"You left our guest alone," the Lady accused. "What if he overhears this insult you bring him?"

"I shut the door, Aunt, and I gave him more tea. He'll come to no harm. Besides, this matter concerns me and I won't be excluded."

"You've involved yourself more than a decent maid ought. Carrying tales about the town. Going to My Lord Ambris!"

"He's my friend."

"How dare you ask him to interfere–"

"I didn't," Laurel answered. "He came of his own accord."

"Laurel spoke to me in great distress yesterday, My Lady. She explained her troubles, and I must take her part," Ambris said quietly, belaying the storm that was about to burst. Nikholas looked extremely grateful. "Perhaps it is not my place to speak of it, but it is wrong of you to plan such a match without your niece's knowledge nor consent. She's not a child to wed to whom you choose."

"She *is* a child, a spiteful, ungrateful child."

"If you please, she owes you respect and a certain loyalty as you are her kinswoman, but she is not bound to express her gratitude in unquestioning obedience against her conscience." He spoke with deliberate and unaffected earnestness. Kaiese didn't interrupt. "You cannot ask so much from your own daughters, My Lady Kaiese. Marriage is a sacred affair, a contract before Our Holy Lord. To press an unwilling maid to wed a man she has no kind feeling for is to condemn her to misery in this life and to purgatory afterwards, for she will have made false vows. She must consult her own heart's truth before any other obligations."

"You speak for a love-match?" Kaiese asked with delicate sarcasm.

"I speak for a match between suitable parties. A union between a pair so opposite in manner and upbringing and position as your niece and the Goldsmith can only bring bitterness. Is this man so important, Lady, that you sacrifice your maidens at his will? There are far better suitors. If your niece chooses from those you have already admitted to this house, she will consult her own preference and she will not disappoint you."

If any but this prominent nobleman had contradicted Kaiese so, she would have exploded with outrage—and Kaiese in a fury could be as fiery as Laurel and twice as fearsome. But the Lady wasn't offended.

Her anger faded while Ambris spoke, and she smiled as she made an answer. "Perhaps you speak rightly, My Lord. It is an unsuitable union."

"You will not pursue me with that creature?" Laurel was skeptical. She wasn't the only one doubtful of Kaiese's ready compliance; Nikholas gaped at his wife.

"I cannot command a maid of age, as you say, My Lord," Kaiese continued to address Ambris.

"She never could, even when the girl was so small," Nikholas added.

"Laurel is no fit wife for a man so sedate in his ways as the Goldsmith," the Lady continued through this interruption. "She'll be the very devil of him. No. Laurel's husband must be another sort."

Ambris nodded.

"Husband, we must untangle ourselves from this unsuitable connection with the Goldsmith. Speak with him. Tell him that Laurel is– Oh, say whatever is convenient so that he takes no more interest in the wretched girl but does not abandon his friendship with our house."

"As you say, Dearest. I'll tell him the truth—that he's had a lucky escape." Nikholas went to greet the guest who waited in the parlor.

Kaiese ignored this too. "My Lord Ambris, is there more you require at present?"

"No, My Lady."

"Then you will pardon us, I pray. Laurel, see our noble guest out."

Laurel waited until they reached the front door before she spoke. "I could offer gramercies a dozen times and more for what you've done, My Lord, and it wouldn't be enough. I never expected to find such a champion."

"Didn't you? Surely you knew I could not bear to see you tormented and threatened. I thought long last night how I might best serve you. There was no other course but to plead with your aunt and hope she would be reasonable."

"You charmed her thoroughly," Laurel answered. "'Twas a wonder to see. I imagined there was no force in the universe powerful enough to sway my aunt from her chosen course. But you must know that you spoke wrongly on one thing. I would never marry any man my aunt approves."

"I only said what she wished to hear." Ambris smiled gently. "You wouldn't, even if he is one to make you most happy?"

"He could not! Not if he is the sort she chooses. No, My Lord. No one could win both the approval of myself and my aunt. But I am grateful to you, My Lord Ambris."

She shut the door behind him and went upstairs.

ten

At the end of March, the tenuous spring relapsed into winter. Heavy rains filled the gutters, cutting winds shrieked through the chinks in doors and window frames, and patches of ice shone on the streets every morning. Then, as suddenly, the clouds cleared and green burst forth in profusion. Bright, blustery days followed.

Geyraulte returned. He made no apologies for his absence; he simply came to the door of the Mayor's Hall and asked Jemrye to announce him within. Kaiese was guarded in her welcome, but she allowed him liberties rare for any suitor. He requested that he escort Igren on a walk. The Lady consented. As Iobethe and Rosandre were in the parlor, they couldn't be excluded. Laurel, again acting as chaperon, led the little party to the wilderness beyond the town.

The paths through the woods and fields around New York were familiar to her and she directed the party to a trail less muddy than most, a cart lane which led along the riverside to the outlying farmsteads through bottom pastures, shielded from the sea breeze by a stout hedge of twisted, gnarled trees. At the top of a hill, they stopped to watch ships sail in from the estuary to the New York docks.

"You'll be leaving for your home soon," Igren said softly to Geyraulte.

"I ought to," he agreed. "Will you be sorry to see me go, Dam'sel?"

She met his eyes briefly. "I will."

Geyraulte smiled. "Then Oerykton be damned."

"Don't you feel your responsibilities to your people?" asked Laurel.

The Earl shrugged. "New York is mine as much as the Northing. Its people are my concern." His eyes remained on Igren. "I'll stay here so long as I please and curse those who speak against me for it. Mama and Gran'ther can care for Oerykton. They did when I was a child."

"You were quite young, I understand, when you came to your title, My Lord," said Rosandre.

"Your father was the Redlyon's lieutenant," Igren added

tentatively.

"Oh, long before he wed Mama or I was born. He came back from the last of the Spanish wars with his legs broken. He'd been run down by a horse on the battlefield, and they didn't heal properly. His knees were all great lumps. He couldn't bend them. I remember—the 'tendants carried him about in a chair."

"How horrid!" said Igren.

"Soldiery was his craft, Dam'sel," Geyraulte replied. "He thought himself well given in King Eduarde's service. When I was a little lad, my papa used to tell tales of his campaigns in the Marches and how he drove the Spanish off our borders at his lord's side. 'Twas his pride. Would that I might serve my liege as well."

"There'll be another war with Spain," Igren offered. "My Lord of Eadeshire says that his sister will call for troops once she is Duke."

"Prince Margueryt?" Geyraulte was contemptuous. "She'd best leave swordplay to men. No strength for warfare, you know. No woman has."

"'Tis not strength that makes a swordsmaster, My Lord, but skill," Rosandre replied. "The art requires much grace and agility, like the dance. It is not to be conducted like a butcher with his mallet and cleaver. I am acquainted with many maidens who are excellent swordswomen."

"They can't be proper maids if they are," the Earl retorted. "We have guardswomen at our castle—big, bony creatures. They laugh so loud and slap their thighs and punch at their fellows in play. 'Tis a wonder they don't grow beards. We don't think much of that sort, my gran'ther and mother and I, but they served with my father and he would have 'em about. We can't cast 'em off now he's dead. 'Tisn't fitting. Now, I like a maid to be gentle. Not over-dainty pets such as your Frankish tarts, but– Well, womanly, if you understand me." He glanced at Igren. "Battle's no place for a woman, Prince or otherwise. I say if My Lord Ambris were a right-made man, he'd see to this Spanish business himself. But he's like the old Duke—a peaceable sort. He's kept a good many warriors from their duties for so many years that they forget what battle is. I'll wager My Lord Dafythe nor My Lord of Eadeshire never swung sword at a foe."

Laurel leapt to her friend's defense. "I will not have you speak slightingly of the Duke or his son."

Geyraulte recoiled—Dafythe was, after all, his liege lord—then he chuckled. "Oh-ho, so *that's* how it is."

Laurel, blushing, flashed at him. "No, it isn't!"

Igren took Geyraulte's arm protectively. "Laurel, I'm sure My Lord Geyraulte means no insult. He has a right to his opinions."

Laurel opened her mouth to retort, but a deliberate, unspoken message from her cousin stopped her: *Please, Laurel, don't hurt him. If you do, I will have to fight you.* Their eyes met: Igren's were apprehensive but unyielding. She would defend this man from any threat, even her beloved cousin.

"You must be friends," Igren said in an effort to have peace, "Laurel, Geyraulte. Please?" Hand in his, she led Geyraulte away from the confrontation. They went ahead of the others in the direction of the town.

"'Tis pity that such a lovely damosel as your cousin must be given to that dragon," Rosandre said.

Kaiese invited the young men to stay to dinner. Geyraulte had a short interview with Nikholas before they came to the table and, after dinner, Kaiese spoke to her daughter and brought Igren to the parlor, where her suitor waited. Laurel knew what had passed long before Igren told her.

"Laurel, can you guess?" The girl burst into the little bedchamber after the guests had gone. "Geyraulte's asked for me!"

Laurel was surprised at the relief in Igren's voice. "You are going to accept him?"

"Yes," Igren answered. "I've thought of him from the day he introduced himself." She sat at the bedside and continued in confidential tones, "He is handsome, do you not think? So bold and outspoken. Like a warrior of old."

"In truth, I must agree with Io. I thought he would have carried you off from the parlor that first afternoon if my aunt weren't there."

Igren smiled. "He said such a thing to me. He said I should be away from here quickly, away from Mama. She frightens him. So do you. You– He saw you cast your spells in the garden. He's heard of the things wizards may do."

"Doesn't he know you–?"

She shook her head. "He calls magic the Gift of the Netherworld. 'Tis the craft of the Faerye and no right pursuit of mortal-folk, he tells me. Geyraulte is a full good Christian."

"God's Spit!" cried Laurel. "My Lord of Eadeshire is as Christian a man as any you might meet and he much admires the greatest of all wizards, our own uncle."

"Geyraulte is not so worldly as My Lord Ambris."

"Then you'll give it up?"

"It is a simple thing for me," said Igren. "I haven't so much to surrender."

"I would accept no man who was not proud to wed a wizard."

"I couldn't do that," her cousin answered. "'Tis an admirable standard, but you must see that you have a choice. I think that if I were like you, I should want more myself. If I had your magic, I should have will enough to do as I pleased." This was an unusual speech for Igren; Laurel stared, wondering if she truly knew the girl after all. "Magic is for the strong. You– You taught me that, Laurel. Do you recall? If you could hurt me without meaning to, how might I fare against one who meant me harm? I don't belong in that world."

There was a sigh of resignation. Laurel leapt upon it. "You don't have to do this if you don't want to. My aunt can't make you. You might come back to Wizardes Cliff with me–"

"No," Igren said softly. "Laurel, I *want* to marry. I am not ignorant of the honor of winning an Earl for a husband." She shut her eyes, then looked up at her cousin, pleading. "Geyraulte loves me. Can I be more fortunate?"

Laurel had no answer.

"Father says we must wait 'til I am of age," Igren went on after a moment. "'Tis only little more than a year and Geyraulte agrees to abide so long. But we shall set the betrothal next week. Mama's insisted on that. Geyraulte wants me to travel to Oerykton this summer to meet his mother and grandmother and see the castle. He's spoken so much about the Ladies' chapel–" She stopped. "Please, say you wish happiness for me, Cousin. For I shall be happy."

The Mayor's Hall burst into a flurry of activity in the days before the betrothal ceremony. Kaiese made all the plans while Igren remained in a dreamy state, awaiting her mother's summons or her lover's visits; others might take charge of the arrangements and negotiations.

Iobethe took more active interest. "My turn next!" she proclaimed, dancing merrily after Kaiese as her mother consulted the dressmaker, wrote out lists for wedding invitations and ordered her household to prepare the troth feast. "My turn next! My wedding will be twice as grand!"

Geyraulte visited daily, but spent long hours shut away with Nikholas and his lawyers. He sent messages to the dowager Earlings to announce his intentions and to call his courtiers and councilors to New York. The dowry and property settlements were rapidly outlined, though no contract would be formalized until Nikholas met with

Geyraulte's mother and grandmother. The Mayor gave careful attention to his daughter's rights, but he lamented that the future Earling of Oerykeshire had no use for a thriving winery. Her inheritance was to be liquidated. Geyraulte would have been contemptuous if asked to participate in mercantile trade on her behalf. Iobethe was now Nikholas's principal heir, but he called her more silly than Igren.

Once, as Laurel passed the door of his office after a prolonged session, he called out to her: "Shall I give it all over to you, Niece? I expect your uncle Redmantyl's taught you to do up mathematics in your head atop all that wizardly uselessness."

"What would I do with a winery, Uncle?" she replied with more affection than she usually gave him. "What sort of wizard should I be if I must leave off my spellcraft every time the latest shipment of Tuscany Red comes in?"

Nikholas chuckled. "You're determined on that then, are you, Laurel?"

"Yes, Uncle."

"It's a good business, you know, but it's lost on your cousins. Rosandre will drag little Iobethe off into the nobility too. Now, what's wrong with a good merchant-man?"

"You might have refused My Lord Geyraulte."

"What? Go against that fierce creature *and* your aunt? Niece, you expect much bravery from an old man. No, I may only hope to hold more firm against young Daubenai when he demands my Io. Or perhaps I may induce him to take up her concerns. A Frankish lad like that must know his wines." He lifted a sheet of paper from his desk, shook the blotting-sand from the damp ink, and frowned ruefully at the writing. "Perhaps not. Well, I'll get it off my hands one way or another."

"I'm sorry, Uncle Nikholas."

He looked up, as if surprised to find her still there. "Don't fret for it, my girl. Can't be helped."

Laurel was rarely at the Hall during this week of commotion, for she was in quest of Alys. She had not forgotten Lord Redmantyl's charge. It troubled her daily. Though she saw her duty clearly, she hoped to avoid the ultimate resolution Redmantyl demanded. Was murder necessary? Alys bore a potential for great evil. Perhaps she had already committed some act which the Empire could call crime or the Church could call sin but, as far as Laurel knew, the girl did not deserve death. No matter what Alys might do if she surrendered her soul to the will of those Outsiders, it was not yet done. Laurel couldn't kill her in cold blood. She was no judge. She had no proof of present guilt. By what right did she act as executioner? One day she must meet other magicians in battle, perhaps destroy them; that was an inevitable consequence of her profession. Death was an accepted possibility; both challenger and challenged agreed to fight according to the traditional rites of their craft and understood that the victor might choose to kill or to be merciful and spare the defeated, as she pleased. Laurel thought she was prepared to do battle under such circumstances—she was warrior enough not to falter before an enemy who challenged her outright, even Olyr or Lord Redmantyl, for they were wizards possessed of sufficient magic and skill to defend themselves if her powers proved the stronger; in any case, she would not kill unless her foe left her no other choice—but this was no forthright battle between matched opponents. *This* enemy was no grown wizard in power, only a girl not yet sixteen. It would be as evil to murder an unready child as any wrong that child might do.

For Alys was still a child. She couldn't understand the damage she might cause. Young girls were always eager for attention. They sometimes took an interest in whatever was weird or unusual or forbidden—if not for mischief's sake or for revenge against a real or imagined slight, then for the notoriety their tricks received. Alys, alone, small, often disregarded, might blunder into incalculable danger simply to show herself as someone important after all. Whatever myths or witches' tales the girl had heard and embraced, they didn't tell her all the truth. Surely she didn't know what she meant to do. Laurel hoped to explain. She must reveal to Alys the very real, horrifying consequences of her plans. She had some authority to make Alys listen: she was older, taller, stronger, more magical. If it came to threats, she could deliver them with credibility. She could carry them out. There was still time; if she spoke now, she might perform her duty as a guardian and avoid disaster without spilling a drop of blood.

While Kaiese upset the Mayor's Hall in preparation for her daughter's betrothal, Laurel wandered the streets, searching for a small, blank spot in the tumult of sensations around her. For weeks, she had puzzled at the paradox: How had Redmantyl sensed Alys? The extended awareness which magic bestowed enabled her to feel the energies of living and inanimate objects; the void that surrounded Alys was neither of these. She should be invisible to magical perception. Yet Redmantyl had discovered her. Was it possible to detect nothingness? Had the wizard somehow attuned his awareness to the gap in natural energies? It must be so. And, if he had been able to do it, so might she. She gave herself to experimentation. The exercise required enormous concentration, but eventually she mastered the newly discovered skill. It required a shift of focus. She must locate an absence, not a presence.

She paced through the town as she had on her winter patrols, psychic senses flung wide, willfully blind to commonplace impressions, so intensely grim in her purpose that the townsfolk stepped out of her way and whispered prayers and charms against a magician's temper. The trick was not difficult to grasp, but it was difficult to maintain. Any disruption jarred her. Just when she found her mark, Alys moved and Laurel lost her again. Then she felt that familiar buzz of warning and turned to find Alys at her elbow.

"You've been looking for me?"

"I have," Laurel began. "I must make you understand. You can't know what you seek."

"I seek power," Alys answered simply. "They will give it me."

Darkness engulfed them. The sun remained high overhead, but its light and warmth were blotted out and a chill fell upon Laurel's heart. There was knowledge hidden from ordinary mortals, knowledge in carefully guarded books, knowledge which she had blundered into and must secure her mind against. There were secrets too vast and horrible, too dangerous, for the uninitiated to comprehend, lest they bring madness. She had sworn most solemnly never to acknowledge the existence of these monstrosities. Yet Alys knew.

Laurel took the girl by the arm and pulled her to the narrow space between two shop porches, out of sight of curious passersby. "How do you *know*?"

"The Old Gods have called me," Alys replied, proud. "In my dreams, they've shown me all manner of wonders. They've promised such things as they'll give to me if I help them return to the places where they belong by rights."

"They are lying! They have no right place in this world. It is Hell to bring Them in. Do you know what they'll do to you? You'll lose your soul if you give over to them."

Alys shook her head. "You'd say such things. You refused. I won't be such a fool. They've promised such magic as yours. More. *You* have power. Why should I not?"

"It won't be yours to control. They'll use it for their own purposes."

"Even the least little scrap is above the wretched mortals," Alys answered. "You don't know what to do with the magic you have. I watched you, before you saw me. You swagger, prideful, and if they hate you, you aren't afraid. They can't touch you for your magic. My father beat me black for it. In Lyngreen, I would've burnt for a witch if the Old Gods hadn't saved me. They meant me for better. They showed me what I might do."

"You burned Lyngreen."

"They gave me fire. Not a one of that wretched lot wouldn't have done the same to me if they had the chance. They hated me that much. If I had magic now, I'd burn this town. Storm Port too, and all the Northlands. I'd burn 'em all to ashes. I'd dance on the fire. I will, when I'm so strong as you."

Laurel had matched her wits with many opponents more skilled, but her words to Alys were not parried; they simply slid away with no effect. Gods, could they speak of such nightmares at midday? "It is my duty to see that this does not happen. I must protect them."

"You! Protect them? You'd care as little to see 'em all burnt away."

"I warn you—If you do not quit this madness, I must stop you."

"If you were going to, you'd have done it before this," Alys answered scornfully. Free of Laurel's grip, she turned and walked away.

As Laurel walked home that evening, she sensed a human presence in the street behind her even before she heard the footfalls on the cobbles. Alys? No; the girl's living essence was not so easily detected. But she felt something odd, something wrong. Dangerous?

Hand on her swordhilt, she turned abruptly. The footfalls stopped.

The street was empty. The rows of shops were dark and only a few flickers of light shone in the windows above. Long and jagged shadows were cast everywhere—a score of places where one might hide. But who would wish to hide? If she were mistaken in her impressions and the presence she sensed was merely one of the tradesfolk in the street or a blameless traveler taking this route from Kalligate Street to the Mayor's Parade, he would have walked on in her sight. This person didn't want to be seen. That in itself was suspicious. Who followed her? A thief? A ruffian? One of her enemies from childhood on a vicious prank?

"I know you're there!" Laurel shouted. "You might as well come out and tell me what it is you want."

No response. She cast her senses wide, searching for that particular shadow which concealed her opponent.

With an outraged yelp—a man's voice—a cloaked form leapt at her just as she located its position. A fist flew at her face. There wasn't time to leap away; Laurel turned swiftly to avoid the full force of the blow and studded leather clipped her cheekbone. Her assailant's outstretched arm shot past her shoulder. It was a clumsy and stupid move, not what Laurel expected from a professional footpad. Such rogues, she knew from experience, could knock their victims into a stupor with a single swift thump and rob them before they fell. They certainly didn't shout before they struck. Whoever he was, he wasn't a thief. Besides, this man wore the gauntlets and cloak of a guardsman. Who was it?

While these perplexing thoughts flashed through her head, Laurel automatically twisted to enact a simple defensive move: she grabbed her attacker's wrist, ducked, and pulled him off his balance. Her foot hooked his ankle and her elbow struck the small of his back. He tumbled to the street, but knocked her feet out from under her as he sprawled. Laurel fell hard on the cold, wet stones, her sword beneath her. For a moment, she lay stunned and breathless, but when flailing arms reached for her and fingers gripped her cloak, she fought herself free with slaps and kicks. She scrambled to a safe distance, arms and knees out to prevent her from stabbing herself until she regained her feet. Her opponent rose more slowly.

It was the sergeant.

She drew her sword as he struggled to his feet and came toward her. Point out, she held him at bay. "No further! What do you want?"

"You want to hurt her!" he cried. "I won't let you!"

"Did she send you?" Laurel demanded. She spun a globe of light with her free hand to see him more clearly. His face was haggard, all jutting cheek and nose and jaw, and the line of his beard was blurred by untrimmed stubble. In the glittering light, his skin looked pale and patchy. Sweat rolled from his brow and his breath fell in furious little gasps. His eyes were not sane.

This assault made no sense. Although Alys had walked away from her this afternoon boldly, did the girl still consider her a threat? Was this man meant to kill her? Or was he meant to warn her away? If Alys truly wanted to be rid of her, why not thwart her with magical trickery instead of dispatching this pathetic bully to do the work? The poor sickly wretch was no more a physical threat than his tiny master. His mind was muddled. He was unsure on his feet. Whatever battle-skill he possessed as a soldier had been forgotten. Had Alys sent him, or was he acting on his own impulse?

"I see how you follow her!" he cried. "Asking questions! Always sneaking about, poisoning my guards' minds against her. I hear them whisper! My sweet child, and you with your suspicious thoughts and serpent's tongue spread filthy lies about her!"

He dodged to one side to escape the extended blade, and Laurel side-stepped with him. The sword point remained at his chest. "Not an inch!" she warned. "If you have half a mind left to call your own, you'll back away." She repelled him again as he made a feint in the other direction. "Listen to me! Alys has done something to you—"

"'Tisn't true!"

"It is! She's evil."

"Lies! Lies! Why d'ye tell such lies? She's done nothing wrong! My poor innocent girl." His eyes glistened with tears. "You're the evil one! I see you! I see what you're about!" He pressed forward, mindless of the sword. He would impale himself in his eagerness to reach her, and Laurel didn't want to kill him if she could avoid it. If Alys had done this to him, then he wasn't responsible for his actions; she wouldn't aid in his destruction.

She tossed the globe into his face. The dazzling little ball of light dispersed instantly, harmlessly, but the flash left him blind him long enough for Laurel to step back and turn her sword to the side, flat out, to form a barrier between them.

"Witch!"

When he ran toward her, she was braced; the blade made a bar against his shoulders and kept his hands from her throat. One fierce shove, and a swift kick to enforce it, sent him down again. This time, he did not rise but lay sobbing in the street. "You give her no rest. Always after her. You'll kill her! Why d'ye have to be so cruel? Can't you let the little maid live in peace?"

No, Laurel knew she couldn't. There was a great deal of truth in his ravings—enough to prick her conscience—but she couldn't explain her actions to this madman. He was past all reason. The sergeant she'd seen last autumn was a hearty, friendly man, not clever, perhaps, but quick on his feet and well-liked by the men and women in his command. A kindly man, the sort to feed a stray kitten or treat a new guard with a welcoming beer. She wouldn't recognize him now. The flesh was eaten away beneath his skin and his mind was a tormented tangle. What had Alys done to him? How? Was it magic? Poison? Had she taken advantage of a natural illness? Did she whisper suggestions to this madman to do her will, or did she have the power to hold him a spellbound slave?

As Laurel stood over him, sword-tip cautiously at the exposed nape of his neck, a multitude of impressions washed through her in a staggering burst. Through the fear and confusion of the people who had overheard the brawl, Laurel sought to focus on the mind of this one man. She met an incoherent jumble: anger, jealousy, despair, pain. Alys was everywhere in his thoughts: the stray he'd taken in. His darling girl. Beloved and feared, despised and cherished as a precious treasure which had fallen into his hands. He would do anything for her. Then Laurel's perception faded and she was left with no better answer than before. Had Alys engineered this assault or had he acted on his own mad impulse? She still didn't know.

She heard the tromping footsteps of the regular guard patrol on their evening rounds. Someone shouted for aid, and their pace quickened. The sergeant's fellows would find him and take him to be either drunk or seriously ill. They would escort him back to the garrison hall. But they mustn't discover her. Laurel stepped into the shadows and slipped away before the patrol arrived.

On Saturday evening at dusk, Geyraulte and Igren met at the tall doors of St. Matthieu's for the handfasting. The church porch glowed with the light of torches and candles and a crowd had gathered on the parvis. Some were acquaintances of Kaiese and Nikholas and the children of these merchants, Igren's playmates not many years before. The Sheriff and his sons were there. Others had come at special invitation: Rosandre, Ambris. The rest were common folk. As the night was clear, more than half the town had come to witness the ceremony.

Handfasting was meant for public exhibition; the prospective bride and groom plighted to each other before all in vows as binding as a signed contract, more than a promise, less than a marriage. Custom decreed that the two were bound together. Igren might go to Oerykton unchaperoned tonight or Geyraulte might take up residence in the Mayor's Hall, though neither would. Children born to a plighted couple between the handfast and the wedding ceremony were considered legitimate, though this also would not happen. Geyraulte intended to return to his home as soon as the weather made travel easy, but he wouldn't leave town until his declaration and his claim to his beloved were secure. Banns were posted and criers would shout the news throughout the fiefdom and its neighbors: the liege lord of Oerykeshire was to wed a Uindaughter of New York.

A tatterdemalion led the procession. This odd little figure in thesperish red and blue striped hose and ragged robe was actually Nikholas's clerk, but his office of recordkeeper required him to serve in the traditional role of matchmaking intermediary. Before sunset, he went to Geyraulte's rooms at the inn to assist the Earl with his wardrobe. Geyraulte wore his best clothes, his silver chains, his heavy signet rings, his circlet upon his brow. His tunic was darkest blue velvet sewn with small gems along the frogged front. He'd brought it with him from France and was obviously ill at ease in it; he had worn it only once before, at his sister's wedding. Accompanied by his friends and fellows from Oerykton, he followed the tatterdemalion to the Mayor's Hall.

"Is this the house wherein dwells the woman?" The question was ceremonial.

"It is," Geyraulte answered.

"I have heard that she is maid passing fair, gentle and pure in her heart. All who know her revere her virtue and all who see her praise her beauty. Her name is Igren, maid born of New York, heir to Nikholas Uinmerchant and daughter of that most honored house. My Lord Geyraulte, is it she you seek?"

"Of course it is!" the Earl snapped impatiently. Some of his companions ducked their heads to hide improper smiles.

"Fortunate is the man who will win her," the clerk continued undaunted. "What gifts do you make?"

Geyraulte had brought a single flower. For common folk, betrothal offerings were usually practical household items: cookery crocks, tools, even livestock. For the wealthy and well-positioned, they were more often symbolic trinkets of affection. A ring or necklace was traditional, but nothing appropriate was available on such short notice. The Earl had taken great care to find and preserve his chosen gift. He and his men had wandered the muddy countryside all morning in search of a suitable early bloom.

"I offer myself and all I possess that she will have." He gave the flower to the tatterdemalion; the emissary went to the Mayor's door and knocked.

Igren answered. Her dress was a fanciful white gown wound with brightly colored ribbons in the traditional colors of wedding garb: gold for prosperity, dark green for fertility, red for the heart's blood. Her hair was bound up in braids and piled upon her head like a crown. A veil held by silver pins fell over her brow and brushed back over her shoulders.

"Igren Uindaughter?"

"I am." Though she answered the intermediary, her eyes were on Geyraulte at the foot of the stairs.

"I present you this man," the tatterdemalion recited, almost in song. "I have heard that he is a nobleman of courtesy, brave and true in his heart. Those who know him admire his bravery and those who see him call him most handsome. His name is Geyraulte, born of Oerykton, Earl of Oerykeshire and son of that noble bloodline. Igren Uindaughter, he asks for you."

"Wh– what does he offer?"

The flower was extended. "Maiden, he offers himself and all he has. Will you have him?"

Igren took the flower.

"Will you come out and pledge with him?"

"I will." She had been well rehearsed, but her voice shook a little as made her response.

She might have walked to St. Matthieu's, but the streets were muddy; Geyraulte's men had made a seat of crossed birch poles and carried her upon their shoulders. The Earl walked ahead and the tatterdemalion led them, whistling through a small flute and jingling bells on a beribboned pole. The Mayor and his household followed and others joined as the procession went past their doors. They sang a song of love and promises.

At the church door, the betrothed couple stood together hand in hand.

"Witness! Witness, all!" the clerk sang out. "I call upon all to witness the handfast of this man called Geyraulte and this woman called Igren. Witness! Witness, all! Know you that marriage is a holy state in which two souls are bound as one before the eyes of our Blessed Savior for all their lives and in Paradise hereafter. It is no contract to be taken lightly. Witness all the promise of these two, man and woman together! See that they willingly accept the charge laid upon them as husband and wife. See that come to this union obedient, chaste, pious and in the blessings of proper love of the spirit as well as the flesh. See that they know well what they do this day for ever and all eternity.

"I bid these two, man and woman, to speak that they have chosen this union freely and without hindrance or impediment. Igren of New York, daughter to the Mayor Nikholas Uinmerchant, Geyraulte of Oerykton, Earl of Oerykeshire, I conjure you to honesty before the Sacred Eyes of Our Most Holy Lord. Is it so?"

"Yes," Geyraulte answered and Igren echoed in a whisper.

A platter containing a small loaf of bread was held aloft for all to see, then the ragged clerk took up the loaf and broke it in two; Geyraulte and Igren each took half and ate. A goblet of wine was offered; each sipped in turn.

"So be it!" the tatterdemalion announced. "You have made most a solemn vow before this gathering. As husband and wife you are pledged together. Thy union may not be dissolved." They placed their hands together, palm flat against palm, and he looped a white ribbon about their wrists to formally bind them. The pact was sealed.

As the night grew chilly, the crowd who had come to witness this ceremony dispersed. Those who were not acquainted with the Mayor's family retreated to their own homes. Others, at Nikholas's invitation, joined the celebration at the Mayor's Hall.

In the house of a Uinmerchant, wine flowed; decanters on tables were filled and refilled and casks in the cellar were emptied. Slices of roast venison, contributed by Geyraulte's men on a series of vigorous hunts, and cakes, offered by friends of the family, were piled high on platters. Kaiese presided over the feast. The merchant-dames were more polite than usual. This alliance with a noble family, liege of the city, was a victory which commanded respect. Tonight, they kept their tongues. Elsewhere in the Hall, music was drowned out by rising laughter. The Earl's men made free with merchant-maids while their mothers and fathers looked on complacently. Geyraulte was red with pride and somewhat shy at his friends' jests and Nikholas's backhanded congratulations. Igren, at his side, smiled and blushed at the toasts and compliments.

Laurel watched this merriment until she was too sickened to bear any more. As she was one of the first to return to the Hall, her cloak lay lost in the pile of wraps spilling from the porter's cubby; she took another and retreated through the kitchens to the garden.

Did Igren understand how she had been matched? Did she know how her affections and interests had been played with? Kaiese had used Geyraulte's infatuation, first encouraging then banishing the young man to force him to an offer. Igren was no fool. Surely she saw. How could she submit?

Every instinct within Laurel protested against such mercenary antics; it was impossible to believe that any young maiden would give herself willingly to them for the sake of a marriage, yet she saw that everyone played the game. The people of the Northlands were free.

They called themselves so. How could the same Norman land which honored Prince Margueryt, praised merchant-dames, respected guardswomen who patrolled the streets beside their men-fellows, and acknowledged, though with distaste, that she would be a great wizard, look upon young girls like Igren and Iobethe as no more than ornaments to be bargained over?

Igren might have refused. Why didn't she? She was in love, true, and love demanded some surrender, but could she cut off her magic for Geyraulte's sake? No, Laurel couldn't believe that. She had heard her cousin's words: Igren desired magic but she was afraid to seek it. Kaiese had taught her daughter to fear her powers, as she feared her own. The merchant society in which they lived held wizardry as disreputable. And, lastly, Geyraulte had called magic evil. Igren knew better, but she was unable to stand against the force of so many contrary opinions. She doubted her ability. She had no will to stand against them. Disapproval crushed her. Perhaps, in her heart, she believed what was said and thought her dissatisfaction wicked. Could she do more than what was expected? It was easier to accept an attractive man and an advantageous match. If she wanted something else, she must forget it.

All of Igren's potential was lost—and there *was* potential. Laurel had seen it. She recalled Igren at Wizardes Cliff: a fragile spell cupped in tentative hands; a trusting sparrow on the maiden's wrist; fingers brushing her temples and the soft urge to *sleep, sleep*. It was magic. Laurel would take Igren back to Wizardes Cliff with her and see that her cousin received proper training, but she knew it was useless. Whatever Igren might have been, she could not be so now. The damage had been done—in her childhood, her young maidenhood, tonight. Her magic had been thwarted for so long that it could never grow to its full promise. She was unfit for a magical life; she knew this for herself and Laurel must reluctantly agree. Igren didn't have the strength to employ the powers she possessed. She was too tender to withstand the intense disciplines of apprenticeship. She wasn't capable of enduring the duties a true wizard must face.

If Igren were faced with the test Laurel now confronted, she would never survive. Dear little Igren could never do harm to a living creature. She would be unable to kill Alys. And Alys would have killed her.

Ambris, at the doorway behind her, coughed softly. "I meant to leave," he explained. "You have my cloak."

Laurel swung the cloak from her shoulders. "You may have it, My

Lord. And my apologies. I took it without knowing—I had to get out of doors."

"I understand." He did not immediately retreat. "You'll return to Wizardes Cliff soon. I wonder that you haven't left already."

"The business which sent me here still keeps me," she answered. "It will be finished soon."

"You've never said what your business is."

"I cannot."

"You've been up to something dangerous, I can see for myself." He gently touched her bruised cheek. "In town, they say you've been walking wild as a banshee, measuring out a curse."

"The townsfolk will talk such superstitious gossip. No, I am not here to cause them harm."

"I didn't imagine you were. I apologize if I seem to pry. I know that wizards have secrets they cannot tell."

"Yes, we do." Shivering a little, Laurel turned away. "Do you ever wonder what's out there, My Lord?"

"Out–?" He followed her gaze up into the night. "The Heavens, of course."

"God, His Angels, the heavenly hosts," she said quickly. "What more? The souls of the dead? The souls of the unborn? Demons?"

"A theologian might answer that question better than I," Ambris replied. "Or a wizard, though I have heard that magicians do not believe in gods."

"That's not true," she responded. "Believe? Yes. We cannot avoid it. Worship? No. There are things out there not– Perhaps it's best if we don't know too much."

"An odd thought for a magician."

"We might all be safer if it were so." Ambris gave no answer to this. "Igren was lovely, didn't you think?"

"She looked very happy."

The corner of Laurel's mouth turned down. "Not so happy as my Aunt Kaiese. The match is her triumph."

"Igren does not wish to wed Geyraulte?"

"'Tis odd, but she does. I think that if she were to choose for herself, she would choose him."

"Then why do you think it strange she consents?"

"How can she submit to the will of any except herself?" Laurel asked in reply. "She is fortunate to have an agreeable match, but it wouldn't signify if she did not. Kaiese has made her plans and Geyraulte his choice and Igren's wishes are unimportant. She deserves better, but she cannot take it. She doesn't know how. Will or no, she cannot refuse. It is too horrible, this buying and selling of people like wares at the market—this one, for 'tis pretty, this one, for 'tis valuable, that one, for 'tis durable and will be of good use."

"An arranged match is not so horrible a thing in itself," Ambris said. "My Lady Margaude and I were introduced and wed within a month."

"But that is hideous!"

"We gave ready consent to the contract. My Lady and I knew that we were suited to each other, far more suited than she would have been to young Kharles."

"Perhaps," Laurel conceded. "You were of like tempers. Igren and Geyraulte are not. 'Tis simply the folly of youth." She saw that Ambris was amused. "I know, My Lord, for I have been so foolish over handsome lads and they over me, and Igren is far more pretty than I."

"She isn't," he said. "You've no good opinion of marriage, Laurel?"

"No, not of the marriages I've seen. Look you, merely, at my aunt and uncle. She cares nothing for Nikholas. He may have loved her once, but now he loves nothing at all. She's killed that in him. He calls himself 'delighted' that Igren has found such a husband, but in truth she might wed the Goldsmith or Rosandre or *you*, My Lord, and he would say the same. He cares no more for her and Iobethe than he does for me, and Kaiese least of all. He's sorry that he wed her and he wouldn't mind if she disappeared tomorrow. I think it would be unbearable to spend all my life shut up with one person under such circumstances."

"As do I. But it is not always so."

"Will you marry again, My Lord?"

"I hope to," answered Ambris. "Father has suggested I may be a proper suitor for Kat."

Laurel felt a strange pang at this announcement. "Prince Kat? But she's your cousin."

"The Pope will give us a dispensation. Cousins among royalty often wed for the sake of the blood. Kat and I were contracted to each other before. I knew when I brought her to Pendaunzel—the little Irish Prince, barely three years old—that she was meant to be my wife. But I was matched with Margaude long before Kat was grown."

"Will you have no choice?"

"My duty lies in my father's service and I must wed where I am bid."

This was by far the most monstrous matchmaking Laurel had yet heard of. "My Lord, how can you bear it? Igren may be bullied, but you–" she stopped. "You are nearly a rightborn Prince. Of all people, can you not choose?"

"We of the Norman royal house are the most privileged people living and we might have all that we desire, if our responsibility did not prevent us from asking for it," Ambris answered. "As it is, we do much that we do not want to do. In our way, we are far less free than the meanest beggars."

"But you wouldn't leave your position for the beggars'?"

"No, of course not. My bondage is preferable, for it is luxury. I'd be a fool to leave it. `Tis rare that one chooses to leave comfort for liberty's sake."

"Then you are as helpless as Igren and little Io."

"Does anyone, Maiden, truly have the right to choose for themselves?"

"*I* can say if I shall wed or no."

"But that choice is not a condition of your place. Were you daughter of a great merchant house or noble family, your marriage would be of some importance. `Tis no matter if a wizard weds. But we all have duties which affect the most private parts of our lives and some of them we do not like, but we must obey. I know a little of wizardry, Laurel. You cannot tell me you embrace the thought of spending the prime years of your youth in magedom."

This was true. She'd said as much to Klyffaude: wizards were not free. The strictures of the magical discipline had kept her from her feelings more than once. It had taken Olyr from her before she'd discovered what a boy and girl might truly mean to each other. It had cast Klyffaude out just as she had learned.

New responsibilities, far heavier, lay upon her now. Three weeks remained before May Night, and Alys was yet unchecked. Lord Redmantyl's message grew more insistent at each repetition.

"Yet you will take your mage vows and keep to them because you must for wizardry's sake," said Ambris.

"I do not have to be a wizard," Laurel answered obstinately.

"You told me yourself a magician must bear responsibility for her powers. You can't abandon them any more than I would leave my duties as Dafythe's son."

"Tell me, My Lord Ambris," she asked suddenly. "What would you do if duty called upon you to perform some act you found repulsive? Would you commit murder, as an example? If your father pointed at a man and commanded you, *Kill him*, would you?"

"My father would never do such a thing."

"My Lord Kharles then."

"Even an Norman Emperor cannot point and have murder done at his bid. We have laws in this land: trials for a punishable offense, judges and juries, writs of execution. As a magistrate, I occasionally hear cases where I might proclaim a sentence of death. If the laws given by my father or my cousin Kharles indicated that execution was a fitting penalty, I would obey. But I judge against such criminals only if they've been proved murderers themselves."

"None innocent of a crime?"

"None innocent."

"If there is a war, you will certainly go with your sister to battle. Innocents will die. You would follow your duty even so?"

"I will not shirk," said Ambris. "But surely you speak of wizardly duties?"

"Yes," Laurel answered. "I'm also bound to do as my duty bids. I am as helpless as you." Mischievous, and a little vicious, she turned to him. "Very well, My Lord Ambris, we would kill for duty's sake. Now I give you a more repulsive case. If your father bids you wed your cousin...?"

"I hope he won't. We are not suited to each other."

"But if he does?"

"Then I shall."

"What if you were to tell him 'No, I have found another and will have her instead'?"

Ambris was silent. Then he said, "It would depend upon who that other was."

"It shouldn't, My Lord," Laurel replied. "If there were such a one, you wouldn't refuse your father's will for her? Duty would overcome love?"

He answered softly, "No, I would defy him."

She smiled. "Then you agree that there are things more important than one's responsibilities?"

"Not more important," he said. "Love also has its obligations."

Laurel studied him. How old was he? Forty-two? Forty-four? No gray wisps streaked his dark hair. Only the littlest lines touched the corners of his eyes and one deep crease had cut up the center of his brow. He wasn't an old man; in truth, he was barely middle-aged. When he spoke, he revealed a poetry of feeling. He couldn't marry for love but surely, in his youth, he'd had romantic adventures? Was there a damosel at some foreign court whom it was impolitic to woo? There might've been many. Certainly, there was one. Ambris was not past remembrance.

"Have you ever loved, My Lord?"

"Yes," Ambris answered. "You, Laurel?"

"I don't know. I thought I had, twice, but I've never known surely. To think of those boys now does not break my heart. If I'd loved either truly, it ought to."

Ambris watched her; a faint light glinted upon his eyes. "If one of these handsome lads had asked," he said, "would you have left your apprenticeship to fly with him?"

"No," she responded immediately.

"Not even for love?"

"I cannot say it *was* love," Laurel reiterated. "Even so, it would be a difficult choice. I can't imagine loving anyone so much to abandon what I am."

Ambris turned suddenly and, bidding her "Good-night," went back into the Hall.

"My Lord Ambris returns to Pendaunzel," Kaiese announced at breakfast the next day.

"He can't be," said Laurel. "He just came from the city."

If the porter had not entered the hall at this moment, an argument would have immediately ensued, but Kaiese was more irritated by this interruption than her niece's impertinence. "What is it, Jemrye?" the Lady demanded.

"'Tis the Captain of the Guards at the door," the boy explained. "He wishes to speak to the Mayor."

"Tell him to go away," Kaiese ordered, but Nikholas had already left the table.

"A strange thing," he said when he returned. "Our Sergeant-at-Arms committed suicide last night. It's rather a shock to the garrison."

"Are they certain it wasn't an accident?" Kaiese asked.

"Oh, yes. The Captain tells me he hung himself from the rafters with his own belt..." He glanced at his daughters; Igren was pale and Iobethe looked a little too interested in the worst details. "He was alone in his room. His squire found him."

Laurel sat, stunned, while her uncle speculated on promoting a replacement from the ranks. Several minutes passed before anyone noticed that she had stopped eating.

"Did you know him, Niece?" Nikholas asked.

"N-no." She wanted to ask after the squire, whom the guards had called the sergeant's pet, but she could not draw attention to any relationship between Alys and herself. Such questions might be remembered. "I saw him. I spoke to him once or twice. He was– He had been sickly."

"Perhaps there was a fever on the brain," Kaiese suggested. "He went mad."

"Yes, I expect that's it," said Nikholas. "Poor wretch."

She must kill Alys. She'd had the opportunity to destroy this evil while it remained fledgling and unexercised, but she hadn't taken it. She'd hesitated. She had let Alys live, and that miserable wreck of man had died. Alys had destroyed him somehow—Laurel was certain of it. She'd driven him mad. She had brought him to this. Less than a week ago, Laurel had spared his life, yet his blood was on her hands. She must kill. It was inescapable. But how? Her instructions were not explicit. What was she meant to do? Blast with fire? Challenge the little squire to wizard-battle? Cut the girl's throat in an alley?

She wasn't ready for this responsibility. She wanted to flee New York, surrender her mission and let Redmantyl deal with this himself. The assassination was best left to him; he had killed a score of times. He could do it and not be troubled. She could not.

Laurel walked through town, trembling, feeling the terrible weight of the act she was called upon to commit. She reached the square before she knew where she was.

With the road now passable, Free Folk returned to town to perform amid the empty market stalls. Though they could not receive much money so early in the year, the thespers and carnies were glad to be out at their trade again. Small groups of travelers had banded together for a time. One entertainment followed another: a conjurer in spangled robes who pulled doves from his sleeves and changed black silk scarves to white was replaced by a spinning pair of dancers; jongleurs and tumblers gave way to a comic scene of lovers who met in secret and made bawdy jokes. Merchant and common-folk gathered on the porches of the inns and shops about the muddy square. Their applause grew more enthusiastic and their shouts more eager as each player succeeded the last. The players laughed at their own games. Laughter filled Laurel's head. She heard the call again, that which she had ignored at Wizardes Cliff: *Come away! Come and join us!* They promised escape. How dearly she wanted to get away!

The minstrel who had once played for Ambris took a place on the base of the market cross and sang:

> *"Love destroys the thing beloved.*
> *'Tis true, 'tis true, I say.*
> *Observe the blooms upon the hills,*
> *The blossoms bright of May.*
>
> *Pluck up a flower, lovers,*
> *Pluck up a flower.*
> *In taking love, we kill it.*
> *For our love, it dies.*
>
> *A pretty fellow passes by*
> *His heart, his heart it beats.*
> *For love of maiden fair he sighs.*
> *The love of maid he seeks.*
>
> *Pluck up a flower, lover,*
> *Pluck up a flower.*
> *In taking love, he kills it.*
> *For his love, it dies.*
>
> *So it is with love, my friends,*
> *Once wooed, once won, it flies.*
> *In our grasp, we kill it.*
> *It withers and it dies.*
>
> *Pluck up a flower, lovers,*
> *Pluck up a flower.*
> *In taking love, we kill it.*
> *For our love, it dies.*

As the crowd dispersed to go on about their business and the lute was set aside, Laurel approached. "You are traveling with this troupe?" she asked.

The minstrel nodded.

"Can you tell me who is their head?"

The minstrel brought her to a caravan parked before the Dolphin Inn and the headethesper, who sat at the back still in costume, smoking a pipe. Laurel explained her request. She would travel with them so far as Storm Port. She had her own horse, but not enough money to purchase food and lodging along the way and she was willing to work if they would take her.

"When do you leave?"

"Friday. Will you be ready to go so quickly?"

"So quickly as I can."

The headethesper didn't ask her reasons; among Free Folk, ones motives for abandoning the old life were given the most respectful silence. "We stop at the inn here. Meet us Friday morning."

Laurel turned to thank the minstrel, but this traveler was looking up, over her shoulder. She turned; Ambris stood on the porch of the Goldbell Inn, looking down at them. "My Lord!" she called out. "I heard that you were gone."

"No, not yet," he explained once he had come down. He looked at thespers. "You are going with them?"

"Yes."

Ambris drew her aside. "I would rather you not," he whispered. "You don't know them."

"They are only thespers, not thieves," she answered. "I am able to care for myself among such folk. Your minstrel travels with them."

"Not *my* minstrel," said Ambris. "Only an acquaintance."

Laurel shrugged. "No matter. I must be out of New York, and soon. My palfrey, as you say, is not a sturdy beast. If she falls on the road, I would rather have friends nearby. The thespers are willing to go with me. If I have no company, I must leave the palfrey and walk alone. I will do it."

Ambris kept his opinion for a moment, then spoke to the point: "Laurel, this is all very silly—this talk of walking to Storm Port. Only a fool will attempt it and I know you are not a fool. I will hear no more of it. If you must go to Storm Port quickly, I shall ride with you."

Laurel had been abashed by his scolding tone—it was folly to speak of going on foot; she knew it—but this offer surprised her into fresh amusement. "My Lord!"

"I must return to Pendaunzel. I may accompany you so far as Storm Port and see you have safe passage to Wizardes Cliff."

"I couldn't," she began.

He smiled. "You will accept the company of strangers, but not of me."

Laurel blushed. "I couldn't object to your company, My Lord," she tried to explain. But what was her explanation? She had some idea that this arrangement was improper, but she'd never cared for proprieties before. Certainly, Ambris meant nothing dishonorable. He was a friend; he planned to go to Pendaunzel and her destination was along the way. It was part of his generous nature to offer assistance. Indeed, he'd provided a most agreeable solution to her problem. Who could accuse her of wrongdoing when she traveled with this nobleman called Just?

"If you are willing," she conceded.

"Then we are settled."

"You travel so much, My Lord Ambris," she observed as they reached the door to the Mayor's Hall. "You go to Pendaunzel again?"

"Yes. Business of vast importance calls me back to court."

"Is one of the boys ill?"

"No, my sons are well." As they entered the hall, he looked about at the closed doors on either side and along the open gallery above. "Where is Mayor Nikholas? I must speak with him."

While the Mayor's Hall was occupied with Igren's betrothal, Rosandre continued his shy courtship of Iobethe. He was at the Hall every day, neglecting his studies in Kallaykirke to listen to Iobethe chatter gaily of her own wedding plans. The young Lord attended her with great interest. He offered suggestions, though he was never bold enough to suggest himself as a bridegroom. No word was yet spoken, but Kaiese was certain that arrangements must be made once Iobethe was sixteen.

Then, Rosandre arrived one day solemn and ashamed. "I am to return to France," he explained to the Lord Mayor and Lady in confidence. "Uncle Lucian writes my mother that my education is completed and I am suited to take the place she has designed for me. But," his face colored, "that is not the truth of it. Your pardon, My Lady. You know I would die rather than bring you insult. My granduncle– He tells Mama that I have made an inferior attachment." He lowered his eyes. "I pray you will not reveal this slander to My Damosel Iobethe."

Nikholas smiled. "It can't hurt the little lass to learn that a Bishop, even a French one, doesn't find her so fine as himself."

"He is an old man and proud of his blood," said Rosandre. "The finest families of the Northlands, such as yours, My Lord, are suspect to him. But I promise you that once Mama hears of my lovely Damosel Iobethe, she will see the truth. She will give consent to my hopes." He smiled beautifully. "I will be here again!"

When Igren and Iobethe came down, he made his farewells; he kissed the hands of all the ladies, then he was gone.

240

"He's gone to tell his mother of me." Iobethe's shining eyes declared her trust. "Mama, it'll be my wedding next! Remember, you promised me a party as grand as Igren's!"

"Yes, Darling. And you shall have one."

The girl bounded happily after her sister.

"'Tis a pity," Kaiese said once the child was out of hearing. "He was a lovely boy. And a Lordling!"

"Well, our Io's young and light of heart," Nikholas consoled his wife. "She can't have a nobleman simply because her sister's got one. She'll forget him when the next pretty lad comes along and we'll see her wed yet before she's grown."

Kaiese ignored the jibe. "But to whom?"

"Peter Sheriffson?" the Mayor suggested. "I don't imagine even our Io is silly enough to like Martin. Or perhaps the Goldsmith. Quite a charming fellow, wouldn't you say, Niece? Shall we call him back to our town?"

Laurel didn't reply. She never learned what explanations her aunt and uncle had used to deter him; there had been a conference in the parlor that afternoon when he'd come to offer marriage to her, and then the Goldsmith had left. He departed New York that same day. Laurel didn't care what lies had been told, what promises and flatteries given. It was sufficient that the threat of him had been removed.

"My Lord of Eadeshire?" said the Lady.

Nikholas chuckled. "I am afraid, my dear, you'll have to give that one up as well. Ambris tells me he plans to marry."

Laurel heard this with dismay: his cousin Kat, certainly, and against his will. Duty had won out. "How dreadful," she said.

Kaiese shot her an intensely searching look.

"My thought exactly," Nikholas agreed. "Marriage is a dreadful business. I can't imagine why anyone would give themselves to it. No, let's not find a husband for our little daughter, My Lady. She's well out of it now My Lord Rosandre's going away."

In the maze of narrow streets behind St. Matthieu's, Laurel slipped from shadow to shadow with only the faintest will-o-wisp light to guide her. She carried her mother's sword; though she was used to handling the weapon, she had never put it to its true purpose before this.

Guards were not always armed. At the gates, they carried iron-sparred pikes. On patrol, they bore swords or staffs, according to their abilities. Laurel had no idea if Alys were skilled with either. It was possible that the girl carried no weapon. Unarmed, she could be overtaken and the task accomplished swiftly. Once it was done, Laurel would leave this town forever.

Lord Redmantyl's message had become urgent and unmistakable: *Do it now.* The words were burned into her brain. No other options remained.

He could have done it himself. He could have been here before May Night and put an end to this danger before it became unavoidable, but he'd given her this mission with certain purpose. He knew that she had a horror of killing and knew that her confrontation with Alys must come to this end. Her first bloodshed. Her test. Perhaps he'd sent her here deliberately, knowing.

Redmantyl trusted that once she had performed this unpleasant duty, she would be fully prepared for the obligations inherent in a wizard's pact. Not all deaths were met in proper battle. Not all her enemies were grown magicians. Where the safety of this little world was concerned, a true guardian must strike unflinchingly. There could be no gentleness. No mercy. She must cast out the weak and malignant without hesitation hereafter, regardless of where she uncovered it. The next kill would be easier.

With further observation and careful questions, she'd learned that the little squire had assumed full guard duty after the sergeant's death. She knew something of Alys's appointments. Tonight, she sat below the gate and waited, but when Alys relinquished her post she did not cross the church green to reach the Tunnels and the garrison halls. Instead, she turned abruptly at a sidestreet and disappeared. Laurel followed.

She heard the brisk, confident click of boot heels on the cobbles ahead of her and she crept more softly behind. Her own boots would clatter as loudly. Turn here. Turn there. Though Laurel had run these twisting streets since childhood, tonight she found them strange. Doorways of familiar shops loomed cavernous. Signs were scripted in alien tongues. Wares left in darkened windows were unrecognizable; bolts of cloth and stacks of pots and plates seemed impossibly like abandoned slabs of butcher's meat. She didn't know where she was, nor whither she was being led in this chase.

Was Alys aware that she was pursued? Did she mean to lose her assassin in this tangle? Laurel's nerves tingled with warning, but the nullity which cloaked the girl's essence was impossible to penetrate. What traps lay ahead? Turn again. Alys led her along a mews behind a row of shops and taverns. A laughing couple emerged from the nearest stable; Laurel stepped quickly into a doorway and pressed herself to the shadows as they passed. They did not see. She ran on in the direction Alys had taken. Another corner. A blank wall. Alys had doubled back. She heard the tapping steps behind her. Laurel scrambled over the wooden fence which blocked her way, up to the roof of a shed and down the other side into the parallel street. She would catch the girl at the alleyway ahead. This was tag, hide-and-go-seek, hunt. This was dodging the children who called her Imp and Changeling. She'd played such games and she was good at them, but the stakes of win and loss tonight were higher. She was in danger, danger as great as that which she had faced last Midsummer. The same danger. What did Alys lure her toward?

Boot heels clicked ahead of her, crossed her path.

Moving cautiously, Laurel reached the alley and crept along its dark length after the receding clatter. She nearly stumbled down a narrow, wet stairway which tunneled beneath two adjoining buildings. Faint light shone beyond.

Laurel went down. The stairs ended against a wall, but another alley crossed and lost itself in darkness in either direction. A lantern in a window above lighted the intersection. Crouched in the shadow at the foot of the stairs, she listened: footfalls echoed against the bare stone walls at the backs of the shops, disorienting, deceiving. Which way? She shut her eyes and let her inner sense guide her. Tentative feelers reached out into the night, searching for that blank spot in the energies of fire and stone and living beings around her. Alys was nearby. Where?

To the right.

Laurel turned and, feeling along the wall once she left the pool of light, turned again. As her eyes adjusted to the dimness, she saw the little figure ahead, walking away. She shrank back against the wall, not daring to breathe, but Alys didn't turn. Did she know she was followed? The girl was strangely attuned to Laurel's psyche, as if they were united by bonds of blood or a sympathy shared. Alys had known of Laurel before she'd come to New York. She'd known precisely when Laurel had arrived, and had watched her enemy for months without revealing her own presence. She always knew when Laurel sought her before this. Where Alys cloaked herself in secrecy, Laurel had gone undisguised; to a child even of undeveloped magical sensitivity, the young wizard's power must blaze in indisputable warning. Alys must sense that Laurel was here tonight. She must know why. Could she be unaware that her death stood so close? Surely not. Why then these games? Why didn't she flee?

Alys went on to the end of the alley without breaking the measures of her stride, paused, then darted around the next corner. Laurel ran after her.

The walls shimmered with unleashed magic. Laurel stopped. A spell had been cast; she felt the waves of its influence wash over her. Something was happening. But what? Danger sang in her ears. She whispered a warding incantation. Did Alys possess such concealed talent?

Abruptly, the ground dropped out from beneath her and she plummeted into darkness.

There was no sensation of striking a surface. When the swirling, sickening, dizziness dissipated and vision returned, she was simply elsewhere. Laurel lifted her head and slowly rose. Where was she? The street was strange. Was this the same alley she had fallen in? No. Not at all like it. Walls rose where none had been before. Narrow crawlways opened where solid brick had stood; she didn't know where they led. Even the stones she knelt upon looked different. The light mist which had blurred the distance all evening had grown into an obscuring fog. She could see no more than a few feet in any direction. Every tentative step revealed another incongruity. Nothing was familiar.

She heard a shuffling noise behind her, a susurrus of leathern skin on stone. Not one pair of boots, but many bare feet. She caught whispers of words, a rhythmic chant that was indistinguishable but eerily familiar. They crawled out of niches in the broken walls, from the shadows behind rocky outgrowths, out of the mists: Monsters, shapes from her nightmares. Laurel shuddered. She turned to escape. More appeared from the joining corridors, voices oddly muted as if they wailed from an immense distance. No matter; she knew what they said. She'd heard the chant before. There was no charcoal landscape, no great door, but she knew where she was. Alys had sent her into her dreams. But how had the girl known? She said she'd seen Laurel in dreams. But *whose* dreams? Was it possible that somehow, in one sphere or another, this place truly existed? Had she been here before? Had Alys seen this too? What did it mean? Gods, she was here. She was really here. This was the crowd. Humanoid forms in ragged garb reached for her with twisted, stunted or elongated limbs, some like claws, some in the semblance of tentacles with a gelatinous sheen upon their surface. Simian faces peered at her eagerly. Yawning mouths revealed vampyric, yellowed fangs. They stretched as they emerged from their hiding-places and came forward her to take her. Take her to the King.

Laurel's sword was up, poised for defense. She wouldn't be captured without a fight. How many were there? A dozen? More? She couldn't defeat them all, but they were a slow-moving mass, languid as they enclosed her. Perhaps she could cut down a couple, break through the circle, and outrun the rest. Where she might run to was a problem to be dealt with afterwards.

A taloned hand swiped at her. Laurel ducked to avoid the blow, then leapt into the vulnerable spot beneath her opponent's outflung arm. The swordpoint drove deep into layers of rags, but apparently did not pierce flesh. The man-beast threw back its head and rumbled with muted laughter. More shambling steps advanced close behind her. Hilt gripped in both hands, cursing, she whirled to fend off the host gathering at her back, and, in the same encompassing swing, struck at a gaping mouth. Her blade sliced through the shaggy head without injury.

She blinked at the creature in amazement, then quickly glanced at the others, hesitating, about her. Then she laughed.

It seemed as if the moon had passed from behind the clouds. The mists had cleared a little and enabled her to see the situation more accurately. Her own shadow lay on the dirty cobbles, cast through the foe she held at bay. The creature had no shadow of its own. None of them did. In truth, the distorted forms were shaky, lacking the lucid edge of reality. It was a poor trick. Godefroi could do better if he were inclined to conjure up illusions so hideous. Yet, they had served their purpose.

She strode boldly to the nearest rocky wall. The ragged creatures danced back uncertainly, breaking their circle about her, yielding. They gestured as if they meant to strike her, seize her, but Laurel ignored them. They were no longer threatening.

She touched the wall—or tried to. Her fingers passed through and met smooth, solid brick a few inches beyond.

"Enough of this game!" she cried. "Begone! Back to Hell with you!"

The fragile spell wavered, warped like a reflection disturbed, shattered like glass. She threw an arm over her face as an icy blast cut her and sparks like snowflakes tickled her exposed wrist and brow. Furious that she'd been deceived, misled, delayed, Laurel shot back blasts of her own fire. That little imp would not play with her this way! Buildings shook. Debris burned in the gutters.

She stood alone in the alley, where she'd been before the

chimerical enchantment had enclosed her. Where she'd been all along. She heard Alys's boots clatter ahead of her, running.

She *felt* Alys. Laurel saw that the girl's powers—mostly mental, precognitive, empathic—were no match for her own. That one illusionary spell had taxed Alys's strength. She held the potential for dangerous magic, but she was young. Her abilities were not developed. She hoped to gain more through her allegiance to the Dark Forces, but she didn't possess such power yet. She survived by deception. Laurel saw now how this child had influenced the unsuspecting sergeant—hinting and lying and worming her way into his mind, not to command him, but to distort his thoughts and shape them to her own. She couldn't overtake anyone stronger. The nullity Alys had wound about herself was meant to hide her thoughts, her magic, and especially her vulnerability.

The cloak of secrecy was torn aside and a multitude of exposed emotions exploded in Laurel's head. She felt everything: frustration that the spell had been unsuccessful. Rage for revenge. Outrage that her camouflage had been obliterated. Fear of the young woman who chased her and had flung that fierce psychic blast to shatter her defenses. Desperation as Alys sought to rally her undefined powers for the final battle. Terror that Laurel saw all of this. Greater fear that Laurel would defeat her. Betrayal. Bestial ferocity. Horrible malformation of the soul like no human Laurel had ever encountered. Hate for her foe, hate for all stronger magicians, hate for the humanity which had cast her out. If she were able, Alys would destroy all the world in this moment.

Instead, she called for help. She invoked names which cut through Laurel's mind, names written in forbidden texts, names of demons and spurned gods, names that defined all that was evil. Names which these same dread powers had called themselves by when they had first touched her. Alys cried out through the depths of night, but she didn't possess the ability to summon them. The time was not right. Tonight, the gates were closed.

The fleeing footsteps stopped abruptly. Despair. Alys was trapped. Laurel flew down the alley.

She ducked through an arch and entered a little courtyard behind the church. The backs of the priory outbuildings enclosed her. St. Matthieu's steeple rose over the brick wall ahead. No doors. No gates. No exit save the archway she'd just come through. She saw nothing but empty crates and scattered, moldering straw. Yet Alys *was* here. Where else she could be? The girl could not escape. But the flood of terror and hatred which had overwhelmed Laurel only minutes before was gone. Alys's concealment had been repaired.

Laurel lifted her sword and whispered a protective spell. Another trap might await her. As she cautiously entered the little yard, keeping her back at the passageway, there was a frantic movement in the shadows. She lunged. The sword caught the thick folds of a cloak. Alys shrieked. Thin arms and legs flailed furiously; knees and feet and elbows buffeted Laurel. Fingernails tore at her face and throat. With her free hand, Laurel grabbed at a wrist, twisted it away from her eyes. She cuffed the girl, then again. She shoved back the bird-light, bony body, banged it against the wall and brought her blade up, slicing cloth and fur, until the point touched beneath Alys's chin. The girl stood perfectly still. Green eyes burned up into hers, bold as a cornered rat.

"You won't."

"I have to."

"You don't want to."

"You've given me no other choice."

"Why should you want me dead? I've done nothing wrong."

"You killed your sergeant!"

"I didn't! He killed himself. You can't prove otherwise."

"You tried to kill me!"

"I couldn't. *You* have the sword."

"You are too dangerous. It isn't right that any mortal have powers such as you seek."

"I might say the same of you," Alys answered. "We are both sisters in our own kind."

"You are nothing like me!"

"No," the girl agreed. "You are stronger. You know more than I do. I can't stop you." Fingers touched the edge of the blade, testing its sharpness. "Why should you begrudge me what you have?" The voice was childlike in its innocence, injured at harsh accusations, without hint of fear nor rage. But Laurel had *seen*; she knew what lay behind the girlish face. This was only another disguise.

"You will work for destruction against all that right magicians fight to maintain," she answered. "You will bring chaos."

"I don't know that word."

"You'll destroy the peace of this world if you live. You'll bring those Others in! I can't let you! It's my duty," she plead hopelessly, for the time for pleas had passed. Alys mustn't leave this cul-de-sac alive.

"You might join me," said Alys. "Teach me. They would

welcome you. They'd give you so much. You might easily be most powerful in this realm, greater than the Red-Lord. You've thought as much yourself. They would make you a Queen of Wizards for your service."

"No!" She would be lost if she let herself listen to more. Reality began to dissolve around her. Alys would suck out her soul with lies.

Laurel drew back the sword. She cried out—"Gods help me!"— and thrust.

Alys slipped down against the wall; steel met stone, grated, snapped. Laurel leapt at the shapeless bundle falling at her feet, and took up an empty cloak. Something moved in the wavering darkness to her left, then darted through the arch. She pursued, dashing down angled alleys until she burst onto the street.

She stopped and stood gasping, heart drumming, breath fogging before her face. Footsteps sounded ahead. Alys was not too far away. She could catch her. She wouldn't; there were other footfalls behind her.

Laurel looked over her shoulder as the guard, not Alys, approached.

"We saw the fire, Dam'sel," he said, "and heard the screaming." Others were arriving now, weapons drawn, ready for battle. "You cried for help." He looked up and down at her torn and muddy clothes, her bruised face, her desolate expression. "What was it?"

"Nothing," Laurel told them. "I'm not hurt."

"Bloody beggars!" another guard said. "The town's not safe for a woman out at night."

"Did you see who it was?"

"No." Alys's footfalls had grown fainter and fainter. The broken sword fell from Laurel's hands and clattered on the cobblestones.

elfen

On Good Friday, Laurel stood on the road to Storm Port five miles beyond New York. The highway was muddy where the stony pavement had deteriorated, but her palfrey had come so far at a goodly trot without difficulty. If it didn't rain tonight, she would ride out again in the morning and leave the town forever.

Her mission had failed. No one had seen Alys since that night: the girl had not returned to the guardswomen's hall and the Captain assumed she'd deserted the garrison. There was no sign of her in the town, nor could Laurel detect that cloaking void in the natural energies about New York. Alys had simply disappeared.

In truth, Laurel was glad. She thought of Alys, throat torn open, blood splashing the walls of the Matthieu Close and spilling at their feet, little hand gripping the sharp blade, body falling, if the fatal strike had not missed. She thought how she might've chased Alys even to the gates of the garrison yard in spite of the enormous risk if the other guards had not come to stop her. She thought of the tragedy which might have been prevented at May Night at the price of her own unstained soul. Laurel was horrified by what she'd nearly done– No, she couldn't have done it. No magical training, no sense of duty, no command from Lord Redmantyl could force her to commit a crime of such magnitude without remorse. Death was an inevitable part of wizardry and this death was especially necessary. She might've done it; someday, she would have to do it. There would be magicians more vulnerable than herself and she must battle them, destroy them: Old wizards, as Redmantyl would be; young upstarts who were not evil, only weaker than herself and foolish enough to stand in challenge; mad, wicked, dangerous creatures who, like Alys, were a threat to the safety of this world. Wizards must battle to the death, but she wasn't yet truly a wizard and she was not yet ready. In time, she might stand as formidable as her uncle, knee-deep in the blood of her enemies, bold of heart and unfaltering her purpose, but not today. She felt it wrong. She could not be a murderer so young. She couldn't begin her career as a guardian of all that was right with a child's blood. Alys's evil did not justify her own. All her best instincts rebelled. She didn't want to do it. She saw now how she had evaded the bloody task until she could no longer turn away and, even at the last when everything had pressed her to it, her aim had struck untrue. Wizardry might demand the sacrifice, but Laurel couldn't give herself to it so easily. In this, she was impotent, bound by too human sensibilities. She was too tender, too squeamish, too infirm of will, too much afraid. This was a surprising discovery; Laurel wouldn't have used these words to describe herself before the past night, but now she knew them to be accurate. She could not kill Alys even if the fate of the universe hung upon it.

She must go to her uncle and confess her weakness. Perhaps, he knew already. The urgent message which had thrummed through her head for weeks had finally ceased. Was this silence meant as a reprimand or as a sign of disappointment? Was Redmantyl's attention turned elsewhere, seeking Alys to dispatch her himself? He would be angry with her—he must be now. He wouldn't understand the reasons for her failure. He would fault her: she had been given a grave responsibility. Much was in jeopardy if Alys were allowed to give herself over to Dark Powers and they found their way into this world. Laurel was aware of the consequences of her inaction. But whose error was it? Hers for being unwizardly, or his for knowing this, yet sending her out to fulfill a commission she was not fit to master? She had come here alone and unready, with no idea what manner of foe she must face nor what duties she must perform at her uncle's command. She had been the best of Lord Redmantyl's pupils, a most promising talent, but she didn't possess the capacities of an adult wizard. Redmantyl knew this. Did he think she would succeed in spite of her ignorance? Did he expect her to return from this test in triumph?

Regardless, Laurel knew that she need not remain in New York. It was time to surrender her duty. If Alys must die, that task was best left to stronger, older wizards who could strike without flinching and live without remorse. She could not. She was relieved that the responsibility was taken from her hands.

Redmantyl would be angry, but he would forgive her. He would do what he must to stop Alys and avert disaster. Laurel would resume her apprenticeship and, in ten years, she would face the responsibilities of a full wizard and prove herself worthy.

In a week, she would be home.

Laurel clicked to the little mare and urged it to turn in the wet roadway. She rode back to town.

Chilled, she stopped in one of the little taverns near the market square. A murmur arose at her entrance and her name was whispered as she crossed the room to take a seat before the fire. The townsfolk must have much to gossip about. She had made sufficient spectacle of herself in her search for Alys: Her spying among the garrison. Her open spell-casting—*walking wild*, Lord Ambris said they called it. Her mysterious fire and fight only two nights ago.

She risked her life and her immortal essence to protect these wretched creatures. They despised her for the very power which made her their guardian. Laurel had long been outraged at this injustice. Why should she battle evil, and for her efforts be looked upon as evil herself? Until her failure, she would have been infuriated. Now, she didn't care. She was not much of a guardian. Let them talk.

A shrill female voice rose from the corner, intending that she overhear: "I can't imagine who would find a wild creature like *that* attractive. She's so tall as a man."

"And so free as one," a male voice added.

Laurel glanced up at the hushed laughter that followed. Martin Sheriffson and Amabel Dyesdaughter, whom Martin had been courting since Igren's betrothal, sat nearby. "What does that mean?" she asked.

"'Tis said that the niece of Mayor Nikholas visits taverns so often as a nobleman," the maid replied, smiling. "With a nobleman."

"You visit taverns yourself," she answered, lifting her mug as if to show them where they were.

"And who do you visit at night?"

Laurel wondered at these odd remarks, but she didn't rise to the bait. If they were looking for a brawl or an explosion, they must be disappointed. Martin made a few more tentative stabs, but they were ignored. The pair were confounded as Laurel quietly drank her cider.

Before she left, she turned to them again. "It doesn't matter, you see," she explained. "Your precious town will be ashes soon enough if all goes wrong. Blame me for that if you will. I won't be back to see this filthy pit again."

A blue cloak hung in the porter's cubby at the Mayor's Hall; Laurel blinked at it, wondering, as she discarded her own gear. Kaiese met her in the front hall. "Is My Lord Ambris here?" If he still meant to accompany her, he deserved fair warning that she planned to leave in the morning.

"Yes, indeed, my dear." The endearment was astonishing; Laurel was even more astonished when her aunt smiled upon her. "He waits to speak to you."

She understood. "He has offered for me?" Though Laurel felt as if she'd been struck by lightning, her voice sounded oddly disinterested.

It didn't seem to be her own. She didn't resist when the Lady took her by the arm and swept her down the corridor; she barely heard her aunt's reply.

"Of course. Silly child! You cannot be so surprised, the way he's paid court to you these months. And after the Goldsmith–" They were at the garden door. Kaiese shoved her gently in the small of the back, urging her out. "Go to him." The Lady went to her parlor windows, out of hearing but not out of sight.

Laurel hesitated before she went to meet him. Ambris was pacing the pebbled paths, but he ceased once he saw her. "Laurel."

"My Lord." She knew that this formality was not what he had hoped to hear.

"Your aunt has explained to you?"

"She has. My Lord, I must refuse."

Injury crossed his face, then was concealed. "May I ask why? Is it myself you object to?"

"No," answered Laurel. "I could not. I am not unaware of the honor you offer. Another woman in my place would think you a marvelous catch."

"I understand," he said softly.

"I hoped you would. I did not expect this– This– How came you to make this proposal?"

"Perhaps I act against my best reason, but I cannot be reasonable in all things." He stepped a little nearer, and Laurel stepped back. She didn't know this man; there was an unfamiliar intensity about him which she found disturbing. "You are like no one I have met before, like nothing I know. Do you remember when we first met?"

She nodded.

"You were only a young maid, but I couldn't forget you. Each time I came to this town, I hoped to hear more news. I didn't expect to see you again, nor did I imagine what might happen if we did meet. Laurel, I did not intend to tell you of this."

"No," she said. "Tell me."

"I suppose I loved you then, though I didn't understand my own heart," Ambris continued. "I thought of you often when I was weary of my life and dreaming of fanciful things—the one wondrous thing I have known. I only come to New York to see you. You welcomed my company. I did not hope before that. Why should I not offer for you? I have spoken to my father and told him of you, who you are. He much admires your uncle, Lord Redmantyl, and he waits to meet you. When I addressed your uncle Nikholas, he likewise approved."

"But, My Lord, I did not approve."

He opened his mouth, hesitated, then plunged on: "I defied my father at your bidding–"

"I never–!"

"You did!" Ambris insisted. "I would've given all I had. I forgot everything for you. I was encouraged to believe that you wouldn't object."

"By whom? Not me," she answered, perhaps too harshly. "My aunt and I are not fond of each other, My Lord Ambris. You know I would not have her approve my suitors."

"I didn't seek her consent."

"You spoke to her before you said a thing to me!"

"I would not have—I vow to you, Laurel—save that she asked to know what I meant by traveling with you to Storm Port and she must know that my intentions were perfectly honorable. I meant that we should speak together before we arrived at the city and, if you were agreeable, I might visit you at Wizardes Cliff. I didn't mean to make an offer yet. But–" He threw a helpless glance at Kaiese in her window. "Having once assured her, I couldn't refuse to speak all. Laurel, I know your feelings for your aunt. You must believe that I would not deliberately bargain with her without your knowledge."

"I know." She could barely stand to think how much he must care for her. No one, not even the Duke's son, could have any practical reason for traveling between Pendaunzel and New York so often as Ambris had these past months. He had come, hoping that he might find her here still. And, finding her, he had been encouraged. How had she not seen? How had she misinterpreted his kindness so? "I never thought you a suitor, My Lord. We never spoke of such things. I thought you and I were friends! If I had imagined you sought more–" She could be calm no longer. "God's bloody eyes! An unmarried woman cannot be pleasant in a man's company without his imagining she looks to him as a possible husband!"

She had meant to be kind, but he was infuriatingly more gentle. Did he have to be so wretchedly courteous? He was even reasonable as he made his unreasonable feelings plain. Ambris must be miserable with disappointment, but he remained entirely sympathetic, with the patience of a lover who sees only what he wishes in the beloved. She was angry that she'd misinterpreted his friendship; she should have stopped this before he made a fool of himself. She wished she could— she simply had to—blast him out of this damnable infatuation. "I am not like anything you know, My Lord, that is surely true. I am not the woman you imagine. So long as we have known each other, I've spoken of nothing but wizardry. Surely you knew I would not quit my magic?"

"I knew that we must wait through your apprenticeship and magedom, but delay is not impediment. Wizards do marry."

"Not I! You don't understand at all if you thought– Do you know what I am? I am the Devil's own—that is what I am called. The witch. The changeling. A magician! I am feared, and with reason. I have duties ordinary folk cannot comprehend. You will fear me for them too and hate that they take me away from you. Will you have such a woman for a wife? You know my uncle Redmantyl. You have heard tales of his battles. I am like him! Do you know what I will be like when I am at my power's height?" Flames roared up from the blossoming trees behind him. "There! That is what I may do."

Ambris stiffened, but he did not look back. "I thought you had command of your powers."

"I have. I can." She was immediately ashamed at her attempts to frighten him. The outburst ended before the tree branches were more than scorched. "You see that we are not suited to each other. I cannot accept you. My apologies, My Lord." She went into Hall, past her aghast aunt, ignoring Kaiese's demands for an explanation. Fresh questions were directed at Ambris, but Laurel was upstairs before she heard his replies.

Kaiese came up some minutes later.

"What did you say? My Lord Ambris has withdrawn his offer! He said that he was mistaken. But it is not his mistake, is it, Girl? Foolish wretch! You have refused Leobolde Goldsmith, and now this most generous nobleman. Is there no end to your pride? Will you keep yourself 'til the Emperor Kharles should ask for you?"

"I will refuse so long you push me at men I barely know!"

"How well must you know him?" her aunt retorted. "They talk all about this town how you behave with him."

"Yes, I have heard it! But your petty, foul-minded gossip is in error! He is nothing to me!"

Kaiese let out a sour laugh. "Such a prominent man! And he obviously thinks more of you than you deserve. Fool I was, I thought you would be glad at this arrangement."

"Seven devils!" cried Laurel. "As if I could ever willingly give myself away in marriage like one of your pretty prize maidens for the distinction of a good match!"

"Oh, you are no pretty prize! 'Tis a wonder any man would think to want you, and more wonder that you can be so perverse to refuse. I cannot say if this obstinacy of yours is stupidity or pure wickedness. This is the taint of your blood! Your mother's curse! Unholy, magical, unnatural—you have the worst of both of them!"

"Both?" Laurel leapt upon this word. "Who–?" She stopped there, for she knew.

Kaiese did not answer.

"I will go," Laurel said quietly. "You cannot keep me."

Her aunt remained silent. The spell had been broken.

Laurel left that afternoon after brief farewells to her baffled cousins and Uncle Nikholas; they knew that she meant to ride in the morning, but this abrupt change of plans and Kaiese's silence told them there was more to this than they would ever hear. The Mayor and his daughters sent her with good wishes and hopes that she would return for Igren's wedding.

The palfrey proved more sturdy than its rider had expected and traveled swiftly over the first miles, trotting through puddles and stepping adeptly amid the mud and rubble of the worst stretches of the road north. Laurel was able to ride on after dark and soon caught up with the thesper troupe which had left New York that morning. She pretended that she'd missed their rendezvous at the inn and joined their company as if she had never made alternate plans.

The next days flowed together so that Laurel couldn't say how many had passed on her travels. She knew that she would not be home before May Night, and so refused to think of the emergency until the time for it was upon her. She gave her hands to the troupe, ate with them, and wandered restlessly about their nightly encampments after the others had gone to sleep. She was never one of them; they would have welcomed her as one out place and therefore as one of their own, but she could never be so careless and easy as one of the Free Folk. She was not truly free. The burden of her failed responsibilities weighed heavily upon her.

They passed the charred ruins of Lyngreen. Laurel knew that this had been Alys's home, and knew what had happened here. If the girl eluded the grasp of more skilled magicians on May Night, the same tragedy would befall New York and Storm Port and all the rest of the world—smoldering devastation so far as Alys's new powers could reach. When the thespers stopped at Gilham and planned to stay awhile, she rode on to Storm Port alone.

She arrived a strange figure, weather-stained and uncombed, with no mark of rank upon her. She might have been a strolling minstrel without instrument, a young soldier who had abandoned sword and shield at the frontier, a Lady in disguise: all these speculations were made at the Salamander Inn after the mysterious traveler took a room for herself. Since she kept within her room for most the day, the servants of the inn were able to weave fanciful tales at their pleasure. Laurel did not emerge until late afternoon, then went out to see the city.

Storm Port's bazaar was just as Laurel remembered, as it had been on that wonderful afternoon when Lord Redmantyl had bought all she dared to ask for. She'd been so frightened to meet her fabulous wizard-uncle, so curious to discover the truth behind the tales, and so surprised to find him kind. What a fool she was! Laurel had always believed her father to be some prominent man who remained unknown to avoid some social or political embarrassment. A common guardsman might have named her; therefore, her father must be a married merchant, a rash nobleman, a Spaniard who had betrayed his country for Tomasin's sake. She had even once imagined—amusing thought now!—that Ambris might be her father. She could account for his attention to her no other way. All her life, she'd wondered at the truth, yet had been too stupid to see it even when he had been before her from the beginning. The guardians of her secret, Lord Redmantyl and Kaiese, had kept it so carefully that their silence fairly shouted.

Her father was no merchant, no Plantagenet, no Spaniard. Mere indiscretion was not the error connected with her birth. Simply, her mother was a wild swordswoman and her father a wandering young wizard. They were cousins to the first degree, a tie of blood only one step removed from that of brother and sister. By the laws of Church and Empire, it was an incestuous union.

Lord Redmantyl's daughter. It seemed obvious now; she looked most like him, more than Orlan, and she had inherited his talent exactly. The bond between them was too great for uncle and cousin's child.

All the rumors she'd ever heard about her mother came together and finally coherently. Laurel knew the story: Tomasin had envied her young cousin's magic. If rumor did not exaggerate, she had dabbled with witchcraft as she sought to develop her own small talent and, when Yryd visited New York, she had seduced him. Redmantyl had told her of his boyish admiration for the wild swordsmaid; he had probably been flattered by her attentions and, newly freed from his mage-vows, surrendered easily. If Tomasin couldn't achieve magic for herself, she would take this unnatural path to try and steal some of her cousin's magic. The widespread myth was not true, but a guardswoman, even one who knew a little magic, would believe it. Perhaps she'd meant to mother a magical child, or perhaps the child had been an accident. Regardless, Laurel had been born.

When Kaiese had learned of her sister's actions, she was horrified. She'd taken the infant from its mother and tried to obliterate all obvious signs of the taint. As Laurel had grown into unmistakable powers, Kaiese's fear of magic and her disgust for her sister were combined in her dislike of Laurel; she had tried to make the young girl like other maidens, as she'd tried to form herself to the common mould, with equal success.

Redmantyl had not stayed in New York to see his daughter's birth. He was ashamed to name her, yet he did love her. He couldn't claim her without advertising his error, but he'd come to see her when her mother had died, he'd watched her grow into her magic—a reflection of his own—and, when her infant powers had gone beyond her control, he'd welcomed her at Wizardes Cliff and brought her into apprenticeship. He had allowed her freedoms of confidence he would allow no other child in his house. He had nurtured her talent above all others. He had entrusted her with this errand, believing her competent because she was his.

For the first time, she truly knew who she was, and that knowledge changed her homecoming: she could bring failure to her uncle, her teacher, her master, but how much more difficult to bring it to her father! He would see her knowledge as soon as they met. His response would not be altered, but her explanation would change. She was as reluctant as she was anxious to see him. What could she say?

At the cathedral, Laurel stopped to light a candle. She was at the middle of an important journey, but it felt like an ending. May Night fell tomorrow and she would not be home. She had fasted and sat sleepless for days. She had rested and spent this day in meditation, and tomorrow she would ride as far as Narby—only fifteen miles. She would make her vigil somewhere in the woods of Greenwaters Island beyond the village, and hope that Alys hadn't escaped Redmantyl's vengeance as she had escaped hers.

At sunset, the bells of St. Khrystopher's began to chime, but Laurel did not stay for Evensong.

Ambris was waiting for her at the Salamander. "You left New York."

"You knew that I meant to, escort or no," she answered.

"But alone! Do you know, once I knew you'd gone I rode out after you, hoping to find you on the road. I asked after you at every stop. Are you safe, Laurel? I worried for you."

"You had no need to worry. I am quite well, as you see, My Lord." Her next words were more biting: "You have no right to ask after me!"

He was taken aback, but recovered himself quickly. "True, I have no business to ask after your welfare," he agreed. "I do not have rights, I know, but I have a concern for you, proper or not. I must ask."

Laurel did not contradict this.

"I know that this has no weight upon you. You do not care."

"That's not so! I am not ungrateful you think me worthy of such honor–"

"I did not intend to bestow an honor," said Ambris. "This is no knighthood. I do not offer you my hand and my heart as a nobleman seeking to title a Lady. I am a man who desires one woman. I love you. You taught me that I ought not be satisfied with what I have. 'Twas true—I did not have enough."

"I spoke of power."

"I do not want power, but I have discovered that I want more than contentment. You may refuse, but why should I not ask? I have done my duty in marriage once and I do not regret it, but I am not called to make another such alliance and, for once, I choose to do something that will simply make me happy." The corners of his mouth moved in the slightest of smiles. "I have been happy with you."

"My Lord– Ambris," Laurel paused. "Ambris, I do feel much for you, but not as you would like. I never meant to make you believe I did. 'Twas all a misunderstanding. I– It is an honor nevertheless."

"If I did misunderstand, I apologize. You cannot change your affections. Indeed, I would think you false if you were to consent against your better feelings." But the hoarseness of his voice suggested otherwise; he wished desperately that she would change her mind. "I came to Storm Port to see for myself that you were safe. I think you will continue to Wizardes Cliff as swiftly." He took her hand. "I remain, always, your friend, Lady. Perhaps we may meet again."

Laurel whispered something; she knew not what.

She knew the expression in Ambris's eyes. She'd seen it in other eyes before this: Olyr's, Godefroi's, Klyffaude's. It was disquieting. She never understood how she could inspire such feelings in any man and, in this gentle nobleman, it was most strange of all. She wouldn't have thought that Ambris could feel so passionately as a hot-hearted boy, but he did.

She understood that he had not had much happiness. Honor and faithful adherence to duty had their merits, but they offered no compensation for that lack. If any man was worth the proper woman's love, he was, but if he imagined her to be that woman, he was mistaken. It was impossible for her to feel differently. She was what she was, and she couldn't return the love Ambris felt. A wizard must always be set apart and keep herself carefully lest she weaken her dedication to her craft. Magic must come first, or it would be lost. Someday, she would take lovers, but Laurel was certain that Ambris could not consent to such an informal relationship. He could never endure a magical woman who appeared from time to time and departed again without giving her heart as fully as he gave his. It was wrong to offer less than a true lover might; she must cheat him with compromise. She respected him, held him in highest regard, troubled that she must spurn him—but nothing more.

When she looked up, she was alone.

She was caught in the midst of a bestial crowd. Ragged bodies pressed her on all sides. Hands plucked at her clothes. A thousand feet raced forward, carrying her along like the force of a fast-flowing river. Voices murmured all about her, softly at first, then louder and louder until the repeated cry was overwhelming:

"The King! The King! The King Comes!"

She stumbled beside the black wall and, grasping for sure holds, began to climb.

"The King! The King! The King Comes!"

This had happened before. Laurel was familiar with the fabric of her dream: the frenzied chant, the glassy surface beneath her fingers, the trumpeting clarion wail, the Door against the night sky. She knew that an ally waited for her at the top of this wall. She knew the words of their conversation like an enigmatic but memorable poem. As she strained upwards, she expected a hand to descend and take her up. She reached up for it.

No one was there. The slippery stone eluded her grasp and she fell back into darkness.

Laurel struck the bedchamber floor and was on her feet before she was fully awake, startled that she had ever fallen asleep. The chant still drummed in her ears.

"The King! The King Comes! The King! The King is Nigh!"

Wizard's Keep was not tomorrow—Tonight! In her room, she was unable to divine the alignment of the heavens, but she could sense that they had *opened*. Vast abysses gaped between the stars, rending space, swallowing all light, seeking life, seeking her.

They poured through the gateway, lost gods, banished demons, the spawn of countless dark and age-obscured legends. It was Time. She did not require the ceremonies of the Keep to call them; they knew of her. They had awaited this opportunity. Drawn by the promise of her power, they reached for her while she remained unguarded.

Laurel scrambled to the fireplace for a bit of charred wood and hastily drew a pentacle on the floor. She wrote all the spells of protection she could remember about the rim and at the points of the star while seated within. Hurry! She felt their glee as they rushed toward her. Wards lifted about her, growing solid as she worked the meaning from the words. She wrote another. Was it enough? Would the circle hold?

Suddenly, as the last spell was cast, reality expanded. The walls gave outward, as if she'd been sitting amidst four stage canvases which had all fluttered at once to show what lay behind scene set in the play. Laurel didn't understand everything she saw, but she thought it was more than she ought to see. There was too much of things: she could look at them from all sides at once—top and bottom, left and right, in and out—and they had more sides than they decently ought. She was still in her room at the inn, but beyond it somehow too, within, without, and above. The pentacle stood like a bright ring of iron about her.

She saw every particle of dust, every point of light in the firmament. She saw the killing cold of the ether and the energies of living matter burning about her in shades of color and intensity which she could not interpret. She saw unmeasured miles, to the rim of the earth, to the edges of the universe and, beyond it, to nothing. She saw the bright glamour of magicians who had likewise passed into this space between: This, she realized, was the magic in its true state, free of human flesh. They were linked together, kindred beings in a common effort. She felt their minds touch upon hers, acknowledging her presence among them. She knew who they were: Lord Redmantyl, nearby, aware of her danger but unable to make himself vulnerable for her sake; Godefroi's mother on her island; an aged wizard at Palefyt; others, more distant and preoccupied with their own defense.

Something touched the barrier about her, pressed against it, but could not penetrate her wards. The pentacle held. Laurel looked up, and saw them.

Creatures of the ether, They were huge beyond comprehension.

She knew she only saw fragments; the rest remained Outside. Little ones, rat-like, snake-like, spidery, fishy, monkeyish, canine, goatish, almost human, or some of these all at once, scrambled like parasites on the surface of their mountainous hosts, and chittered as if they were laughing. She would have cowered, shrieking, and covered her eyes like a frightened child, but all her training had prepared her for this trial. She held her place. She remembered her exercises with Redmantyl. She mustn't panic. Fear now was fatal. She mustn't lose herself in anger or terror or expectations of failure. Her father had taught her to protect herself and trusted her to survive. He sought, even now, to distract them from her, but this was her battle. She possessed powers sufficient to deflect them, if she kept her self-command.

Steeling herself, she confronted these monstrous shapes whose forms pushed her to the edge of sanity. She blasted.

The impact of her magic surprised her. The little ones retreated, squealing. The vast forms flinched, then pressed forward again, eagerly, as the brilliant light faded. She blasted a second time, with more precise aim. An intense spurt of fire shot into what she imagined to be an eye. Another form extended a tendril of darkness toward her back; she spun and shot frantically. The damaged appendage fell away as if cut, but fresh tendrils soon stretched out against her barrier, fumbling like blind fingers for an unguarded opening. The little ones, emboldened, returned to swarm about the rim of the circle. Sparks caught their fur; they wailed and bit at themselves as they burned. Their bodies puffed to distended and grotesque proportions, then burst. Other guardians fought at their flanks. The blaze of magic glowed everywhere. Thousands of the vermin exploded, banished, but there were always more. The vast ones stood like quivering black mountains, flinching at each blast but resuming their assault once the light was gone. On and on they pressed, inexhaustibly patient.

As she fought, Laurel heard a soft and melodious voice calling to her; it urged her to cease this foolishness. It spoke in favor of its masters: They promised greater power in their service than any mortal could possess. They threatened punishment. They praised her magic. They offered everything she could desire, for her surrender.

"No!" She sent her last blast in all directions, blotting out the dark shapes with blinding light. She knew that when this shield of light failed, her powers would be exhausted. She couldn't fight like this much longer. They were immortal; she was not. They could wait until her defenses were weakened. The pentacle would hold, but as an empty fortress; her energy spent, she was weaponless within. They would breach her wards at the first spell's weakening. She couldn't last until the Time was ended, but she would not be taken helplessly. She was, after all, a guardian. She would die before she gave herself over.

She called to every force of good she'd ever heard of with every prayer or incantation she could think of. It didn't matter if she believed or not.

Then, she heard it: a cry in the night so far away that it must be impossible for the sound to carry. No. It was far away Inside. In the place between, time and space were not given the same measurements. She heard the summons: Alys called to them.

There was a hushed moment. They forgot their siege upon her and rushed to take the more willing sacrifice.

The guardians turned their attention from her too, attempting to defend this dangerous point, but the battle was lost before any magician could move to distract. They had her. They *had* her.

It happened quickly. Laurel felt their caress upon the child as their tendrils wound themselves into her receptive essence. There were no wards to breach. Alys welcomed them. They wormed into her flesh, her nerves and organs, her brain. It was too much for the girl. She screamed beyond pain as she was taken, then changed. Madness filled her. At the shrieks, Laurel covered her ears and shouted "No! No! No!" until there was silence.

The glimmer of infant magic was put out. Destroyed? No. They did not burst through the open gateway in invasion; instead, they pulled their newly claimed minion Outside. Alys was removed from this sphere, body and soul.

The door between shut.

This was not the end of it.

Laurel was in her room. She had never left it. The battle was over and the weary young woman sank down on the floor within her circle. She did not pass her fading wards. Hours passed before she fell into an exhausted sleep.

She rose at first light, cold, bleak-hearted, desolate, like a wounded warrior who has fallen before a vastly powerful foe and is surprised to find herself still living. A strange numbness lay over her. There were injuries that would never show, but she felt them as deeply as mortal cuts. Her mind was scorched. Nerve ends were seared away—Not their work, but her own doing, for her own protection. They couldn't reach her now. She'd been lucky; her magic had not saved her.

She knew how the true guardians must view her: a meddlesome

girl who had endangered herself and forced them to draw their attention away from the threat of Alys in order to assist her. She'd been a hindrance at the Keep. And it was through her error that Alys was there in the first place. Because of her mistake, Alys had survived to draw the Outsiders away and they had found their way through to her. They would reshape the girl and return her as their agent. Whatever chaos fell when Alys returned in her new form, Laurel was responsible.

She wasn't fit to be a wizard. She couldn't bear to think of the danger she had put herself, her kind, her world through. If she hadn't been such a reckless fool none of this would have come about: They would not have known of her; Alys would have been destroyed by a guardian who did not flinch; They would have been held at bay by stronger wizards not distracted by a foolish child. She couldn't go home now, with so much laid upon her even before she could call herself a true magician. But where else could she go?

Later that morning, Ambris prepared to leave his room at the Grey Knightes Inn and thought sadly that he might never see Laurel again. Then there came a knock at his door.

She was there.

"Ambris, if you truly care for me as no one ever has, you will let me in."

He saw that something had frightened her badly; all her self-reliance had been shaken away and left her very young and unsure. He didn't understand what had happened, but she had come to him in this trouble and that was all that mattered to him.

"Certainly," he said. "Come in."

tuelfe

There was much surprise at the marriage: conventionally minded folk marveled that a man so sensible and conscious of his duty would involve himself with a guardswoman's unnamed daughter. Ambris had once wed a princess and might easily wed another! The girl wasn't even the sort of pretty schemer who made middle-aged men forget themselves. Others, with more imagination, wondered that a young woman so obviously magical would accept a staid nobleman twice her age with seven children and only a modest inland earldom. But Ambris's betrothed was at Pendaunzel throughout the summer and the consensus of the Duke's court was that it must be a love match.

Laurel hadn't meant to marry; she'd gone to Ambris because she couldn't go home and could not return to New York. Who else could she turn to? Ambris's offer had seemed like sanctuary. She agreed to go with him to Pendaunzel that same day. Duty obliged Ambris to return to Eadeshire soon after, but he left her in the care of his family with the understanding that nothing was fixed between them and she might leave whenever she changed her mind. She stayed.

While the court murmured its speculations, Duke Dafythe and his daughter and niece welcomed her without reservation. Ambris had spoken so much of Laurel that they had expected her long before her arrival. They assumed that she had already given her consent to wed Ambris.

Laurel had been a little afraid to meet Dafythe, who had ruled the Northlands for more than seventy years, but she found him a warm and unassuming elderly man, ninety-four, and much like Ambris in looks, manner and philosophy. At her introduction, he kissed her with fatherly affection. "Do you know," he confided, "when my Ambris first told me of you, he asked if I believed in the Faerye? I'm delighted to find he did not exaggerate. You don't know the change you've brought upon him, my dear. He was always a quiet lad. I never expected he could feel so strongly for anything. 'Tis enchantment. We don't have enough of that sort of thing in the world these days, and we sorely need it."

The Princes Margueryt and Katherine were cautious at first, knowing that Laurel was a student of magic, but they were prepared to like her for Ambris's sake—Kat, especially, was pleased, for she would not be forced to wed Ambris herself if he chose to marry elsewhere. When they found that Laurel was not at all bookish, their admiration increased. Both were bold, athletic young women. Margueryt was the ideal of a Plantagenet Prince: fierce, forward, visionary. Kat was her cousin's lieutenant: smaller, younger, but ready to follow Mara to the ends of the earth on any quest. Like Dafythe and Ambris, like their legendary ancestor, Eduarde Redlyon, their faces were broad-browed, square-jawed, proud and stern, framed by dark chestnut hair. Both respected anyone who could ride and shoot straight and wield a sword with skill. Laurel ceased to wonder how Ambris could admire her when he had such kinswomen; it would have been strange if he preferred the company of more delicate ladies. She joined the Princes at jousts and rode with them into the hills above Pendaunzel, though they could not bring falcons or dogs. They often spent their evenings in the city, attending plays by the Duke's troupe, watching gamesmatches or visiting taverns. In the Princes' company, Laurel was as well known about the city as in the palace.

She had worried that she might not be suited to the niceties of the Duke's court, but Dafythe's kindness and the Princes' enthusiastic companionship put her at ease. With them, she was free from responsibilities. She had cut all her bonds and had no future except what she decided for herself. Ever resilient, she swiftly regained her health, her spirits, even her damaged magic. Fear had not cowed her, but it made her extremely cautious. From time to time, she thought of returning to Wizardes Cliff. She knew she had a duty to resume, but she was not yet ready to face Lord Redmantyl. His disappointment at her behavior must grow each day she stayed away. There was no excuse she could offer: the fear that had brought her here, kept her here, was more difficult to explain than her initial failure.

Midsummer and Maryemas passed quietly. Laurel did not go out on the Keeps; she was prepared to shut herself against any sign of danger, but she *felt* the calm of each night. For now, the Outsider powers had what they wanted. There was no reason to break through until their agent was prepared to return.

Ambris returned at Mykhaelmas. Laurel was out riding with Mara and Kat when she saw him alone on the road beneath the hills and she urged her palfrey down to catch him before the city gate.

He saw her coming and stopped and dismounted. "You haven't

gone."

"I couldn't." She leapt from her saddle, mindless of the smiling Princes who had raced behind her, and threw her arms about him. "Ambris, I missed you." Her uncertainty fell away as his embrace tightened. She hadn't truly felt safe since he'd been gone and she didn't want to be parted from him again.

Ambris spent the rest of the day closeted with his father, but in the evening, they found a private moment to speak seriously together. Laurel wrote to Lord Redmantyl and her aunt in New York, announcing her intention to marry. Banns were posted and the news sung across the Northlands.

The wedding on the Feast of St. Stephan followed soon upon the betrothal, but it was the greatest spectacle seen in Pendaunzel since Margueryt's christening. The city became a festival: Chinese rockets exploded and bonfires blazed even in the daylight hours; parties were given in honor of the bride and groom; alehouses which Laurel had visited dispensed free wine; ballads were written for the occasion. The Duke's thespers performed *Rhyannen*, the tale of a Faerye queen who left her realm for love of a mortal Prince.

Guests arrived from all over the world, as many as could reach Pendaunzel on such sudden notice. Ambris's younger children were brought up from Samandra Abbey. Earls and Marchions from all parts of the Northlands and the borderlands, the Prince of Uinlande, and the granddaughter to the Duke of Burgundy attended. The Emperor Kharles was too busy to appear himself, but he sent representatives. Ambassadors from German and Italian courts brought the compliments of their sovereigns. Even the Spanish Emperor sent an emissary with lavish gifts.

Kaiese, Nikholas, Igren, Geyraulte, and Iobethe traveled to the Duke's city for the ceremony. Laurel didn't particularly want her family there but Ambris and, even more so, Dafythe would not dream of slighting any relation of blood or marriage. Kaiese took credit for the match and was so glad to see her niece—if not her daughter—so successfully placed that she readily forgave or ignored every impertinence Laurel uttered during the festivities. She would have complimented the bride on her good sense, but did not wish to offer insults now.

Lord Redmantyl and Orlan had also been invited, but did not attend. This wounded Laurel, but she couldn't expect her father to be pleased at her decision.

At Stephansmas, she entered the Pendaunzel cathedral of St.

Othelie and stood, dazzled by candlelight, as Igren and Kat helped her out of her cloak and led her the altar where Ambris waited. She didn't hear the bishop's words. Her own voice sounded unfamiliar, echoing against the ancient stone in the expectant silence. Then, Ambris took a ring from his own finger and placed it upon her hand and she, with surprising poise, gave her own ring. They kissed for the first time since the betrothal.

Hand in hand, they walked back to the palace on snowy streets lined with cheering crowds and joined the singing and dancing and feasting at the palace. The celebration went on past midnight and at last, the bridesmaids accompanied the bride to her bedchamber. Ambris followed soon after and the maids left them alone together.

In the morning, Laurel rose first and sat at the window, watching the snow fall. She had known that sex was part of marriage, part of her consent. She was not apprehensive of the act itself, but she'd always associated it with love and passion and had worried that Ambris would notice how little she gave of either.

Though she had not imagined Ambris as a lover in the early days of their acquaintance, he was the most solicitous and attentive of husbands, afraid that she might regret her decision. She'd felt the apology in his touch. Before they had gone to bed, he had stood for long, timid minutes before the fire, not looking at her, and confessed that he had not lain with any woman before his marriage to Margaude and he had never been unfaithful to his first wife.

"I had known women, but it would be unseemly to bed with one as an amusement and no more. You may think this odd."

"No," she had said. "It's entirely like you. I would think it more strange if you said you had given yourself wantonly."

"Laurel, you told me once– No, I vowed I would not ask."

"What?" she asked, with a kind of panic; he would ask why she chose to stay. What answer could she make?

But Ambris said, "You once spoke of two boys you thought you had loved. It is none of my concern. Yet I cannot help but think of it."

Laurel laughed. "You are jealous?"

"Ravingly."

"You mustn't be. After all, I am here and they are nothing to me now. `Tis unlikely I shall ever see either again."

He smiled. "You are so young, Laurel, and you have an energy I did not even at one and twenty. I do not want to be a disappointment."

That night, he gave his heart entirely to her; she could not hurt him. As she watched the snow and Ambris slept, Laurel began to understand what responsibility she took when she promised to receive such a love.

In the spring, Igren married and went to Oerykton. Ambris and Laurel attended, stopping on their way to Eadeshire.

After the winter at Pendaunzel, Ambris felt he must resume his responsibilities. The little village of Eadbury was surrounded by an untamed land; thick forests covered the mountains and hid valleys and rivers in its greenery, crowded the edges of the carefully cut pastures and fields, pressed close even to the castle walls. A few miles from Ellsrood, Laurel could believe that Eadeshire had never been touched. The people, too, were not entirely tamed. Norman citizens and Christians, they kept the customs of their native ancestors just the same, mixing one tradition with the other. They had firm ideas of what a leader ought to be and were accustomed to Earls of their own blood who knew the old ways well. Ambris was an outsider to the shire and he found his people foreign to his understanding, but his father had taught him that a good governor served as well as ruled. He gave attention to the advice of his steward and sheriff, who were both natives to the land, took the trouble to learn the ancient ways, and smoothed over conflicts between native custom and Norman law. He heard his tenants' grievances and sometimes rode out for days to the remote corners of the shire at their summons. He stood austere as their lord, but always with a deference that let any of his people know that they might approach him for justice. The people of Eadeshire, if they found their lord equally foreign, were pleased at his efforts.

Eadeshire had, of course, heard of Ambris's marriage to a most remarkable woman. The peasants traditionally petitioned their Lady for charity or mercy and the yeomanry tendered humble invitations, but it was obvious from the first that Laurel was not a Lady of customary tribute. How were they meant to address this silver-fair bride who rode the countryside in plain courier's garb and spent her days shut in her chambers reading? The villagers were respectful, curious, reserved. The folk of the little farms and woodlands were more enthusiastic; they called her one of the Old Race which had lived there before their own ancestors had come, and who had left crumbling circles of ancient standing-stones atop the nearby mountains. They'd heard of the powers of great magicians and assumed it her natural ability to bring rain, to heal the ill and injured, to aid the infertile, to bring new milk to dry cows and new life to straggling crops. The good harvests of 1951 and '52 were attributed to the Lady's magic, though Laurel knew she had nothing to do with it.

Laurel found little to occupy her days. Ambris's library contained few books of interest beyond the classic Roman authors—Livy, Ovid, Horace, Virgil. The younger children loved her as a playmate, but Arthur and Bertrande, like their elder brothers, remembered their own mother too well to readily befriend her replacement; Laurel was relieved when the boys returned to the Abbey to continue their education. The servants had grown used to managing Ellsrood after Lady Margaude's death and during Ambris's long absences; they would have consulted their new Lady, but she did not take much interest in the keeping of her house. The normal pursuits of Ladies bored her. She nodded when the steward showed her the household accounts and she occasionally looked into the kitchens and storerooms to see that everything was in order. It always was. She interviewed new servants. She heard the pleas of the most unfortunate peasants and, when she could, gave aid. She received Ambris's small circle of local councilors and the most prominent families of Ellsrood, presided over a tea table in her sitting room and feigned polite interest in her guests' gossip. She taught little Guylliame his letters, played at archery with Mathilde and Marcius and rode with them when they trotted their ponies around the stable-yard. She read through the small library. And, when she grew too restless to stay within the castle walls another moment, she took her palfrey into the wilderness and returned by moonlight.

Ambris had never requested that she give up her magic; in fact, he was perplexed that she had. He sometimes asked why she chose not to pursue wizardry, but Laurel never answered these questions. How could she in honesty? Any attempt to describe what had happened that May Eve recalled more than she wished to think of.

Since she had entered the space between her own world and what lay Outside, she *saw*. The veils were sometimes very thin; the shadows beyond grew bright and her own world faded dim and ghostly. At unexpected moments, she caught glimpses of grotesqueries out of the corner of her eye. She heard sighs, murmurs, an occasional muted scream, or whispers so low that the words were not distinguishable. Did they speak of her? Did they call? She refused to listen. She wouldn't look. When familiar shapes dissolved into an alien guise, she shut her eyes and clapped her hands upon her ears. She could never look into the night sky.

She couldn't explain this to her husband. She could not even tell him the most simple truth: she hadn't given up wizardry for marriage; she'd given it up because she could not bear the consequences of her actions. The eternal vigilance against the Others was more than she could withstand. She didn't want to know that there were such vast and dark forces in the universe. She did not want to share in that secret. She wanted her magic, but not all its responsibilities. She wanted to be free of the terror that chilled her. She wanted to feel as if she were not pressed on all sides by dangers. Above all, she wanted to be human. Wizardry did not offer the security and comfort of an ordinary mortal's life.

Yet, even as she was afraid, she was ashamed. At least, there was some honor in surrendering for love, but none for cowardice. Could she tell Ambris that she had married because she didn't know what else to do and he was willing to have her?

She shut and locked the chambers of her mind, closing away secrets she could not endure. She put it all away from her, as a bad dream, and tried to forget. Ambris helped her in this. He offered a haven; he was so sane within the boundaries of his own perceptions that her knowledge of the Outside seemed like madness. Surely, if she told him, he would think her insane.

Her first child, a son, was born in November of 1952. Laurel named him Tomyas.

That winter, Ambris was appointed Lord High Chancellor of the Northlands and they returned to Pendaunzel. The position brought new duties: Ambris still gave attention to Eadeshire, left under direction of his steward and his eldest son Eadryk, who had just come of age, but his duties there took a subordinate place to his responsibilities in his father's domain. He worked with the Duke's ministers to draft and revise laws, briefed his father in imperial and international matters, received foreign ambassadors. He tried to ease the strained relations with Spain, repaired broken treaties, sent urgent messages to the Emperor, and finally, published the declaration of war and called for the release of the city garrisons in Margueryt's name. He sometimes spent twenty hours a day in the management of the Northlands and the strain of it began to show in his face, but he thrived under the burden. This was the place he'd been born to occupy.

As the spouse of so prominent a statesman and a member of the royal family, Laurel took part in processions, sat in the pew at the Duke's chapel, had her likeness taken to hang in the portrait gallery. She greeted visiting courtiers. Once, she welcomed Rosandre, fresh from his success at Paris, accompanied by a timid little wife. He'd asked eagerly after Iobethe and Laurel had told him that her cousin was married now too, to a younger son of one of the New York merchant families; Nikholas was teaching his daughter's husband the wine trade to look after her interests.

Courtly clothes were made for her: long velvet skirts, tight-bodiced tunics, silk petticoats and heavily embroidered robes, finer than any merchant-dame could ever wear. She was surprised how heavy a Lady's garments could be and, like Margueryt and Kat, she reserved her finery for ceremonial occasions. Like the Princes, she became a model for courtly fashion; she brought ribbons and lace back into vogue simply by wearing her riding garb about the palace; the breeches and short tunic of noble blue were more becoming than common brown.

Andemyon entered the court as one of the Duke's heralds when he was fourteen, and Lord Redmantyl and Orlan escorted him to Pendaunzel. Laurel had looked anxiously forward to their coming; she had so many things she wished to say to her father, explanations, apologies, questions, confessions. Redmantyl, however, cut this hope for reconciliation. She saw that he knew she knew who she was, but he didn't invite her confidence. When they met, he did not reproach her with harsh words and he showed interest in little Tomyas, but his anger and his hurt were always apparent even as he shut his mind against her. He didn't speak to Ambris except when compelled by courtesy. He could not forgive her for abandoning her talents and he held her husband responsible. Orlan and Andemyon didn't understand why she had left Wizardes Cliff, but they were glad to see her regardless. She spent most of her time with the younger boy, who was bewildered by the palace's size and the unending activity with it. Orlan was quickly taken up by the pastimes and fads of Pendaunzel's young courtiers and became something of a dandy; Laurel could see that this was his first experience of life beyond Wizardes Cliff and, at twenty-two, he was beginning to question wizardly ways. She was not extremely surprised when she heard that he left home suddenly, his apprenticeship unfinished, only months later. Letters from Igren informed her that Orlan had gone to Oerykton and continued his newly-found rakish ways there, then left Igren's house; she heard no more of him. The storms that covered the sky, centered at Wizardes Cliff, told her of Redmantyl's misery. He had lost his son, too.

A daughter was born in July of 1954, christened Laurel Ambrosia and called Lauret.

As the years passed, Laurel sometimes believed she'd made a terrible mistake. She had hoped that she would come to love Ambris in time, but she did not—not in the heart-quickening, playful, earnest way she'd known as a girl. She admired him as an important man in the greater business of the world. She saw the good that Ambris had done for his country; she caught the look in his eyes, tone of his voice when he urged the Duke's ministers to institute some policy for the benefit of the Northlands. She respected his intelligence and the strength of his convictions. She was proud he had chosen her and pleased that he still loved her after nearly so many years of marriage. She was grateful for his tenderness and the comfort of his steadfast presence. She knew that, in some way, she fulfilled a need of his—not love nor passion nor companionship; he had desired something strange and wonderful in his otherwise duty-bound life and sought it in her. She'd tried to give him that sense of wonderment, though she knew that she wasn't truly what he had wanted. Laurel liked to think that if she'd gone to Wizardes Cliff and emerged ten years after as a full wizard, she would have sought him out again and they might have been happy, but she did not love him as a wife ought to.

Ambris knew her well enough to see that she was unhappy. Her growing discontent disturbed him; he would do anything for her happiness, if only he knew what to do. Laurel might have abused this power if she were another sort of woman. To appease his guilt, she might have asked for jewels, or taken lovers without reproach, or made the Council dance her bidding—but these were not things she desired. As it was, she kept her silence. For all his talk of people who were content only in their proper place, Ambris did not see that *she* was sadly out of place. No fault to him, however; she hadn't seen it herself.

Though she did not want to make a show of her regret, she couldn't avoid disagreements, for as her understanding of Pendaunzel intrigue increased, her opinions frequently differed from her husband's. Laurel was always quick—quick to pronounce judgment, quick to anger, quick to speak her thoughts and quick to apologize when she saw she had acted rashly. Most of their arguments were no more than heated discussions which were soon forgotten, but they fought at length when Andemyon became a favorite of the aging Duke. Ambris refused to believe the most vicious gossip—he preferred to think that Dafythe was in his dotage and had paid too much attention to this one, pretty herald—but, intent on the truth, he conducted a private trial and practically accused the boy of causing a scandal, which Laurel found unforgivable. The scandal was hushed up, but the conflict was not satisfactorily resolved. The rift between Laurel and her husband never completely healed.

That summer, she returned to Eadbury with her two small children. During Dafythe's final years, while Margueryt and Kat were away at their wars and later, during the beginning of Margueryt's absentee reign, Ambris was Regent of the Northlands. He was too occupied with the business of the Dukedom to follow his family into retreat.

Alone except for the children and servants in the solitude of Ellsrood, Laurel began to exercise her magic again. She had occasionally used the toys of light to amuse the children and the Pendaunzel courtiers, and she always lit fires and candles by sparks from her fingertips. She'd done nothing more wizardly since the day she'd gone to Ambris. She hadn't dared to do more, but now she began to see that cowardice for what it was. In her youth, she'd been a swaggering child who was good at games and certain that all in life could be so easily conquered. Once she had faced a challenge, she had wept and fled and refused to play again. She had always known that she had done a cowardly thing in flying with Ambris, but she now faced the full truth of herself. She had tried to hide, to deny what she truly was—there was no excuse. Her actions were despicable.

Now that she was a grown woman, her duty became imperative. She understood what her father had meant by guarding his world. This was *her* world: the green hills of Eadeshire, the country-folk who brought their calves and kittens to her to be healed, the music of her minstrels, the laughter of her silver-haired children. These were her people, as were Igren, Iobethe, Andemyon, Orlan, Olyr, Godefroi, Klyffaude. She hadn't seen them in years and didn't know where many of them were, but as she had once loved them, she still desired to see them safe. She wouldn't see Ambris endangered by an evil he could not comprehend. Even those she didn't care for—the dull merchants of New York, the callous court of Pendaunzel—and the millions more she'd never seen all deserved a better fate than that which the Others would mete if they had opportunity. If the people one by one did not matter to her, the world as it was did. This was her responsibility. A guardian must have a greater love than for the individual, a love for the living itself, for humanity as a whole, for the substance of their secure existence. She understood that Lord Redmantyl had made himself into a sentinel to protect all of this and thus removed himself from it. That was the price for their safety.

She understood that Lord Redmantyl, too, had a weakness to the distraction of his magic. If he had been a wizard of the strictest principles, he wouldn't have allowed his love for her to dissuade him from his duties. He would have removed the renegade before it became dangerous. He ought to have killed her that Midsummer morning after she'd first intruded on his Keep. He couldn't. His weakness. Her weakness. His mistake. Her mistake.

Alys had returned. Laurel had felt the battle which announced the agent's return on another Midsummer eve, but she did not participate. Now, she regretted that. Her powers might have made a difference in the struggle lost. When Laurel heard news of the slaughter at the Spanish fort at Iagoburso, which even Margueryt's most loyal and zealous followers called atrocity, she knew that it had been more than the usual mishap of war.

She saw that she had not escaped her duty. Even if she didn't use her magic, it was part of her, necessary to her being, and desirable to Others who would employ her for their own ends if she relaxed her guard. She felt them at times. They had placed one minion in this world to do their work, but they had not forgotten her.

In her self-imposed exile, she tested herself against the spells she knew, studied books brought down from the library at Maryesfont, and determined that her abilities had developed greatly during those quiescent years. It was joy to be able to release those energies she had for so long concealed. It had been waiting all along, the satisfaction which had been here for her in her right place if she would take it. She did not fling aside her defenses nor open her senses indiscriminately, for that would be past folly in these dangerous days, but she was no longer afraid to take her place. Though she couldn't be sorry for the time she'd lost in her marriage—how could she regret Tomyas and Lauret, or all her relationship with Ambris?—she recognized that it was time to put things right.

When Ambris came to Eadbury that autumn, she told him of her plans. "I want to return to Wizardes Cliff and complete my training."

Ambris readily agreed. He grasped at it as a hope for both of them. "I am pleased that you came to this decision."

"I shall take Tomyas and Lauret with me. They are too young to be left behind here and I will not have them at an Abbey." Even now, the piping voices of the little ones at play rose from the courtyard. The older children had gone to Samandra Abbey, but Laurel's children were only seven and five and not yet of an age to be sent away alone.

Ambris went to the window to look down at the silver-curled pair, laughing and squealing, running about the flagstones in a private game. "Do you think they'll be magical?"

Laurel came to his side. "They aren't old enough to show. Magicians don't come into their first powers 'til they are twelve or fourteen."

"You told me once that you were eight."

"Yes, and Igren tells me that Orlan's little daughter is already bursting with magic to fright the poor country-folk of Oerykton, and *she* cannot be more than three. It is not the usual, I assure you."

"I'd like to think these two are not usual. They are yours." He put his arm about her, tentatively, and when Laurel smiled, kissed her. "It will not be an unpleasant distinction," he said, "to be husband to a wizard."

But before arrangements could be made, Laurel discovered that she was pregnant again. Her magic must be put aside a little longer.

When she woke, Ambris sat at the foot of the bed, peering into the cradle.

"He's a wrinkled little elf now," he said. "But I think he'll be a handsome lad. His hair will be so fair as yours." He smiled at her. "Have you decided upon a name?"

They had discussed many names these past months: Dafythe, Margad, Denys, Rolande, Theodore. "Parsyfal," she said.

"The name of a holy knight."

"No. I was thinking– Remembering. A play I once saw...." She shut her eyes, and forced them open again. She mustn't sleep! She would not have darkness close over her! She was no frail little creature to die in childbed. She had birthed twice before without difficulty. But this time, something had gone wrong. The labor had been too painful. The child had been days in coming and she'd fallen into a fever before the actual moment of delivery.

In delirium dreams, she had seen her newborn son as a grown man, a magician. It was promised in his birth. She felt the potency of the moment, the magic of one generation bearing the magic of the next on a most powerful day. The last of April. They had noticed. *She* had noticed. Laurel couldn't recall whom she had spoken to, what promises she'd made for the safety of her child, but she had bought his life. She must not sleep!

But sleep she did, and wake, and sleep again. Sometimes the baby cried and was hushed by the nurse. Sometimes Ambris sat at the bedside with tear-bright eyes and told her it was all his fault. He had done her great wrong. Always, she was surrounded by midwives and healers who offered potions to ease her and whispered apologies to her husband. They marveled that her will alone kept her alive; another woman would have died days ago. A priest came and smeared oil on her brow and said prayers for her soul.

Laurel ceased to notice these ministrations. Her efforts were directed elsewhere. As she slipped from that material plane that was easiest to understand and command, she concentrated, focusing the energies of her fading body into what lay deeper within.

Her father had not taught her this. Perhaps he didn't know it himself. *Here* lay the source of human magic. The power was not merely a part of her; it was, in truth, the essence of her self. It didn't end with the cessation of her body, for it was far more *her* than her flesh. The body was like a chrysalis, a fragile shell wrapped about the living energy. If it were possible to free herself, she would. This was the proper end for all great wizards if they could find the avenue of escape before death. She would go as others had already gone—as she might have gone herself, a dying Redmantyl years from now if she hadn't lost her way. The release was perhaps premature, but it was the inevitable step.

She opened her eyes at the sound of her baby's cry. It wasn't the same plaintive tone she had heard may times before, but something more urgent. What was wrong? Where was the nurse? She lifted her head. There was no disturbance. The hour was late, long past midnight. She was alone; no nurse or healer sat in attendance and Ambris had gone.

As she looked to the cradle, her eyes were caught by a shadow cast in the corner, in the niche between the fireplace and the closed chamber door. It looked odd somehow. Was it cast by the cradle? No. The shape was wrong, and it was out of line with the firelight as well as the single candle left flickering on the table. Had it always been there? She couldn't recall. It seemed to stretch further back than it possibly could, beyond the wall she knew it must cast itself against.

Alys stepped out of the shadow. In ten years, she had not aged. Her form was that of a young girl, but she was nothing of the sort. Laurel saw too well to be deceived. Whatever flesh and blood and bone Alys had once been, she was now made of the substance of the Outside. True human elements were taken from her. She was a focus. A tool designed to pass between the spaces.

As the little shape crossed the room, Laurel left her bed and placed herself between the child and her foe. "Stand away."

Alys stopped. "He is mine. You promised him, for your life."

"I did no such thing!"

"You take back your word, Lady?"

"I never gave it. Not to you."

"Then your life for his. We will rather have you than the child." Eyes ran down her body, assessing the growing magic beneath. "You were always a fool. So much power and you never knew what to do with it. You feared it. You denied it. What can you do now?"

The time of Wizard's Keep was upon them. The mechanisms of the cosmos had turned into place; trembling, Laurel waited for the exact moment when the gateway opened. Thunder drummed in her ears. Power burned within her, consuming the little substance that remained. Her body felt as light as dry tinder. Veins blazed bright beneath the translucent flesh. Her blood was aglow. No need for rituals—words to be spoken, devices written, gestures made. No need to cast spells. What were they, after all, but the physical representation of her will? She was past that now. If she could live until the Time arrived...

"I can fight you."

"You can barely stand," Alys answered with contempt. "You forget yourself, Lady. You are not the white knight any longer. No more than mortal woman. You are still in the flesh and you won't live to pass over. You can't command such powers as you have. They'll burn you through. You might as well give over."

Time. As every perception expanded around her, she threw her failing body at Alys and pulled them both into the space between.

It was all here, exactly as she remembered: the wall, the night sky, the chanting crowd far below the perch where she clasped her foe, the enormous door flung open. Her old dream. Her battlefield. None of it was truly there—like their Outside forms, like her own form, this place was only symbols. She saw what she could comprehend.

Her glamour burst outward. Yet she survived. She was still Laurel—her sense of her identity, her awareness, remained unchanged, but there was so much more as well. She *saw*. She *knew*. She *felt*. She *was*. This transformation from matter to energy was not oblivion, but completion. It was what she was meant to be. There was no pain as the husk burned away, crumbled from her as the magician's soul swelled unrestrained. She found the power to defend herself in this realm; she had possessed it all along. She was ready to employ it. She was not afraid.

The shape that Alys wore dissolved away in the burning embrace. The small, struggling body blurred into a mass of black streamers which tangled about her to swallow her brilliance and engulf her will. Yet she held on. She cast her own bright forces around the spewing tendrils to contain them. The barrier would not endure for long. Soon, Alys would break free. This was not the little magician Laurel had overpowered in her youth. Alys's masters had given their agent vast powers—a fraction of their own, but how much beyond mortal limits! She knew she couldn't defeat this dark force, but she might hold it until the vulnerable time had ended and the gates were closed against them.

Somewhere far away, her newborn son slept undisturbed and Laurel wished him well. She wished she could see the magician he would become. She wished she could know what Tomyas and Lauret would grow to be. She wished she could have made her farewells to them, for she would not return. She must leave all she cared for to protect it. For the safety of her world, she must forever guard against this creature, block Alys's ability to enter and exit at will, hold her, distract her, thwart her schemes for destruction. This was not the duty of a moment's Keep, but an eternity. As her lapse had first brought about the danger, she must be the one to put it right. It was time to take up the responsibilities she was meant to fulfill.

A light shone in the darkness.

When the Earl's household discovered the Lady gone, there were frantic searches through the castle, then through the village and the wild hills in the first morning light. With the nurse in her cubby, Ambris in the adjoining chamber, and servants up and down the corridor at all hours, it was improbable that Laurel could leave Ellsrood unseen. It was impossible, in her condition, that she could have gone far. Yet she had disappeared.

The search went on for days, but Laurel's body was never found. Common opinion held that she had fallen into the creek and been swept away, or had wandered deep into the woodlands and lay hidden under bracken. Ambris was frantic as he lead the searches, and overcome by grief when he called them to a halt; he was wretched at the thought of Laurel lost forever, but he had heard legends of how the bodies of many great wizards had disappeared at their death and he took what comfort he could in that. Perhaps, he hoped, she did not lie forsaken.

Laurel's son was christened Parsyfal in accordance with her last wish.

Igren

Oerykton

1960

The Lady Igren returned from her chapel below the castle, dropping her white gossamer cloak over the arms of a waiting attendant as she passed the lowest gate. Like one blind, she moved with hands brushing the stone walls as she went through the corridors. Brother Kai, who accompanied her, took her arm at the foot of the great stairway.

"Are you well, My Lady? Shall I come with you?"

"No," she answered.

"Brother Anselm and I shall stop in Oerykton tonight before our return to the Abbey. You may call upon us if we are needed."

Igren brushed at her tears and bestowed a gentle smile on the young Brother. "Gramercies, Kai, but I will be fine. I would like to be alone for a time, in peace."

There was no more to be said; Brother Kai made his farewells and slipped away silently. Igren went up to the nursery.

Her small son was wailing. Igren dismissed the nurse and took the seat beside the cradle herself. As she touched the baby's cheek, his sobbing ceased. Pale blue eyes found her face. Little hands reached up and she offered a finger to the tenacious grip. "My poor little one," she whispered. He was tiny, frail, and flaxen-haired, but nearly six months old. None of her other children had lived beyond their first days.

Geyraulte came in. "Is it finished then?"

"Yes. They'll be gone soon," she answered. "There's no reason to remain." Her eyes misted.

"Are you so sad to see Orlan go?"

Igren shook her head.

"Alen then? Ah, well, I'm sorry for that, Dearest, but I never thought her a proper companion for My Lady of Oerykeshire. Mama's said that that marriage has lowered your cousin Orlan's place beyond recovery. Oh, Alen was sweet enough—a respectable peasant-lass— but I never could see your fondness for her above the ladies here at court."

When Igren had arrived at Oerykton as a bride, Geyraulte's mother and grandmother had received her with cold and formal courtesy. The chill of that welcome had not warmed in the years since. They disapproved of her; she was not the wife they would have chosen for their boy and they made her feel it. The ladies of the little court—the dowager's well-born attendants, vassals and the wives and daughters of vassals—followed this lead. They smirked at Igren's shyness and easy tears. They whispered that her silvery fairness gave her a sickly complexion. They blamed her stillbirths and miscarriages on her delicate health. They scorned the compliments she received from Geyraulte's men and wondered what had possessed the Earl to choose her. She was, after all, a merchant's daughter, no better than a tradeswoman. She was no one of consequence.

"She was my friend."

Geyraulte scowled. "There's altogether too much of that cousin of yours and his family about my house." Old jealousies rang in his words. "I didn't like it when he was here before with his dandy's ways and wizard's tricks. I call it too much magical influence for my tastes. 'Tisn't godly. You fuss over that daughter of his as if she were your own."

"Before," Igren glanced at her baby, "I did imagine..."

"You give her ribbons and laces and sew little things for her frocks. Not that I don't like the child—for I do. She's a pretty little thing, but she's blasted odd. Daughter of a magician–! That sort of witchery tells in the blood."

"It is my blood also, Geyraulte," she reminded him. "You knew that when you courted me."

"Yes, but I thought you'd left it behind when we married. Your mother, your cousin Laurel, that wizard you call uncle. I brought you away from that taint." New tears began to fall; Igren bent her head over the baby so that Geyraulte did not see. "Now, blasted Orlan must come again to my lands with a peasant-wife and witch-child and you welcome them as if you'd never had a better friend in all the world! I give you all a wife could want. And for what pleasure? You shut yourself up in your chambers and refuse the companies of the court and weep so that anyone who saw you would think you were kept a prisoner! You are Lady of my house! You might behave so! Damned ungrateful, I call it!"

"Hush, I pray you," said Igren, laying fingers against her own lips. "You'll wake the baby."

Geyraulte was cut short by this, for he worried for the health of his heir as much as she did. "Is he–?"

"Nurse tells me he doesn't sleep so much as he ought." She tucked the quilt up around the infant's chin. "Please, leave us. We shall speak later."

Her husband hesitated in the doorway, then left.

Life with Geyraulte had promised to be such an adventure. Her husband was handsome and exciting, a man of strength and boldness. His home was far from New York, a castle at the foot of great mountains with a little chapel in a willow garden just for the Oerykton ladies. Deer ran to the walls. This would be her home too.

She had not known how lonely she could be. After eleven years, she was still a stranger here.

Geyraulte gave her the most passionate attention in the first months of their marriage, and Igren had hoped that all their happiness would grow from this early ardor. She'd hoped to be a friend to her husband, to join in his interests and to share in the management of his fief as a true wife ought. But while Geyraulte was eager enough to make love to her at night, in the daylight he preferred the company of his attendants; he rode to the hunt with them, gamed with them, drank with them. Ladies, he maintained, were not suited for such sport. His Lady, especially, was too gentle. She watched from her chamber windows as he charged from the stable-yard roaring in delight amid his friends and the baying hounds. She heard the loud laughter in the feast hall as she followed the dowagers upstairs after dinner.

She had hoped to have freedom here as Earling that she hadn't found as a merchant-maid, but the dowagers were more exacting of her behavior than her own mother had ever been. She was Lady of Oerykeshire, but only after Lady Emma and Lady Syolfe. They frowned upon her worldly ways. Veiled and wimpled, they called her long, unbound hair urban vanity, in spite of the fact that Geyraulte protested any covering to the silver-white plaits. If one of the young maids dared admire or attempt to copy Igren's fashion, she was scolded for it. The dowagers managed Geyraulte's house and his lands as they had since his childhood; any curiosity expressed by Igren on such matters was called ambition. They crossed themselves at the mention of her magical relations, and looked at her as if they expected some witchery. Igren knew it was common gossip that she had ensorcelled her husband.

She had hoped to have children. With each pregnancy, she reopened the nursery and made her plans anew, then, each time, shut the nursery door and put the baby-things away. She envied news of Laurel's children and occasionally thought of inviting them to Oerykton. She wondered who would care for Laurel's baby, born so soon after her own son. It was true, she had loved Orlan's daughter as her own. It was easy to pretend that that silver-curled sprite was the child she might've bourn. Now, she had a new, fragile hope. If she lost this little one, she didn't know how to find the heart to go on. Geyraulte did not blame her, but he was disappointed.

There had been no funeral for Laurel. Official mourning was proclaimed to honor the memory of the Lord Regent's wife, but for Igren, of course, the grief was much deeper. She remembered Laurel, little hoyden, her infant idol, face dirty, elbows scraped and bruised, fighting with the other children, weeping furiously at their taunts, urging her timid cousin into mischief. Laurel, half-grown, hot-tempered and impulsive, bursting with new and uncontrolled powers, setting the house so carelessly afire. Laurel, returned from Wizardes Cliff in her shabby beribboned breeches and stained cloak, striding about New York as if it were too small for her, out at night on unimaginable errands—more magical than Igren could understand. Laurel, a bride, strangely silent, an ivory statue in her white shift and veil. Igren recalled that her cousin had stared at the candles above the altar as if she didn't know what they were. What could she have been thinking on her wedding day? The Lady Laurel, whom she had corresponded with in affectionate terms. Laurel, gone.

Always, always, there was a vivid impression. Laurel, so vibrant that she left her mark on the memory as the sun leaves a burnt spot on the eye. It was impossible to believe she was really dead. Igren felt herself a pale second: her cousin had been stronger, brighter, swifter, more willful, more magical than she could ever be. Even her mother and father, who didn't like Laurel much, called her more clever and able to make her way in the world. Everyone had wondered when Laurel had given up her magic to marry. No one, except Laurel, had ever lamented that *her* talents were lost.

Yet, Igren wasn't jealous. She had loved her spectacular cousin, her friend, nearly her elder sister. Laurel had been all that she wished she could be. Laurel was meant to live a remarkable life, to do everything Igren had never found to courage to do. She should have been a great wizard.

Something had happened to alter that fate. Igren didn't know what. This was a confidence her cousin had never shared. Laurel had sworn she would never marry. She had refused Ambris once and set out for Wizardes Cliff to resume her apprenticeship, then had fled with him to Pendaunzel and announced her betrothal. What had changed her so suddenly? With so much else before her, would Laurel so abruptly decide to turn her back on her magic and pass the rest of her life quietly?

Igren understood that most women lived their lives this way; only the most extraordinary took other paths. But Laurel *was* extraordinary.

If Igren wept today, she wept for Laurel as well as Alen and for all her own children. She wept that so much promise had gone to nothing.

She was meant to love one man, but Geyraulte did not care for the heart she readily offered; he trampled recklessly over the tender parts and wondered at her injury. She was meant to be mother to many children. She was meant to be more than this, a woman sitting still.

Could it all be irredeemably lost?

She wondered what it would be like to use the magic she'd never dared acknowledge. She possessed a little—not much, not enough to attain wizardry, but a little. She did not aspire to wizardry: its disciplines were not hers; she couldn't survive that harsh and dangerous life; the thought of Laurel's mysterious errands in the night still alarmed her. She could never do battle. She was too timid, too tender. Her magic was likewise gentle. The blasting powers wizardry valued were not hers, and the subtle powers she did have would be dismissed as unimportant, a trifling, to the great magicians. They would overlook her. She would be as out of place among the ranks of the magical as she was among the hard, bright ladies of her husband's court. But there must be a place where she would be proper. There were other ways to exercise her abilities.

She saw that it was not the limits of her talent which bound her, but her infirm will. She was meek. She was gentle. She was afraid. She had let herself be guided by others: her mother, her husband, whoever would direct her. They had taken command of her, for she did not command herself.

She might use what small powers she possessed to do something to make herself more happy here. She might make her little one live and thrive. She might gain the strength to stand up to Emma and Syolfe and the other ladies here. She might make Geyraulte look at her as he had in the first days of their marriage—or, if not that, at least make him stop shouting. In truth, Geyraulte would be a satisfactory husband if she could have him be silent from time to time. Oerykton could become the home she'd once dreamed of. *That* was in her power, if she would take it. Laurel had taught her how and she had not forgotten.

Once the baby was peaceful, she ascended to the hall between her boudoir and the chambers she and Geyraulte shared. He was there, alone with his dogs at his feet, still sulky from their quarrel.

"The little one's asleep," she said. "Is there more you wish of me?"

"No, My Lady. Stay or go as you please."

Igren stood behind him, hands gently on his shoulders.

"'Tis pleasant as we are," Geyraulte said after awhile. "You see how things might be between us?"

"Yes, Geyraulte."

"We were pleasant together when we first wed. Remember, Igren? I know it can't be so lovesome through all our lives, but you've changed so from the pretty maid I asked for. You used to be such a sweet, gentle girl, like a little dove. You fair made the castle a courtly place—I was blasted proud to show you about." He leaned back against the chair. "What happened to your pretty ways, Lady? You go about so mournful and weepy I cannot bear to see your face for fear 'tis gone red with your blasted tears. 'Tisn't proper for a wife to behave so sadly. You spoil your looks."

Igren whispered, "I will try to be better."

"I don't know why you can't be happy. You might have all you ask for at the twist of a finger. I'd give it you if it were in my power."

"Let it not trouble you, my love. Rest your head. Sleep." She touched his temples, pressed lightly before his ears. The dogs looked up and whimpered.

"Hush," she told them, and they were still.

Geyraulte slept.

About the Author

Kathryn L. Ramage has a B.A. and M.A. in English lit and has been writing for as long as she can remember. She lives in Maryland with two aging and chronically ill cats. "Maiden in Light" is her second novel. Like her previous novel, "The Wizard's Son," "Maiden in Light" is set on an alternate Earth whose history has diverged from ours somewhere during the medieval period. Both are part of an intended series of fantasy novels that mostly take place in a dukedom called the Northlands, a part of the Norman Empire that roughly covers the north-eastern U.S.

About the Graphics

Northlands map by Molly Kiely, www.MollyKiely.com

Cover design by Michelle Mauk, www.MichelleMauk.com

Cover photo of the Shambles courtesy of www.FromOldBooks.org, http://www.fromoldbooks.org/RedBookOfYork/pages/18-The-Shambles This image is in the public domain. Our thanks to FromOldBooks.org for hosting it where we could find it on the internet.

www.ingramcontent.com/pod-product-compliance
Lightning Source LLC
Chambersburg PA
CBHW070303260626
47160CB00003B/691